MW01043556

Warrior Priest

Mike Johnson

1663 Liberty Drive, Suite 200
Bloomington, Indiana 47403
(800) 839-8640
www.AuthorHouse.com

First published by AuthorHouse 10/10/05

ISBN: 1-4208-8948-6 (sc)
ISBN: 1-4208-8947-8 (dj)

Printed in the United States of America
Bloomington, Indiana

This book is printed on acid-free paper.

For Uncle George

This is a work of fiction. All of the principal characters and most of the secondary or supporting characters are entirely fictional. Some supporting characters were real-life people, and a roster of them appears at the back of the book.

All locales and ship names are authentic, and cited statistics are accurate in so far as my research showed. References to actual historical events and real people as well as locales are intended only to give the fiction a stronger sense of reality and authenticity.

The chronology of the story is historically accurate with the exception of one incident that I have advanced by three weeks to strengthen the story's flow.

CHAPTER 1

John "Jack" Brecker slipped on his priestly collar before saying his first solemn high Mass. It was early June 1942, in Shelby, Ohio. The town of 10,000 people had given birth to America's seamless tube industry in 1890. It was also home to the Shelby Cycle Company and its renowned Shelby Flyer bicycle – its frame shaped from locally made seamless steel tubing. The tallest structure in town was the Moody Thomas Milling Company – 6 floors – and the largest was Most Pure Heart of Mary Church – seating capacity 900 -- where Jack said his first Mass.

Two weeks later, Jack began driving west, 1,800 hard miles to Tucson, Arizona, then still designated as mission territory by the Vatican. The newly ordained priest was piloting a very much used Model A Ford he had purchased for $500 from his uncle on a promise to repay when he could. Along the way, Jack was stopping to take black and white photos. In a little Arkansas town, he took one showing a white horse pulling a wagon with lettering on the side that read Southern Ice. One taken in a small Texas town showed a Texaco gas station sign in the foreground and mountains in the background. Many of the photos were of metal mileage signs screwed to wood posts. Tucson 108. Tucson 24. Tucson 5.

Jack Brecker, fresh out of Josephinum Pontifical Seminary in Worthington, Ohio, en route to his first assignment, didn't know it yet, but he was one of the coolest men ever to wear a collar. In later years, some would say, he was one of the coolest men – with or without a collar.

Theresa Hassler thought Jack Brecker was cool when she first kissed him – in a cloakroom at St. Mary's School in first grade. She still thought he was cool when he left Shelby after one year at St. Mary's own two-year high school to go to St. Joseph's Seminary in Vincennes, Indiana. As Jack boarded a train at Shelby's Baltimore & Ohio station, family and friends were there to bid farewell. Theresa was among them. She gave Jack a St. Christopher medal – and another kiss on the cheek. That was in 1932, when they both were 15. She felt a lump swelling in her throat as questions pounded her mind. Will I ever see you again? Do you know how much I love you? Will I ever kiss you again?

Theresa knew Jack liked her, but she also knew how set he was on the priesthood. Why? Why would such a cool, outgoing, handsome lad begin to pursue a life without large, frequent doses of fun? Without girls?

At age 15, Jack already was close to the six feet one inch he would reach within a year. His brown eyes and coal black hair could easily have given him a dark demeanor. But his gregariousness and genuine friendliness toward all lightened and brightened his appearance.

He liked girls. He had teased and joked with them. And he had sneaked his share of kisses in the cloakrooms. Jack also was a superior athlete, with baseball his first athletic love.

So why a seminary? In 1932, for large numbers of Catholic boys, it was the thing to do. Jack Brecker's choice of the priesthood was very much a result of his environment. His household, headed by parents Anthony and Virginia, was intensely religious. They followed all church rules scrupulously. No meat on Fridays. Fasting from midnight before taking Holy Communion. Mass every Sunday. Confessions nearly every week. A family rosary was said nightly. Jack and his St. Mary's schoolmates attended Mass every morning, Monday through Friday. Every Friday afternoon, they went to confession, often fabricating or exaggerating the sins to which they confessed. Franciscan nuns taught them, daily hammering into their impressionable minds the strictures of the Baltimore Catechism.

"Everyone stand," said Sister Take-Your-Pick in her black-robed Franciscan imperiousness. "This half of the class form a line on the left side of the room. This half on the right." Then she would begin firing questions from the catechism. Answer correctly and return to your seat. Answer wrong and go to the rear of the line and try again. This every day immersion swamped Jack's mind, helping condition it toward a journey to ordination.

Then there were the semi-annual visits by missionaries on home leave to their Sacred Heart Seminary just four miles south of Shelby. Jack had gone not to Sacred Heart but to St. Joseph's because he wanted to be a diocesan parish priest and because the Toledo Diocese had funded his attendance there. Each visit to St. Mary's by a Sacred Heart priest began with kindly pastor Michael McFadden leading a robed missionary into a classroom. "Children," Father Mac would say in his Irish-tinged brogue, "today we have a very special guest. He is Father Thomas Hogan of the

Missionaries of the Sacred Heart. Father Hogan has been working the last two years with the poor people of the Belgian Congo. He wants to share with you what he has seen and learned. Father..."

After Father Hogan gave his lecture, emphasizing the faith of the poverty-stricken Congolese, he would encourage the boys and girls to listen for "the voice of God" in case He wanted them "for a vocation." In those years, a goodly number of boys and girls heard that voice. Seminaries and convents had no trouble filling their ranks with eager, putative priests and nuns.

No one was surprised by Jack Brecker's choice. And many were thrilled, beginning with his parents and Father McFadden. Did anyone feel otherwise? Theresa Hassler was hurt. Deeply. She had been smitten with Jack from their earliest days at St. Mary's, and she had fallen in love with him during a party at Julie Ryan's house in the autumn of their eighth grade year in 1930. She knew it was love when she first slow danced with Jack in the basement of Julie's house. Julie's mom Gladys had decided it was time that her daughter's classmates began learning the arts of dancing and mixing. She mailed invitations to the homes of Julie's classmates. Most accepted, including Jack, with his parents' blessing. But there also were objections, and one of the protesting mothers mailed her complaint not to Julie's mother Gladys but to St. Mary's Franciscan principal, Sister Mary Elizabeth. By the time Sister received and read the letter, the dance had taken place. So, the next Monday after school, she phoned Gladys.

"Hello?"

"Mrs. Ryan, this is Sister Elizabeth."

"Hello, Sister, how are you?" Actually, Gladys' quick mind already had an accurate fix on Sister Elizabeth's feelings.

"Frankly, Mrs. Ryan, I'm troubled."

"Oh?"

"About the dance."

"I see," said Gladys. "The children had so much fun. I had fun watching them." Gladys had, in fact, done some observing but mostly stayed upstairs. "They were so well behaved."

"Don't you think," said Sister, "that it is inappropriate for boys and girls to be dancing so young?" Sister had posed a question, but Gladys knew it was an accusation.

"Oh, Sister, just the opposite. Don't you think it is important for boys and girls to learn to socialize and in a carefully supervised way?" Gladys, too, knew the value of using questions to make points. Her daughter Julie would have been proud of her mom had she been listening in.

"Yes, Mrs. Ryan, but I think thirteen or fourteen might be too young."

Might be? Gladys Ryan sensed victory and she wasn't one to flinch. "Sister, next year most of these young people will be going to Shelby High. There will dances during school, after school and on weekends. Most will be chaperoned. But not as carefully as the dance at our house." Okay, thought Gladys, so I'm exaggerating a little. "I prefer that our St. Mary's children have a good social grounding before they begin high school."

"Mrs. Ryan, I respect your feelings but-"

"I respect yours, too, Sister. You and the other nuns do a wonderful job teaching and building strong Catholic values. But teaching and building values also must take place in the homes."

In the spring, Gladys hosted an eighth grade graduation party and dance at her home. Sister Elizabeth knew about it in advance but didn't phone to protest.

At both parties, Jack danced with all the girls. Among them were three or four that he especially enjoyed holding. Julie Ryan was one of them. But his favorite was Theresa Hassler. Like so many girls, Theresa seemingly had raced to her full height of five feet seven inches. She was lithe and moved with understated athletic grace. She was very intelligent, perhaps the smartest girl in the class. Her memorization skills were extraordinary; rarely did she miss answering questions from the Baltimore Catechism or the multiplication tables. She was pretty. But more than pretty, her luminous brown eyes and small mouth, framed by shoulder-length brown hair, made her look perpetually serene. Her soft, almost musical, voice accentuated the serenity.

As to Jack's answering the call to the priesthood, Theresa felt helpless. In the 1930s, it was well beyond the imagination or initiative of a good Catholic girl to question a boy's choice of seminary. As demonstrated by the stolen kisses she had shared with Jack and their closeness while dancing, Theresa was no shrinking violet. But there were cultural inhibitions aplenty, and they exerted tremendous pressures and restraints. That, of course, was their well-understood purpose.

So Theresa was making her own career plans. After eighth grade, she went to Shelby High School. She continued to score high academically, and she stood out athletically and socially – cheerleader, thespian club, basketball and, her favorite activity, biology club. Indeed, her biology studies led her to a conclusion that surprised and concerned her parents.

One evening at the dinner table in September of her senior year, three Hasslers were happily chattering. Theresa, the fourth, was pondering.

"Mom. Dad." They looked at her. "I want to be a nurse. I want to go to nursing school."

Joe and Eleanor Hassler looked at her and at each other. Younger daughter Bridgett quieted. Money wasn't a big issue. Although the Depression was at its worst in the mid-1930s, Joe Hassler managed plant operations at the Shelby Steel Tube Company and made a good, steady salary. Location and distance were their worries.

"That's very nice," said Eleanor. "Good nurses are needed.

"That's true," said Joe. "Getting a job after nursing school shouldn't be a problem."

"Where would you go to school?" said Eleanor.

"Probably Cleveland or Columbus," said Theresa. "I hear that Mount Sinai in Cleveland has a very good nursing school."

"Cleveland. That's a good ninety miles," Joe said contemplatively. "And it's a big city." His mind was already picturing the dangers to a pretty young woman in a city full of strangers. "Couldn't you study nursing at Mansfield General?" Mansfield was a scant 12 miles southwest of Shelby.

Theresa's mind was picturing those big city dangers as vividly as her dad's, but she knew what he was thinking. She ignored his comment about Mansfield General where nurse training paled compared to that at Mt. Sinai. "I've heard the girls live right at the school which is part of the hospital. You wouldn't have to worry." Which, of course, Theresa knew full well, was precisely what her mom and dad would do.

CHAPTER 2

During the Depression years, money was a chronic issue for the Breckers. Jack's dad Anthony also worked at the Shelby Steel Tube Company, known locally as the Tuby. But as a pipefitter, not a manager. His pay was enough for the family to live on, but work in those years wasn't steady. Anthony frequently worked short hours or was periodically laid off. Money for extras was out of the question.

The Toledo Diocese had been paying Jack's tuition and living costs at St. Joseph's. It had been doing likewise for five other boys from northwestern Ohio towns. Then the diocese itself ran short of money and informed the boys that they would have to pay their own way or withdraw.

Most Pure Heart of Mary pastor Michael McFadden had money. Reputedly, lots of it. The source of his rumored wealth remained unclear. It certainly didn't derive from the diocese that paid his meager salary or from the parish's long-handled collection baskets. Yet he always drove a nice car, traveled annually to his native Ireland, and often had St. Mary's boys lugging boxes of books to the Shelby Post Office to be shipped to schools in Ireland. Speculation held that Father Mac had been named beneficiary in a number of parishioners' wills. He never said and no one worked up the courage to satisfy their nosiness by quizzing him. Balding, gray, bespectacled, slightly stout, not tall but still physically imposing, Father Mac could be intimidating, enough to ward off others' curiosity.

In the spring of 1935, Jack returned from Vincennes, glumness initially shadowing his usual ebullience. He wasn't sure what he would do next. He had thought of no career other than the priesthood. He was deeply disappointed and resigned to a life outside the clergy. But he soon moved past moping because that wasn't Jack's way.

That same spring, Theresa Hassler was anticipating graduating from Shelby High School. She heard that Jack had returned home and was planning to go to his house on Raymond Avenue to visit. Her pulse quickened at the thought of seeing Jack, and she began rethinking her decision to go to Cleveland – if Jack would be staying in Shelby and not as a priest.

Father Mac beat her to the Brecker's door. He had waited until after 4 p.m., so Anthony would be home from his shift at the Tuby. He wanted Anthony and Virginia present when he spoke with Jack. Father Mac knocked on the door and Jack answered.

"Oh, hello, Father. This is a surprise – a pleasant one." Jack was holding an edition of The Saturday Evening Post.

"Hello, Jack," said Father Mac. "I know you were returning from St. Joseph's, and I wanted to speak with you and your parents. Are they available?"

"Sure thing, Father. Come in. Mom! Dad! Come here. Father McFadden is here."

Virginia quickly shook off her surprise at Jack's announcement and came walking toward the door from the kitchen, wiping her hands on a colorful apron. Anthony came down the stairs, having changed out of his gray Tuby work clothes. Curiosity was consuming him. He and Virginia both extended their right hands and Father Mac shook them.

"What brings you here, Father?" said Anthony.

Before Father Mac could reply, Virginia said, "Come, let's go in the living room and sit."

After they were seated, Father Mac spoke. "I know about the financial plight of the diocese and what it means for Jack and the other lads at Saint Joseph's."

"A shame," said Anthony. "We can't afford the tuition and living costs and not many other parents can either. Even Sacred Heart Seminary is beyond our means."

"Tis true," said Father Mac. "And I detest the prospect of the church losing so many good young priests because of money problems."

"A terrible shame," Virginia echoed sadly.

"I've been doing some inquiring," said Father Mac, "and I think I see a way around this for Jack." Anthony, Virginia and Jack all looked at Father Mac uncomprehendingly. He smiled ever so tightly, his lips barely creased. "Jack was getting excellent marks at Saint Joseph's. In all subjects." Where was this leading? Jack wondered. "I know the church doesn't want to lose these fine young men. In Worthington, just north of Columbus, the Vatican operates a pontifical seminary. The Josephinum, it's called. Very difficult to gain entrance. Only the brightest are admitted.

I've petitioned on Jack's behalf. Because of his excellent marks and my strong recommendation, the Josephinum will accept him."

There followed a long moment of silence.

"Father Mac…I don't know what to say," said Jack.

Anthony cleared his voice. "You might want to say thank you."

"Oh, yes. Thank you, Father McFadden. Thank you so very much."

"Yes, Father, we deeply appreciate your thoughtfulness, your kindness," said Virginia. "But who will pay his tuition and living costs? The diocese doesn't have the money and heaven knows we don't."

"Not to worry," said Father Mac. "The Vatican is only too happy to cover Jack's costs."

That was true in so far as it went. What the Breckers didn't know and would never learn was the condition under which the Vatican had agreed to cover Jack's tuition and living expenses. Father McFadden had agreed to reimburse the Vatican for fully half of Jack's bills. Father Mac knew he could afford it. Two recently deceased parishioners, as had others before them, had left him generous bequests. And the trust set up for him as a young priest by a benefactor in Ireland provided generously for his needs. The trust's only requirement called for Father Mac to make an annual trip to Ireland to say Mass for the benefactor's own son, a young priest who had died during the deadly global flu epidemic of 1919. The son and Father Mac had been best friends in Dublin.

Chapter 3

Theresa's family lived on Grand Boulevard which had supplanted the east end of Marvin Avenue as the street of choice for Shelby's affluent. Grand Boulevard, situated adjacent the town's picturesque Seltzer Park on the east side, was an oval, with the widest pavement of any street in Shelby, and with a center island 150 feet across and four blocks long. Although only about a mile and a half from Jack's home on Raymond Avenue on the west side of town, two days passed before word of Father Mac's initiative for Jack reached Theresa. The news hurt. To spare herself more pain, she changed her mind about visiting Jack. She resumed her focus on nursing school in Cleveland.

Two others close to Jack were ambivalent about his pending departure for the Josephinum. His brothers, Paul younger by four years and Tom by six, idolized Jack. They didn't yet feel his pull to the priesthood, but their worship of him was complete and unconditional. In Jack, they saw high intelligence, amazing wisdom, bottomless patience, and a boon companion. They had missed him terribly while he was at St. Joseph's, and they would miss him when he left for the Josephinum.

One quiet evening in that June of 1935, the three brothers were sitting on the wood steps of their home's front porch. The steps and porch were painted gray, the boxy, two-story house white.

"Boy," said Paul, then 14, "Father Mac must really like you. The Josephinum sounds like a nifty place."

"Yes," said Jack, "I suppose it does. But I think pride is part of it, too. He wants to see some of his St. Mary's boys become priests. He made one thing clear; I'll have to work hard. He stressed that the Josephinum works it seminarians very hard."

"You'll do fine," said Tom, 12. "You always do. You'll be the smartest guy there."

Jack threw his head back and laughed his rich, bass laugh. "I doubt that. Seriously doubt it. I'll just be happy to make it all the way through. But when I do, little brother, you can call me Father." Jack chuckled at his own teasing and so did Tom.

"How long will you be there?" Paul asked.

"Seven years."

"Seven years!" exclaimed Tom. "Geez, that's a long time. I'll be a grown man when you get out."

"Almost a man," Jack gently corrected him, smiling. "Nineteen."

"I bet I can beat you in arm wrestling then," Tom said, defensively. "How often will I get to see you?"

"Not very often, I'm afraid," said Jack. "At Christmas, maybe Easter. Summers…I don't know how much time off they'll give us in the summers."

"It sounds like they'll really keep you hopping," observed Paul.

"Yes," said Jack, "and I'm sure the next seven years will go by in a flash."

Chapter 4

Thaddeus Metz was sitting astride his white stallion in a large expanse of thick forest. The young soldier was a corporal in a brigade of Polish lancers. The horse was fidgeting excitedly. Thaddeus looked across the broad plain of western Poland at the wide rank of advancing panzer tanks. Behind them came striding German infantry. It was September 1, 1939.

Today I will die, Thaddeus was thinking. He crossed himself. Coursing adrenalin and abiding anger were keeping his fear at bay. He had never before seen tanks, but he had heard about their amazing speed and terrifying firepower. And German infantry, he knew, were well armed with rifles, machine guns and grenades. Thaddeus was keenly aware of the futility of medievally equipped cavalry resisting Hitler's ultra-modern army. But I'm a Pole, he reminded himself, and I'm duty-bound to serve my homeland. He sucked in a deep breath and blew it out.

The German tankers and infantry were nervous. They could see they were enjoying superior numbers and weaponry, but this would be their first taste of combat, and they knew some would be killed or maimed.

Thaddeus had grown up in Cracow, near the city's large central plaza and Jagiellonian University, a center of learning since 1364. That's where Thaddeus was – at the university studying history and planning a career in law or government – when Germany swept into Austria in March 1938. As with many other students pursuing similar interests, Thaddeus also was studying French and English. On September 29, 1938, when Germany won Czechoslovakia's Sudetenland, Thaddeus decided to leave university and join the military. Despite Hitler's pledge to make no more territorial claims, Thaddeus felt certain that Poland, often overrun by great powers over the centuries, soon would tempt Hitler's ambition.

His horse reared slightly, and he patted its neck to calm the animal. Some 300 yards to the east of Thaddeus across the grassy plain from the German tanks, a company of Polish lancers sat astride their mounts, waiting. Thaddeus and the rest of his brigade were well hidden in the large copse of forest on the northern flank of the advancing Germans.

The lancer company facing the tanks knew their mission. It was not to fight. Certainly, it was not to resist tanks. Their job was to serve as a temptation, to create separation between the fast-moving tanks and their supporting infantry. As the tanks continued to close, the lancers' commanding officer spotted swiftly moving dots in the sky. He had been briefed. Immediately, he shouted the command to wheel eastward, disperse and retreat. The white horse-mounted lancers obeyed at once and none too soon. The German tankers accelerated their steel-treaded monsters, and the dots in the sky soon began swooping low. German stuka dive bombers.

In the forest, Thaddeus watched as the tanks began spitting fire and steel and the screaming dive bombers began strafing and dropping explosives. In the next moment, flesh – human and horse – began ripping apart. Many of the retreating lancers would escape. Some would not. But their sacrifice was working as intended. The space between the fast-advancing tanks and trailing infantry was widening.

Thaddeus and his fellow lancers felt their anger growing, their eagerness to defend their homeland swelling. They all had rifles strapped to their backs, but they would charge as Polish cavalry traditionally charged. Better to surprise and terrify the enemy, Thaddeus was thinking. Besides, firing a rifle from horseback likely would accomplish little. Many of us will fall, but we will make these invaders pay a steep price.

The line of German infantry, at least a thousand strong, had nearly passed by the waiting lancers. Thaddeus glanced at the brigade's commanding officer. His right arm was upraised. He nodded to his second-in-command. "At a gallop!" came the shouted command. The line of cavalry began easing out of the forest and went surging forward, their long lances still pointed skyward. Then came the command to "Charge!" The lancers lowered their staffs, and their exquisitely trained horses strained and went thundering toward the left rear flank of the German infantry.

For a long minute, the only sounds were horses' pounding hoofs and lancers' shouted battle cries.

The German soldiers, intently and exultantly watching the rear of their fast-moving tanks, were slow to see the onrushing lancers. A German private, Hans Muller, on the far left, was the first to spot the charging white mounts, and he reacted as the Poles expected. Hans was flabbergasted then terrified – the reaction for centuries by foot soldiers facing cavalry. Hans wanted to shout, but a surge of terror silenced his voice.

Thaddeus and the other lancers pressed toward the Germans. The gap between lancers and infantry was narrowing quickly. Thaddeus felt no elation. Instead he was experiencing grim determination.

Hans Muller at last found his voice and screamed a warning. Germans nearby heard him and pivoted. They reacted as Hans had – with shock and terror.

The lancers kept pounding closer. Hans raised his rifle, pointed it toward Thaddeus and fired but wildly. Thaddeus' long lance impaled Hans who fell screaming, the first German to die in Poland.

Thaddeus pulled his horse up sharply and jerked his bloodied lance free. Other lancers were spearing German prey. A ragged chorus of agonized screams was piercing the air. But the lancers knew they couldn't long engage the better-weaponed Germans. Thaddeus hadn't heard a bugler sound retreat, but he saw fellow lancers wheeling their mounts and racing in all directions except west. His quick mind digested the situation, and he went riding eastward, toward the rear of the tanks. He felt that the safer alternative to riding across the front of the Germans' line. Many other lancers made the same choice. As Thaddeus approached the tanks, still intent on chasing the diversionary company of lancers, he wheeled his warhorse to the south.

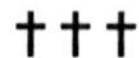

Chapter 5

Ribeauville is one of France's prettiest villages, and in 1939 Lea Peiffer was one of its prettiest residents. The village, its roots dating to the 1200s, was long and narrow, nestled among foothills of the Vosges Mountains in the Alsatian region near the Rhine River and Germany. The village's main street, Grand' Rue, meandered gently and on a slight upward grade from south to north for nearly a mile. About mid-way was the main village plaza, Place de la Marie. Another, Place de la Sinne, lay farther north after another bend in the street. From the main street, homes, restaurants and shops, mostly dating from the 16th and 17th centuries, spread only two or three blocks, then came vineyard-covered hills sweeping up and away. Atop the highest mountain at the village's north end were the ruins of St. Ulrich castle, constructed in the 1200s and belonging to the Ribeaupierre family who built it until the 1789 revolution. Two other castle ruins built by the same family sat atop nearby mountains.

At age 19, Lea Peiffer's universe was limited principally to Ribeauville and the nearby villages of Hunawihr and Riquewihr, fewer than three miles to the south, and Bergheim, three miles farther north. She easily could walk from one to the others and did so often, generally on business for her father, Klaus. Infrequently, she journeyed with Klaus in his delivery truck to the wine exchange in Colmar, a city of about 50,000 people about eight miles south of Ribeauville.

The Peiffer family – Lea, Klaus and Klaus' wife Sonia – were, like many other Alsatian families, winemakers. Their nearby vineyards weren't especially large nor were their cellars underneath a block of Ribeauville. But they were widely respected for the quality of their specialties – rieslings and muscadets.

In early September each year, visitors from throughout France, Germany and Switzerland crowded Ribeauville and other villages along the wine route for wine festivals. Ribeauville had an additional attraction; the first of September saw the feast of the menetriers or wandering minstrels, also called Pfifferdaj or Piper's Day.

"Mama, where is my minstrel costume?" Lea asked Sonia.

"Where it always is," she smiled. "In the chest of drawers by the stairs."

"Why do I never remember?"

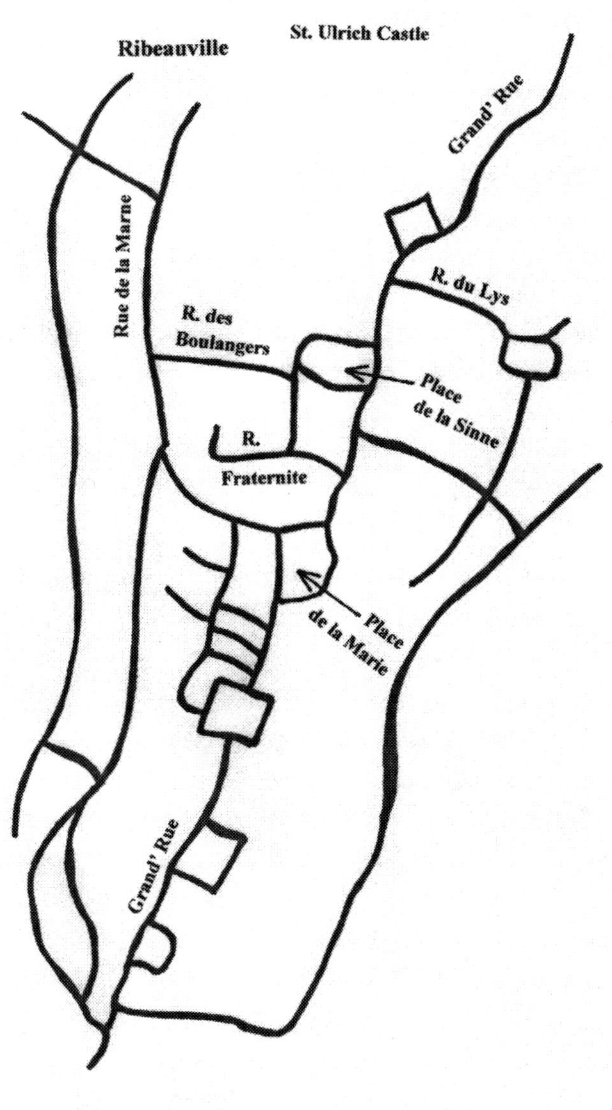
Ribeauville
St. Ulrich Castle
Grand' Rue
Rue de la Marne
R. du Lys
R. des Boulangers
Place de la Sinne
R. Fraternite
Place de la Marie
Grand' Rue

"Because you are so young and so busy – and because you have me to remember for you." Sonia laughed softly at her own little joke.

"Do you think the parade will be as big as usual?"

"Yes," replied Sonia, "I think so."

"And visitors, do you think we will have as many?" Lea was alluding to Germany's invasion of Poland, just days before.

"I think so," said Sonia. "The war is hundreds of kilometers from here. I think the people who usually come still will want to taste our wines and see our parade."

"I hope so," said Lea. Her brown eyes were sparkling in anticipation. Her five feet three inches, topped by shoulder-length light brown hair, went bouncing from the kitchen toward the chest to search for her festival costume.

Moments later, she returned to her mother. "I'm so glad the counts of Ribeaupierre protected the pipers and minstrels," Lea said. "They made so many people happy."

"Yes," smiled Sonia, "just as you will tomorrow."

"Mama?"

"Yes?"

"I can't help wondering what is happening in Poland. I can't get it out of my mind."

†††

Neither in Shelby, Ohio could Paul Brecker. It was evening, and he and his brothers Jack and Tom were sitting on the front steps of the Brecker's home on Raymond Avenue. Within days, Jack would be returning to the Josephinum in Worthington, and Tom would be suiting up for the season's first high school football game.

"You just can't trust Hitler," said Paul. "He's a born liar."

"He's that and more," agreed Tom. "He's a bastard. Oops, sorry Jack."

Jack smiled and shrugged his broad shoulders. His years at seminary notwithstanding, swear words were hardly foreign to his ears.

"How long do you think Poland can hold on?" Paul asked.

"Not long," replied Jack. "It's a mismatch. It's sort of like the New York Yankees playing the Saint Louis Browns. The Browns might win a game or two, but the Yankees will dominate the season and crush 'em."

"That bad?" said Tom.

"How long do you think horse cavalry and infantry can stop German tanks and dive bombers?"

"It's strange," Paul observed solemnly. "Right now Hitler's army is slaughtering Poles, and here we sit. Peacefully. No danger. It's like we're in two different worlds."

"Thank God for the Atlantic Ocean," said Tom. "At least we don't have to worry about Hitler."

"Actually, we might," said Paul.

"What do you mean?" Tom asked.

"Well, England and France have declared war on Germany. If they actually end up fighting Germany, watch out. The war might not jump the Atlantic, but we might jump the Atlantic to help the British and French."

"Good point," said Jack. "But I hope you're wrong. But if you're right," he smiled sadly, "I'd rather be a priest than a soldier. Saving souls seems more up my alley."

†††

The next afternoon, Tom went for a last swim at the Seltzer Park pool before it closed for the season. He loved cavorting with his friends, splashing with them, playing submarine and "attacking" girls from below the surface. Most of all, he loved diving from the three boards – two springboards and a tower platform. With some dives, he was the picture of grace, with others a study in athletic explosiveness.

"I'm meant for the navy," he said to Bridgett Hassler, Theresa's younger sister. They were sitting on towels near the pool's edge. "If there's a war, I'll go navy."

"I hope you don't go anywhere," Bridgett said softly, pulling off her yellow rubber bathing cap. "Not in the Navy. Not in war."

"Paul thinks the U.S. might go to Europe to help England and France."

"I hope he's wrong," she said. "Maybe France and England can beat Hitler by themselves."

"Maybe."

"But you don't think so…"

"I don't know." There followed long moments of silence, then Tom spoke again. "Bridgett, I'd like to ask you something."

"What?"

"Well, you know football season begins this Friday. There are dances at the Eagles after the games. Would you go to them with me?"

Bridgett brightened at the unexpected request. "Yes. I'd like that."

"Terrif! Let's meet there after the game on Friday."

"You'll shower first?" she teased.

"Nah, I thought I'd come in my shoulder pads and helmet." They both laughed.

That autumn of 1939 was a football disappointment for Tom. In 1938, the team had gone undefeated and won the North Central Ohio League title. But in 1939, the team finished with just four wins in nine games. Tom was a guard on offense and linebacker on defense. The defense played well, holding scoreless three opponents. But the offense struggled and was shut out four times.

Removing some of the sting from the losses were those Friday night dances at the Eagles lodge on Main Street. Tom and Bridgett treasured dancing, holding each other, talking, laughing. After each dance, Tom walked Bridgett to her home on Grand Boulevard, and they kissed on her front porch. Love was taking root.

†††

At a dance in Cleveland that autumn, Theresa Hassler met Hal Walker. There was a strong, fast mutual attraction that would grow stronger.

Theresa was working in the emergency room at Mt. Sinai Hospital near University Circle on Cleveland's east side. While studying nursing at Mt. Sinai's own nursing school, Theresa had been surprised by how much she had come to like living in Cleveland. A product of quiet Shelby, she had become fond of the big, vibrant, noisy city on Lake Erie's south shore.

At that dance, Hal saw Theresa standing along side the dance floor with three of her nurse friends. With the orchestra beginning a new tune, he approached them.

"May I please have this dance, Miss?"

"Yes," Theresa smiled politely.

The orchestra began playing another waltz, and Theresa realized quickly that Hal Walker was an experienced, accomplished dancer.

"You and your friends," said Hal, "do you live near each other?"

"Very near," Theresa smiled. "We're all nurses at Mount Sinai. We share an apartment near Little Italy."

"I see. I'm impressed."

"And you? Where do you live?"

"On the west side," said Hal. "Near the airport. It's convenient."

"You work there?"

"Yes, I'm a pilot."

"Oh. What kind of flying do you do?"

"American Airlines. I fly a DC-3."

"I'm impressed."

"That's a good sign, I think," he smiled.

"How many people does your plane hold?"

"We can take up to twenty-one passengers. Plus our crew of four."

"That's huge!"

"Have you ever seen a DC-3?"

"Just in the sky."

"We'll have to change that. How would you like to see the inside of one?"

"That would be exciting."

"I'll arrange it."

"Where do you fly?"

"Mostly from here to Chicago and New York."

"That sounds exciting, too."

"They are great cities. Much bigger than Cleveland."

"I'd love to see New York," said Theresa. "To see the Empire State Building and the Chrysler Building."

"Yes, but do you know that the Terminal Tower right here in Cleveland is the tallest building outside New York?"

"It's stately. I love looking at it."

"Have you ever been inside it?" Hal asked.

"No."

"Tell you what. We'll go and I'll take you up the observation deck. On a clear day, you can see Canada."

"That would be wonderful," Theresa smiled. "It might give me a feeling for what you see when you're flying."

Hal chuckled. "It just might."

†††

At the Josephinum, Jack Brecker found himself unexpectedly thinking about Theresa. He was in the library, browsing through the new edition of LIFE magazine. A story on hospital emergency rooms included photos of pretty nurses.

I know she's still in Cleveland, Jack was thinking. I wonder where she's living, what she's doing. How long has it been since we've seen each other? His right hand reached toward his throat. He tugged lightly on a chain around his neck and fingered the St. Christopher medal Theresa had given him when he went off to St. Joseph's Seminary back in 1932. The memory was a pleasant one – his family and friends at the Baltimore & Ohio station to see him off to Vincennes, Indiana...Theresa stepping toward him, handing him the medal, kissing his cheek. Another lifetime, thought Jack, it all seems so long ago. We were children, kids. I wonder if we'll ever see each other again. Heaven only knows where the church will send me. Probably far from Worthington and Ohio. The Vatican likes to send Josephinum graduates to places that have shortages of priests. If I had her address handy, I'd send her a note. Ask how she's doing. Oh, well, time to get back to the books.

And that's what Jack did.

†††

Lou Boudreau also was reading a book, a biography of General "Black Jack" Pershing. Given Lou's occupation, that was unusual. Of course, Lou was unusual in that he was a Major League baseball player who had graduated from college – the University of Illinois where he had played both baseball and basketball in 1936 and 1937. Indeed, he had captained the basketball team. Although ineligible to continue playing sports in college after signing his first professional baseball contract, Lou continued taking classes until he graduated in 1939.

That September afternoon in 1939, he was sitting in a rocking chair in Cleveland Municipal Stadium's locker room before the season's last game. The Cleveland Indians had signed him in 1938 and sent him to their minor league team in Cedar Rapids, Iowa. During the second half of the 1939 season, the Indians had summoned him to Cleveland from their Buffalo farm team of the International League.

Like Jack Brecker and Theresa Hassler, Lou Boudreau had been born in 1917 – on July 17. Like Jack, from childhood, Lou had developed a zest for sports. Unlike Jack, who possessed good athletic ability, Lou early on showed signs of athletic brilliance. Lou grew up in Harvey, Illinois and three times was named an all-state basketball player.

Like Jack, Lou was dark-haired, tall and strong. Like Jack, he was a thoughtful, caring man. Like Jack, he was religious. Like Jack, he saw his future in a uniform, but not the black robe and white collar of a priest.

†††

George Patton was a religious man, too. One night in the autumn of 1939, while his wife Bea readied herself for bed, he knelt beside their bed and prayed – for war. More precisely, for a war in which the United States and he – a descendant of a long line of warring Pattons -- could strive for and achieve victory and glory. Lasting fame would be nice, too.

Dear God, George Patton prayed, I know World War One was a bloody and deadly affair, but I thrived in it and I achieved victory for the greater good of mankind. I was one of your most dedicated, ablest servants. A crusader. And, Lord, I beseech thee to let me crusade again.

That 1939 autumn found Colonel Patton at Fort Meyer, Virginia, commanding the post and the 3rd Cavalry Regiment. He was itching to fight and had been since World War I ended. Back in 1925, while stationed in Hawaii, Patton had written to his father: "Personally, I am in hope that the Russians and Chinese combined may start a war and that I can get in it…I would not get excited over it yet as China is difficult to arouse and we are hard to insult. Too damned hard."

†††

Thaddeus Metz was not engaged in prayer, although his thoughts were focused tightly on survival which, he realized, at the moment was far from certain.

It was late afternoon and the two milk cows were lowing. Inside the barn, in the small pen, they were not used to so much company. It was unsettling to the gentle creatures. With them in their cramped enclosure were Thaddeus Metz and 10 other Polish soldiers.

One of them, older than the rest, addressed Thaddeus. "What is your name, Corporal?"

"Metz, Sir."

The older man looked hard at Thaddeus' uniform. "You are cavalry, a lancer."

"Yes, Sir."

"You have seen action against the Bosche?"

"Yes, Sir, on the first day of invasion."

"Did you draw blood?"

"Yes, Sir. Once. And then I rode hard away from the German guns."

"Your brigade?"

"Some were lost. Some escaped. Some were captured. Like me."

"It is difficult for horses to outrun stukas and panzers," observed Major General Stanislaw Sosabowski. "My men and I, we, too, were surrounded. Outgunned. Everything is happening so fast. The Germans don't even have proper facilities for prisoners. So they put us in this cow pen." The general, a husky man with a matching voice, paused and smiled. "And the cows don't like it."

"I was trying to head south to Cracow when we were cut off," said Thaddeus. "Where are we?"

"Near Zyrardow," Sosabowski replied. "About forty kilometers southwest from Warsaw. Trying to flee south was wise. That's still the direction to take...toward the Ukraine."

"Escape?" said Thaddeus.

"If we can."

Standing outside the cow pen was a German soldier armed with a

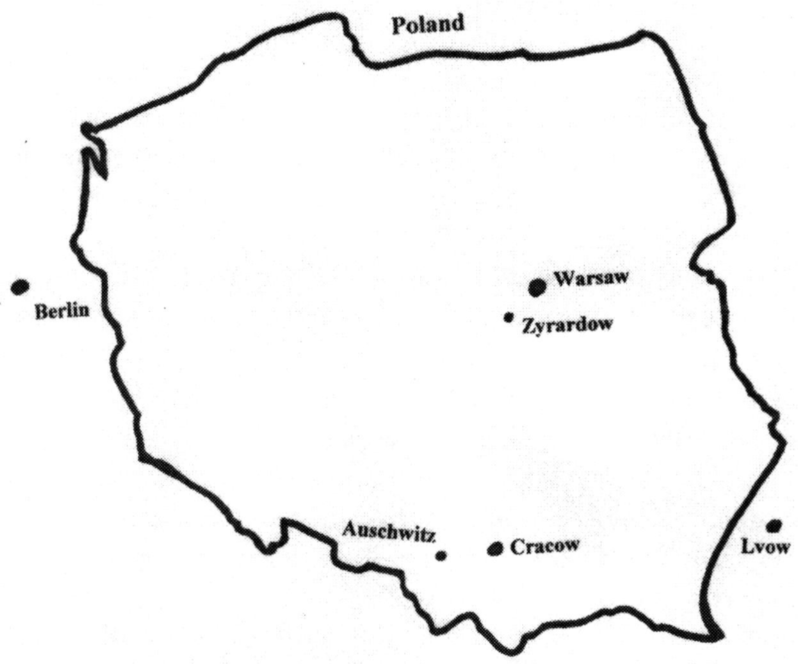
Poland
Warsaw
Zyrardow
Berlin
Auschwitz
Cracow
Lvow

schmeisser machine pistol. A second guard, similarly armed, was posted outside the main entrance to the barn. Close by, perhaps 100 feet, was the farmhouse.

Thaddeus and General Sosabowski and the other prisoners in the pen didn't know it yet, but they had been extraordinarily lucky. On September 1, some 250,000 German soldiers in 60 divisions, nine of them armored, had gone sweeping into Poland. Their panzers, supported by infantry and stukas, had encircled and then began squeezing Poland's hard-fighting troops. Their luck? Hitler had ordered his generals to be harsh and remorseless, to close their hearts to pity, to bear in mind that it was the stronger man who always was right. And before five years would pass, Hitler's vicious, unrelenting reign of savagery would kill some five and a half million Poles – or 16 percent of its pre-war population, a higher percentage than that suffered by any other nation. Yugoslavia would be hit second worst with 10 percent of its population killed. Russia would lose five percent.

But on September 6, 1939, the day Thaddeus found himself penned with General Sosabowski, the wholesale slaughter was just getting started. The lust for wanton murder had not yet permeated German ranks. It was on that day, the 6th, that, unknown to General Sosabowski and his fellow prisoners in the cow pen, the Polish government had fled Warsaw to Lublin. On the 17th, it would flee farther east and south into Romania. Eventually, the government would establish itself in Paris, then London. In the interim, though, Poles in Warsaw, soldiers and civilians alike, fought on bravely until surrendering on September 28.

"What do you think the Germans will do with us?" Thaddeus asked.

"Shoot us," said the general. "Or build a prison camp and take us there. I don't know. Maybe they don't know yet."

Neither General Sosabowski nor Thaddeus was worried about being overheard. They spoke no German, and they were certain their young German guards spoke no Polish.

"I would feel much safer if we were out of here and moving," said Thaddeus.

It was a statement of the obvious, and General Sosabowski felt no inclination to reply. But he was taking a quick liking to the young lancer.

†††

Bernadeta Gudek never had thought of herself as brave. Indeed, she had had little reason to think about courage. Her life on the small farm had been one of pleasant sameness. She and her younger sister Barbara helped their parents Jszef and Tosia with both daily and seasonal farm chores, with the gravest dangers being occasional hail storms and drought. Now, though, she found herself entertaining strange and unsettling thoughts. Can I help those soldiers? Can I give them some food? Can I possibly help them escape? If I tried to do that, what reprisals would we suffer? Torture? Rape? Would we be executed?

Bernadeta looked at her sister and parents. Tosia and Barbara were beginning to prepare supper, pealing potatoes and onions. Jszef was sharpening a scythe. Motorized farming had not yet arrived in rural Poland. Bernadeta was holding a pail; it was nearly time for the late afternoon milking.

From the house's front doorway, Bernadeta looked at the guard outside the barn door. He was smoking a cigarette and seemed thoroughly bored. Bernadeta stepped outside the house, then paused. Her mind flashed back to her father inside, methodically sharpening the scythe. It was early September, harvest time, a time for cutting. Bernadeta turned and stepped back inside. She put the pail on the floor, then went to the kitchen and removed a small basket from a wall hook.

"What are you doing?" Tosia asked.

"I'm taking some bread and cheese to the guards."

"What?"

"They must be hungry, standing so long."

"They are Germans," Tosia protested, "the enemy."

"It is the right thing to do," Bernadeta said firmly and Tosia objected no further. Bernadeta opened a drawer, removed a bread knife, then sliced a newly baked loaf. Then she stooped to the floor in a corner and took the top off a round, white ceramic container decorated with an image of red roses. She removed a wheel of cheese, stood and broke off several chunks. Bernadeta then glanced at Tosia and Barbara who were continuing with supper preparations. Bernadeta returned to the knife drawer, reached in and removed a small roll of brown twine. At the kitchen table, she put the bread and cheese into the basket, looked once more at Tosia and Barbara, and hid the knife under the basket. She left the kitchen and walked to the small bedroom she shared with Barbara. Three minutes later, she emerged, holding the basket, and walked to the house's front door and picked up the pail.

†††

Outside the barn door, the guard had finished his cigarette and was pacing back and forth. He yawned, then rotated his head and scrunched his shoulders.

Inside the barn, the two cows were lowing their impatience, amusing the prisoners. Thaddeus smiled and patted each of the cows on their backs. Across from their enclosure was a second pen, holding the ox that powered the farm's plow. The second guard eyed the livestock and the prisoners with near total indifference. No one had told him anything about relief, he was thinking. But soon he and the other guard should be receiving relief, instructions or food or all three.

Bernadeta approached the barn door and the guard. She smiled shyly, hoping it would mask the nerves shrieking in her stomach. Without speaking, she held out the basket and gestured. The German smiled, shouldered his machine pistol and removed two slices of bread and two chunks of cheese. "Danke," he smiled again.

Bernadeta gestured toward the door and the guard understood. He pulled open the door for her and she passed through, the basket in her left hand, the pail in her right. She walked calmly toward the second guard who was eagerly viewing the bread and cheese. Bernadeta handed him the basket. "For you," she smiled, knowing her meaning was understood. Then she held up the pail and gestured toward the cows. The guard paused. Bernadeta raised her left hand and, blushing, made a squeezing motion. The young, boyish guard smiled, his face reddening, and nodded his assent.

Bernadeta stepped to the pen's gate. She picked up the milking stool, then slipped the short rope loop from the gatepost, pulled slightly, and stepped through the opening. Slowly, the prisoners parted as she moved toward one of the cows. Bernadeta positioned the stool and sat. She glanced up and caught Thaddeus' attention. With the forefinger of her left hand, Bernadeta beckoned him. Thaddeus, uncertain, looked to his right and left and back at Bernadeta. Again, she beckoned.

Thaddeus stepped to her side. With her hand, she motioned for him to squat beside her. The other prisoners were watching. They closed the gap they had made for Bernadeta, obscuring the line of sight between her, Thaddeus and the guard who was chewing contentedly on the bread and cheese.

Bernadeta placed her lips next to Thaddeus' right ear. "Say nothing," she whispered. "Make no sound." Thaddeus pivoted his head so that his eyes met hers. Bernadeta Gudek's eyes were deep blue and showed seriousness of intent. Her blonde hair was pulled back into a long ponytail that was held in place by a blue bow. Her complexion was creamy. From the left corner of her mouth, a thin scar ran for an inch to the left and slightly downward. Bernadeta hiked her ankle-length brown dress to her knees and then farther back along her thighs. Thaddeus watched, puzzled and entranced. What on earth is she doing? General Sosabowski was watching, equally mystified. Bernadeta's right hand then reached to the inside of her left thigh and pulled steadily toward her lower abdomen. The two circles of brown twine remained snug against her skin.

Thaddeus' eyes widened. So did the general's. Bernadeta handed the bread knife to Thaddeus. Quickly, he slipped it inside his cavalry tunic.

Bernadeta then went about milking the cows, first one and then the other, as methodically as her thumping heart would allow. Gradually, her adrenalin eased its flow and her pulse slowed. Thaddeus, General Sosabowski and the other prisoners who had seen the knife pass were amazed – and thinking.

After she was finished milking, Bernadeta stood and whispered to Thaddeus, "I will return in a few minutes. Be patient. Watch for your opportunity." Her clear eyes were at the level of his chin. The prisoners parted and she exited the pen, holding the full pail in one hand, the stool in the other. She put the stool down, closed the gate and slipped the rope loop back over the gatepost. Then she walked away, left the barn and returned to the house.

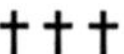

In Ribeauville, the annual Piper's Day parade had been a great success. Thousands of visitors had lined the winding Grand' Rue to watch and applaud the passing parade units. From her perch atop a horse-drawn wagon piled high with hay and festooned with colorful ribbons, Lea had smiled and waved merrily. Many of the visitors also had bought bottles and cases of the Peiffer family's muscadets and rieslings.

Lea was exuberant. After the parade, although 19 now, she went skipping along like a small child toward her home in Rue des Boulangers. At that moment on that stunning early autumn day, the thing farthest from her mind was war.

†††

Minutes later, Bernadeta was walking back toward the barn. This time she didn't even hesitate as she reached and opened the barn door. She merely smiled and nodded to the guard. Upon entering, the second guard glanced toward her, as did the prisoners in the cow pen. Bernadeta strode to a wheelbarrow and maneuvered it beneath a large hook hanging at the end of a thick rope. "Time to feed the stock," she said, knowing the youthful German didn't understand her Polish words but confident that he wouldn't interfere.

She then moved to a wooden ladder that was permanently nailed in place. Quickly and lightly, she began climbing to the loft. The guard and prisoners watched with curiosity. Thaddeus edged to the front of the group by the gate.

In the loft, Theresa tugged at a pulley, raising the rope and hook. She fastened the hook to a bail of hay and began lowering it to the wheelbarrow. As she did so, Thaddeus slipped the rope loop off the top of the gatepost, then reached inside his tunic.

The guard glanced back at the cow pen, and Thaddeus froze his movement. Then the guard redirected his eyes to watch Bernadeta descend the ladder. Her plain, modest dress notwithstanding, the guard couldn't take his eyes from her behind. About half-way down, she let her right foot slip off a rung. "Oops!" As she was regaining her balance, the guard instinctively stepped toward her, ready to help. At that same moment, Thaddeus eased through the gate and closed on the guard. Simultaneously, his left hand closed tightly over the guard's mouth and his right plunged the knife blade hard into the young German's back, just below his shoulder. Shocked, the guard wriggled. In the next instant, one of the cow pen prisoners, Stefan, was helping to restrain the guard while Thaddeus continued to apply hard, twisting pressure. Soon, the guard's body grew limp, and Thaddeus and Stefan lifted and carried it to the cow pen. Another Polish soldier, Jerzy, had opened the gate wide and Thaddeus and Stefan quietly laid the body down.

Back on the ground, Bernadeta paled and shivered and squeezed shut her eyes for a long moment. Then she whispered to them, "Follow me to the barn door. I will try to distract the other guard. He is the only other one."

They nodded and followed her.

Her heart still racing, Bernadeta pushed open the door part way, stepped through the opening and said, "Ouch." She looked at her right hand, then smiled at the guard. "A splinter." She held up her hand. Solicitously, the guard stepped toward the friendly farm girl who had generously given him the delicious bread and cheese. Bernadeta stepped away from the barn and turned to face the opening. As the guard reached for her right hand, Thaddeus repeated his action of moments ago. As the blade pierced the guard's tunic, skin and flesh, his eyes widened in terror and disbelief. The face of approaching, violent death stunned Bernadeta and she averted her eyes.

Thaddeus eased the guard's body to the ground, and General Sosabowski and the other soldiers quickly exited the cow pen, the last soldier closing and securing the gate.

Thaddeus looked at Bernadeta and shook his head. "Thank you."

Bernadeta gulped, swallowed and nodded but said nothing.

Other soldiers murmured their gratitude.

General Sosabowski then spoke. "We need to get moving but first we must dispose of the bodies and hide any trace of blood. Or the girl and her family will face execution." They might anyway, he was thinking.

"When the Germans return," Bernadeta said quickly, "I will tell them simply that the guards moved the prisoners. There are shovels in the barn. You can bury the bodies in the woods behind our house."

"Let's use the wheelbarrow to move the bodies," said Thaddeus. "No trail of blood."

"First, put some hay in the wheelbarrow," Bernadeta advised.

Several of the soldiers smiled in admiration and then went to fetch the barrow and shovels. They needed an hour to transport the bodies, bury them and spread undergrowth over the graves. While they were completing their task, Bernadeta returned to the house to inform her family. She was anticipating an eruption of emotion, chiefly panic.

Minutes later, she came back outside with her father, Jszef, a hardened farmer and Polish patriot. Together, they walked the short distance to the woods. There, much to Sosabowski's surprise, the farmer seemed not at all unnerved by what Bernadeta had just told him.

"Here," said Thaddeus. "You should keep this." He handed her the bread knife, now clean of blood.

"I'm sure we'll be baking and slicing more bread," Bernadeta said, smiling thinly.

"I hope that's the only use you'll need to make of it," said Thaddeus.

"I, too," she smiled.

"We'll be taking these," said General Sosabowski, pointing to the guards' machine pistols in the hands of Stefan and Jerzy.

Bernadeta nodded. Then her father stepped forward. "We will need the bread knife, but perhaps you can use these." He handed a dagger and a bayonet to Thaddeus. "Mementos from The Great War. Against the Russians," said Jszef. "You might need them."

"Thank you, Sir."

"Yes, thank you," said Sosabowski, who now had a greater understanding of the farmer's calm.

"Where will you go," Bernadeta asked.

"South, toward the mountains," said the general. "I hope we can gather enough men and weapons to fight the Bosche another day."

Thaddeus was eyeing Bernadeta intently. Her eyes, hair, skin, scar, they were imprinting in his mind an indelible image far sharper than any picture taken with a camera. He held out his hand and she took it. "Another time, perhaps," he said.

"Perhaps," she smiled slightly.

Chapter 6

Spring, a time of reawakening, sees grasses greening, flowers blooming, trees budding, farmers plowing and planting, and neighbors emerging from homes for evening chats. Smiles abound.

Early on a spring evening in 1940 in Ribeauville, Lea Peiffer was chatting with her good friend, Marie Kieny. They were standing by the ornate fountain, erected in 1536, in the center of Place de la Marie across from the town hall on Grand' Rue.

"I wasn't so worried when Germany attacked Poland," said Lea. "I felt bad for Poland, but it is far to the east, like Austria and Czechoslovakia."

"But now?" said Marie.

"But now that Germany has invaded Denmark and Norway, I'm not so sure."

"And we are so close to Germany," Marie said worriedly.

"Only twenty kilometers from the Rhine," said Lea. "Too close."

"If the Germans come," said Marie, "what will you do?"

"I don't know. Here in the Alsace, most of our ancestors are German. Mine, yours." Lea shook her head slightly and smiled ruefully. "We Alsatians are like ping-pong balls. For hundreds of years we were part of Germany. Then France took us over in the fifteen hundreds. Then Germany got us back in the Franco-Prussian War. Then after The Great War, France reclaimed us. Will we bounce back to Germany again?"

"I hope not," said Marie. "Our names are German, but our hearts are French. So is our language." A pause and a small smile. "Well, for the most part anyway." In the spring of 1940, most Alsatians spoke French, but some spoke German and others a hybrid Alsatian dialect. Many could speak two or three of the languages. But from the French Revolution onward, Alsatians increasingly thought of themselves as French.

"If the Germans come," said Lea, "what will *you* do?"

"I don't know either," Marie replied. "Perhaps we will meet nice young German soldiers and then...who knows?" She smiled playfully.

"If we see soldiers, any soldiers," Lea said somberly, "I hope they are French. Only French. No Germans."

†††

For Theresa Hassler in Cleveland, Ohio, spring meant the ice melting on Lake Erie and fingers of warmth beginning to infiltrate the winter's arctic winds. After five years of living in Cleveland, Theresa wondered why it was Chicago, not Cleveland, that was called The Windy City. After all, Chicago sat west of Lake Michigan while Cleveland sat exposed south of Lake Erie across which northern winds rose and rushed unimpeded by hills, trees and buildings. Winters in Cleveland, Theresa knew, were, in a word, wicked.

But for a particular reason, this past Cleveland winter had seemed considerably less hostile. Theresa and Hal Walker had seen much of each other and were growing close. Among other examples of his thoughtfulness, the American Airlines pilot had delivered on his pledge to take Theresa to the top of the Terminal Tower. He had phoned her on a crystal clear January morning, one of the few during Cleveland's normally gray winter months. Now, three hours later, they were standing side by side.

"What do you think?" Hal asked. They were peering from the tower's observation deck, more than 700 feet above Public Square.

"It's marvelous! You were right. I think I can see Canada. And the ice on the lake. From up here, even the ice looks beautiful. Maybe we could take a walk to Canada."

They laughed.

"It would be a very breezy walk," said Hal. "Not to mention a long one. Here," he said, handing a pair of powerful binoculars to Theresa, "try these."

Theresa took the binoculars and adjusted the focus. "Oh, wow, yes! I can see the Canadian shoreline. This is wonderful! I think I really see now why you like to fly. What views!"

Hal smiled. "I still need to get you into a plane. That's next."

They hugged and Hal kissed Theresa on her cheek.

†††

Spring found Lou Boudreau not in Cedar Rapids, Iowa as had been the case in 1939 but in Cleveland. 1940 would be the young Cleveland shortstop's first season as an every day player. He would quickly establish himself as a standout, batting .295 and driving in 101 runs. Lou was on his way to stardom. Along the way, he made time for reading and daily prayer.

†††

When Jack Brecker wasn't studying or praying or reading the sports pages of The Columbus Dispatch or Columbus Citizen, he, too, often was playing baseball, not in a major league stadium but on the packed clay diamond at the Josephinum. During one game that spring, while batting, he lined a ball sharply to left centerfield. He was running hard to first base, intent on a double. When his right foot struck the inside edge of the first base bag, he tripped and went sprawling. Standing back on the bag and dusting off his uniform, he said, "It's a good thing I'm going to be a priest and not a ballplayer." He laughed at himself.

Jack also read other sections of the newspapers and was particularly following events in Europe. "It's ironic, isn't it?" Jack said one evening to classmate and best friend Mark Hood.

"What is?" Mark asked.

Jack flicked the gray ash from his White Owl cigar into a heavy glass ashtray and put down that day's edition of The Columbus Dispatch. "Hitler is one thing. Overrunning Poland, Norway, Denmark. But Mussolini is another. Here we are, studying at a pontifical seminary when the Vatican is surrounded by Mussolini and his adoring mobs. His army slaughtered Ethiopians and you can bet he wants more."

"And the Vatican – our Vatican – does nothing," said Mark.

"A few words now and then," said Jack, "but Mussolini has ears only for his own ambitions – and Hitler's."

"So you think they will both keep invading other countries?"

"Yes, I do," said Jack. "I wouldn't be surprised if France was next on Hitler's list." He puffed his White Owl thoughtfully. "He's probably mad for revenge against France for the way World War One ended."

†††

In fact, Belgium, The Netherlands and Luxembourg as well as France were next for Hitler and his mechanized legions. The assault began on May 10, 1940. Luxembourg fell in one day, The Netherlands in five. Belgium held on for 18 days. As the Germans raced for the English Channel coast, hundreds of thousands of British, French, Belgian and Polish troops were cut off in Belgium and isolated from the main body of the French army. Among the Poles were General Stanislaw Sosabowski, Captain Thaddeus Metz, and the other nine cow pen soldiers.

After their escape from the barn near Zyrardow, General Sosabowski, Thaddeus and a growing throng of other Polish soldiers fled southeast to Lwow in Ukraine. During their flight, the general promoted Corporal Metz to captain. "You've earned a battlefield commission," said the general. "And I need a strong aide with officer status." Jerzy, Stephan, Piotr, Henryk, Marek and the other cow pen soldiers shouted and applauded their approval.

After resting briefly in Lwow, they went hiking through the Carpathian Mountains into Czechoslovakia. From there, they continued southwest into Hungary. There the general talked his way onto a plane headed to Venice. He took with him Thaddeus, the other nine cow pen soldiers and 10 more troopers. In Venice, Sosabowski again talked his way onto a plane, this one bound for Paris.

Many other Polish soldiers made their way southeast through Romania to the Black Sea and beyond to Syria, then a French protectorate, before heading west to France and England. In all, some 165,000 Polish soldiers, sailors and airmen made their way to France and England, most by Polish navy and merchant vessels plying the Mediterranean Sea, smaller numbers via the Baltic Sea. In France, the Polish government in exile established itself in Angers, some 150 miles southwest of Paris. Commander-in-Chief General Wladyslaw Sikarski had with him about 100,000 men.

"I am disgusted," General Sosabowski said bitingly to Thaddeus a few days following Germany's strike west. "We come to help the French. We stand and fight. But the French, they turn tail at the first sounds of artillery or the first strafing run by a stuka."

"Not all the French are running," Thaddeus observed softly.

"I know, I know. Some are fighting bravely. But they have inferior leaders. Reynaud telephoned Churchill almost immediately to say that France was beaten. Disgusting." He spat the word. "Despicable."

In fact, early the morning of May 15, just five days after Germans began cutting across northern France and Luxembourg and then into

The Netherlands and Belgium, French Premier Paul Reynaud telephoned British Prime Minister Winston Churchill and blurted in English, "We have been defeated."

Churchill was aghast. The very next day, May 16, he flew to Paris to check things out for himself and attempt to brace up the defeatist Reynaud. Churchill would fly to Paris twice more before France capitulated on June 22.

By May 26, two French armies plus British, Belgian and Polish forces were squeezed into a narrow corridor running inland from the English Channel. This corridor extended 60 miles from southeast to northwest and just 15 to 25 miles east to west. German forces – armor, artillery, infantry -- were pressing to squeeze the corridor still smaller.

It was in this shrinking pocket that thousands of Poles found themselves on the morning of May 24. General Sosabowski and Thaddeus were outside the village of Hazebrouck on the western edge of the pocket. All around them, Allied soldiers were smashing and burning howitzers, vehicles, great coats and blankets – anything that might be of use to the Germans. The preferred method for disabling a vehicle – a bullet to the radiator and leave the engine running until it seized up. Stukas were attacking constantly, often indiscriminately. One stuka target was a convent at Carvin, near the south end of the escape corridor; 60 convent girls were killed. By May 24, stukas, dorniers and heinkels had been pounding and strafing Dunkirk for five days.

"How near to Dunkirk are we?" Thaddeus asked.

"As best I can tell, about forty kilometers," said the general.

"A hard forty kilometers. Why Dunkirk?"

"It's the only major port we have a chance to reach, and the canals that surround it might slow the Germans just long enough for some of us to escape."

"Yes," said Thaddeus, "to England – which puts us even farther from Poland."

"We all want to return to Poland and drive out the Bosche," said the general.

"How likely is that now?" Thaddeus asked.

"We will need much help. From the British. From the Americans if they enter the war. Even the accursed Russians."

"It could be years," Thaddeus said softly.

"Oh, yes, it *will* be years." There followed a long interval of silence. Then Sosabowski spoke again, equally softly. "You are thinking about the farm girl?"

"Yes," Thaddeus sighed. "I know it's foolish but I think of her often. I wonder what has happened to her and her family." At his waist, Thaddeus fingered the hilt of the dagger that Bernadeta's father had given him.

"It's not foolish," the general said gently, "but try not to dwell on her. There is nothing we can do for her or her family. Nothing."

†††

Near Zyrardow, on the evening of Thaddeus' escape from the barn back in 1939, a German lieutenant, Gerhard Blatz, had arrived at the farm with relief for the two guards. He was surprised to see no guard outside the barn. He jerked open the barn door and was more surprised to find no prisoners inside. The lieutenant spun around and led a squad to the farmhouse door and knocked roughly.

Bernadeta opened the door.

"Where are they?" Lieutenant Blatz asked through gritted teeth in surprisingly good Polish.

In that instant, Bernadeta knew she shouldn't play dumb. Instead, she answered quickly and evenly. "A German officer and his men – a group like yours – came late this afternoon. They and your men removed the prisoners from the barn." She pointed in the direction opposite from the house and forest behind it. "They all walked that way." A field with young shoots of wheat lay in that direction.

"And?"

"A little later, I heard shooting."

Lieutenant Blatz looked hard into Bernadeta's eyes. She met his gaze and then looked downward for a moment and then back upward.

"Nearby?" said Blatz.

"I'm not sure. We were afraid to come out of our house."

Lieutenant Blatz pursed his lips and nodded slightly. Should I believe you? My instincts say no, but there is no other apparent explanation. Saying nothing more, Blatz abruptly turned away and motioned to his men to follow.

"Do you think some of our men executed the prisoners?" a sergeant asked the lieutenant.

"Possibly, but I hope not. I wanted to interrogate the prisoners myself. Then I might have had them executed."

Bernadeta watched the Germans walk away and then she began to tremble, as she had earlier in the day. She had told the biggest and most dangerous lie of her life. Jszef approached from behind and placed his hands on her shoulders, and gradually Bernadeta stopped shivering.

From May 5-25, 1940, George Patton was serving as an umpire. Not for baseball games or tennis matches but for military maneuvers. Near Alexandria, Louisiana, he watched tankers outmaneuver and easily defeat horse cavalry. He was surprised and chagrined. As recently as 1938, Patton, a tank commander in World War I, still had advocated retaining horse cavalrymen and their swords. Now, he saw matters differently. If I get a chance to kill Germans, Patton ruminated, it will be with tanks. I think I will have to trade my horse for a jeep. Now if the goddamned Germans would just give us a half-decent excuse to go after them, I could put these tanks and my men to a use that the Lord would assuredly approve.

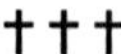

Late on the afternoon of June 3, the Poles had passed through Teteghem, a village fewer than three miles from Dunkirk and its funereal canopy of slowly drifting black smoke. General Sosabowski and Thaddeus Metz could see the Dunkirk-Furnes Canal just behind and to the immediate south of Dunkirk. They also could see the bridge spanning the canal. Behind them were their nine fellow Poles from the cow pen and some 3,000 others.

"French, Sir," Thaddeus said to the general.

"Getting ready to blow the bridge." They could see French army engineers setting explosives.

"It would be good to be north of the bridge while there is still a bridge," Thaddeus said dryly.

The general nodded, looking straight ahead. "Let's move out."

Thaddeus elevated his left arm and motioned the troops to advance. As they were nearing the bridge, a French squad providing cover for the sappers saw the Poles and leveled their weapons, poised to fire.

General Sosabowski himself raised both his arms in a crisscrossing wave. "No. No!"

"Maybe I should speak to them," Thaddeus suggested softly.

"Given my poor French, you seem a good choice," said Sosabowski. "Take the lead." At university, Thaddeus, like many others, had been studying French and English.

Thaddeus quickly made himself understood to the lieutenant commanding the French unit. "He says we must cross quickly, General. He is under firm orders to blow the bridge as soon as possible."

Sosabowski nodded. "Pass the word. Tell the men double-time. You lead. I will bring up the rear."

Exploding German artillery shells nearby underscored the urgency felt by both the Poles and the French. Thirty minutes later, General Sosabowski was the last of the Poles to cross the bridge into Dunkirk. "Merci," he said to the French lieutenant who had crossed with him. Thaddeus was waiting. Moments later, a short series of explosions raised and splintered the bridge.

"What now?" Thaddeus asked.

"Let's move into town and to the waterfront," the general replied. "Assess our options, if there are any to assess."

All around them were destroyed buildings, many burning or smoldering. Occasionally, in and around the city, German artillery shattered more walls and windows. Beneath their feet, the Polish troops felt and heard the crunch of glass fragments. "It's been like we're walking on eggshells," observed Thaddeus.

"Or on broken dreams," replied Sosabowski with his customary growl.

Moving through town, the Poles learned that virtually every basement was crammed with British and French troops, trying to stay out of harm's way while still hoping for deliverance. The Poles' first view of the waterfront staggered them. To their left or the west were two long breakwaters that extended 1,400 yards out to sea and, angling gradually toward each other, formed the gateway to Dunkirk harbor. The eastern breakwater was crowded with thousands of troops, waiting patiently for evacuation vessels.

In front of the Poles and to their right were long, snaking lines of troops on the beach. Thousands of them. At low tide, nearly a mile separated the rear of the beach from the water's edge. The Poles could see beach marshals keeping order in the queues. Some soldiers were digging foxholes in the sand. The lines were broken only where men clustered around comrades felled by stuka bombs and artillery shells. Farther out to sea, the Poles could see vessels burning, victims of stuka attacks. By the time the evacuation would end, 243 rescue vessels would be lost to aerial bombs and torpedoes from fast German schnellboats, teutonic cousins to American PT boats.

"It looks like we have a choice," said Thaddeus. "Stay here in town, queue up at the breakwater or move onto the beach."

The general surveyed the scene. "It looks like the Germans have been concentrating on hitting the city. It seems smoke from the burning refinery tanks is obscuring the breakwater and beaches from stukas. The breakwater is too crowded. The beach would seem the best of poor choices."

"Stefan has heard that this will be the last night of evacuation," said Thaddeus. "The Germans are closing in – as we know."

The evacuation, dubbed Operation Dynamo, had begun on May 26. The first ship – Mona's Isle – dispatched from Dover had departed at 9 p.m. and arrived at Dunkirk at midnight. It took on 1,420 British troops. On its return voyage, six stukas dived on Mona's Isle. The attack killed 23 men and wounded 60. It arrived at Dover at noon. Its experience was indicative of what would happen over the next nine days. And the German planes didn't wait only for loaded vessels to begin their return trips. Some vessels were hit so badly on the eastward crossing that they had no choice but to turn back to England before reaching Dunkirk.

On May 27, only 7,669 men were evacuated. Churchill and other senior British leaders were estimating glumly that the total might reach only 30,000-40,000 troops.

On May 28, 17,804 were evacuated and Allies' spirits rose. To slow the advancing Germans, French troops had begun flooding the low-lying land south of the coast.

On May 29, 400 German planes, including 180 stukas, attacked Dunkirk. As the smoke from the burning oil tanks cleared, they began attacking the breakwaters.

On May 30, vessels ranging from British destroyers to small pleasure craft combined to shatter estimates. They lifted off 53,823 troops. Churchill's morale went soaring.

On June 1, the Luftwaffe sank or knocked out of action 17 rescue vessels. Brave crews making multiple crossings – the destroyer Malcolm made eight – with no sleep and under heavy attack were exhausted, with nerves fraying by the hour. Astonishingly, another 64,429 men were evacuated. That total included 35,013 French troops -- plus British General Bernard Law Montgomery, and Augusta, the French bride – wearing army fatigues – of British Army Private Bill Hersey.

On June 3, the day the Poles arrived in Dunkirk, supplies were running low. There was no more fresh water or bandages.

General Sosabowski looked skyward. "It will be dark soon. Too many fires are burning, but we shouldn't be so visible. God has been smiling on the Bosche too long. Let's go."

During the nine days of the evacuation, despite the heavy loss of vessels and men, the Allies had some good luck. The often turbulent English Channel had miraculously been as smooth as bath water. That saved countless lives. With little breeze, smoke from the burning refinery tanks had hovered over the breakwaters and beach, barely drifting. It had taken the Germans three days to discover how much the Allies were using the breakwaters. Light winds meant troops wading into the water up to their necks weren't swamped and were able to climb into the small vessels taking them to England or to larger ships waiting farther out to avoid grounding on the gently sloping sea shelf.

Allied troops were lucky, too, in another respect. While German planes were pounding Dunkirk and rescue vessels, they seldom strafed the beach and didn't drop fragmentation bombs. Even Hitler's indecision helped. As the evacuation was just getting underway, he had ordered the panzer units to stop their advance on Dunkirk and begin their drive on Paris, the chief target of the Fuhrer's lust. By the time Hitler changed his mind, three valuable days had been lost – or, from the Allied perspective, gained. But the Allies' luck had its limits.

"Well, General, what happens when we get to England?" Thaddeus asked.

"I've been thinking about that. The central question is how do we get back to Poland the fastest way? That's my goal."

"That suits me fine," said Thaddeus, "and the men, too."

The Poles had just begun moving onto the beach when they heard the whine of incoming artillery shells. Scores of Polish voices began shouting, "Down! Get down!"

In quick succession, three explosions blew sand and shrapnel in punishing waves. As Thaddeus went diving, one of those waves struck and spun him around in mid-air. As he dropped to the beach, he felt hot metal piercing his uniform and flesh. He screamed primally.

†††

Near Zyrardow that night, it was two hours later than at Dunkirk. In recent months, Bernadeta Gudek and her family had learned the extent of their luck. They were lucky to be farmers. The food they grew was needed by their German occupiers. They were lucky not to be Jews, Gypsies, homosexuals, intellectuals or Polish military officers. More than once, Bernadeta had watched helplessly, mournfully, as German soldiers marched groups of Poles into the nearby woods. Gunfire would erupt, then the Germans would reappear – alone.

"I am thinking of joining the Home Army," Bernadeta said to Jszef on that night of June 3.

He looked at her calmly. A small smile formed. "I'm not surprised. But I don't know if I should be pleased. The Home Army..."

"Yes, Father, I know," said Bernadeta, "it's dangerous."

"For all concerned," Jszef added.

"Yes, I know it could be bad for you and Mama and Barbara if I'm caught or seen fighting."

"Or," observed Jszef, "if you are merely suspected. We have learned how easy it is for Germans to murder."

"That's why I think I should join the Home Army."

"Do you think Barbara will want to join with you?" Jszef asked.

"I don't know. I'm not sure."

"If she wants to, we can't let her. It would be too obvious if both of you joined. The risk of discovery would increase too much."

"I agree."

"Good. The pain of losing you would devastate your mother and me. But losing both of you would simply be too much to bear. I don't know how we could carry on."

"Are you telling me not to join?" Bernadeta murmured.

"Not at all. I just want you to have a complete understanding of the situation. And if you see combat, well, it is much harder than most people dream. Much harder."

"I think –"

Jszef cut her off. "I know you watched that young soldier stab the Germans. And you've watched Poles taken to their executions. But the intensity of combat is on another level. A higher level. Stress you can barely imagine. You could be killed but worse, you could be maimed for life."

"I understand."

"I hope so."

"How long do you think Germany will rule us?" she asked.

"I don't know. A long time. Who is going to stop them? Drive them out? Not the French. Not the Russians. Not the British."

"America?"

"America doesn't want to fight another war in Europe," Jszef asserted. "Who can blame them? They lost so many men in The Great War. No, I don't think America will fight the Germans again, not unless Hitler does something incredibly stupid."

"Such as?"

"Attacking America."

"Would he?"

"If he takes England. Perhaps." He smiled. "Remember, Bernadeta, I am but a simple farmer. Yes, I fought in a war, but I am a farmer. I have no great wisdom."

"I think Copernicus might disagree." She smiled, and they both chuckled.

"Warsaw?" he asked.

"Maybe. Probably. That's where the Home Army is based."

He nodded. "I will pray for you. And I have a suggestion."

"What is it?"

"Dye your hair dark."

Bernadeta looked at him blankly, slow to grasp his meaning. He smiled lovingly and she understood. "It would be dangerous to look too Aryan, too blonde."

"Or," he said, smiling wryly, "too beautiful and too visible."

†††

In the darkness on the beach, a Polish medic was tending to Thaddeus Metz and Marek Krawczyk, a cow pen soldier who also was hit. General Sosabowski and the other cow pen soldiers were watching.

"Well?" said the general.

"They will live. Private Krawczyk's wounds are bloody but minor. Gashes on neck and buttocks. Captain Metz…I think I have the splinter from the boardwalk out. And the shrapnel. I've got the bleeding stopped."

"Can they walk?"

"Not tonight."

The large splinter from the boardwalk had stabbed Thaddeus in the side of his right shoulder. A painful and bloody injury, but not debilitating. More seriously, one shard of shrapnel had penetrated high on the outside of his right thigh. A second shard had hit just above his right foot.

"Just leave me here," Thaddeus groaned through clenched jaws. "I can survive as a prisoner. They might even send me back to Poland." He didn't really believe that, nor did any of his cow pen comrades.

"I think," said General Sosabowski, "it is far more likely that you would be executed or forced to fight for Germany."

Jerzy spoke. "He is going with us. Stefan," he said, "let's find stretchers." It was now past midnight.

About 30 minutes later, Jerzy and Stefan returned with two stretchers borrowed from the French. They placed them beside Marek and Thaddeus. Gently, they and two other cow pen soldiers, Henryk and Piotr, lifted Marek and Thaddeus and positioned them on the stretchers.

At 2 a.m. on June 4, two small French torpedo boats, loaded with French soldiers, left the harbor. At 2:25 a.m., the British gunboat Locust received her last load of troops. At 2:30 a.m., the last French ships, a convoy of trawlers, packed with troops who had been fighting off the closing Germans, headed to Dover.

At 3 a.m., the destroyer Shikari was nearly finished taking on 400 French troops. It would be the last British warship to evacuate soldiers. But the rescue would go on for another hour or so, with commercial and smaller vessels still taking on troops as German artillery continued to pound the city and the waterfront.

"It will be dawn soon, Sir," said Thaddeus. "Our time for escaping is shrinking fast. If the men have a chance to evacuate, I don't want to be slowing things down."

General Sosabowski nodded. "We might all end up as German prisoners," he said, "but we will not fight for the Bosche." And, young man, he was thinking, we all have been together since the cow pen in Zyrardow, and we are staying together.

†††

At the Josephinum in Worthington, just north of Columbus, it was still June 3. 10 p.m.

"It's late, Jack," said Mark Hood. "I don't know about you, but I'm heading for bed."

"Yeah. Okay. I'm just about ready to hit the sack," said Jack Brecker. He folded the Columbus Dispatch with its daily report on Dunkirk and put it on the small end table.

"Something wrong?" Mark asked.

"Dunkirk. I was just trying to imagine what it must be like. Waiting on the beach. Gunfire. Bombs. Explosions. Death and destruction all around. Ships going down. Men thrashing and drowning. More men shot and burned. Dying horrible deaths. All those poor young men. Our Lord…He cannot countenance all this hatred and violence. It's hard to understand. Really hard."

"Faith, Jack. I realize that it sometimes sounds simplistic, but it's the only way. You have to keep the faith. You have to."

"Yeah, I know," Jack said, sighing. "But I'd like to be doing something more."

"Take it easy, Jack. Don't beat yourself up. We aren't even in the war."

"I wonder if our Lord is."

†††

"Everybody up! Up!"

It was Piotr, one of the cow pen soldiers. He was shouting and sprinting across the sand from the water toward Polish soldiers lounging at the back of the beach near the splintered boardwalk. Piotr was breathing hard from the exertion of running across the spongey sand. He stopped in front of General Sosabowski, his face appearing to be orange-tinged from the refinery oil tank fires. "Sir," he said, panting, "a steamer has agreed to take us. The Abderpool."

"Good." Sosabowski wanted to ask several questions but settled for posing only one, "How far out is she?"

"Not far. She is sending in her small boats. But we must hurry. Her captain says he must be underway before dawn. That's when he expects more stukas."

"Right. Good work, Piotr. Start spreading the word. We will move quickly but orderly. The wounded will go first."

Men began scrambling to their feet, brushing sand away from their uniforms. Nearby, Jerzy, Stefan, Piotr and Henryk lifted two stretchers bearing Thaddeus and Marek and, with help from other soldiers, hoisted them onto shoulders. Thaddeus gripped his stretcher's rails. At that moment, he was feeling no pain. The medic had injected morphine.

"So," said Thaddeus, "I will stay dry while you get soaked." They heard the affection in his words.

"Bite your tongue, Captain," Jerzy said, "or we might just slip in the water."

"And stain these French waters with Polish blood. Seems almost traitorous."

"You've got a point," replied Henryk, and there was laughter all around.

Into the English Channel they waded. They carried Thaddeus and Marek to one of the Abderpool's small boats that quickly motored to the mother ship. Coming along side the big steamer, there was no gentle way to take Thaddeus and Marek onboard. Silently, Thaddeus thanked God for the morphine.

The Abderpool, overcrowded with 3,200 Polish soldiers, was the last rescue vessel to leave Dunkirk. The evacuation had ended. The Poles were among 338,000 men to be rescued. When the Abderpool got underway, though, some 40,000 troops, mostly French, were left behind. There was no panic, no shouted recriminations. Many of the remaining French saluted the last British and Poles to leave.

The danger was not past. Everyone knew that, and tension remained high. About 6 a.m., a French auxiliary dredge, the Emile Deschamps, was nearing Dover. It struck a magnetic mine, exploded and sank in less than a minute. Some 500 struggling, screaming men went down with her. The Emile Deschamps was the 243rd and last vessel lost.

At 10:20 a.m. on the 4th, a squad of Germans raised a swastika over Dunkirk's eastern breakwater.

Chapter 7

Within minutes, Hal Walker would be fighting for his life. Simultaneously, Theresa Hassler's bloodied hands would be working to save lives. Both were where they never expected to be when they had first gazed into each other's eyes on a dance floor in Cleveland, Ohio.

Hal was running across the grass at Tangmere airbase, near England's southeast coast, to a waiting Hurricane fighter. Theresa was at St. Thomas Hospital in London, tending to airmen wounded in combat and civilians injured in bombings.

Hal's dash across Tangmere's grassy expanse and Theresa's ministrations were rooted in a conversation that had taken place earlier in Cleveland on a mid-July day – the day when Hal was fulfilling another of his pledges to Theresa. Dunkirk and its aftermath had been weighing heavily on Hal.

"What do you think?" Hal had asked, pointing to the Luscombe 8A side-by-side two-seater plane.

"It's nifty, and I love the colors," Theresa replied. The single-engine, 65 horsepower aircraft was painted pale yellow with twin, front-to-back reddish yellow stripes.

"Here we go," he said as he helped Theresa ease into the plane's passenger side.

"Oh, my! This is so exciting."

Hal smiled and strapped her in place, then settled himself into the pilot's seat. Intently, he did a thorough check of dials and gauges.

"Nervous?" he asked.

Theresa laughed. "I'm too excited to be nervous."

It was Hal's turn to laugh. "Good." He had borrowed the Luscombe from the owner of an aircraft maintenance company based at Cleveland's airport.

The morning was sun-splashed, with the rising sun transforming Lake Erie's gloomy gray surface into a shimmering blue. After receiving clearance from the airport tower, Hal taxied to the runway.

"We'll take off the west," Hal said, briefing Theresa, "then sweep out over the lake and swing east into the sun. You'll get a much closer look at Canada."

"Could we actually fly over Canada?" Theresa asked. "That way I could say I've been there. I've never even been out of Ohio."

"No problem," Hal smiled. "Happy to oblige. I'll just circle a little farther north and take us over Canada's shoreline."

Theresa was rubbing the palms of her hands back and forth against each other in happy anticipation.

Hal then accelerated the frisky plane which went zipping down the runway. It needed only about 1,000 feet for liftoff. As the wheels left the tarmac and the plane's nose rose, Theresa was forced against the back of her seat. "Oh my! This is…this is gorgeous, Hal. Thank you, thank you so much. I've never felt so…so…"

"So free?"

"Free! Yes, that's it. I feel so free. Like an eagle!"

"Or," Hal grinned, "those seagulls below us."

Theresa looked down at the swooping white gulls, diving into Lake Erie in their quest for breakfast. She shook her head in incredulity. "Above the gulls…I can't believe I am actually flying."

"You mean you doubted my word?" Hal teased.

"No, no. Not for an instant. It's just so fantastic. I can't wait to tell my family and friends. I don't think any of them has ever been inside an airplane. How fast are we going?"

"About one hundred miles per hour."

"That fast? It seems so much slower, like we're barely moving."

"At this altitude, yes. When we get closer to the ground again, you'll have a much better idea of our speed. Besides seeing Canada," said Hal, "I'll give you a different look at Mount Sinai. We'll go north over Canada, then east for awhile. Then we'll head south and swing back west over the Lake Erie shoreline. I'll take us right over the hospital."

"That sounds wonderful. How long will we be up here?"

"About forty minutes."

"Oh good. It's so peaceful up here. Oh, Hal, now I understand why you really love flying. Even if I fly again sometime, I'll never forget this morning. You are truly a man of your word. Thank you so much."

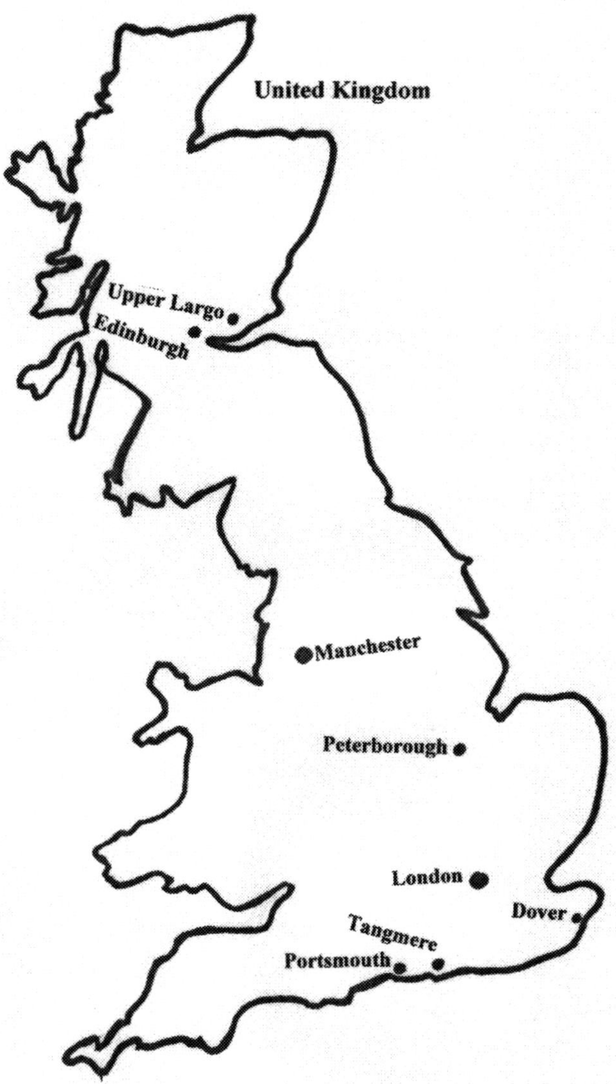
United Kingdom
Upper Largo
Edinburgh
Manchester
Peterborough
London
Dover
Tangmere
Portsmouth

"You are very welcome, Theresa. Of all my flights, I think I'll remember this one the most, too."

†††

Back on the ground, Hal opened the passenger side door of his car for Theresa. He then bounded around the front and slid in behind the steering wheel. "Hungry?" he asked.

"Not really. I think I'm still too excited to have much of an appetite."

"Well, Ma'am, I'm hungry so what say we head into town for a bite of breakfast?"

"Of course, we can't have a pilot going hungry," Theresa replied, smiling happily.

Twenty minutes later, they were sitting in a deli on Euclid Avenue near Halle Brothers department store. "I love the lox and bagels here," said Hal, "and their coffee. Try some?"

"Sure," smiled Theresa. A mischievous smile formed on Theresa's lips. "Hal, I think my life is now complete."

"What do you mean? You're only twenty-two years old."

"Twenty-three, Sir. But I'm also a nurse in an emergency room. That was a major goal. I've been to the top of the Terminal Tower and I've flown. What else is there?" Her brown eyes were twinkling in merriment.

"Actually," Hal said, grinning, "I can think of something else that just might make your life even more complete."

"And would that be, Mr. Walker?"

"Well, it would involve me asking you a certain question and you giving a certain answer."

"I would like very much to hear that question, Mr. Walker, but not quite yet. I'd like a little more time...to get to know each other...before answering that question. Even though I think I know what the answer will be. Okay?"

"Okay. That's fine." Hal sipped his coffee and sighed. "You know, Theresa, there's been something else I've been thinking about. Quite a bit, actually."

"Planning to start your own airline?" Theresa teased. "Take on mighty American Airlines? Bring them down to earth?"

"Not exactly. But I am thinking about taking a leave of absence from American."

Theresa realized immediately that their conversation's path suddenly had taken a sharp turn. "Why?" she asked soberly.

"England. You've been reading what the Germans have been doing to England for the last few days."

"You mean the bombing?"

"Yes."

"It's terrible."

"Yes, it is. And now that Hitler has taken France, it's clear that England is next on his agenda." Hal again sipped his coffee. "It's also clear that the Royal Air Force doesn't have enough planes or pilots to stop the Luftwaffe. If Hitler gets control of the air, he will try to invade England. Well, at least that's one man's opinion."

"I think I know where this is going."

"Have I mentioned that my dad was an aviator in World War One?" Theresa shook her head. "He was. He was shot down over France. Luckily," Hal smiled, "he survived. Managed to bail out. Lucky to even have a parachute. Early in the war, pilots weren't given parachutes. The Army thought giving them chutes would make them cowards. Can you believe that? If they were hit, they had a choice – jump and die for sure or stay in the plane, ride it down and hope to get it on the ground before burning to death. Fortunately, wiser heads prevailed. Anyway, I've been hearing that pilots from other nations are volunteering to help the RAF. French, Polish, Canadian, Irish, Australian, Czech. A few Americans."

Theresa reached across to Hal's plate and picked up a small piece of bagel. Deliberately, she placed it on her tongue, chewed and swallowed, all the time looking unblinkingly into Hal's eyes. Then she picked up her cup and sipped. "And you mean to be one of them?"

"It seems like the right thing to do. I think I can help."

There followed a long interval of silence. Theresa and Hal both sipped coffee.

"Well," he said, "what do you think? I really want to know…need to know."

The merriment had deserted Theresa's eyes. They now were reflecting a very different emotion, one that Hal had not before seen in Theresa. She nodded slightly. "I'm going, too."

"What?" Hal spluttered.

"I'm going to England, too." Her words were spoken with great calm, also with great determination. "The way I see it, the hospitals in England could use another experienced nurse. Don't you agree?"

"But, Theresa..." Hal's customary poise had deserted him. "Theresa, you don't know a soul in England."

"When I came to Mount Sinai as a high school graduate from a small town, I didn't know a soul in Cleveland either."

"Touche."

"You're darned right."

He smiled. "You don't have a passport."

"Do you?"

"No. Touche again."

"You're darned right again."

"I think I might be about to make a concession."

"I think that might be a wise flight plan, Mr. Walker."

He smiled. "I'll bet we can get them fast when we explain our intentions. A call to our congressman, if need be."

"The passport clerk might think we're nuts, " Theresa smiled. "Of course, perhaps we are."

†††

In July 1940, the RAF had formed into four groups, numbered 10 through 13. No. 11 Group was under the command of 44-year-old Air Vice Marshall Keith Park. The group included 18 airfields and was England's first line of defense in southeastern England against the Luftwaffe. One of the 18 was Tangmere, near Chichester and the English Channel. Tangmere was home to four squadrons, each numbering 20 fighters with two in reserve. Tangmere is where Hal Walker received his fighter training and where he quickly was made to feel welcome. His Squadron 43 flew Hurricanes which were formidable fighters. Forty feet long, with a 31-foot wingspan, they were agile, armed with eight .303 caliber Browning machine guns mounted in their wings. They could climb to 34,000 feet, achieve a maximum speed of 328 miles per hour and had a cruising range of 500 miles, far fewer in the rigors of aerial combat. Hal loved flying them.

Theresa had shocked the head nurse at St. Thomas.

"Yes, Miss Hassler, I understand you've been asking for me," she said, her voice as chilly as the gray lobby.

Theresa extended her hand, and the head nurse looked at it before taking it in a gentle shake. "I think I could be of service here."

"You're American?"

"Yes."

"In what capacity do you think you can assist?"

"I'm an experienced nurse."

"No doubt. But we are dealing with war wounds, many of them quite horrific. It can be quite jarring."

"I'm an emergency room nurse," Theresa said calmly. "By both training and experience."

"I see," said the head nurse. "But why have you come to England? Really? You're the only one."

"Why did you become a nurse?" Theresa asked pleasantly. She thought it best not to mention Hal Walker.

"Yes. I see. But London is a great distance from..."

"Cleveland, in Ohio. Mount Sinai Hospital."

"And Saint Thomas could be a dangerous place to be...as you no doubt have observed."

"I've noticed the preparations for bombings. Very thorough."

"Thus far," said the head nurse, "we've been fortunate. No bombs have fallen on London."

When German planes had begun attacking England on July 7, their initial targets were British airfields and ports. Mainly. As early as the first day of attacks, German bombs killed 62 civilians in the southern villages of Godalming, Aldershot, Haslemere and Farnborough. In London, St. Thomas was just across Westminster Bridge from the House of Commons. Anticipating that the Germans might begin to bomb London, staff at St. Thomas had moved the surgical theaters to the basement, sandbagged ground floor windows, and closed the top floors.

"But," said Theresa, "your casualty registration rate is climbing nonetheless."

"Yes," said the head nurse. "Injured pilots. Civilians from the countryside. I cannot deny our need." Her voice was warming slightly. "I will introduce you to the ward sister in charge of emergency treatments."

"Thank you."

"Do you require lodgings?"

"Yes. But I'm used to modest quarters."

"Good," said the head nurse, a small smile surfacing. "They are a hallmark of ours."

†††

The Battle of Britain. Of the 2,365 pilots who flew for the British, 348 were killed in action. About 80 percent of the airmen were British.

Of the other 13 nationalities, Poles were the most numerous with 141 -- of whom 29 were killed. All the Poles were volunteers and virtually all had come to Britain at their own expense and some after harrowing escapes from their homeland. Consistently, they fought with enthusiasm and fierce determination.

Of all the RAF pilots, including the British, the Poles were the most experienced, many having dueled Luftwaffe planes right up until Poland was forced to surrender. They had to learn to fly Britain's higher performance fighters, but from the start the Poles were extraordinary marksmen. In one RAF Fighter Command gunnery contest, three Polish squadrons won the first three places. The best British squadron finished fourth. In September 1940, one Polish squadron achieved the highest "kill rate" in Britain's Fighter Command. Their squadrons "swing into the fight with dash and enthusiasm," wrote Air Chief Marshall Sir Hugh Dowding. "They were inspired by a burning hatred of the Germans, which made them deadly opponents." In the end, six of the top 12 Fighter Command aces were non-British.

Hal Walker proved a fast learner. Quickly, he learned to scramble, getting his Hurricane into the air within the required two minutes from alert. So much for the detailed, long pre-flight checklists of the commercial airline industry, he reflected. The RAF's rapid response was crucial. German fighters needed only five minutes to cross the Channel. British fighters needed 15 minutes to scramble and climb to the altitude – about 15,000 feet -- necessary for successful intercepts. Hal learned to zero in on targets and to fire. He also practiced evasive maneuvers, including quick, twisting dives. He learned never to fly in a straight line for more than 30 seconds in a combat zone.

Within two weeks after arriving at Tangmere, he felt comfortable at the controls of the Hurricane. Britain was desperate for pilots. Hal's first combat took place on August 18, two days after a German raid had heavily damaged Tangmere, shattering buildings and pocking taxiways and runways. During that August 16th attack, Hal and others had gone sprinting for protective trenches. Most made it but two WAFs, their skirts shredded and bloodied, lay motionless just 30 feet from the nearest trench. Hal had heard their screams.

On the 18th, a brilliant sun quickly was warming the air. A phone call received in the Dispersals Building and a flare sent skyward immediately afterward signaled the scramble. Hal and the other Squadron 43 pilots went sprinting across the grass, pulling on parachutes as they ran. Hal vaulted onto the Hurricane's wing and climbed into the cockpit. A ground crewman assisted with his leather helmet and straps. Two more pulled chock blocks away from the plane's wheels. Hal ignited the fighter's engine and immediately was taxiing toward the runway, accelerating all the way. He felt sweat dripping from his brow and forming in his armpits. At altitude, he knew, it would be much colder. The Hurricane went rocketing down the runway and into the air – in just under two minutes.

This is it, Hal thought as the Hurricane began its steep ascent. No DC-3 with a co-pilot, a stewardess and 18 passengers. No redundant systems. No small talk. This was my choice.

†††

For Theresa, the morning of the 18th heralded the start of another grueling day. It would include treating the newly injured and tending to the recovering. But more than that, there would be endless boiling, scrubbing, wiping and buffing to combat the viruses and bacteria rampant in hospitals. In her small room above a bicycle shop in nearby Carlisle Lane, she heated water on a hotplate for tea to sip with day-old bread. As she pulled the bread apart into bite-size pieces, her thoughts turned to

Hal. She hadn't seen him since arriving in London. He was too consumed with training. They had spoken twice by phone. Despite everything, Theresa was thinking, coming here was the right choice. Yes, there are the terrible injuries. Amputations. Burns. Gashes. The long, long hours. But I am making a contribution, and I feel closer to Hal. And I know he's thinking about me. She smiled and sighed. She was remembering the St. Christopher medal she had given Jack Brecker in 1932 and was wishing she had thought to give one to Hal. Jack, she thought, if you could only see me now. I'm a long way from Cleveland and even longer from Shelby. I doubt if you even know I'm here. I wonder if you still think of me. I don't think I'll ever get over you. Not entirely. First love and all that. But now there's Hal, and he is a truly wonderful man. I've been blessed, Jack Brecker. She sipped her tea. Enough, she told herself, it's time to be off to Saint Thomas.

Lying just a block east of Carlisle Lane and St. Thomas was hulking, bustling Waterloo Station. Theresa marveled at the swerving taxis and scurrying pedestrians headed for the station. I sometimes wonder if they know there's a war on, she mused. They seem to be taking everything so much in stride. As Theresa neared St. Thomas, some of those taxi drivers and pedestrians might have noticed a spring in her own stride. She was glad to be alive, in London and working for the greater good.

†††

Hal and the other flyers in Squadron 43 had climbed to more than 15,000 feet above the English Channel. Scant moments later, a voice barked through Hal's headset. "German bombers to the east and below. Let's knock the bloody Bosche from our skies."

Hal looked down on a huge formation of twin-engine enemy bombers. Far below they were silent and appeared to be gliding.

"Any fighter escorts?" another voice radioed.

"None yet" was the reply.

"Sitting ducks" called a third voice.

"Keep watchful for their escorts," cautioned the initial voice. "They prefer to follow and pounce."

Hal and his squadron mates rolled into their attack dives. The distance between predator and prey began closing rapidly.

"Attack at will" came the order. "Good shooting."

From above, Hal locked onto the starboard side of a bomber. Once it was squarely in his gun sight, Hal's right thumb deliberately depressed the red firing button. A two-second burst of machine gun rounds went tearing at the bomber. Its tail gunner was killed instantly and its tail splintered badly. Hal saw smoke begin to trail from the starboard engine. Immediately, he recalled one of the RAF's "Ten Commandments:" Don't watch your flamer go down except out of the corner of your eye.

Hal zeroed in on another German bomber. Simultaneously, his headset again came alive: "Escorts coming out of the sun. One-O-Nines. Break off. Break off now and evade!"

Hal didn't hesitate. Driving his action was another RAF "commandment:" If attacked from a superior height, wait until your opponent is well committed to his dive and within about 1,500 yards of you. Then suddenly turn toward him. Hal obeyed. He put his Hurricane into a gut-wrenching dive. Then moments later, he swung the agile craft around and upward. His decisiveness startled the German pilot who swerved to evade Hal's fire.

With no warning whatsoever, though, Hal was under attack from a second German. Hal rolled quickly into another steep, twisting dive, then swooped upward to try to gain advantage. In the next instant, his canopy's windscreen shattered and he heard and felt rounds ripping through his port wing.

Again, his training kicked in. When hit, Hal knew it was crucial to bail out as quickly as possible, before overwhelming G-forces developed in the plunging aircraft. He reached for the latch on his canopy. It was stuck. Sweet Jesus, he murmured, release! He pushed hard. The latch wouldn't budge. Frantically, Hal glanced in all directions. No flames yet. He punched the latch with his leather-gloved right hand. The latch held. Shit, Hal hissed, Shit.

†††

That evening, on the walk back to Carlisle Lane, the spring was gone from Theresa's step. She was bone tired. Pedestrians exiting Waterloo Station, she observed, also were striding less purposefully. As she was nearing the door that led to the upstairs rooms, Ronald Turner, the bicycle store owner and repairman, stepped from his shop. "You've a phone call, Miss Hassler."

"Now?" she asked.

"Yes, Miss."

Her upstairs room had no phone. Turner, a pleasant man in his mid-40s, had informed his tenants that they could use his shop's phone to receive calls and to place outgoing local calls. For long-distance dialing, they needed to use the corner phone booth.

Theresa stepped inside. Who would be phoning me? she wondered. So far, the only incoming calls had been from Hal. "Do you know who it is?" she asked Turner.

"Can't say. It's a woman."

Theresa felt alarm knifing into her stomach. Nervously, she followed the shopkeeper inside. She walked behind his sales counter and picked up the receiver.

"Hello?" she said.

"Miss Hassler?"

"Yes, who's this?"

"I'm calling for Mr. Walker."

Calling for, Theresa's mind was racing, not calling about? Why? What's wrong? She wanted to hold her breath but knew she must speak. "Yes, what is it? Is he all right?" She felt her throat constricting and chest tightening.

"Just a moment, please," the woman said.

A moment later. "Theresa?"

"Hal?"

"It's me."

"Oh, my God. I'm so glad. I was so scared. Are you okay? Are you hurt?"

"Slow down," said Hal. "I'm a little dinged but in one piece."

Theresa felt her knees buckling and reached for the counter top for support. Standing by his shop's entrance, Turner was trying not to watch or overhear. "Where are you?" Theresa asked. "What happened?"

"I'm in a farmer's cottage. He tells me the nearest village is Middleton. Not far from Tangmere."

"I don't understand. What are you doing there?"

"Waiting for a pickup. Back to Tangmere."

"I still don't understand," Theresa said, far more unsettled than at any moment at St. Thomas.

"I had a little accident today. I didn't want you to hear rumors, so this kindly lady phoned you for me."

Hal's "little accident" had been a very close call. Unable to open the cockpit latch by pushing or punching it, he had considered briefly trying to bring the Hurricane down at Tangmere – or even on the Channel beach. Then he saw flames sprouting behind him. No time to bring the Hurricane down. Instantly, he decided to take an alternative, chancey course. He removed his sidearm from its holster, placed the muzzle against the latch and fired, hoping no ricochet would hit him. The latch shattered. He pushed hard and the canopy gave way.

"When I came down," Hal was saying, "I sprained my ankle pretty badly. No break so far as I can tell. These people – Mr. And Mrs. Sutton – helped me from the field into their cottage."

Theresa felt an immense wave of relief washing over her. She leaned against the shopkeeper's counter. "Remember this, Hal. I do not want you for a patient at Saint Thomas. Is that clear?"

"As clear as a squadron leader's orders."

"Nor do I want you copying your dad's daring-do any more. Is that clear?"

"Equally."

"When can we see each other?" Theresa asked.

"This injury won't keep me off the flight line long," said Hal. "Wouldn't want that any way. Still, they'll probably insist that I take a couple days off. Wouldn't want me to be a liability in the sky. Maybe I can get a ride into London tomorrow or catch a train into Waterloo."

"Please try. I need to see you."

"Same here."

"I'll leave my room key with Mr. Turner. If you can make it, just walk over from the station. Look for Turner's Cycle Shoppe in Carlisle Lane."

"Right. Got it. See you, Theresa." He handed the phone back to Mrs. Sutton.

Ronald Turner had stayed discreetly by the door to his shop. Now he approached Theresa, still leaning against his sales counter. "Are you all right? Is everything okay?" His concern for the overworked young woman was genuine.

"Yes, I'm fine. Well, a little shaken. I might be having a guest for a day or two. If that's okay."

"That's fine, Miss."

"I'll leave my key with you in the morning."

"No need. I have the extra. I'll be happy to let your guest in."

†††

The next evening, Theresa left St. Thomas for the short walk to Carlisle Lane. Her step had more than a morning spring. It was akin to a late-for-the-last train stride. Strong, long, purposeful. As Theresa rounded the corner into the lane, she looked up. A light shone in her window. Her heart leaped and she covered the remaining distance in a half-run. She was through the door and up the stairs in scant seconds. Theresa twisted the knob on her room door, swung it open, saw Hal in a large upholstered chair and went rushing to him. He started to rise but before reaching his feet, Theresa was crushing herself against him, forcing him back into the chair. Her lips met his with an impact that rendered him deliciously mute.

When she pulled back at last, Hal smiled and said, "This could lengthen my recovery time."

"Or speed it up. I'm a very experienced nurse."

"How experienced?"

"Well, actually, I'm still a virgin."

Hal nodded. "Do you want to stay one?"

"I think I've been one long enough."

"Think we should close the door?"

"Good idea."

Hal was watching her eyes. "Getting pregnant in a war wouldn't be good. Even for an experienced nurse."

Theresa smiled lovingly. "There's a pharmacy around the corner on Taur Street."

"I'll go."

CHAPTER 8

"Do you want to go with me?" Lea Peiffer said to her friend, Marie Kieny.

"Why?"

"Because it's a gorgeous morning and we haven't done it in a long time. The weather is perfect for climbing. I don't need to tell you how beautiful the views are." It was September 1940, and the pair of young women were strolling along the northern or upper end of Grand' Rue, the village's main street.

Marie looked gravely at her friend, her best friend since early childhood. "The views now would not be so magnificent. Too much gray, if you know what I mean."

"I know what you mean. Too many German uniforms. But from the walls, the gray will not be so obvious. It will be a way to escape the gray for awhile."

Lea was referring to St. Ulrich, the largest of three castles that perched atop the mountains overlooking Ribeauville. All long had been deserted.

"Do you think the Germans would be angry?" Marie asked.

"We won't ask them."

"What if they see us? They might accuse us of spying. You've heard what they do to spies."

Lea shook her head in affectionate exasperation. "I will tell them I wanted to show you our family's vineyards."

"From the castle walls?"

"Oh, Marie. Use your imagination. I would simply tell them we are on a harmless diversion...that we are using a favorite way of seeing our lovely village and all the vineyards."

"I'm not so sure," Marie said, still plagued by uncertainty. "It could be dangerous. The Germans don't trust us."

"Marie, have we given them any reason to not trust us? No. They have been here for four months, and we have been cordial to them and they to us. I think they are enjoying life in our little village. It's pretty and it's quiet. They eat well. They certainly enjoy our wines. I can testify to that. They buy from us almost daily."

"I'm surprised they haven't persecuted our Jewish neighbors," Marie said.

"They might not know we have Jewish neighbors."

"What?"

"Well, you know there are just two Jewish families here," Lea observed. "Unless the Germans have asked, they might not know. I hope that's the case, especially given what we've heard they've been doing to Jews in Germany and Poland."

"We know they are persecuting Jews," said Marie. "That's a fact. But I hope those stories are exaggerated."

"I hope so, too."

Half a platoon – 27 men – comprised the German occupying force in Ribeauville. And for this quiet village, the local German commanding officer, Captain Gerhard Oberster, thought that might be too many. He had two lieutenants, Karl Hoffman and Paul Kohler, and had given each a dozen troops. It was boring duty, with far too little of significance to do. Germany had swiftly conquered all nations it had invaded. For the moment, there was no more pressing need for his men.

The people of Ribeauville hadn't welcomed Oberster's men. That would be too much to ask, he realized. But he had seen little overt sullenness and no armed resistance or sabotage. He hoped it would stay that way, as he had no desire to take up arms against these villagers. Oberster viewed himself as a good soldier, but not one who looked forward to fighting. That was a reality that he hadn't shared with anyone else and wouldn't, knowing that disclosure could be ruinous to his career.

Captain Oberster was trying to keep his men sharp. He had ordered Lieutenants Hoffman and Kohler to drill their men, meet with them daily to remind them of their responsibilities and expected behavior, and he required the lieutenants to file typed daily reports, however brief and repetitive. Oberster wasn't at all certain what the future might bring, but he found it difficult to imagine staying in Ribeauville indefinitely. He was harboring a hope that Hitler's ambition would be fulfilled soon so that he could return home.

On this warm, dry September morning, Lea had at last persuaded Marie to join her for the climb to St. Ulrich castle. They went strolling unhurriedly north on the Grand' Rue. In front of a café, four German soldiers, all young, were sipping coffee, chatting and occasionally laughing. As the young women passed by, they drew admiring glances and could hear murmurs of appreciation.

"They make me nervous," whispered Marie. She looked back and saw one of the soldiers stand. "Do you think he will follow us?"

"Why would he?" replied Lea. "They see us every day. Nothing special about today."

"Some of them are learning French," Marie observed. "I don't like it. I don't want them to understand us. We should have our secrets."

"That could work to our advantage as well, the Germans learning French."

"How?"

"I'm not sure. But I think it could."

At the north end of the village, Lea and Marie paused and peered upward. The path to the top of the mountain was well worn after centuries of use, but it remained a steep, challenging climb. They made no effort to hurry. Still, by the time they reached the summit, the exertion had caused both of them to begin sweating.

"Well?" said Lea.

"As beautiful as ever," Marie conceded readily. "We are lucky to live here. I can't imagine a more beautiful place to live than the Alsace. The mountains, the hills and rivers, the vineyards and sunflowers. The storks with their huge nests."

Lea was smiling during Marie's recitation. "Come on," Lea exulted, "into the castle! Let's storm the ramparts! Charge!"

Marie laughed delightedly. "We shall conquer all! Drive the Germans from our midst. Charge!"

The two young women, this morning sounding and looking more like rambunctious school girls, went running into the castle and scampered up the decaying stone steps to the high battlements. At the top, both were bent at the waist, sucking in deep breaths.

"The air up here is a little thinner," Lea gasped. "And we are not in such great physical condition, are we?"

"We can see all the villages," Marie marveled, ignoring Lea's question. "Riquewihr, Mittelwihr, Bennwihr, Beblenheim, Zellenberg, Bergheim,

Ostheim. Even Colmar. You were right, Lea. From up here, we can't see any gray."

"But we can see Germany," Lea said, still breathing heavily. She pointed toward the Rhine, a broad, shimmering ribbon. "I want to visit Germany some day. Perhaps visit Freiburg. I'm told it's a lovely town. A university town. We can almost see it from here. But when I go, I want to go as a free Frenchman. Free to go, free to return."

CHAPTER 9

September 7, 1940 brought the first major Luftwaffe assault on London proper. Previous attacks on the capital had been confined largely to port facilities, rail yards and airfields. What prompted Hitler's reversal of policy against bombing London was the first Allied air attack on Berlin. The raid angered Hitler and bewildered Berliners who had been assured that their skies were safe from enemy marauders. Afterward, in front of a huge throng of adoring countrymen, Hitler vowed swift and ruthless retaliation.

"That sounded close, closer than usual," Theresa Hassler remarked to the ward sister. Her words were barely spoken when a series of even closer blasts rocked St. Thomas. Involuntarily, Theresa hunched her shoulders.

"Quickly," said the ward sister, "check on all patients. Hurry!"

They both went scurrying toward their ward. Other nurses were hustling to their stations. Outside, the blasts kept growing closer and louder. Inside the hospital, light fixtures were rattling, bulbs cracking, windows shattering.

"Don't they know this is a hospital?" Theresa cried in exasperation.

"I don't think they much care," replied the ward sister. "I just hope our RAF lads exact a heavy toll from the Germans. This is despicable. Lord, have mercy on us all."

At mention of the RAF, Theresa's mind switched immediately to thoughts of Hal Walker.

At the first alert to the waves of oncoming German planes – some 1,000 in all – Hal Walker and his Squadron 43 mates went sprinting to their Hurricanes. From the Tangmere runways, they quickly began ascending steeply. They saw the first German aircraft before reaching attack altitude. "Keep climbing" barked the voice coming through Hal's headset. He could see the other Tangmere squadrons as well as those from other Number 11 Group airfields positioning for the intercept. Hal found himself thinking that the favored British adjective bloody would be appropriate today. Stay with us good guys, Lord, he prayed.

His headset came alive again. "They are headed north…toward London. They are passing over our airfields. Bastards are going to bomb the city."

The squadron now had cleared 15,000 feet. At the mention of London, Hal's thoughts turned immediately to Theresa. Stay safe, Sweetheart. Follow procedure. And to himself, he cautioned, stay concentrated on the Germans. Then came the command to pounce. "Get Jerry! Remember, these are British skies."

Hal's first target was a bomber. He dived, fired, saw smoke begin trailing from the plane, and shifted his attention to another bomber. In the same instant, his headset screamed a warning. "One-O-Nine on your tail, Yank! Evade now!"

Without pausing to glance, Hal broke off his attack on the bomber. He dived sharply, training and experience driving his actions. He swung sharply again to face the ME-109, and now it was the 109's pilot's turn to evade. The German pushed his control stick forward and dived away at full speed. Hal pursued. On the ground far below, six-year-old Peter Bloomfield was standing in the street in front of his family's home, watching in awe. The two dueling planes seemed to be diving straight down on him. He stood still, transfixed.

The German kept plummeting, finally pulling out of his dive at near ground level, wings still fluttering from the stress. He looked behind. Hal's Hurricane still was dogging him. The German pilot took no time to draw a breath. He went speeding toward the Channel, hedgehopping over trees and houses. He couldn't shake Hal, just 100 yards behind. Little Peter Bloomfield waved at Hal's plane. The two fighters flew out over Dover, just above the wave tops. Hal blinked away sweat behind his goggles. So did the German. He is flying magnificently, the 109 pilot was thinking. But he must be running low on fuel. I am.

Hal could see the French coast looming and reached for the firing button. He pushed – and the 109 jinked left. Hal's rounds splashed harmlessly into the Channel. The ME-109 skimmed over the bluffs behind the beach, not more than six feet separating fuselage from earth.

Shit, hissed Hal, and he backed off. During the moment Hal pulled up, the German saw a sliver of opportunity. He jerked his 109 around and upward in a tight bank. His engine howling, he went tearing up at the Hurricane. From nearly point-blank range, the German fired.

During that September 7th attack, 448 British civilians were killed. Thousands more were injured. Of their nearly 1,000 attacking aircraft, the Germans lost 39. The RAF lost 31 fighters. Some of the German and British flyers were able to bail out.

Chapter 10

"This weather is dreadful...brutal." Thaddeus Metz was shivering. "The air...I don't think I've ever felt air quite like this."

"It's not as frigid as a Polish winter," replied General Stanislaw Sosabowski, shoulders hunched against the penetrating cold. "Just miserable."

"*More* miserable," said Thaddeus. "Cold but also so wet and windy. I do not understand why Scots ever began wearing kilts. And some still do. Amazing."

"Sheep."

"Sheep?"

"Most of their clothing was made from sheep's wool. Very scratchy," the general said, smiling, one eyebrow arched in amusement. "Too scratchy in the wrong place."

"Hmmm, yes," agreed Thaddeus. "And they say necessity is the mother of invention. In this case, though, necessity might have mothered a cure for itching."

General Sosabowski chuckled. "Very good, Captain."

Many of the Polish soldiers, sailors and airmen who had escaped to England via Dunkirk and the Mediterranean and Baltic Seas now were concentrated in Scotland. They had been designated the First Polish Army Corps, and their mission was to defend Britain from possible German attack via Norway. By early 1941, the Poles had been awarded full British Army status, and Stanislaw Sosabowski, born May 8, 1892 in Galicia in Ukraine, had been named its commanding officer. Thaddeus had continued to serve as his aide, and the other nine cow pen soldiers were never far removed.

On this raw February morning, General Sosabowski and Thaddeus were in Leven, a village overlooking the Firth of Forth, close to where it joins the North Sea. Across the Firth was Edinburgh. Thaddeus and General Sosabowski were walking slowly along side the Firth, Thaddeus limping noticeably from the lower leg wound suffered at Dunkirk.

"Do you think the Germans might actually invade from Norway?" Thaddeus asked the general.

"Look at this sea," Sosabowski replied. The waters were gray, choppy and white-capped. "It is wide, cold, rough. These Scottish shores would be easy to defend, virtually impossible to storm."

"Then," Thaddeus said pensively, "it would seem we are not serving much purpose here. It seems an awfully slow way to get back to Poland."

"I've been thinking the same thing," said Sosabowski. "And I've been making some inquiries."

"Oh?" Thaddeus was hoping that he wouldn't have to prod the general – whom he now regarded as a mentor and friend as well as commanding officer – for more of his thinking.

"You were a lancer, Thaddeus."

"Still am. Although horses here in Scotland," Thaddeus added dryly, "are in rather short supply."

"Yes. Still are. You are very skilled on horseback. How do you feel about airplanes?"

"Not so good. Dodging stukas in Poland and again at Dunkirk. Airplanes seem to me very nasty birds."

Sosabowski nodded. "How do you think you might feel about being in one for a change?"

"A stuka?"

"No, a British plane."

"Flying one? As a pilot?"

"Not exactly." Sosabowski half-chuckled. "Actually, I mean jumping out of one."

Thaddeus' head rocked back. "Joining the British Airborne?"

"No. Helping me form the Polish Airborne."

"Whew. Well…I…"

"As an airborne force, we could drop into Poland. Surprise the Germans. Shock them. Liberate our countrymen."

Thaddeus' thoughts immediately switched to Bernadeta Gudek, and that surprised him. Yes, he thought of her often, but to think of her so suddenly upon learning of the general's plan? He and Bernadeta had met just once and only briefly. But that encounter had been intense and memorable. "Is this possible?"

"I think so. At least I hope so. I should be hearing soon from the British if they will let us begin training some of our men as an airborne brigade."

"This is very exciting, General. It would take time to train our men. Equip them. One problem I don't see is volunteers. We should have more than enough." He smiled. "I'm ready...your first volunteer. And before you say anything about my leg, it is healing well. Really."

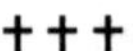

CHAPTER 11

In the spring of 1941, just two days before the Cleveland Indians opened their regular 154-game season, they were scheduled to play an exhibition game against the minor league Columbus Clippers. The game was to be played at the Ohio State Fairgrounds just a few miles south of the Josephinum Pontifical Seminary. Jack Brecker and Mark Hood were in the stadium's front row along the first base line.

Before the game, Lou Boudreau and other Indians were playing catch. With the season about to open, the atmosphere was relaxed and festive. Players were joshing and laughing. Fans watching the players were caught up in their high spirits. The operative word seemed to be fun. A thrown ball went rolling past Boudreau, and he casually turned and went trotting toward the stands to retrieve it. As he picked up the ball, a voice said, "Hello, Mr. Boudreau."

Boudreau looked up. "I'm not often called Mister. I answer to Lou."

"Okay, Lou," Jack smiled. "Nice to meet you."

"Nice to meet you." Lou sensed that Jack and Mark were together. "Are you and your friend from Columbus?"

"Yes and no," said Jack. "I'm from Shelby, Ohio, up north. And my friend Mark – Mark Hood" – Lou stretched out his right hand to shake Mark's hand, then Jack's – "is from Manhattan – New York. We're here in Columbus at the Josephinum."

"The what?"

"A seminary," Jack clarified.

"Priests?"

"No. Seminarians."

"Do I call you Father?"

"Call me Jack."

"Okay."

"Are you Catholic?" Jack asked.

"Born and raised. In Illinois. You're from Manhattan, Mark. Near the Polo Grounds by any chance?"

"Hell's Kitchen. My team is the Dodgers." Mark was beaming. "Hate the Giants and Yankees."

"A good team to hate," Lou smiled, "the Yankees, I mean. You an Indians fan, Jack?"

"For as long as I can remember. I listen to Jack Graney announce the games on radio."

"Graney's the best," said Lou. "Sometimes we have a radio going in the locker room to hear his comments before games. Say, Jack, did you ever play baseball?"

"Some," replied Jack.

"A lot," interjected Mark. "He's good."

Jack was reddening.

"Well, Jack, want to play catch with me for a few minutes?"

The question caught Jack off guard, much like a runner trapped between first and second bases. Then he recovered. "Sure. When?"

"Now."

"Now? I don't have a glove."

Lou laughed. "Shouldn't be a problem. Come on."

Jack shrugged and climbed over the railing and Lou handed him his glove. Jack looked at it with more than a hint of wonder. Then Lou borrowed a glove from third baseman Ken Keltner. "Fellas," he said to his Indian teammates, "this is Father Jack Brecker. Well, almost a Father. He's at a seminary here. Big Indians fan. I've invited him to play a little catch with me."

The other Indians smiled, and the four nearest Jack came over and shook his hand, then made way for him and Boudreau.

"Not too hard," Boudreau teased Jack. "My glove hand isn't calloused yet."

Jack, a trifle nervous, laughed. "And you can see I wear glasses. From studying all that Latin."

Other players laughed heartily, and Jack was feeling more comfortable by the moment. For the next few minutes, Jack and Boudreau threw soft tosses back and forth. Then Jack put some zip on a throw. Boudreau smiled and did likewise. Soon the sharp pop of hard ball meeting their leather gloves became louder than that of any of the other pairs of Indians. "Just one more," said Jack, "and then I'd better quit before my hand looks like a ripe tomato."

After that final throw, he and Boudreau came together to shake hands. "Glad you're up to trying new things," said Boudreau.

"That's never been a problem with Jack." It was Mark Hood, voicing the affection and pride he felt for his friend. "Jack's game for just about anything."

Chapter 12

At the same time Jack Brecker and Lou Boudreau were playing catch in Columbus, Germans were engaged in a construction project not far northwest from Ribeauville. They were building a concentration camp in France near the village of Natzwiller, about 30 miles southwest of Strasbourg and about half-way from there to Ribeauville. The camp, the only one that would be built in France, was located on high ground, a rounded peak 2,500 feet up in the Vosges Mountains in a popular skiing area. Views from the camp were spectacular.

Building the camp were 300 prisoners brought from Germany. During construction, they were housed in temporary barracks near the Hotel Struthof, about a half-mile from the base of the mountain. Overseeing the work were Nazis, many of them SS. Designed to hold up to 1,500 prisoners when completed, the camp would include the commandant's house and swimming pool, a guards' camp, barracks for prisoners, workshops, garages, a kennel, gallows, gas chamber and crematorium. Surrounding it were watchtowers and barbed wire. Nearby was a quarry and that explained the decision to locate the camp. The site was controlled by an SS-owned business, Deutsche Erd Und Steinwerke -- German Earth And Stone Works Ltd. Prisoners would be quarrying indigenous granite that would be used in general construction and highway building.

On May 21, 1941, the camp was ready to begin fulfilling its intended purposes – helping assure a supply of slave labor for Germany's war effort and exterminating those the Nazis deemed undesirable – criminals, Jews, Gypsies, Polish officers, homosexuals, socialists and others considered insufficiently Aryan and unappealing to Hitler. Almost immediately upon completion, Natzwiller's prisoner population grew to 800, all Germans. That would change.

In Rue des Boulangers, Lea Peiffer answered the sharp knock at the front door of her family's home.

"Have you heard?" Marie Kieny asked breathlessly.

"Heard what?" said Lea.

"About the new concentration camp near Natzwiller," Marie said, speaking with a conspiratorial urgency.

"A rumor now and then. Nothing more."

"It's true. A German concentration camp. Right here in France. *Our* France." Marie was speaking with an energy born of anger. "Close to Ribeauville. Close to *us*."

Lea reached out and put a hand on her friend's shoulder. "Try to calm down. Have you ever been to Natzwiller?"

"No."

"Nor I," said Lea. "It's pretty isolated in the Vosges. Do you know who's there? I mean who the Germans are putting there?"

"Other Germans, I'm told," said Marie.

"Jews?"

"Probably. Maybe Gypsies and criminals, too."

"French?"

"Not so far as I've heard," said Marie.

There followed silence for about 20 seconds. "I think we're thinking the same thing," Lea said. "It's only a matter of time before French people are taken to a concentration camp in France."

"We should warn our Jewish neighbors," said Marie.

"Yes, I agree."

"Maybe they will flee. To Switzerland."

"Perhaps," said Lea, "but I don't think they will run yet. I think they will wait to see what happens. They don't want to leave their homes and businesses any more than we do."

"But waiting could be dangerous," said Marie.

Lea nodded in agreement. "Or fatal."

†††

In Warsaw, violent death already had become a daily occurrence. In addition, death from starvation was becoming more commonplace. To Bernadeta Gudek, what she was witnessing in Warsaw seemed almost otherworldly. Yes, she reflected, I saw death in Zyrardow, but nothing like the mass cruelty I am seeing here. It's like a disease, a contagious disease. German soldiers are murdering innocent civilians as casually as a cow's tail swats at a fly. Some of the murders are my fault, I know. Reprisals for the work of the Home Army. The sabotaging of German equipment. The killing of German officers. I pray to you, God, for understanding, for

France
Bastogne
Metz
Strasbourg
Nancy
Paris
Natzwiller
Ribeauville
Colmar
Mulhouse
Basel

forgiveness. I could never do this work on my own. Not after knowing how the Germans will react. Dragging innocents from their houses and shops and shooting them in the streets. Or hanging them from lamp posts. Too sad. Too sickening. The Home Army gives me strength. I wonder if Father sensed all of this would be happening when I left Zyrardow.

Bernadeta lit a cigarette. She inhaled deeply. I never smoked at home. I had no desire. Here, it seems necessary. Steadies my nerves. Keeps the hunger pangs at bay. She inhaled again. Living in a cramped room and in basements. Hardly sleeping. Just dozing and napping. And for how long? How long can we resist? How long before the Germans tire of our presence and just slaughter all of us? She looked at the cigarette in her left hand. Her right hand fingered a confiscated German luger. Zyrardow. It seems so far away. So much time has passed, yet so little. I must get home for a visit. Breathe farm air. See Barbara. Father and Mother. That young soldier. Thaddeus Metz. I wonder if he ever thinks about me. Remembers me, yes. But thinks about me? If he is still alive...We could use him in our Home Army. Such a brief meeting. Yet, I think I will remember him always.

"Bernadeta."

She looked up, startled from her reverie.

"It's time for our meeting." The voice belonged to a Home Army captain, Kaz Majos.

She nodded. Then, slowly, for the moment feeling drained and much older than her years, she rose to her feet. She holstered the luger. As Bernadeta followed the captain, she puffed on the cigarette, then ran her tongue around the inside of her teeth, stretching the thin scar that ran for an inch slightly downward from the left corner of her mouth. Whatever the new plan, she was thinking, it will involve danger and possibly death. I really do need to get home for a visit.

Chapter 13

On June 22, 1941, a month and a day after the Natzwiller concentration camp in France became operational, Hitler's ground and air forces again struck eastward. The onslaught -- Operation Barbarossa -- was code-named after a medieval German emperor who had won great victories in the East. Barbarossa now was Hitler's plan to attack and crush Russia. So much for his August 1939 non-aggression pact with Joseph Stalin.

Under that pact, Russia had been sending trainloads of oil, food, minerals and other materials to Germany. But Hitler wanted more. He wanted to control the Soviet Union's vast resources directly. Besides, he regarded Slavs as sub-human and unfit for anything other than slave labor.

Barbarossa shocked nations around the globe, but to Hitler's senior staff, it came as no surprise. Three months earlier, on March 21, Hitler had drafted his Commissar Order: all Soviet commissars – political officers – who would be captured were to be executed summarily. Still earlier, in July 1940, Hitler had decided to invade Russia. In fact, from 1939 onward, Hitler knew his forces would one day invade Russia. The only issue in question was timing, and losing the Battle of Britain settled the matter.

In England, for a brief while, Thaddeus Metz thought that Hitler's attack on Russia might relieve some of the suffering in Poland. He soon learned otherwise. One piece of news in particular both infuriated and saddened him.

"In Cracow," Thaddeus said to General Sosabowski, "the Germans continue to terrorize. There is no let-up."

"Your hometown is suffering greatly," the general said soothingly. "It is hard, I know."

"A couple days ago," Thaddeus said, "I heard that Germans went into Saint Stanislaw Kostka. A church. My church. Eleven priests. The Nazis took away nine and imprisoned them. Priests. Men of the cloth. They could be dead by now. Executed." A pause. "General, we must return to Poland. We must."

The general made a gesture rare for him. He extended his left hand and affectionately gripped Thaddeus' right shoulder. "Before we can return to

Poland, there is much we must do here. You must concentrate on our work. It's hard, Thaddeus, I know, but you must. Come with me."

Limping, Thaddeus went walking with the general to his quarters. Sosabowski wanted Thaddeus to be the first to learn some big news; the general had received permission to form the Polish Airborne Brigade.

CHAPTER 14

Bernadeta had left the luger in Warsaw. Being seen or caught with it would mean instant execution. Traveling at night, walking, she believed she could arrive at the family farm in two days. She had neither seen nor communicated with her family since coming to Warsaw some seven months ago. Although in the company of Home Army companions in Warsaw, she missed her family terribly.

How are they? she was wondering. Are they healthy? Are they still alive? Have the Germans ever discovered the two graves in the forest?

That first night on the road to Zyrardow had passed uneventfully. In her work with the Home Army, Bernadeta had learned to walk with an athletic stealth. No wasted motion. Little if any sound. Constantly alert. On the sun-hardened earthen road, there was some traffic, both motorized and horse-drawn, and it was all German, much no doubt headed east to support the invasion of Russia. The Germans were confident and noisy. Why not? she thought. They are in control. They are winning. But their carelessness provided Bernadeta with ample warning each time they neared her.

As daybreak approached, she began to look for a place to hide and rest. Ahead and off to her right, she saw a barn – one badly in need of whitewashing and new roof thatching. There was as yet no sign of activity around the barn or the nearby house. She dropped into a squatting position. Still too early, she thought. She would need to be careful to avoid startling any livestock, including any rooster ready to crow a morning reveille. She stood and went walking closer.

At the barn, she surveyed her surroundings. Immediately, she felt a sense of comfort. No rooster or hens on the loose. She could see now that they were confined to a nearby, small coup surrounded by wire fencing. Carefully, slowly, she opened the barn door. It creaked slightly, and Bernadeta held her breath. As she eased in, she saw two pens, one holding an ox, the other a milk cow. Just like home, she thought. She went directly to the wooden ladder and climbed to the loft. She knew the farmer would be coming soon to do the morning milking, and she would need to stay awake until after he had finished. She would not ask for food. She was carrying a loaf of bread and a small flask of wine.

Hours later, Bernadeta awoke. She had slept well, much better than in Warsaw basements or in her own small room there. She could judge by the sunlight pouring through the loft opening that it was around noon, perhaps a little after. She began chewing on the bread and sipping the wine. The bread was far from fresh and the wine too warm, but she was grateful for the nourishment. Many in Warsaw had less.

After finishing, Bernadeta moved to a rear corner of the loft to urinate onto some straw. Afterward she moved to the loft opening. The earthen road lay about 100 yards away. No vehicular traffic to be seen. Bernadeta breathed in the farm-scented air and shook her head, her blonde hair still dyed brown. So peaceful here, she reflected. So vastly different from Warsaw. Right now, it's hard to imagine we are at war. In the distance, walking briskly, a lone figure was nearing the farm. Bernadeta watched idly. I have many hours to pass before I can resume walking safely, Bernadeta mused. Oh, to be as carefree as that Pole.

The walker's long stride was admirable. Nearly like mine, Bernadeta reflected. In that instant, her curiosity came alive. She looked hard at the figure, wearing a black, brimmed hat. Look this way so I can get a better view, Bernadeta commanded silently. She continued watching intently. The walker had drawn even with the path that led from the road to the farmhouse and barn. I wish I could call out but I can't, Bernadeta was thinking. Too risky.

The farmer with his hulking ox was at work in the field. His wife was hanging laundry from a line strung between poles at the rear of the house. Both seemed thoroughly absorbed in their work. Bernadeta took another look in both directions for signs of German traffic. To the south, she could see nothing, but she could hear distant rumbling. German convoy. Bernadeta decided to take a chance. She quickly stepped away from the loft opening and crossed to the ladder. Down she went.

By the time she pushed open the barn door, the walker had passed 100 feet down the road beyond the path to the farm. Bernadeta jogged as lightly as possible down the path. At the road, she turned left and continued jogging, quickly closing the distance. She then stopped and looked behind her. The farmer, behind his ox, now was watching her but showing no evidence of strong curiosity.

She continued walking rapidly until she was within about 20 feet of the walker. “Ahem,” Bernadeta cleared her throat. No reply. A few seconds later, Bernadeta said forcefully, “Excuse me.”

The walker halted and turned. The recognition was instantaneous and mutual. The two figures went hurtling toward each other, arms outstretched.

“Barbara!” cried Bernadeta, caution momentarily deserting her.

“Bernadeta!” came the exultant reply.

The two sisters threw themselves together, laughter and tears of joy commingling. They pulled apart, grasped each others’ shoulders and smiled widely.

Bernadeta was the next to speak. “Where are you going?”

“To Warsaw, looking for you.”

“What? Why? Is something wrong at home? Are mother and father all right?”

“They are fine,” said Barbara. “Well, they worry about you, and they miss you terribly. It has been so long since we have seen you. I had to see you. I’ve missed you. Even more than I thought I would.” Another tear trickled down Barbara’s cheek.

“It is dangerous in Warsaw,” said Bernadeta. “It is dangerous on this road.” She pointed to the farmer who was now giving them his full attention. Then he surprised them by waving and smiling. The sisters waved back. “Listen,” whispered Bernadeta. “Do you hear them? Those are German vehicles. If the Germans see you, they could kill you. For traveling without permission, without proper papers. For spying. For no reason at all. I see it almost every day.”

“Yes, but –“

Bernadeta cut her off. “What did Father say?”

Barbara lowered her head. “I left a note.”

“He doesn’t know you are doing this?”

“He does by now. I’m sure they have seen the note.”

“They must be worried sick. He will come after you.”

“I told him not to…in the note. I said I would go to Warsaw and find you. I would try to get you to return home…or join you in the Home Army.”

“No.”

“No?”

"You are not going to Warsaw, and you are not joining the Home Army." Bernadeta's sharp tone surprised her sister.

"Bernadeta?"

"What is it?" she replied brusquely.

"Where are you going?"

"Home…to visit you and Mother and Father." A brief pause, then Bernadeta spoke accusingly, "You are changing the subject."

Barbara ignored the accusation. "You look thinner."

"Not much home cooking in Warsaw."

"Mother will change that."

"I'm sure she will."

"Where did you spot me?" Barbara asked.

"From that barn." Bernadeta turned and pointed back toward the farm. "I missed you, too. I needed to see you."

Barbara's eyes softened. "Then let's go home."

Bernadeta smiled and nodded.

"Did you hide there?" Barbara asked, pointing toward the barn.

"Yes. It's not safe to walk during the day. Especially when you are far from home."

"Should we be looking for a hiding place? Another barn?"

Bernadeta paused before replying. The German convoy soon would be coming into view. "No, I don't want to endanger another family today." Across the field, she saw a copse. "Those trees. We'll hide there until the Germans pass. Then, we'll head for home, but we'll be staying off the road as much as possible."

"Will you be staying? Home, I mean," said Barbara.

"For a few days."

"That's all?"

"I have to get back to Warsaw. I'm needed there." The sisters had begun crossing the field.

"I'll go with you."

An unequivocal No was forming on Bernadeta's lips when she swallowed it. "Let's talk about it…at home."

†††

Chapter 15

On Sunday morning, December 7, 1941, after attending Mass, Jack Brecker returned to his room at the Josephinum. His spirits were buoyant. Only six months to my ordination, he was musing. Then I can get on with my life's work. My calling. I wonder where I'll be going. Some place where I'm really needed. That much I know. The Vatican considers us missionaries-in-the-making. It's pretty clear they want a good return on their investment in us. They want us to build parishes. I'll probably be heading to the Pacific Northwest or the Southwest. Growing areas for the church. They told us we would have a choice -- as long as all eight of my classmates don't choose the same place. Still, I was surprised. I had been just assuming the Vatican would tell us where to go. No choice at all. I was prepared for that. But we do have a choice in the matter. I kind of like the idea of going to Arizona. Mountains. Desert. So different from the green of Ohio. I'm ready. More than ready. I've been a student my whole life. It's time I was a working priest. Priest. Has a nice ring to it.

It was cold but sunny that day in Worthington, Ohio. At lunch, the nine members of the Josephinum class of '42 were occupying two round tables in the dining hall.

"Want to help me after lunch?" Mark Hood asked Jack and their two tablemates.

"With what?" Jack replied.

"Putting up the nativity scene in the chapel."

"Sounds good. I like the big and colorful pieces. When do you want to meet?"

"How about at two?"

"Okay. Chapel at two." Which would be 8 a .m. in Hawaii.

†††

Tom Brecker's emotions that day were mixed. He was slowly pacing the flight deck of the Hornet. The new carrier had been commissioned just six weeks before on October 20. It had yet to leave port at Norfolk, Virginia. Tom hunched his shoulders inside his wool navy p-coat against the chilled sea breeze. He was pleased because he was confident that Bridgett Hassler would like the white cashmere sweater with blue trim that he was about to mail to her in Shelby. Simultaneously, Tom was saddened that he would be unable to see her or his family at Christmas. Walking the deck, he also felt pride in being a crewman – fireman – on this spectacular new ship. 809 feet long. A flight deck 127 feet wide. Capable of knifing through seas at 34 knots and carrying 81 warplanes. For defense, it carried eight five-inch guns and 16 1.1-inch guns. Tom was one of 2,072 crewmen.

At the fantail, he breathed deeply the brisk air. A good choice, he was reflecting, joining the Navy, and good luck, being assigned to the Hornet. He was jolted from his reverie when, unexpectedly, the klaxons sounded Battle Stations. A drill, thought Tom, a Sunday drill and then, with no hesitation, he went sprinting down the long deck to don his fireman's gear.

In Shelby, Bridgett Hassler was decorating the tree her dad had put up in front of the living room window. She was humming Christmas songs to herself while stringing lights and hanging glass ornaments and garland. She would miss not getting to spend time with Tom, but she would visit the Breckers' home and get to visit with Jack and Paul.

Her humming was serving another purpose; it was helping to avoid dulling her spirits with the heavy knowledge that, come Christmas, her sister Theresa would be an ocean away in London.

During the 15 months since Hal Walker had been reported missing in action, Theresa's life had seemed to come nearly to a standstill. Her work at St. Thomas was now proceeding much like it had been at Mt. Sinai in Cleveland – busy, demanding, but not overwhelming.

I'm glad I've stayed on in England, Theresa had concluded. Hal might be dead. That's a horrible thought, but it's possible. No wreckage has been found. But he might be a prisoner or wounded and still recovering in a French hospital. In any case, I feel better for being closer to him. And I've grown fond of London and her people. The other nurses are friends, good friends. And Mr. Turner couldn't be a better landlord or friend.

Another thought crossed Theresa's mind: I'm glad Jack is at the seminary and not in harm's way. I wonder if he is still wearing the Saint Christopher medal.

On December 7, 1941, when it was 8 a.m. in Hawaii, it was 7 p.m. in London. There were no Christmas lights to see. No lights at all. London was in a blackout that would eventually extend for nearly five years. Still, Theresa felt secure enough to decide to take an evening stroll through her neighborhood. It's brisk, she thought, but not uncomfortable as she went walking toward the Thames. When I get back to my room, I'll turn on the BBC nine o'clock news.

†††

In Ribeauville, it was an hour later than in London. I can't believe it, Lea Peiffer was fretting, as she and her parents listened to the news that night in their home in Rue des Boulangers. Japan attacks Pearl Harbor. America will go to war against Japan. This should please Hitler. Now he can concentrate on conquering Russia. He doesn't have to worry about America coming to the aid of France. England can't do it, not alone. Not without America's help. My poor country. My beloved France. My wonderful Alsace. We could be doomed to a lifetime of German domination. She was buttoning her red cardigan sweater against the chill brought on by winter and worsened by this news. Is there any hope for us? Lea wondered. Any hope at all?

†††

The next day at Fort Benning, Georgia, Brigadier General George Patton was euphoric. Hitler had shocked him, indeed, shocked much of the world, by declaring war on the United States. Goddamned lunacy, Patton was thinking. Hitler's an utter idiot. He'll have us standing on the doorstep of Germany before he realizes he's made a fatal miscalculation. Mark my words, fatal. I'll bet he didn't pay a whit of attention to his generals. He has some damned fine generals. They would know how foolish it is to bring America into the war when they are struggling to take Russia. I can't wait. I love it. I hope I get to shoot the son-of-a-bitch Hitler myself.

At Fort Benning, Patton had been promoted to brigadier general on October 1, 1940. Just six weeks later on November 16, he had been given command of the 2nd Armored Division. He was hoping for, in his words, "a long and bloody war."

Three times in 1941, in June, August and November, he had put the 2nd Armored through challenging maneuvers in Tennessee, Louisiana and the Carolinas. His mantra on rigorous training was "Hard on maneuvers, easy in war."

His energetic leadership was not going unnoticed. In July, he had been pictured on the cover of LIFE magazine.

†††

In Ribeauville, the next night's newscast lifted the gloom that had enveloped Lea the night before. I simply can't believe it, she thought. Hitler and Mussolini have both declared war on America. I don't think I could ask for a better Christmas present. Her parents, Klaus and Sonia, agreed. An idea popped into Lea's excited mind. I think I will start knitting a sweater and give it to the first American soldier I see. And a bottle of our best riesling.

†††

The war declarations – America's against Japan, Hitler's against America and America's quick reply – brought cheer elsewhere in the world as well.

"What do you think it all means, General?" Thaddeus asked Sosabowski. "What do you think it means for us?"

"It means we need to step up our airborne training."

"For jumping into Poland."

"Eventually," said Sosabowski. "First, though, I think we will be jumping somewhere else. Probably into France."

"When?"

"Not soon enough."

†††

For the third Brecker brother, Paul, as with millions of fellow Americans, the Japanese attack on Pearl Harbor and the exchange of war declarations brought overnight change to his thinking and his plans.

Following his graduation from Shelby High School in 1939, Paul had been content to take a job at the Shelby Salesbook Company, a large commercial printing firm, and to continue living at home with his parents. At the Salesbook, Paul had been apprenticing as a press operator. He liked the work and the people he was working with. They liked him as well. Paul was eager to learn and friendly to all. Now, on the morning of Tuesday, December 9, they were feeling proud of him and worrying, too.

Out in the plant, a veteran pressman approached Paul. "Is it true?"

"Yes, I'm going over to Mansfield to enlist tomorrow." Mansfield was the county seat, 12 miles southwest of Shelby on winding state Rt. 39.

"Navy like Tom?"

"After Pearl Harbor, I don't think so. One of us on a ship is enough. I'm worried about Tom. The Hornet isn't going to stay in Norfolk forever. It's bound to sail to the Pacific."

"You?"

"Army. I'm not sure where it will take me, but I like the idea of solid ground under my feet." Paul was smiling and so was the pressman.

The pressman reached out to shake Paul's hand. "Well, good luck. America needs you and many more like you. I almost wish I was young enough to enlist. Almost."

"You fought in one war. That's enough," said Paul.

"I won't argue with that. It was no picnic. I still have nightmares now and then. Paul," the pressman said, his tone turning grave, "keep your head down. Don't go out of your way trying to be a hero."

"Thanks," Paul smiled, "I'll try to remember that."

At work that day, Paul found his mind often shifting away from the huge press and the heavy rolls of paper. Tom, Jack and myself. A sailor, a stinkslinger and a soldier. Stinkslinger, Paul smiled. That was his very private, affectionate word for the parish priest, Michael McFadden, who swung the incense burner back and forth during benediction after the last Sunday Mass. Soon the word would apply to Jack as well. Paul smiled again.

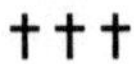

Chapter 16

"I don't get it," Tom Brecker said to fellow Hornet fireman Sam Tortino. "We're supposed to be carrying fighters, dive bombers and torpedo planes. Well, we are. But why the hell are they loading those two B-25s onboard?"

"Beats me," said the black-haired Sam in his distinctively Brooklyn accent.

"Heavy bombers can't take off from the Hornet. There's just plain not enough flight deck."

"Agreed," said Sam. "And it doesn't make any sense for us to ferry them to the west coast. They could fly and be there in a day or two."

It was Tuesday, February 3, 1942, and the U.S.S. Hornet was about to get underway for her maiden voyage. Destination: San Francisco.

"Who are those guys?" Tom asked. He was pointing to two young officers coming aboard. "They're not Navy."

"Don't know," said Sam, "haven't heard a thing. They're not very big."

"Army lieutenants," Tom said, noting the rank insignia – single silver bars – on the Army officers' uniform jackets. "Army lieutenants on a carrier. Heavy bombers. I just don't get it."

"I'm sure great minds are at work," Sam said, winking at Tom.

"Greater than ours," Tom said dubiously. "Can't wait to get the poop on all this."

†††

As winter edged into spring, Lou Boudreau's mind was tussling with more than the inherent challenges of playing shortstop, widely regarded along with catcher as the most demanding of baseball positions. Back on December 10, 1941, Lou's teammate and future Hall of Fame pitcher Bob Feller had enlisted in the Navy. The right thing to do, Lou was thinking. For himself, he already had learned that his bad ankles would bar him from military service. Still, he was feeling guilty. Lou was 24, soon to turn 25, the same age as Jack Brecker. Lou, like Jack, was self-confident and mature beyond his years. He also was hungering for leadership. The Cleveland Indians were a good team, Lou knew, and he believed that stronger leadership would drive them to the American League championship and a World Series title. As the 1942 season drew closer, Lou worked up the courage to address team owner Alva Bradley.

After the 1941 season had ended, team general manager Cy Slapnicka had resigned. Bradley then had moved manager Roger Peckinpaugh to the general manager position. Upon learning about that development, Lou Boudreau had taken pen in hand and written Bradley. Soon afterward, Bradley and Boudreau had met.

"That was an interesting letter," Bradley said to his young shortstop.

"If we had a stronger manager," said Lou, "I think we could win the American League pennant."

"And you think you could be that stronger manager..."

"Yes."

There followed a very pregnant silence. Lou wasn't certain what would come next. Derision? Anger? A trade to another team? To Lou, they all seemed like possibilities.

Bradley finally ended the awkwardness. "Lou, you're my shortstop."

"I can be both. Shortstop and manager."

"Player-manager."

"Right."

"You're only what? Twenty-four? Twenty-five? That combination would be a heavy load. Probably too heavy."

"Does anyone know this team better than I do?" Lou's confidence was showing plainly. "Does anyone know more baseball than I do? I can do it, Mr. Bradley."

"Well..."

"It would save you money, too," Lou asserted. Bradley looked at Boudreau with growing appreciation. "You'd save a salary."

"You've been thinking about this for awhile."

"All winter, actually."

"Maybe getting that college degree was worthwhile after all," Bradley observed dryly. Although ineligible to continuing playing college sports after signing a professional contract, Boudreau had continued attending classes, graduating from the University of Illinois in 1939.

"I think our players would go for it. I think they'd like the idea of having their manager on the field with them."

"You sure about that?"

"No," Lou admitted, "not sure. But pretty confident."

"Okay, Lou, you've persuaded me. We'll give it a try. But if it looks like it's not working out, I'll fire the manager side of you. And don't say anything until I tell Peckinpaugh. I doubt if he'll be very keen on the idea since he's no doubt counting on picking his own manager. And keep a lid on it until I can get a press conference scheduled. This will be big news."

†††

"This should be interesting," said Hornet fireman Sam Tortino.

"I think that's what they call an understatement," Tom Brecker replied dryly.

They and other Hornet firemen were poised for action. The Hornet was at sea now, 100 miles off the Virginia coast.

"Think they'll make it?" Sam asked.

"Geez. I don't know. I've heard B-25s need a quarter mile to take off. The Hornet can't give them half that. Plus, the B-25 tails are so high off the deck there's no way to install a landing hook. I've also heard their tails are too weak to handle the shock of sudden-stop landings. On the other hand, they've been stripping them of every ounce of excess weight. Right now, those two babies are basically flying cigar tubes with gas tanks."

The two young Army lieutenants, John Fitzgerald and James McCarthy, climbed into the B-25s. The Hornet was steaming into the wind. Tom Brecker and Sam Tortino joined the team of deck crewmen who maneuvered the two bombers into takeoff position. They then moved away and saluted.

Fitzgerald and McCarthy began revving their engines to maximum power. Navy Lieutenant Edgar Osborne waved a black and white checkered flag, Fitzgerald replied with a thumb up, deck hands dashed underneath the plane and pulled away the wheel chocks, and the B-25 went roaring down the slightly sloping flight deck. It had 500 feet of usable space. Tom and Sam and hundreds of other Hornet seamen were holding their breaths. To their surprise and relief, the B-25 lifted off with space to spare.

Without thinking, Tom began applauding. He wasn't alone. On the flight deck and on the Hornet's tall island, there was the kind of excitement that might be seen in the closing seconds of a hotly contested basketball game.

Next it was Lieutenant McCarthy waiting for the checkered flag. Tom was covering his ears. Moments later, the second B-25 was underway. Once airborne, McCarthy and Fitzgerald began piloting their planes west toward Norfolk.

Tom inhaled and then forcefully blew out a long breath. "Whew! I had my doubts."

"Me, too," said Sam. "I had my fingers crossed. At least, they aren't going to try to land those babies on the Hornet. That means fires we don't have to worry about fighting."

"Saint Christopher was on the job today," Tom observed.

Still, no one on the Hornet, including Captain Mark Mitscher, knew why this unprecedented experiment had taken place. Nor would they for another six weeks.

†††

An ocean and a continent away to the east, Bernadeta Gudek was back in the basement of St. Anne's church in Warsaw...planning and participating in more sabotage...plotting the ambush of German officers... mourning the thousands of Poles starving or being executed.

Barbara Gudek was not with her. Back on the farm, Bernadeta had emphasized not the danger to Barbara but to their parents if both sisters were found to be missing. Bernadeta also had emphasized their parents' need for Barbara to help operate the farm.

"Please, Barbara, I want you to promise me you'll not follow me to Warsaw. Please."

At barely more than arm's length, Barbara had looked Bernadeta squarely in the eyes while considering the request. The younger sister was no longer a girl, Bernadeta was thinking. She is her own woman now. "All right," Barbara murmured. "All right."

Bernadeta merely nodded. Any words, she knew, might sound patronizing.

"I will pray for you," Barbara said.

"I know."

"When will you come back to visit again?"

"I don't know. I haven't thought about it yet."

Barbara smiled. "Not too long, I hope."

"Me, too."

It was dusk now, with darkness not far behind. The two sisters embraced lovingly. Not another word was spoken. They pulled apart and Bernadeta began her long walk back to Warsaw.

†††

"Ever see a parade like that one?" Tom Brecker asked Sam Tortino.

"No and I doubt if we'll ever see it again."

Colonel Doolittle makes for one heck of a grand marshall," observed Tom. "He's not very tall but look at that build and that stride...the way he carries himself. Confidence and pride. Impressive guy."

Lieutenant Colonel James Doolittle was, indeed, short of height but impressive nonetheless. A shy, self-deprecating man, he nonetheless walked jauntily and smiled easily beneath eyes that twinkled mischievously. Colonel Doolittle had bearing but wasn't overbearing. Men gravitated to him with an unforced naturalness. In the days to come, aboard the Hornet, he would make a point of walking about, greeting as many crewmen as he could spot. His friendliness and his pedigree of daring speed and distance records inspired quick admiration and respect.

Early on the morning of Tuesday, March 31, 1942, Lieutenant Colonel Doolittle had left the B-25s and their crews at McClellan Field near Sacramento and flown down to Alameda Naval Air Station, directly across the bay from downtown San Francisco. The Hornet was waiting there. On the morning of April 1 at Alameda, Doolittle greeted the crews of the arriving B-25s. As soon as the pilots shut down their engines, Navy crewmen began swarming over and around the B-25s. They drained gas tanks and connected tow bars to the nose gear of each plane. As firemen, Tom and Sam were on standby for the delicate operation.

A Navy "donkey" began the parade, towing each B-25 down to the pier. Their crews followed solemnly behind each plane. At dockside, a huge crane reached down, snagged the bombers and slowly, gently hoisted them aboard the Hornet.

Tom and Sam and the rest of the Hornet's crew were intensely curious about this most unorthodox of aircraft carrier operations, but they had not been told and had the good sense not to ask.

After the loading process was completed, the Hornet moved to the middle of the bay and dropped anchor. The next morning, April 2, the Hornet weighed anchor, got underway and passed beneath the Golden Gate Bridge, heading west. Now, in addition to the crew of 2,072, the ship was carrying 16 B-25 bombers and their 80 crewmen, including Lieutenant Colonel Doolittle plus 80 other Army Air Corps men in supporting roles. Only then did Colonel Doolittle inform his volunteers of the specifics of their mission. In his plainspoken but not unkind fashion, Doolittle told them, "Some of you are going to get killed." He was thinking they all might perish. Again, as he had several times before, he said, "If anyone wants to bow out, he can still do so and no questions will be asked." Not one man had taken him up on this frequently repeated offer.

Afterward, Captain Mitscher passed the word on the nature of the mission to the entire Hornet crew.

"Can you believe it?" Sam said to Tom. "It's only been four months since Pearl Harbor and we're going after the Japanese."

Tom nodded but, to Sam's surprise, said nothing. He was staring at the Pacific which, beyond the Golden Gate, spread out before them.

"What are you thinking?" Sam asked his friend.

"That we going to be a long way from home. A long, long way."

†††

It's ironic isn't it, Bridgett Hassler was thinking. I'm in love with Tom but I'm filling in for Paul. With the help of an experienced operator, Bridgett was loading black ink into a press at the Salesbook. Well, it makes me feel closer to both of them. And all the factories in town needed women after so many boys had volunteered. She smiled ruefully. At least I could have picked a cleaner job. Even wearing gloves when I can doesn't keep all the ink off.

After loading the ink, she removed the gloves. Look at my hands. In addition to smudges, there was evidence of paper cuts. They were healing quickly. It's a good thing I'm learning how to handle the sheets and rolls, Bridgett reflected. In fact, it's a very good thing or by the time this war is over, my hands would look like raw liver – part black, part red. Small sacrifice, though. They do need us here. That's obvious. Business is booming. Everyone needs business forms. Other factories, offices, stores, restaurants, the government. Especially the government. They must live on forms. That's good, though, more people bringing home money. Even, she smiled, if there isn't much to spend it on. Rationing. I don't think I ever heard that word til recently.

When Bridgett's shift ended on that April afternoon, a gentle rain was falling. But there was no wind, not even a breeze. Unusual for an April afternoon.

"Want a lift home?" another woman asked.

They had just inserted their time cards into the clock and then placed them in the adjacent rack.

"I don't think so," said Bridgett. "Thanks anyway, but I think I'd like to walk."

"Okay. Suit yourself."

As Bridgett stepped through the doorway, she extended her umbrella and pushed it open. She was in no hurry. Strolling along, it would take about 20 minutes to reach her parents' home on Grand Boulevard. I have a boyfriend in the Navy, she was musing. His brother is in the Army. I have a sister in England. I can't believe how the world has changed. It seems so long ago that we were all here together in Shelby. Happy. Will it ever be that way again? Could it ever be that way again?

The rain was dripping steadily off her umbrella. I wonder where Tom is now? Still in San Francisco? He couldn't tell me much more in his last letter. He knew he was shipping out but not when or to where. And Theresa, I know she misses Hal. If only there was some word. I think Theresa is still holding out some hope. Poor thing. I miss her so. I would give anything to hear her voice. It's been almost two years now. I wonder if it's raining now, in London.

†††

In London that night, it was, as with every night, inky black. Everything was damp to the touch from an all-day drizzle. Theresa knew, though, that the rain had stopped because she no longer could hear it pattering outside her window. She was sitting with a tablet on her lap and a pen in her hand.

She had intended to write her parents, but unexpectedly found her thoughts turning to Jack Brecker. He's getting close to ordination, she thought. It would be nice to talk to Jack. About London, my work, my friends, the war. About Hal, about everything. Hal. Where are you? How are you? She felt a too familiar stab of pain. Theresa drew a deep breath to relieve the pressure in her chest and put the pen down on the small chairside table. She looked at her watch. 9:30 p.m. She placed the tablet on the table and stood. I'm not ready for sleep, not yet. She pulled on her raincoat, looked at her umbrella and picked it up. Just to be safe, she thought.

She descended the stairs and pushed open the door. As she stepped outside into Carlisle Lane, her thoughts shifted. I've heard the U.S. is building up its Army Nurse Corps. They aren't here yet, but they could be soon. If America is going to help Europe, that will mean American soldiers coming here. They will need lots of Army doctors and nurses. Maybe I'll join.

The U.S. Army Nurse Corps had a rich history. It began on June 14, 1775 when Major General Horatio Gates reported to George Washington that "the sick suffered much for want of good female nurses." Washington then asked the Continental Congress for "a matron to supervise the nurses, bedding, etc," and for nurses "to attend the sick and obey the matron's orders."

That first matron was paid $15 a month plus a daily food ration. Her nurses started at $2 per month. On April 17, 1777, nurses' pay was raised to $8 a month plus a daily food ration.

In 1918, during World War I, the Army School of Nursing was authorized, and instruction began at several Army hospitals. At that time, upon graduating, Army nurses received no rank, retaining civilian status.

After the war, the Corps dwindled. In June 1940, there were only 942 Regular Army nurses. Another 15,770 were in the First Reserve of the American Red Cross and were available for military duty if needed. With Germany and Japan having invaded much of the world, on May 27, 1941, the White House declared a State of National Emergency. It became necessary to begin activating those First Reserve nurses. By December 7, some 7,000 Army nurses were on active duty. Within six months, the total would climb to 12,000. Those and other new recruits were receiving their training at the nation's 1,300 schools of nursing. Trainees were part of the Cadet Nursing Corps but, as cadets, still were not part of the military.

As Theresa went strolling along the Thames, she reached a conclusion. I'm going to inquire. Tomorrow at the U.S. Embassy. Of course, I'll tell my ward sister first. I think she'll understand. I hope so. Right now I'm probably one of the few American nurses with experience treating war wounds...or dealing with soldiers and civilians who have been traumatized by bombings. The ones at Pearl Harbor. Manila. I might be the only one in Europe. One thing I won't need is basic training.

†††

During the first two weeks of April, Tom Brecker could feel tension rising aboard the Hornet. The ships steaming west, dubbed Task Force 16, included the cruisers Nashville andVincennes, oiler Cimarron and destroyers Gwin, Meredith, Monssen and Gruyon. On April 12, they joined the carrier Enterprise, cruisers Northampton and Salt Lake City, oiler Sabine, and destroyers Balch, Benham, Ellet and Fanning, which had departed from Hawaii on April 7.

Despite all these vessels and their firepower, Tom was edgy. Because the 16 B-25s were too large for the Hornet's elevators, they were lashed to the flight deck. That meant all the Hornet's normal complement of planes were below on the hangar deck. If attacked by Japanese planes, Tom and his fellow crewmen had been told they would have to push the B-25s overboard before bringing the fighters up to the flight deck. This very possibility was keeping Jimmy Doolittle on edge, too.

One evening, Tom was standing near the stern where the tail of the 16th B-25 was hanging out above ocean air. He saw someone walking among the B-25s. Though nearly dark, he knew it was Doolittle. His build and his penchant for inspecting the B-25s had become well known to the crew. Tom felt no compulsion to move. Doolittle drew closer, intently checking each plane.

"They're in good shape, Sir."

Doolittle looked up, saw Tom and smiled. "Can't be too sure."

"Our men are taking good care of them."

"I know that and I'm grateful."

"I'd be worried, too, Sir."

"About the planes."

"About your men."

"Some of them are going to die. I've told them that."

"But it's still eating at you."

"Right in my gut."

"Where will you land?" Although no one had said so, Tom knew the B-25s wouldn't be returning to the Hornet. Even stripped down and low on fuel, they were too big and ungainly for carrier landings.

"We'll be aiming for airfields in China," said Doolittle. "Russia, but only if necessary. The Chinese are supposed to be expecting us. Well, they will be after we tell them about the mission. We haven't told them yet for fear of leaks or intercepts."

Tom nodded. "I hear the Japs are overrunning more and more of China," Tom said quietly.

"You've heard right. Let's just hope they don't overrun the airfields we're planning to use."

"If you don't mind me asking, Sir, what will you do if you're shot down? Over Japan – or territory controlled by Japan?"

"I'll tell you what I've told my men. If my plane is hit, I won't be taken prisoner. I'll order my crew to bail out and then I'll drive my plane into the most valuable Japanese military target I can spot. But I'm forty-five years old and my men are much younger. If they have to bail or ditch, I've told them they are in complete charge of their planes and themselves after we leave the Hornet. They will be free to make any decision they feel is best."

Tom looked up at the B-25 tail that was looming in the enveloping blackness. Then he looked down at the churning foam of the Hornet's wake. "I hope it doesn't come to that, Sir."

†††

At that moment, in China, Japanese forces were attacking the airfields where the Doolittle raiders were planning to land and refuel before beginning long flights to the west. In addition, China's leaders, now informed of Doolittle's plan, were nervous about the raiders using their airfields. Their concern was deep and understandable. They knew full well the Japanese penchant for massive retaliation against Chinese whenever there was even the slightest indication that China was supporting American efforts.

Meanwhile, Japan, despite an unbroken string of victories in China, Malaysia and the Pacific islands, was strengthening its defenses. Part of its growing defensive capability was a line of some 50 radio-equipped fishing boats that were to form an early warning surveillance network.

On April10, these vessels intercepted Task Force 16 radio messages. After analysis, Japan's leaders concluded than an American force would be arriving in Japanese waters on Tuesday, April 14. When the Americans were within 600 miles of land, Japan would dispatch its first wave of bombers. If deemed necessary, it then would send a second wave – torpedo bombers. Japan's leaders fully expected to wipe out America's Pacific carrier strength.

Within days, though, their confidence was ebbing. Their fishing boats had intercepted no more U.S. radio messages, and the 14th came and went without incident. Japanese leaders now concluded that the task force was headed elsewhere. Still, they left in effect a state of alert.

As Task Force 16 steamed ever closer to Japan, Tom Brecker and his shipmates grew ever more tense. Their concern over aerial attack was compounded by a high desire to be part of the first American retaliation against Japan for its perfidy and deadly aggression. They were praying that nothing would go wrong.

On Thursday, April 16, Tom was resting in his bunk. Absentmindedly, he was fingering the small silver crucifix that he kept on the same chain with his dog tags. A thought occurred to him, and he vaulted down from his bunk. Quickly, he climbed several flights of steel stairs. On the wooden flight deck, Tom looked upward at the Hornet's tall island and then toward the parked B-25s. He saw Doolittle speaking with two Army Air Corps aircraft mechanics – sergeants by rank – and went walking slowly toward them. Tom watched as the mechanics nodded their agreement at something Doolittle had said. Then they saluted, turned and left. Doolittle saw Tom approaching.

"Don't you ever sleep?" he asked Tom.

"I was wondering the same thing about you, Sir." Tom snapped off a salute and Doolittle returned it.

"I'm a talented napper," Doolittle winked. Tom chuckled. It was abundantly clear to him why Doolittle commanded so much respect and affection from his men.

"Colonel, I had an idea – a small one."

"What is it?"

Tom unfolded the fingers of his left hand. "I know you've planned this mission very carefully. Six ways from Sunday, I heard one of your men say. But I was thinking that it wouldn't hurt to have something more in your plans."

Doolittle eyed the small crucifix. "You're absolutely right, Seaman. This should be an integral part of our strategy."

"We're almost in Japan's backyard now," said Tom. "If you don't mind..." Tom extended his right hand. Doolittle didn't hesitate. He shifted the crucifix to his left hand. With his right, he gripped Tom's hand firmly and shook it solemnly.

"Let's hope your crucifix sees both of us through this war," said Doolittle. Then he slipped it into a pocket of his leather flight jacket.

They released their grips and saluted each other.

†††

On the 17th, Doolittle and his B-25 crews, Captain Marc Mitscher and several of his Hornet crewmen, including Tom Brecker and Sam Tortino, were assembled around a bomb that had been brought up to the flight deck. Mitscher was holding three medals commemorating the 1908 visit of the U.S. fleet to Japan. Secretary of the Navy Frank Knox had sent them to Admiral Chester Nimitz at Pearl Harbor with the request that they be returned "via bomb to Tokyo."

Mitscher handed the medals to Doolittle who attached them to the bomb. Then Tom spoke up. "Do you mind, Sir?" He held up a piece of white chalk.

Doolittle saw Tom and smiled. "Step right up."

Fireman Tom Brecker stepped close to the bomb and began printing neatly: Your one-way ticket to hell. Laughter and applause broke out. Then Tom handed the chalk to a B-25 crewman who printed on the bomb: You'll get a BANG out of this. Another crewman printed: I don't want to set the world on fire – just Tokyo. There followed more laughter and applause and photos taken by a Navy photographer which, in the years to come, would be published often in pictorial histories of World War II.

†††

On Saturday the 18th at 5:58 a.m., a Task Force 16 patrol plane spotted a Japanese fishing vessel 42 miles away. Too far to have seen the plane or the task force. At 7:38 a.m., a lookout on the Hornet saw another fishing vessel – just 11 miles away. A quick conclusion: if the Hornet could see the fishing vessel, the reverse was true. Moments later, the Hornet's radio operator intercepted a message in Japanese that had originated closeby. At 7:45 a.m., the distance between the Hornet and the fishing vessel was seven miles.

Immediately, Admiral Halsey on the carrier Enterprise ordered the cruiser Nashville to sink the Japanese vessel – which within brief minutes it did. In the next instant, Halsey flashed a message to Captain Mitscher: "Launch planes. To Col. Doolittle and gallant command, good luck and God bless you."

Doolittle was standing with Mitscher on the bridge when the message arrived. They shook hands and then Doolittle scampered down to this cabin. On the way, he shouted to everyone he saw, "Okay, Fellas, this is it. Let's go!" At the same time, the Hornet's klaxon sounded. Then came the announcement: "Army pilots, man your planes."

Hornet crewmen, including firemen Tom Brecker and Sam Tortino, were racing to their stations. Other crewmen were ripping away engine covers that protected against salt water spray, unfastening tie-down ropes and pulling away wheel chocks. Simultaneously, the Hornet was accelerating to full speed into the wind. The Hornet's bow dipped and towering waves went roaring across the front of the flight deck.

Tom saw Doolittle and his four crewmen sprinting toward the lead B-25. Tom shouted, "Colonel!" Dootlittle glanced toward Tom who was flashing double thumbs up. Doolittle, not breaking stride, patted his jacket pocket. Then he was at the open belly of the B-25, climbing up and in.

Moments later, at 8:20 a.m., Doolittle's plane was up and away. Tom and Sam saw deck hands wrestling the remaining B-25s into takeoff position. The strong winds and heaving sea were complicating their labors. Sam nudged Tom and pointed to the stern. There, deck hands were struggling to maneuver the 16th B-25. Six deck handlers were straining to hold down the nose wheel while the pilot taxied forward slowly on the bucking deck. "Of all the lousy times for rough seas," Tom muttered. Then he and Sam went running to help. Then the pilot began revving the B-25's powerful engines. Just then, Seaman Robert Wall, one of the six, began losing his footing. Tom and Sam watched in silent horror as Wall slipped into the spinning left propeller. It sliced into Wall's left arm and hurled him to the pitching deck.

In the same brief instant, Wall screamed, blood shooting from his left arm. Tom and Sam went sprinting to his side, and two medics were just steps behind them. Their first move was to get Wall out of the way of the plane.

The 16th B-25 lifted off at 9:20 a.m., an hour after Doolittle. Soon afterward, in sick bay, Wall's arm was amputated. By then, Task Force 16 had wheeled around and was steaming east toward Pearl Harbor at full speed. Tom Brecker's face, hands and uniform were stained with Robert Wall's blood. Tom went walking tiredly toward his quarters. "A shower." Tom looked at himself. "Lord, I need a shower."

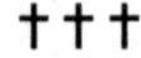

CHAPTER 17

Anthony and Virginia Brecker had set their alarm clock for 6 a.m. An hour before then, both were wide awake and stirring.

"Let's get up," said Anthony. "You know we're not going to sleep any more."

In the darkness, Virginia smiled. "Okay. I'll go downstairs and make coffee."

"Good. Better to be early."

"You mean really early," Virginia teased. She snapped on a bedside lamp, rose and pulled on a robe.

"This is a great day," Anthony said cheerily, "a great day."

†††

At 11:00 that morning in Worthington, Ohio, at the Josephinum, Jack Brecker became Father Brecker. It was Sunday, May 24, 1942. The occasion was intimate. The only attendees were Jack, his eight classmates and their families, younger seminarians, and seminary faculty and staff. He was pleased to have Anthony and Virginia there. He was disappointed that Paul and Tom had to be away.

As the ordination ceremony proceeded, Jack found himself thinking that the long haul was behind him. Ten years since I first left Shelby for Vincennes. I'll be forever grateful to Father Mac. Without him, I simply wouldn't be here today. I'll bet he's grinning right now. And the friends I've made here at the Josephinum. Especially Mark Hood. Friends forever, even if we never see each other again after leaving here. Tomorrow we get our orders and get ready to get on the road.

†††

The Tokyo raid and its aftermath were weighing heavily on Jimmy Doolittle. He was sitting dejectedly on a wing of his wrecked B-25. At that time, as he was to say years later, "I felt lower than a frog's posterior." This is what he knew at that moment. Of the 16 B-25s, 10 had bombed their primary targets and had inflicted varying amounts of damage. Five others had missed their primary targets but still had hit industrial sites. One had had to jettison its bombs without hitting a target. Over the Yellow Sea, all 16 had run perilously low on fuel. Some pilots had been able to reach China and crash land their planes. Others and their crews had bailed out, landing in the surf or farther inland. One plane had made it safely to Vladivostok where Russia interned its crew until near the war's end, although they were visited several times by American diplomats. Russia, which resisted releasing them, kept billing the U.S. for the crew's food and lodging.

Japanese troops, hunting for the downed crews, captured eight of Doolittle's men. Three of those, Doolittle would learn later, were executed. A fourth would die. In addition, two men drowned during crash landings, and another died jumping from his plane. Doolittle was feeling these losses deeply. He also was learning about the dramatic impact of the raid on Japanese military thinking. Japan's leadership, stung severely by the raid, already was pulling back forces from the farthest reaches of its empire to further strengthen defenses. Doolittle also was learning about the tremendous lift the raid had given to the morale and determination of American soldiers, sailors and civilians.

What Colonel Doolittle didn't know at that time was that the raid had so embarrassed and angered Admiral Isoroku Yamamoto, commander-in-chief of Japan's Combined Fleet, that he had vowed to take retaliatory action as soon as possible. His target: Midway Island. Nor did Doolittle yet know of the furious retribution that Japanese forces would exact on Chinese suspected even remotely of having assisted Doolittle and his crews. Japan sent 53 battalions smashing through Chekiang Province where most of the raiders had landed. The Japanese searched 20,000 square miles, plowed up landing fields, burned entire villages, committed countless rapes and murdered villagers by the hundreds on the scantiest evidence of having aided Doolittle's men. The three-week campaign was estimated to have cost 250,000 Chinese their lives.

†††

A Pacific breeze was cooling Tom Brecker as the Hornet steamed west from Pearl Harbor toward Midway Island. It was May 28, 1942, and the

Hornet now was part of another task force. U.S. intelligence had concluded that a Japanese attack on Midway was imminent.

Between launching Doolittle's B-25s on April 18 and sailing now toward Midway, the Hornet also had sailed to the Coral Sea on April 30, but had arrived too late to participate in that battle. Once again it had returned to Pearl Harbor.

Morale among the Hornet's crew was high, but there was disappointment from having missed out on the Coral Sea engagement, and boredom was weighing more heavily. This was troubling to Tom, and his restless mind had spawned an idea. He was wondering how it might have been received when he heard a voice say, "Brecker?"

Tom turned and saw a senior non-commissioned officer approaching. "Right, Chief," Tom replied.

"The captain will see you," the chief petty officer said. "Now, on the bridge."

Moments later, Tom, slightly winded from hustling up the stairs, was saluting the Hornet's Captain Mitscher.

"I'm told this was your idea," said Mitscher.

"Yes, Sir, it was."

"It's not conventional."

"No, Sir."

"There's no precedent."

"I'm sure you're right, Sir."

"We're in the middle of a war – and we're not winning."

"Yes, Sir. I know, Sir."

Captain Mitscher looked in all directions at the seemingly endless expanse of Pacific water. "The sea is calm. No wind to speak of."

"Right, Sir," Tom said, beginning to think that the captain might be veering the conversation in an entirely different direction. Tom was wrong, as he would learn with Mitscher's next words.

"Well, despite everything," said the captain, "even though there is nothing to cover it in regulations, your idea is a damn good one."

Tom smiled. "Thank you, Sir. Thank you very much. The men will be very grateful." Tom felt like shouting in triumph but restrained himself.

"Yes," said Mitscher. "Daily calisthenics can be boring, and we can't be sure when we'll next see action. The competition would be good for the men. Go to it."

Tom hesitated a moment, then decided to take one more plunge. "I have a favor to ask of you, Sir."

"Another one?"

"Yes, Sir. Would you please consider presiding over our opening ceremony?"

Mitscher smiled broadly. "Happy to. And I'll go one better and have ribbons made up to award the winners."

Tom Brecker's brainchild, the Navy's first Flight Deck Olympics, was on, and Tom would be their lead organizer and promoter. He also would be a multi-event competitor. Two days later, on May 30, the flight deck was crowded with eager competitors and cheering spectators. The Hornet's island was packed with more spectators, including Captain Mitscher with Tom Brecker at his side. With Mitscher's voice booming through a bullhorn, the captain addressed the men. "Gentlemen of all ranks, may I direct your attention to the mast." All eyes looked upward and were amazed to see a homemade Olympic flag, with five interlocking circles, being hoisted. Then he raised the bullhorn to his lips and proclaimed: "The U.S.S. Hornet's first Flight Deck Olympics. Let the games begin!"

Tom quickly descended from the island's heights to join hundreds of men, all wearing the same uniform – boxer shorts and deck shoes. They spent the day running, jumping and shouting. They competed in the 100-yard dash, long jump, standing broad jump, 4 X 100-yard relay, and half-mile and mile runs.

Captain Mitscher watched – and enjoyed -- every moment of it. That Brecker lad is a good man, he reflected. Imaginative. Takes initiative. Excellent leader. The men all respect him, that's for sure. I wonder if he might be interested in becoming an officer.

Tom finished second in the 100-yard dash finals and anchored a relay team that came in fourth in the final heat. He relished every second of that long but invigorating day. Not once, he realized that night, had he thought about Bridget Hassler or his brothers, Jack and Paul.

†††

Five days later, on June 4, the Battle of Midway was raging. This time the Hornet did not arrive too late. That first day of engagement was a long, heart-wrenching one for Tom and his shipmates. There were many takeoffs and landings to prepare for. The Hornet's bombers and fighters found and attacked Japanese carriers but unsuccessfully. Worse, in one of the attacks, the 15 planes of the Hornet's Torpedo Squadron 8 spotted a Japanese carrier and went diving in for the kill. But Japanese anti-aircraft fire plus protective fire from carrier escort vessels and Japanese Zeros downed every one of the 15 planes. Fifteen brave pilots, Tom was thinking. He didn't know them personally but mourned for them deeply. He found himself wishing he'd had 15 more silver crucifixes to hand out.

Then the tide of battle turned. Two days later, on June 6, the battered Japanese fleet was in retreat, and the Hornet's remaining planes were in determined pursuit. They helped sink the cruiser Mikuna and damaged several other Japanese ships. The Japanese had sent 150 ships, including five aircraft carriers, into the battle. They lost four carriers, the cruiser Mikuma, and suffered major damage to six other ships. They also lost 332 planes. American losses were costly but less -- a carrier, a destroyer and 147 planes.

When it was over, Tom Brecker had never felt so utterly exhausted. Not after a long summer football practice on a steamy August day. Not after a grueling day of boot camp. Physically and emotionally, Tom felt as spent as the uncountable shell casings around the Hornet's island guns. God, he prayed silently, if we never see action again, that'll be plenty fine with me. For all the men we've lost the last couple days, please have mercy.

Chapter 18

Just a day after Tom Brecker offered up that prayer, his brother Jack offered his first Solemn High Mass in his hometown church, Most Pure Heart of Mary. The church was packed, with nearly 900 family members, friends and admirers crowding the freshly polished wooden pews. Among the five priests who would be assisting was the parish pastor, Father Michael McFadden, who had paved the way for Jack to enter the Josephinum.

Before the Mass, inside the sacristy, adjacent the large sanctuary, Jack's cold, stiff fingers were adjusting his collar and robes. He also was wishing fervently that the butterflies in his stomach would cease fluttering. Saying a Mass in front of Mom and Dad and a small gathering had been one thing, Jack was thinking, but a whole churchful is something else. I feel like I'm about to go on display in a department store window. A male mannequin with a collar and cassock. Nah, probably wouldn't be a big seller.

Jack sensed that someone was watching and turned. Father Mac was smiling, kindness, pride and affection clearly evident. The other priests and the four altar boys all were chattering quietly, busy with their own preparations.

Father Mac stepped close to Jack. "Tis a fine day," he said, barely above a whisper.

"It's been a long time coming," Jack replied quietly.

"For you, Yes. For me, it's all happened so fast."

"You realize I can never thank you enough."

"This is thanks enough, Lad. Tis grand to see trust and faith fulfilled." Father Mac placed his hands on Jack's shoulders. "You've done us proud. Me. Your family."

"Thank you, Father." A brief pause and then Jack inhaled deeply.

"Nervous?" Father Mac asked.

"It shows?"

"Oh, no more than the gold trim on your vestments," Father Mac joshed, eyes twinkling.

"That's reassuring," Jack said, managing to smile ruefully.

"These Solemn High Masses can be unnerving for anyone," said Father Mac. "It's likely you'll not say more than a handful of them during your entire life. Don't worry. I'll stick close to you, and I know the script." He patted Jack on his left shoulder, then looked up at the sacristy clock. 10:29. "Well, as I'm the master of ceremonies, it's up to me to be sure we begin on time. And," he smiled, "we wouldn't want all our parishioners remembering that you were late starting your first Mass in Shelby. That would be almost sinful."

Jack's jumpy stomach notwithstanding, he nearly chuckled aloud.

Father Mac turned away from Jack and cleared his throat loudly. "Everyone. Please. Let's all get lined up."

The subdued chattering halted abruptly. Priests and altar boys formed up, Father Mac in the lead, Jack bringing up the rear. As the procession entered the sanctuary, ablaze with bright lights and burning candles, Jack was smiling inwardly. A new chapter begins, he thought. Let's see how it unfolds and where it takes me.

†††

Not far at first, it turned out. After the Mass, Jack had walked about 200 yards from the church with his mom and dad and fellow new priest Mark Hood to the family's home on Raymond Avenue for a chicken dinner. After the meal, still seated and sipping coffee at the dining room table, Jack's dad Anthony reached into his suit jacket's inside pocket and extracted a white envelope. He handed it to Jack.

"What's this?" Jack asked.

"Just open it," Anthony smiled.

Jack flipped up the envelope's flap. As he removed the contents, a smile slowly formed. "Very nice, Dad. Thank you."

†††

"That was very thoughtful of your dad," said Mark Hood. It was the following Tuesday morning, and he and Jack were in the used Model A Ford they soon would be driving west. Today, though, they were driving north from Shelby to Cleveland. "Two tickets to an Indians game. Box seats. Betcha they're great seats. Your dad certainly knows his son."

"And his son's best friend," Jack replied. Both new priests laughed joyously.

At Cleveland's cavernous Municipal Stadium, built in 1932 on the Lake Erie waterfront, Jack and Mark learned just how great were the box seats Anthony had purchased. They were in the front row and right next to the Indians dugout. When an usher led Jack and Mark to their seats, the Indians were taking batting practice. Jack thrilled to the sound of hardened ash smacking against hide-covered ball.

"Oh, man, this is a great spot," said Mark. "These seats could spoil a person."

It didn't take long for Lou Boudreau to spot Jack and Mark, and the recognition was immediate. He came trotting over to the stands. "How're you guys doing?" Lou asked.

"Just fine," said Jack.

"Couldn't be better," said Mark.

"So," Lou said, smiling impishly, "is it time for me to start calling you two Father?"

"You could say so," said Jack.

"Then I will," said Lou. "Father Brecker. Father Hood." Lou bowed slightly. "Welcome to our ballpark."

"Very nice to be here, Mr. Boudreau," Jack smiled, "but don't overdo it."

"Mr.? Oh, please. I told you back in Columbus, it's Lou."

"Then let's keep it to Jack."

"Touche," conceded Lou.

"And Mark," Mark added.

"Done," said Lou. "When were you ordained?"

"Couple weeks ago," Jack replied. "Said my first high Mass last Sunday. Mark does his next Sunday back in New York. Felt he needed to learn from my experience," Jack teased his friend.

"Hey!" said Lou. "We're going to be playing the Yankees in New York then."

"You're invited to my Mass," Mark said excitedly. "All the Indians."

"I accept," said Lou. "Thank you. I don't know how many of the guys will want to join me, but I'll be there. Count on it. And I'll leave tickets for you and your family at Yankee Stadium."

"That's great," said Mark. "Thank you. My family will be thrilled. They've been to Ebbets Field many times to see the Dodgers, but as certified Yankee haters, I doubt if they've ever been inside Yankee Stadium."

"Well," said Lou, "they'll just have to be Indians fans for a day."

"I think they can manage that," Mark said, smiling gratefully.

"Where are they sending you?" Lou asked.

"Arizona," said Jack. "Both of us."

"Wow! A long way from home," said Lou.

"Still classified as mission country by the Vatican," said Jack. "This might be the last time we see each other, so we're counting on you to bring us a win today."

"I don't think so," Lou said, shaking his head soulfully.

"You think you're going to lose?" Jack asked, surprised by both Lou's words and tone.

"I'm not referring to the game," said Lou. "I'm talking about not seeing each other again."

"I don't follow you," said Jack.

A smile began to crease Lou's face. "We do our spring training in Tucson."

"Oh."

"Right. So depending on where you guys are stationed, there's a good chance we'll see each other next year. And I'll tell you what. Next spring, I'll leave passes for you. Just walk up to the ticket window before any exhibition game, and there will be tickets for both of you. How does that sound?"

"Like a grandslam homerun," Jack said, smiling broadly.

Tucson. June 1942.

"As you've been told, Rome still regards Arizona as mission territory. I sometimes wonder if the pope still thinks we're under attack from Geronimo and his marauders," said Bishop Wilhelm Metzger. "But as you can see, we have a very nice cathedral here in Tucson. And we have a few nice churches scattered around the state. But this is a very large state. Four times the size of Ohio. My home state, too. Near Toledo. Many of the more remote towns need churches, rectories, schools, convents. Then there are the Indian reservations. They take up a good bit of the land here in Arizona. But their reservations tend to be primitive – both in general and as to churches."

"We're ready to get to work," said Jack.

"Eager, actually," said Mark.

"Very good," said Bishop Metzger. "We need young priests who are willing to work hard under challenging conditions. A spirit of adventure can't hurt. I'm told you both have these qualities."

"Well," said Jack, "we did make it across country in a used Model A."

The Bishop laughed. "That qualifies. We will need you to build parishes. That will mean organizing, fund raising, managing, leading, teaching, communicating. You might need to heft a few bricks. You both speak Spanish?"

"We've studied it," said Jack.

"Good," said the bishop. "You'll need it. First, though, we need to get you settled...help you get your feet on the ground. Here is what I have in mind. Father Hood, I'm sending you to Green Valley. It's a pleasant little community about twenty miles south of here. You'll minister there and to some nearby villages. Plus the San Xavier Indian Reservation and the eastern portion of the Tohono Indian Reservation. I think you'll be kept sufficiently busy."

"Thank you, Bishop," said Mark. "That's fine. It's what I was hoping for."

Bishop Metzger nodded in satisfaction. "Father Brecker, I'm sending you to Ajo. "It's a little town – a copper mining community, maybe four thousand souls – about eighty miles west of Tucson. That's as the crow flies. More like a hundred miles on the road you'll be driving. Lots of curves through the mountains, lots of cactus. Besides Ajo, you will also be serving a couple other small communities plus the biggest part of the Tohono Indian Reservation. That covers a lot of territory. You'll need to keep that Model A in good working order."

"Very good," said Jack.

"We'll have to get you a car, too, Father Hood. It will probably be much the same vintage as Father Brecker's"

I've helped Jack change the oil on his car and the tires."

"Which reminds me. Always – both of you – keep jugs of water in your car. For your radiator and yourself. Running out of water out here can be fatal." They both nodded. "Well, I think you'd both should get a day or two of rest here at the diocese, then head to your new assignments. May God travel with you both."

Chapter 19

Brigadier General George Patton could sense the coming combat. He remembered well the sights, sounds, smells and tastes of World War I, and he was more than ready to experience them again. His fervent prayers of the past 20 years were being answered, and the white-haired general was grateful.

His excitement had begun to build in earnest earlier in 1942. With the British and German forces slugging away at each other in the North African desert, the U.S. War Department began to see the need for specialized training. Patton was ordered to reconnoiter southeastern California for a desert warfare training site. On March 18, he selected 10,000 square miles that covered parts of California, Arizona and Nevada and was named Camp Young. He surveyed his choice with satisfaction and anticipation.

On July 30, he was ordered to Washington, D.C. for briefings and on August 5 he was flying to London for more meetings. At least I'm getting closer to some real action, he reflected as he peered down from his window seat into the blackness of an Atlantic night. By the time I'm finished whipping my boys into shape, taking on the Germans will seem like a Sunday stroll to church. In the darkness, he closed his eyes and smiled. George Patton lived for making war.

†††

For Tom Brecker and his Hornet shipmates, the sights, sounds, smells and tastes of battle had become all too familiar. Tom's prayer at the end of the Midway battle had gone unanswered. On August 17, the Hornet began sailing westward from Pearl Harbor toward the Solomon and Santa Cruz Islands. Mission: provide air cover for the Marines invading Guadalcanal, where Japanese forces were constructing an air base. Its purpose: sever the U.S. lifeline to Australia with land-based bombers.

The fighting on Guadalcanal and in the surrounding waters would remain fierce for the next six months. For the first two of those months, the Hornet remained unscathed. That would change on October 26.

On the night of October 25, Tom Brecker eased himself onto his bunk. Enervating fatigue seemed to have wormed its way into every bone and muscle. He was nearly at that point where exhaustion is so overwhelming that a person just doesn't care what happens next. Seven months of accumulating stress, diminished only occasionally and never for long. On his bunk, he stretched his body taught, squeezed shut his eyes and slowly inhaled, filling his lungs. Then he sighed audibly. Bridgett, Paul, Jack, Colonel Doolittle, his mom and dad…these and other faces and voices went parading through his thoughts. He longed to see them, to hear them again. Eventually, sleep came.

Not long afterward, a shrieking klaxon ended sleep. It was 6:58 a.m. Tom and fellow fireman Sam Tortino hurriedly pulled on their fatigues and went scrambling up to the flight deck. They knew this was no drill, and as veterans they knew that every second could demarcate survival from disaster. Darkness was just giving way to daylight, and Hornet pilots were sprinting to their planes. The Battle of Santa Cruz Island was on.

The Hornet's planes would soon be attacking a Japanese task force that had arrived north of Guadalcanal in mid-October. It included four carriers. Positioning to oppose them were two U.S. carrier task forces, led by the Hornet and the Enterprise. Tom and Sam watched as Hornet planes went roaring off the deck, climbing steeply. Soon there was reason for optimism. Word was radioed back that Hornet planes had severely damaged the carrier Shokaku and cruiser Chikuma.

Shortly after 8 a.m., Tom and Sam and other firemen were told they could go below for a quick breakfast. Shaving could wait.

"Hungry?" said Sam.

"Not really," replied Tom. "You?"

"Coffee would go down good."

"Yeah, I guess. Better grab it while we can."

As they turned to descend, the klaxon shrieked again. "Battle Stations! All hands to battle stations!" the loud speakers were blaring. The klaxon continued its piercing alert.

In the next instant, Sam's right arm pointed skyward. "Look!" he shouted. "Bad guys coming at us."

"Holy shit," was Tom's studied reply. Quickly, he put on his steel helmet. Sam did likewise. Tom glanced at his watch. It was 8:22 a.m. The sky was filling rapidly with Japanese dive bombers and torpedo planes and a blizzard of exploding anti-aircraft rounds from the Hornet's island guns.

For awhile, they seemed to be keeping the Japanese planes at bay. Then from directly overhead, a dive bomber began its screaming descent.

"Sweet Jesus!" Tom shouted above the din. "That one's coming straight down on us. Stay low!"

The Japanese pilot released his bomb but kept on diving. Ack-ack from the Hornet went shooting up at him. His plane was hit several times.

"Pull up! Goddammit, pull up!" Tom screamed.

"I don't think he can," shouted Sam.

Sam was right. The Japanese pilot was dead, and his plane kept plunging, seconds later smashing onto and partially through the Hornet's wooden flight deck. An explosion and searing flames followed immediately.

"Hoses!" shouted Sam, and he and Tom and other firemen went racing to fight the flames.

They barely had begun dragging hoses toward the wreckage, when a second Japanese dive bomber took aim at the Hornet. All the firemen heard its howling engine. They stood transfixed as sweating Hornet gunners tried to shoot the bomber to shreds. Pieces of wings and fuselage were shot away and the windscreen shattered. The mortally wounded Japanese pilot tried and failed to release his bomb. Still, he kept control of his plane and dove it onto the Hornet's flight deck. Another explosion, more flames and more firemen struggling to control the damage. The strain and pace of their exertion soon had sweat cascading from them.

"Oh, my God!" It was the frightened, panicky voice of another fireman. Tom and Sam, their faces, hands and arms already blackened, looked up. Japanese high-level bombers were maneuvering over the Hornet. They released their loads and several bombs were falling unerringly toward the Hornet.

"Hit the deck," Tom shouted. "Everybody down!" All the firemen dropped their hoses and quickly flattened themselves. Scant seconds before the falling bombs made contact with the Hornet, two Japanese torpedo planes went screaming over the Hornet just above the ship's island.

"Where the hell is our cover?" Sam screamed. "Somebody goofed and left the goddamned screen door wide open."

Seconds later, two torpedos struck, detonated and rocked the ship. Then the bombs hit and a blizzard of shrapnel went slicing through the air.

Tom heard a nearby piercing scream. It was Sam. Agony was contorting his face as blood reddened his left arm.

"Medic!" Tom bellowed. He could see that a smallish piece of shrapnel, shaped like an arrowhead, had sliced through Sam's arm and embedded itself in the wooden deck. He looked around. Fires everywhere. More men bleeding and screaming. No medic in sight. Tom jerked his t-shirt over his head, pulled it off, twirled it into a bandage, wrapped it tightly around Sam's arm and tied it off. "Come on," Tom shouted, "we've got to get you below."

"I can make it on my own," Sam protested. "You stay and fight the fire." Then Sam bent double and vomited what little was left from his meal last night.

"Yeah, sure," muttered Tom, as he began half-carrying, half-dragging Sam toward the island.

†††

Returning from taking Sam to sick bay, Tom knew the Hornet was in serious trouble. Dead in the water. Fires raging. He picked up one of the many hoses strewn across the deck and again went to work.

Not long afterward came the order to abandon ship. No one was surprised. Support vessels began edging toward the Hornet, ready to rescue her crew. Silently, for a long moment, Tom surveyed the situation. He made a decision. "I'm not leaving," he said to other nearby firemen. "Not yet." A long pause, as other firemen absorbed Tom's words. "If enough of us stay, I think we can get the fires under control. It's worth a try."

"What about the engines?" another fireman asked.

"If the engineers know we're staying, maybe they will, too," Tom replied.

"I'll go below and tell them what we're doing," said one of the firemen.

Meanwhile, crewmen continued climbing down ropes or jumping from the Hornet into the sea and swimming toward rescue vessels. On the Hornet, Tom and his fellow firemen continued to fight the inferno.

Minutes later, Sam Tortino emerged onto the flight deck and went to pick up a hose near Tom.

"What the hell?" Tom said dubiously.

"Pain was worse than the injury," Sam muttered. "Doc sewed me up. Then a shot of morphine. Sorry for all the commotion but I couldn't let you guys have all the fun."

Tom smiled, teeth a slash of white surrounded by blackened skin. "No problem."

In just seven minutes, between 9:10 and 9:17 a.m., the Hornet had been hammered by two dive bombers, seven falling bombs and two torpedos. Soon, largely abandoned but with both firemen and engineers still aboard and working feverishly, along with new Captain Charles Mason (Captain Mitscher had been promoted after the Battle of Midway), the Hornet was taken under tow by the cruiser Northampton.

†††

By midafternoon, Tom's hose was turned off. So was Sam's and the other firemen. Still under tow, the Hornet was moving slowly.

"I'm beat," said Tom. "Just plain butt-whipped."

"Everyone is," Sam said, breathing heavily.

Everyone was. Fuel-fed flames combined with scorching ambient heat and suffocating humidity had seen to that.

"Look," said Tom.

It was Captain Mason emerging from the island, his khakis thoroughly besmudged, trudging toward the firemen. They waited.

Captain Mason saluted them wearily. "Well done, Gentlemen. You've got the fires out here, and your fellow firemen below have contained the fires there." Mason would have smiled but he was too tired. "The engineers say we can get underway on our own. Not to fight. To get repairs. Quite an accomplishment. I'm very proud of each of you. We'll have the Northampton break off the tow and make ready to get underway."

Some of the firemen nodded. None spoke. They were too tired.

"Take a break," said Mason. "We'll start getting our crew back on board." He motioned with a downward sweep of his right hand for the firemen to rest. He then turned and began walking away. He had taken no more than a few strides, when he stopped and turned. Something had caught his attention. Tom and the other firemen looked back in the same direction.

"Christ almighty," muttered Sam.

"Would that he were," murmured Tom.

Six Japanese torpedo planes were abreast, sweeping low, skimming over the sea and taking dead aim on the crawling Hornet. Tom, Sam, Mason and the rest of the firemen knew they had to flatten themselves. Still, they stood, watching the oncoming planes. With the Hornet largely abandoned, there were no gunners to oppose them. Then almost simultaneously, six torpedos fell from the planes and came slicing toward the Hornet. For a long moment, the men continued watching. The thought that was going through Tom's mind was this: it's like watching the bullet with your name on it. Then the men lay flat on the deck and waited. Seconds later, the explosions began. After one of them, Tom felt his body being lifted from the deck.

†††

In London, Theresa Hassler, knowing that American soldiers, sailors and airmen soon would be in harm's way in Europe and probably elsewhere, already had left St. Thomas to join the U.S. Army Nurse Corps. She had been right in her thinking. She and her experience treating war wounds were welcomed warmly and she immediately was commissioned First Lieutenant Hassler.

Theresa had been assigned to a newly formed unit named the 48th Surgical Hospital. Later, as combat began taking its inexorable toll, the hospital would be reorganized as the 128th Evacuation Hospital. Commanding the nurses was Lieutenant Colonel Marilyn Carter. Although they didn't know it, in fewer than two weeks, they would be treating American soldiers on another continent.

†††

George Patton had been ordered to help plan Operation Torch. Its aim was to capture French Morocco and Algeria, wresting it from Hitler's Vichy puppet regime. Now, Patton was back at Camp Young, preparing to bring his 2nd Armored Division to North Africa. Under a blistering desert sun, he addressed his men: "Well, they've given us a job to do. We can go down on our bended knees, every one of us, and thank God the chance has been given to us to serve our country. As for the damn Germans or the yellow-bellied Eyetalians, we just won't shoot the sonsabitches. We're going to cut out their living guts – and use them to grease the treads of our tanks. We're going to murder those lousy Hun bastards by the bushel."

†††

"Am…Am I going to make it?" Tom Brecker asked haltingly. Even speaking quietly, his voice sounded barely like his own. But then he wasn't feeling like himself. He was hurting, bleeding and filthy. A medic already had jabbed him with a strong dose of morphine, dulling the most excruciating pain Tom ever had endured. "I feel cold."

"You'll make it," Sam said with certainty as the medic tended to Tom. Sam didn't know that for a fact, but he knew enough to answer in the affirmative.

"In one piece?" Tom asked.

Sam's left hand moved across his mouth and chin. He glanced at the medic who shrugged. "We're going to get you sewed up," said Sam. "Then we'll get you off the Hornet and onto a hospital ship. We'll know more then. Just hang in there."

"You gonna make it in one piece?" Tom asked.

"No problem," Sam replied, lying more easily than he had thought possible. Part of him already was gone, and he wasn't sure how much of the blood on him was his and how much was Tom's.

The medic stood and motioned for Sam to step away with him from Tom. "Getting him off the Hornet and onto another ship won't be easy on him," the medic said. "If you're up to it, you should stick with him."

"No problem."

†††

At 4:25 p.m. on October 26, Captain Mason again gave the order to abandon ship. He knew there no longer was hope for the Hornet. She was ablaze from stem to stern. Tom, Sam and other injured and dying sailors were eased off the carrier. The dead soon would be buried at sea.

The Hornet herself stubbornly continued to fight off death. After Captain Mason was the last to leave her, nearby U.S. ships fired on the crippled carrier, trying to scuttle her. She stayed afloat. Darkness enveloped the sea, flames silhouetting the Hornet. About 1:00 a.m. on the

27th, Japanese destroyers closed on her. They finished her off with four torpedos. At 1:35 a.m., the Hornet slipped below the surface on her way to her grave in 16,000 feet of water. Her end came just one year and six days after her commissioning.

Chapter 20

Solomon Island in Chesapeake Bay bore only the faintest resemblance to North Africa. George Patton knew that, but also knew it would have to suffice, and he shook his head in resignation. My men need a dry run, he was thinking. Hell, I do, too. Amphibious landings are a very different matter from horse cavalry and sabers. Or tanks. But to use my tanks in North Africa, I've got to get them and my men ashore.

It was late October 1942, when Patton brought his 2nd Armored Division east from Camp Young. "What is thoroughly pissing me off," Patton growled to his chief aide, Colonel Charles Codman, "is that the goddamn Vichy French might actually oppose our landing. Shoot at us. We're trying to save their cheese-eating country, and they might try to kill us for the favor. I'd like nothing more than to strangle Petain. Skedaddling from France to their African colonies and still puffing out his chest as only the French can do. What a posturer. And he's senile to boot."

Patton knew he had to have himself and his men ready for a range of contingencies. The confusion in Africa and in France – part occupied, part under Marshall Philippe Petain's Vichy regime, part in limbo – was at the root of Patton's uncertainty and anger. Some French soldiers in North Africa wanted to join General Charles DeGaulle's Free French in England. Others wanted to fight with General Henri Honore Giraud who had recently escaped to France from a German prison camp. Still others felt obligated to support Petain and his Vichy commander-in-chief, Admiral Jean Darlan. The rest were content to wait and see which way the winds of war would be blowing.

In 100 vessels, Patton and his men and their equipment and supplies sailed for Africa. They would be joined by 700 ships and thousands more men – and a few women – sailing from England. The small group of women on the British flotilla were the American nurses, including Theresa Hassler.

Theresa was standing by the rail, watching the English coast slowly fade. This is what I need to be doing, she mused, but it is taking me farther away from home and Hal. Part of me says he must be dead or I would have heard something by now. At least a little something. Two years and no word. If he's alive, dear God, I pray he's well. If he's gone, I pray to hear something final.

Theresa reached into her jacket pocket and extracted an envelope. In it was a letter from her sister Bridgett in Shelby. It had arrived just before embarkation, and Theresa wanted to read it when she wasn't pressed for time. Now, onboard a ship bound for North Africa, seemed an appropriate moment. Slowly, gently, her right thumb broke open the envelope's seal. She pocketed the envelope, turned her back to the ocean breeze, unfolded the letter and began reading:

"October 15, 1942

Dear Theresa,

A cheery letter is no doubt what you need to read and what I need to write. But I don't know if it's possible to write that kind of letter now. Oh, I'm fine and so are Mom and Dad. And everything is okay at the Salesbook. I'm actually enjoying the work – especially now that I've learned most of the do's and don'ts. Picture your little sister with ink-stained hands and messy hair. And yet, after the war, I think I'd like to stay – if they'll let me. Most of us 'Rosies' expect to lose our jobs when the men return. I guess that's only fair since they had to leave for the war.

It's been so long since I've heard from Tom. And I know he doesn't tell me everything about his experiences. He glosses over the war stuff and mostly talks about his friends, especially Sam Tortino. Their friendship obviously means a lot to Tom. I think it's cute. A boy from little old Shelby, Ohio and an Italian from Brooklyn. They've been through a lot together. I haven't received any letters from Tom since they left Pearl Harbor for Guadalcanal. I'll probably receive a whole batch at the same time. It will be so nice to see him again. I wonder how long that will be.

How are things in London? Do you still remember what it was like living in Shelby? Just teasing, Sis. Wouldn't it be fantastic if you heard from Hal?!! Or just learned where he's at? I pray for him every night. For you, too.

I need to get to bed, so I better close for now. We start early at the Salesbook, you know. The presses won't wait! You stay safe and be sure not to take any chances. I love you lots!!

Bridgett"

Theresa sighed and smiled. How would Bridgett react when she learned that her sister no longer was in London but in Africa? But then, thought Theresa, I expect to be returning to London. I'm continuing to pay rent on my room so Mr. Turner will hold it for me. I want to have a place to come back to. I need that. Strange. That room in Carlisle Lane now seems more like home than Shelby or Cleveland. I feel like I've lived two separate lives, one in Ohio and one in England. I never would have dreamed it.

Slowly, Theresa folded Bridgett's letter and slipped it into her pocket. She would reread it later. For now, she pivoted, again turning her face into the wind.

†††

George Patton noisily sucked in a breath of bracing sea air. Though long a cavalryman and tanker, Patton had developed a deep love of the sea. At this moment, he was contemplating the yacht he had sailed with his wife, Bea, family and friends in 1935 from San Pedro, California to his posting in Hawaii. A grand adventure, he recalled, and now I'm on another. He smiled in anticipation.

Patton's force was one of three converging on North Africa. His included 35,000 men and 250 tanks bound for the Atlantic coast of Africa. He and some 19,000 of those men would push to take Casablanca, about 200 miles southwest of the Strait of Gibraltar. The second force, with 39,000 mostly British troops, was under orders to seize Oran on the Mediterranean coast of Africa, about 280 miles east of Gibraltar. The third force, the one Theresa was part of, had embarked from England with 23,000 British and 10,000 Americans. Their mission: take Algiers, about 200 miles farther east from Oran on the Mediterranean shore.

†††

Jack Brecker's first months in Arizona were proving the accuracy of Bishop Metzger's prophecy. The work was hard and required a spirit of adventure. His daily efforts left him both exhilarated and exhausted. The surprises were many. One came on the first Sunday he was to say a Mass on the Tohono Indian Reservation. With Ajo parishioner Luke Haynes serving as his guide, they set out soon after sunrise.

"Ever been to the church there?" Jack asked.

"Yeah."

Silence.

"Well, what's it like?" Jack asked.

"I'm not sure how to describe it," said Luke, who stood nearly six feet three inches but weighed only about 180 pounds. A Stetson was covering his sandy hair, and he was wearing blue jeans, boots, a long-sleeved beige shirt and a brown corduroy jacket.

Jack smiled. "Well, give it a try."

"Mmm…I'm not so good with words" Luke said laconically. "Best to let you see for yourself."

Jack eyed Luke and concluded that probing further would be decidedly unproductive.

They had driven from Ajo on Rt. 85 and then bore east on Rt. 86 into the Tohono Reservation, bound for a mission near Charco.

"What's Charco like?" Jack asked.

Luke, both hands resting on the top of his Ford pickup truck's steering wheel, laughed. "You're just too dadgum curious, Father Jack. It's like the rest of what you've seen out here. Small, dusty, dry, hot, mountainy. Let me put this way. Your black robe and collar's gonna feel mighty uncomfortable. I doubt if you'll want to take your vacation there."

"Hmmm," Jack smiled. "Might be the perfect place for vacation. Out of the way, quiet."

Luke looked at Jack to see whether he was being serious or silly. A wink from Jack provided the answer.

A few minutes later, Luke pointed in the distance toward a group of about 150 men, women and children. "There's your Charco congregation, Father," said Luke.

Jack smiled. The Indians he could see through his gold-rimmed glasses were dressed modestly but neatly. The women and girls were wearing colorful, homemade, knee-length dresses and the men and boys jeans and long-sleeved shirts open at the neck. "Where's the church?" Jack asked.

Luke smiled wryly. "See that little white cross sticking up above their heads?" Jack nodded. "That's it," said Luke.

"Short church."

"Real short."

As Luke pulled the pickup truck to a stop, smiling, expectant faces pressed forward, crowding around the truck, straining for a first look at their new padre. A hand reached out and opened the passenger side door.

"Welcome, Padre," a male voice said.

"Thank you. I'm very glad to be here." Jack meant that. "I've been looking forward to my first visit." He meant that, too.

"Come with me, Padre," the voice continued. "I will lead you to our chapel and there you can speak to our people."

The people parted, making way for Jack and the elderly, gray-maned, distinguished-looking man leading him. "Hello, hello," Jack kept repeating, shaking hands with many of his new mission flock as he neared the chapel.

"Here we are, Padre."

Jack looked up at the small white, wooden cross Luke Haynes had pointed to. It stood atop the peak of a roof, no more than 14 feet above the baked ground. The cross' base was screwed to the front of the chapel. The chapel itself was a large garage with a single, open door about 20 feet wide and eight feet high. Well, Jack was thinking, the Lord was born in humble lodgings.

"We hope to build a new chapel," the elder said, explaining but not apologizing. "Money is short."

"This will do fine," said Jack. "I'm sure the Lord is smiling on us today."

Well said, Padre, Luke remarked to himself. He was smiling approvingly. You're off to a good start, Father Jack.

†††

The elderly men, 20 of them, had just been rousted from their homes in a Warsaw neighborhood near the Vistula River. They were confused and frightened. Nazis had targeted them in reprisal for sabotage – the destruction of railroad tracks that led south to the death camps – carried out by Poland's Home Army.

Bernadeta Gudek would have felt unutterably sad at the men's plight were it not for the intense concentration she knew she must maintain. Only seldom did the Resistance receive word in advance of Nazi atrocities. Generally, they were carried out as quickly as they were mercilessly, often on the streets. Sometimes, though, the Nazis sent out advance word when they wanted executions to serve as a deterrent to partisan actions. And sometimes there were leaks. This morning was one such occasion, and Bernadeta's Home Army cell had been alerted and a plan quickly devised. As with other such plans, Bernadeta had doubts about this one's efficacy. The risks, she was thinking, always seem so enormous.

A Nazi lieutenant, a sergeant and four privates began escorting the 20 luckless men. Their destination was a nearby cemetery. Awaiting them there were two cemetery grave diggers and 20 shovels. The men would be ordered to dig their own grave – one long one -- before being forced to kneel beside it and executed with a shot to the nape. No stone of any size or shape would mark their burial site.

As the procession continued, the men did not speak to the Germans. Nor did they protest. From three years of brutal occupation and repression, they knew it would be useless. They had shaken off their initial confusion and clearly knew their fate. Since the Germans had arrived in September of 1939, the elderly men had witnessed or heard about countless executions and even more deportations to the death camps at Auschwitz and Birkenau. Violent death was the everyday companion of Poles.

At the cemetery, the German lieutenant dismissed the two gravediggers. He then ordered the men to pick up the shovels and begin their excavation. About two hours had elapsed and they were nearing its completion. The Germans had been standing by, chatting, occasionally barking at the men to hurry. The Germans were bored and well beyond feeling sympathy for their victims. The soldiers had received their orders and were carrying them out without question – which would have been out of the question.

Unobtrusively, Bernadeta Gudek, wearing a dark blue headscarf and long brown cloth coat, stepped toward a gravestone about 40 feet away from the mass grave and knelt down. She did not so much as glance at the men and their waiting executioners. Her thoughts turned momentarily to Thaddeus Metz, the young lancer she had helped free more than three years ago. Please, God, if he is not already with you, stay with him. Please. Then she willed herself to concentrate on the here and now.

The men kept digging, sweating despite the early November chill. A few minutes later, Bernadeta rose and turned to face the doomed men. This time, she stared, motionless. The six Germans were watching her. Deliberately, she made a sign of the cross. Then slowly, gracefully, she knelt again and pressed her hands together in prayer.

One of the privates chuckled derisively and pointed dismissively at Bernadeta.

"Shut up!" snapped the lieutenant, disgusted with the private's unseemly behavior. The Polish men, startled, paused and looked up. They saw Bernadeta, kneeling for them in prayer. She was fingering a simple, black-beaded rosary. "Keep digging!" the sergeant barked.

Bernadeta got to her feet and began walking toward the grave.

"Stop!" the lieutenant ordered firmly.

Nearby, from behind a thick stand of trees that bordered the cemetery, Kaz Majos and four other Home Army members emerged. They began moving quietly, efficiently toward the mass grave.

Bernadeta paused. Again, she pressed her hands together in prayer. Then she took another step forward.

"Stop, I said," repeated the lieutenant. Now, all eyes, soldiers' and men's alike, were on Bernadeta. "Come no closer," the lieutenant commanded.

Bernadeta pretended to not understand his warning in German. She was surprised by the absence of fear, perhaps because she had been half-expecting to die for more than two years.

"Stop!" This time the lieutenant raised his right hand in an unmistakable gesture. Bernadeta halted. She forced the smallest of smiles and shook her head slightly.

"Do you think she is addled?" the sergeant asked the lieutenant. "Look at her face. She looks…stupid."

"I don't know," the lieutenant replied. "She looks harmless. Just don't let her get any closer to this grave."

"Yes, Sir."

Kaz and his companions edged closer. About 20 feet from the Germans, they took careful aim at their targets. Silently, Kaz extended the fore and middle fingers of his left hand and pointed them toward himself. Then Kaz nodded to the others. Five captured German lugers crackled, and five German soldiers crumpled. Kaz fired a second time, and the sixth German fell. Four of the Germans died instantly. Two, including the lieutenant, were moaning.

The 20 elderly Poles were dazed. Kaz and his companions stepped closer. Two took aim at the pair of dying Germans.

"No."

They all looked at Bernadeta.

"No," she repeated firmly. With steps that seemed almost robotic, Bernadeta closed the remaining distance to the mass grave. Once there, she loosened the clasp on her cheap, brown purse. She removed a luger. She held the gun to the nape of one wounded German and pulled the trigger. A sharp crack. Then she stepped to the second injured German and did likewise. She looked at the men she had killed. She was feeling no anger, no remorse, no real sense of satisfaction. There seemed at that moment a vast emotional emptiness. Then she looked at Kaz and nodded.

"Stand back," Kaz said to the 20 incredulous men. Then he and his fellow partisans used their feet to topple the Germans' bodies into the grave. "Fill in the grave," he said to the men. "Quickly. We'll help." Kaz and his men took shovels from five of the men and, with the others, went silently to work. It didn't take long before the job was completed.

Everyone stood looking at the filled-in grave, the loose dirt mounded higher than the surrounding earth. Then Kaz spoke to the men. "You could return to your homes, but you know that would mean certain death. For you and perhaps for others as well. Family members. Or you could follow us. We will turn you over to other Home Army members. They will take you into hiding. You might survive. You might not. But at least you will have a chance, and that seems better than no chance at all."

Most of the men nodded. Then for a few moments, there was barely audible murmuring. Then one of the 20 Jews spoke. "We will take that chance. We are old, but we would like to keep living."

"Good," said Kaz. "Let's get moving over to those trees."

"One more thing," said the Jewish elder. "Thank you." He smiled at Bernadeta and bowed. "Thank you all."

†††

"Will you at least consider it?" Maurice Trimbach asked Lea. He was speaking quietly but with a sense of urgency.

"I'm not sure."

The two of them were standing by the fountain in Place De La Sinne, one of the plazas along Ribeauville's Grand' Rue. The sound of the spilling water assured they wouldn't be overheard.

"It is only a matter of time, you know," Maurice said quietly. "So far, the Germans have not taken any French to Natzwiller, but they certainly will. They've been executing German Jews there...hanging, shooting, gassing. There's a crematorium. Eventually, French Jews will be killed there. Others, too."

Lea nodded. "You are probably right.. I know the Germans have begun asking whether we have any Jews in our village. I don't think anyone has informed on them. If only we could persuade them to leave."

"They are in denial," Maurice said. "The Steiners, the Somers. Like so many Jews in so many places, they can't bring themselves to accept the full evil of the Nazis."

"The mountains," said Lea. "So far they seem to be protecting us from witnessing the worst of the war. So little seems to be happening now."

"That will change," said Maurice. "When America comes to our aid – and I truly believe America will help us – everything will change. And that is why the Resistance needs you."

†††

At 3 a.m. on November 8, 1942, the 800 warships and transports of the Allies' North African force began landing troops on the continent's Atlantic and Mediterranean beaches.

At Casablanca, Patton's men met sharp resistance from the French. Patton was incensed. "The French, at least these French, don't deserve our help," he snarled to Colonel Codman. "We have to persuade Petain to stop this nonsense and damned fast. This is a job for Ike."

The French also fired on the British troops coming ashore at Oran. In total, at Casablanca and Oran, the Allies suffered 800 casualties, the French many more.

At Algiers, Allied landing craft dropped their ramps on the beach. British and American troops went dashing across the sand, expecting to fight but meeting no opposition. Still on their ship, several American nurses were clustered, watching the soldiers storming ashore, one carrying a U.S. flag.

"We were lucky this morning," said Lieutenant Theresa Hassler.

"Very lucky," somberly echoed Lieutenant Colonel Carter.

"I wonder how long our luck will hold," said Theresa.

"Not nearly long enough, I'm afraid," said Colonel Carter. A pause and then she added, "They'll be taking us ashore soon. Is everything ready?"

"Yes, Colonel," said Theresa. "We've double checked to be sure all our supplies are loaded."

"Very good. We may not need them this morning but soon enough…"

†††

During the next two days, General Dwight Eisenhower negotiated feverishly to persuade the French to put down their weapons. On November 10, he offered Admiral Darlan, the Vichy commander-in-chief who had arrived in Algiers, the post of governor general for all French North Africa – provided Darlan could persuade French soldiers to lay down their arms. Quickly, Darlan accepted Eisenhower's proposal and the fighting ended. Six weeks later, on December 24, Darlan was assassinated.

†††

On the 24th, Jack Brecker said midnight Mass for his Immaculate Conception Church parishioners in Ajo. The little church was packed, and Jack was exhilarated. During the service, he smiled often. Afterward, in his bedroom in the small rectory, he removed his glasses and pulled his vestments over his head. He hung them carefully and then stretched out on his bed. He checked his clock, pulled out the alarm pin, and switched off the bedside lamp.

Two hours later, the alarm jarred Jack awake. He groaned once and rubbed his eyes. Then he swung his legs over the side of the bed and stood. Quickly, he shaved and ran a comb through his coal black hair. Then he fixed coffee and poured it into a glass-lined thermos bottle. Church rules required strict fasting after midnight for communicants, but Jack felt no guilt as he poured a little milk into the thermos of coffee. Better than falling asleep at the wheel in the desert, he told himself. Jack gathered up his vestments and a felt-lined wooden box of Communion wafers.

Minutes later, he was driving his Ford Model-A southeast toward Charco. Lateness of hour and fatigue notwithstanding, Jack was feeling satisfaction. Christmas morning in the desert. When I first went to the Josephinum, I never dreamed of this.

Darkness had not yet given way to dawn when Jack arrived at the garage-as-chapel. Not to his surprise, the congregation elder was waiting for him.

"Merry Christmas," said the elder, offering his right hand.

Jack took it. "Merry Christmas to you, too."

"This must feel different from your Christmases in Ohio," said the elder, starlight glancing off his neatly trimmed, shoulder-length gray hair.

"They do tend to be a little colder and whiter," Jack said, smiling in the desert night. Then Jack shivered. "Of course, the desert itself is chilly enough at this time of day." He looked up. "It looks like the Lord has painted the sky with stars. Here in the desert they are so bright they remind me of the Christmas lights back in Ohio."

The elder smiled. "It will be awhile before our people arrive."

"Would you like a cup of my coffee?" Jack asked.

"Yes, if you will have one of my cigarettes."

"Christmas presents to each other," Jack said. "Useful ones."

"The best kind."

The two men stood under slowly fading stars, smoking, the elder sipping the last of Jack's coffee.

"I don't believe I've ever been anywhere so quiet," Jack said softly. "This is beautiful country, your home."

"You are a good man, Padre," murmured the elder. "My people respect you. Like you."

"I like and respect them, too."

"Coming out here in the night to say Mass for my people on Christmas morning. This means very much to them. You are a true desert priest."

Part Two

Chapter 21

Unbeknownst to each other, Paul Brecker and Thaddeus Metz were about to begin engaging in the same kind of training. Each was standing on a platform atop a tower. Paul was with the 101st Airborne Division at Fort Benning, Georgia. Thaddeus and the other cow pen soldiers were with General Sosabowski's newly formed Polish Airborne Brigade at Upper Largo near the North Sea.

Paul tugged at his parachute straps and breathed deeply. He was tethered but still a trifle nervous. Nobody made me do this, Paul reminded himself. I'm a volunteer.

From behind, Paul heard a familiar voice. "Hey, Paul, remember to keep your eyes open. Think your stomach will stay where it's sposed ta'?" The voice laughed merrily. It belonged to Roscoe Remlinger. Everyone, including the platoon sergeant, called him R, his preference. R was from Douglasville, a rural community set at the intersection of winding roads 20 miles west of Atlanta. In the center of the village was a single traffic light. When Paul first asked Roscoe why he had volunteered for the airborne, R had replied with a voice as smooth as fresh cream, "When I was jus' a boy, I liked to jump off a high rock into the fishin' hole. It was scary the first time but fun. I figured jumpin' from an airplane would be a mite higher and lots more fun."

There had been a brief pause and then, "How about you, Paul? Why'd you join the paratroopers?"

Paul smiled and shrugged. "Curiosity, I guess. I've never been in a plane, much less jumped out of one. Curiosity and a weak moment. That pretty much sums it up."

"Aww, come on, Paul, there's gotta be more to it than that."

"Not much more," Paul had replied. "Maybe a feeling that I'd be doing something important... something that might help beat Hitler."

Now, at the edge of the high platform, Paul bent his legs, then sprang outward. The jump went fast, faster than he had anticipated, and the sharp, upward jerk at the end punched out his breath. Then his feet touched the ground. Not bad for the first time, he thought. Kept my eyes open. More exciting than any ride at an amusement park. R was right.

At Upper Largo, Thaddeus looked down. He was less nervous about his first training jump than about the integrity of the training tower. General Sosabowski had succeeded in obtaining permission to form his airborne unit, but he had failed to win approval to train with British airborne forces at their training center near Manchester. He and his men would have to scrounge and improvise to train at Upper Largo. The tower was a strong testament to his men's talent for scrounging and improvising. From scraps of steel, its quality open to question, they had welded together their jump tower. Standing atop it, Thaddeus was thinking that someone had to be first to climb to the top of the uncertain structure. We are short of materials and technology, Thaddeus reflected, but long on spirit and determination. We must keep in mind our goal – beating the Germans and freeing Poland. He stepped to the platform's edge and leaped.

†††

Bridgett Hassler was walking slowly across the parking lot, flanked by her parents, Eleanor and Joe. As they started up the steps, Bridgett's knees weakened, and she felt a chill.

"Are you all right?" Eleanor asked.

"I think so. Just a little nervous."

The February air was arctic, with a biting wind that made breathing painful. The Veteran Administration Hospital was in Brecksville, a southern suburb of Cleveland. Driving there from Grand Boulevard in Shelby had taken about 90 minutes.

"May I help you?" asked the clerk at the reception desk.

"Yes," said Bridgett. "We're here to see Tom Brecker."

The clerk began running a finger down a roster sheet. "He's in room three-twenty. Elevator is down that hall on the left."

"Thank you," said Bridgett. She was desperate to see Tom yet dreading the moment. More than two years had passed since they had last seen each other. Last hugged and kissed. Their letters, written almost daily for most of those two years but received in batches, had sustained their love. In recent months, since the Hornet had gone down, Tom's letters had been less frequent. That's understandable, Bridgett was thinking as the elevator ascended. His letters also had been less passionate, less certain about things. That's understandable, too, she was musing. Nothing to fret about overly much.

The elevator door opened and they stepped out. Eleanor spoke. "Do you want to go in alone first, or would you like us to go in with you?"

"Alone, I think."

"I think that would be better. For you and Tom. We'll wait here at the nurse's station until you're ready for us."

"Thanks, Mom."

As Bridgett went walking slowly down the hall toward Room 320, Eleanor and Joe exchanged brief parental half-smiles that bespoke deep concern and bottomless affection for their younger daughter. Bridgett felt unsteady, as though she might faint. Her stomach seemed to rotate, stirring its bitter gastric juices. Once, twice, she breathed as deeply as she could. Then she lowered her head and swallowed. Room 320. Gently, she pushed the door. Silently, it swung inward. Tom was lying still and his eyes were closed.

Bridgett hesitated and then whispered, "Tom? Tom?"

His eyes opened. Bridgett was holding her breath. Then he smiled, an incredibly warm smile. Bridgett, arms at her side, began sobbing and shaking. Tom watched for a moment, then extended his arms. Bridgett reached for them and their hands came together.

He was the first to speak. "I love you, Bridg."

Bridgett tried to stop weeping but laughter began forming before her tears stopped cascading. "I love you, too, Tom."

Hands still joined, Tom pulled her toward him, and their lips touched lightly.

"Oh my," said Bridgett.

"What's wrong?"

"I might faint. Again. I almost fainted in the hallway." She laughed at herself.

"Sit," Tom said, patting the edge of his bed. "Just don't let go of my hands."

"I won't. Don't worry."

"Your mom and dad with you?"

"Yes, they're at the nurses' station. They offered to wait until we're ready."

"Good. I was hoping for some privacy. Bridg, I can hardly begin to say how glad I am to see you. Every day, every night..." Tom faltered as his throat thickened and eyes misted. He forced a swallow.

"I missed you, too," Bridgett said, voice cracking. "I know I said that over and over in my letters, but I missed you even more than I could say. I truly ached."

"Bridg, you know, uh...It's going to be awhile before...uh..." Tom breathed deeply. "Before I can walk without crutches." He looked at where his left foot used to be.

Tears were welling again in Bridgett's eyes. "Tom, all that matters is that you're back and safe. That's all."

He sniffled. "They'll be fitting me with a prosthesis. Soon. I'll need to get used to that before they let me leave here. And my other wounds, they're basically healed. Some ugly scars..."

"I could care less about scars, Tom. Or about the prosthesis. I'm just so happy to have you back."

One large piece of shrapnel had nearly severed Tom's left foot, just above his ankle. Amputation had followed quickly aboard a hospital ship. Several smaller shards had ripped into his left leg nearly to his buttocks. No one had bothered to count the number of stitches.

"I'm not sure what I'll do when I get out."

"You'll marry me," Bridgett said spunkily. "Darned fast, too."

"Yes, I will. And I've been thinking about that."

"How?"

"Well, wouldn't it be great if Jack could marry us?"

"Oh, Tom, geez. That would be wonderful! Truly wonderful."

"I don't know if he could get away. It's a long haul from Ajo to Shelby. But it won't hurt to ask."

"Do you know when his first home leave will be?" Bridgett had grown quickly excited at the prospect of Tom's brother conducting their wedding ceremony.

"No. Probably not for a while. But we can wait awhile if Jack thinks he can get back to do it. Besides," Tom chuckled, "I'd like to be able to walk out of the church with you and without crutches or a cane.

Bridgett laughed. "I could be your cane."

"And a pretty one at that."

They both laughed.

"It feels good to laugh," Tom said.

"I'll tell your doctor to make it part of your therapy."

"My doctor might need laugh lessons himself." They both laughed again.

"I'd like Sam to be my best man if Paul can't be there. Otherwise, I'd like him to be my head usher."

"I'd love to meet him. Your letters made him seem so real, so special. How's he doing?"

"Pretty much like me. He left part of himself back on the Hornet. Shrapnel carved a chunk of flesh from his left side. His left knee was shattered. He's in a VA hospital in Brooklyn."

After the Hornet went down, Tom and Sam Tortino had been put aboard a hospital ship. After treatment to stabilize them, they were taken to the Veterans Administration hospital in San Francisco before being transported by train to the hospitals in Brecksville and Brooklyn.

"I've prayed for him, too," said Bridgett.

"I know," he sighed. "Neither one of us will be running any more dashes. That's for sure. And I don't see us as civilian firemen. Climbing ladders is out. But if I know Sam, he'll probably still take New York by storm. I can see it now – Mayor Sam Tortino."

"How about Mayor Tom Brecker? In Shelby?" said Bridgett. "You'd get my vote."

Tom laughed. "Just don't stuff the ballot box and land yourself in jail."

They hugged and kissed, tenderly and long. "I hope your mom and dad don't get tired of waiting and walk in on us. Not quite yet."

Bridgett smiled and they kissed again, this time more urgently.

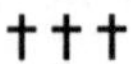

Chapter 22

George Patton's triumphs in North Africa were winning him publicity, enemies and even a measure of sympathy. In January of 1943, he met with President Franklin Roosevelt and Prime Minister Winston Churchill at Casablanca. On February 16, his son-in-law, Lieutenant Colonel John Waters, was seriously injured and captured by Germans in Tunisia. This news hit Patton hard. He cared deeply for Waters and knew how hard the news would be for his daughter.

In March, he began planning the invasion of Sicily, but occasionally took time for diversions, chiefly horseback riding and wild boar hunting. It was during this period that he uttered one of his more oft-cited quotes: "God favors the brave; victory is for the audacious." On April 12, Patton was pictured on the cover of TIME magazine, which devoted three pages to examining the general's strengths and weaknesses. His reaction: "The story is too goddamned balanced." He dropped the magazine on his desk and strutted across his office to the door. He was hungering for his next joust with the Germans – the blessed American warrior squaring off against the godless Hun. He would be pictured on TIME's cover a second time later that year.

†††

It was a June morning in Ajo and already blisteringly hot. Luke Haynes removed his hat and wiped a large blue kerchief across his forehead.

"Dry heat," Father Jack Brecker teased him. "Isn't that what you told me on my first day in Ajo? You really don't have any sweat to wipe."

"Good memory, Father Jack. We sweat here, but it's just so dry it evaporates as soon as it breaks the skin. Except under your hat band."

"What brings you here so early? And on a weekday?"

Luke passed his tongue over his dry lips. "Mountain lion."

"Mountain lion? Here?"

"Killing a lot of the Indians' sheep out near Charco. Gotta get him."

"And you want me to bless your gun," Jack teased.

"Not exactly. Actually, I thought you might like to go with me."

"Why on earth why?"

"To help."

"Help? I'm sorry, Luke, but you're flying way over my head."

"I brought two rifles, Father Jack. Thought you might help me get the cat."

"Me?" Jack's surprise was bordering on astonishment. He laughed. "You want me to shoot a lion? I've never killed anything. Well, flies and ants and a few spiders. But nothing else. Why should I go mountain lion hunting with you? What on earth ever gave you that idea?"

Nothing Jack said surprised Luke. He had deliberated a good while before deciding to come to the rectory. "Somebody's got to. One lion has been slaughtering sheep over on the Tohono. That's their food and blankets."

"I see. But why you? Why are you going after the lion on their land?"

"Because, like I said, I have the guns. A seven millimeter Browning and an M-1."

"Hmmm...Bishop Metzger said a spirit of adventure would be helpful."

"He was right. Father Jack, come with me and I'll bet you'll see a new mission chapel at Charco faster than you ever thought possible."

"What?"

"Word will get around. Wallets will open. Not just the Indians'."

Jack smiled and nodded. "You're a smart man, Luke, as smart as you are tall."

"Just practical, Father Jack."

†††

Outside Ajo, Luke pulled his pickup truck off the side of Rt. 85. "Time to teach you how to handle the M-1."

"Father Mac would never believe this."

"Who's Father Mac?"

"The priest who really helped me become a priest. A great man."

"Well, if he's great," said Luke, "if he was here, he'd understand."

For the next hour, Luke instructed Jack in the basics of riflery. First, he explained the rifle's operation and capability. Then how to load it, how to carry it, how to quickly and quietly get into firing position, how to breathe, how to sight, how to squeeze the trigger. "If you get a clear chance to shoot a lion," said Luke, "you gotta make the most of it. You'll only get one shot."

Luke set up a few small rocks as targets, and Jack fired practice rounds. He surprised himself with his accuracy. "Not bad for a priest who wears glasses," Jack said dryly.

"Not bad for anybody," Luke replied sincerely. "You'll make a good hunter."

Jack was dressed for hunting. He was wearing khaki pants and a long-sleeved white shirt. He had learned quickly that white and long-sleeves protected better against the intense desert sun and aided comfort by trapping more perspiration, which quickly evaporated and cooled. He also was wearing a gray Josephinum baseball cap with a large script J on the front and new hiking boots, courtesy of Luke who had pointed out that Jack's black leather dress shoes would be ruined by a single trek into the desert mountains.

They returned to the pickup truck and continued south, then east. On Rt. 86, nearing Charco, Luke braked the pickup. "This is where we stop. Last kill was over there." He pointed toward the mountains to the north.

Jack looked at the vast panorama. "Finding a lion out here can't be easy."

"Never is."

"How do we find him?" Jack asked. "If it's a him."

"We look for scat – cat droppings."

"What does that tell us?"

"If it's full of sheep's wool," said Luke, "we'll know it's been chewin' on the Indians' stock."

"How often have you done this?" Jack asked. "Hunted mountain lion."

"Not that often. A few times. Enough to learn a few lessons."

"How big are the lions?"

Luke smiled. "Big enough to cause problems. Females run maybe seventy-five to a hundred pounds. Males can go two hundred."

"You were right," said Jack. "That's big enough."

"After we find some," said Luke, "we'll let the lion come to us."

"What do you mean?"

"Just wait and you'll see."

A few minutes later, the mission elder arrived in his well-worn pickup. He warmly greeted Luke and Jack.

"Padre," said the elder, "my people are very grateful you are helping Luke. We do not like to kill the big cats, but we must when they kill our stock."

"I understand," Jack said softly. He was thinking that Luke must have assumed he would help and that at no point in his seminary education were there ever lessons on relations with Indians and killing lions. There should have been, he concluded.

The elder stepped to the rear of his truck, reached over the side and returned holding a lamb.

"You carry the rifles," Luke told Jack. "I'll carry the lamb." Luke knew the question that Jack was about to ask and provided the preemptory answer: "Bait."

The elder smiled wryly. "Padre, if the lamb dies, its sacrifice will not be in vain. One more kill for the cat will save many sheep."

Jack's face was clearly registering his discomfort with the notion of sacrificing this young creature to lure another hungry creature to a violent death.

"It's the best way," Luke said to Jack. "And if we're lucky, the lamb won't get killed." Then to the elder, Luke said, "We'll let you know at the end of the day – luck or no luck."

Luke and Jack began walking across what passed for high desert grazing meadow toward the nearest ascent into the mountains. "Be careful you don't kick rocks, Father Jack." Jack looked questioningly at Luke. "Rattlers."

"Oh my. I think seeing a rattle snake scares me more than seeing a lion."

"It should," said Luke. "There's lots more rattlers around than lions, and rattlers don't like folks interruptin' their siestas."

"An understandable sentiment." Lions, lambs and snakes, Jack was thinking. That's definitely a course that needs adding to the Josephinum curriculum for missionaries. Maybe I'll write the good fathers back in Ohio a letter with a few of my thoughts. Of course, if I did, they might think the desert heat had fried my brain.

†††

Dry desert heat notwithstanding, the climb was tiring. "Wish I was in better shape," Jack said.

"At least you're still young," said Luke. "I've had more years to get out of shape."

"How many years has that been, Luke?"

"Nuf to be your father, Father."

Jack chuckled. At the moment, despite the newness of virtually everything he had been encountering, he felt truly blessed with his assignment. The desert priest, the elder had called him. Jack liked the sound of that. And the stories he would have for telling his brothers and parents back in Shelby...Well, they would have the sound of fiction more than fact.

"Ah," murmured Luke.

"What?"

"Scat. Just ahead of us."

They walked to the droppings. Wool hair was clearly visible. Luke surveyed the surroundings. "He could be watching us. Let's hope not. They're smart creatures. Real smart. Come on."

They climbed a little higher and stopped. They were standing in a slight depression bordered on three sides by steep heights. "Here," Luke said, "put the rifles down and hold the lamb." He then set about gathering some smaller rocks. He piled them in the center of the depression. Then from his belt he removed a length of rope.

"I was wondering what you'd be using that for," said Jack.

Luke looped one end around the lamb's neck, took the small creature from Jack's arms and carried it to the rock pile. He put the lamb down and tied the opposite end of the rope around a rock and piled the other rocks on top of it.

"Okay," said Luke, "let's take up position there." He was pointing to higher ground. "Looks like decent cover." Luke took the Browning from Jack who kept the M-1.

They had barely begun climbing when the lamb began bahing.

"He sounds scared," said Jack.

"He is."

From behind a large boulder, Jack and Luke each took long pulls on water from their canteens. The boulder was warm to the touch.

"Stay ready," said Luke. "Remember what I said. If we get a chance, it'll likely be a short one."

†††

In Warsaw, the Ghetto uprising was over, and Bernadeta Gudek still was trying to come to grips with the helplessness she had endured during the Jews' lashing out at their Nazi tormentors.

Initially, the Germans had confined some 500,000 Jews to a section of Warsaw they called the ghetto. By April 1943, most had starved, been executed or sent to concentration camps. Only 60,000 remained, and they decided to strike back.

Their uprising was the first armed revolt in occupied Europe. It had begun slowly in January 1943 when the Home Army provided 10 pistols to Jews in the ghetto. Later, the partisans smuggled in 60 more pistols, most by skulking through sewers. The smells, thought Bernadeta, were worse than the odor of farm manure. There was no air to freshen the sewers. Then the partisans supplied some rifles, machine guns and grenades.

When the uprising spread throughout the ghetto in April, SS chief Heinrich Himmler paid a visit and then cockily predicted to Hitler that he would have it suppressed within three days.

"We have given them weapons," Bernadeta said, "but I wish we could do more."

Homeland Army Captain Kaz Majos smiled wearily. "You've been saying that every day."

"I know. It's the way I feel."

"Right. So I will say again that trying to do more at this time would mean certain death. The Germans have the ghetto completely sealed off. They are even guarding the entrances to the sewers. Our mission is to stay alive and keep resisting just like we have been. Maybe later we can attack in force."

"Later…"

"We need more weapons," said Kaz. "You know that."

"So many of them are dying," Bernadeta murmured sadly.

"Yes, but the Jews know if they don't die fighting in the ghetto they will die in the camps or be executed right here in Warsaw."

"Sometimes it's so sad I just want to sit and cry. Or go back home to Zyrardow. Be with my family. On our farm."

Kaz sighed. "I understand."

"But I will stay."

"I know."

What Himmler had pledged to achieve in three days took more than four weeks. More than 15,000 Jews were killed during the battle. So were 300 Germans. Himmler was stunned by the Jews' tenacity and Hitler was infuriated. Most of the remaining 45,000 ghetto Jews were executed or sent to death camps.

†††

After about two hours of waiting and watching, Jack felt Luke's hand on his shoulder. Luke put his lips next to Jack's left ear and whispered, "Look up there." He was pointing with the forefinger of his partially extended left hand.

Jack saw nothing except barren rocks. "Where?" he mouthed.

"Follow the line of my finger."

Jack squinted behind the lenses of his glasses. Atop the highest rock surrounding the depression was a pair of eyes set amidst grayish beige hair mottled with small patches of black. The creature blended virtually perfectly with the high desert rockscape.

"Shoot now?" Jack mouthed nearly silently.

"Not yet. I think he will get lower and closer before he attacks the lamb. Shoot then if we have a clear shot. If not, we wait until he has the lamb."

Moments later, the eyes and graying beige fur disappeared.

"Are you ready?" Luke whispered.

"I think so."

"Remember the lessons. Take a couple deep breaths. Relax your trigger hand. Flex your fingers."

Jack complied. Then, on a lower rock, the lion reappeared. Its left flank was visible to Jack and Luke. The lamb, sensing danger, began to bah again.

"Now," whispered Luke. "Breathe in and out. Aim for just behind his shoulder. Squeeze the trigger gently."

Jack nodded, breathed and squeezed. At the M-1's crack, the lion half-leaped, spun in a scattering of pebbles and dust, and disappeared. The lamb was terrified.

"Did I get him?" Jack whispered.

"No need to whisper now," Luke smiled. "Let's find out. Keep your M-1 ready. Got my Browning ready, too." They stood. "Stay a step behind me and to my right. I want to know where you are."

"Okay."

They began climbing toward the rock where the lion had been stalking and crouching. Cautiously, they circled up and behind the rock. At its base lay the lion's corpse.

"There's your answer, Father Jack." Blood was seeping from a wound behind the lion's shoulder.

Jack gazed down silently for a long moment. "It's such a beautiful animal," he murmured.

"Yes, it is," Luke said. "A shame he had to die. Just keep in mind that taking this one life will save many more. Plus you've helped the Indians...your desert congregation."

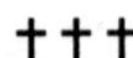

Chapter 23

It was early July 1943, and the first of the men jumped down from the railroad cattle cars. They all were members of the French Resistance, and they were the first French prisoners brought to the Natzwiller camp. Two days later, a second train brought more French partisans and, two days after that, a third train delivered still more. In total, among the prisoners delivered to Natzwiller that week were 167 French partisans who went trudging up the road from the rail station to the mountaintop concentration camp.

"I'm surprised we're still alive," said one of the partisans as he passed through the camp gate.

"Agreed," replied his friend, "I thought they'd shoot us on the spot."

They wouldn't have long to wait. Some of the 167 were executed that same day. Some were shot, some hanged. All murdered that day were incinerated that night, with the camp band playing outside the crematorium.

The lucky ones were put to work quarrying granite and excavating nearby for the planned construction of underground factories. The prisoners, underfed, would slowly starve. Their daily diet: for breakfast, a pint of ersatz coffee or watery soup; at noon, two pints of liquid soup; in the evening after work, a pint of ersatz coffee, 12 ounces of bread, a spoonful of marmalade and a small piece of cheese or scrap of sausage. As they grew too weak to work, they were executed, their deaths often recorded as "shot while attempting to escape."

†††

"You've heard?"

"Yes."

Maurice Trimbach and Lea Peiffer were standing in the doorway of the Peiffer home in Rue des Boulangers. Although only 9 a.m., the brilliant sun was heralding a hot Alsatian summer day.

"You can guess why I'm here," Maurice murmured somberly.

"Yes," replied Lea, "it's about the partisans at Natzwiller. I've heard what's happening there."

"The Nazis are murdering them," Maurice said, his full fury barely concealed. "Shooting, hanging, injecting them with poison, gassing. Starving them. Soon they will be rounding up Jews in the villages, including ours."

"You want my help," said Lea.

"Yes."

"What are you thinking?"

"We want the Germans here in Ribeauville thinking about something besides our Jews. We want to create a distraction…one that will last."

"Revenge?"

"That, too."

"And?"

"And we think the best way is to make one of their officers disappear."

"Kill him?"

Maurice, knowing Lea as well as he did, hesitated. He expected her to have moral qualms with his plan. He pursed his lips and nodded. "Yes, but not so they can confirm that. We want them to think he is missing. Raise questions about him. His loyalty to the Nazis. We hope to do this without causing reprisals."

"Is that possible?"

"To be honest…We're not sure."

"This would be murder."

"Murder is a sin," Maurice said, still laboring to keep his fury from erupting. "Is it a sin to strike back at those who have taken our freedom? Who are executing fellow Frenchmen and women? Who are rounding up Jews?"

"But not here. Not these Germans in Ribeauville."

"They are part of the evil that is murdering freedom. If killing Germans here will spare some of our people, I am prepared to commit that kind of murder."

"Does Mayor Javelot know about this?" Lea asked.

"No."

"He is our village leader. Don't you think he should know?"

"Frankly," said Maurice, "I'm not sure about his stomach for something like this. A good man, yes. A nice man. I voted for him. But I worry that he might try to talk us out of this. Or, worse, say something to Oberster. No, I don't think he would implicate any particular individual, but I could see him possibly alerting Oberster to be more cautious. I'd rather he didn't know."

"I'm not sure I agree," Lea said, "but I understand." Stonily, she eyed her friend of many years. Lea didn't see herself as a soldier, much less an assassin. Inwardly, she was recoiling at the notion of involving herself in killing. But their freedom was being suppressed and her Jewish friends were at risk. And perhaps, given what was happening at Natzwiller, Maurice was right in saying that the risk was growing. Lea closed her eyes and sighed. "And how do I fit in?"

†††

Twice during the next few days, Lea made a point of crossing paths with Lieutenant Karl Hoffer. The first time, she smiled and said, "Bon jour, Lieutenant." Hoffer was taken aback. Up to now, the young woman had studiously avoided Hoffer and his fellow occupiers. She was nearly past him before he regained his wits in time to reply, "Bon jour, Mademoiselle."

The second time, Hoffer saw Lea standing by the fountain in Place de la Sinne. She smiled at him. He paused. She is used to seeing us, he was thinking. We have been here for three years. Three very boring years. We have posed no danger to the people here. Maybe she is becoming more comfortable with us. Accepting. He smiled and began walking toward her.

"Bon jour, Mademoiselle," he said again.

"Bon jour, Lieutenant."

He smiled a genuinely warm smile. He would welcome having a friend among the locals, especially one so striking. "You know, your village is very pretty. I wish I could be here under different circumstances."

"It's sad," Lea said, nodding in agreement, "that you have to be our enemy."

"I really don't feel that way."

"But you are. That's the reality. Denying it doesn't change things."

"I know," Hoffer said almost sheepishly.

"Where is your home, Lieutenant? A village like ours?"

He brightened and laughed. "No. No. I am from Frankfurt. A very large village, I'm afraid." They both laughed. Hoffer hadn't felt so good in ages.

I could like him, Lea was thinking, but don't think like that, she warned herself. "Frankfurt isn't so far away."

"Have you been there?"

"No. I haven't traveled far. Not to Germany."

"My country is beautiful, too."

"And you are so close to it. The Rhine we can see from the hills. Don't you get homesick?"

"Sometimes. Yes, of course."

"Your family must miss you."

"We write to each other. Often. And I've taken my yearly home leave."

"A girl friend?"

"No one serious. Well, there is one girl I like." Hoffman's face reddened. "We go dancing when I am home on leave."

"Is she pretty?"

"Yes." Hoffman's eyes again brightened. "Very. And lively. She laughs a lot."

"You miss her. She is so near, yet so far. That is very sad."

Hoffman sighed. "Yes. It's a long time between home leaves."

"Do you talk to your friends – the other soldiers here – about home?"

"Only all the time," Hoffman said, smiling.

†††

This time Bridgett Hassler had made the drive to the Veterans Administration Hospital in Brecksville alone. She parked her dad's car and went skipping across the parking lot. She nearly vaulted up the steps. She couldn't remember when she last felt so gloriously, deliriously happy. In her right hand was the handle of a shopping bag filled with home-baked goodies. At the reception desk, she said brightly, "Tom Brecker. Room three-twenty." The clerk nodded and Bridgett walked – wanted to run – to the elevator.

At the third floor, the elevator door opened, Bridgett exited, turned right and froze, eyes wide and mouth agape in astonishment.

From half-way down the hall came an exuberant, "What do you think?!"

Tears sprang instantly from Bridgett's blue-green eyes.

"Tom! You're walking!" She dropped the shopping bag and went running toward him.

"Whoa," he said, smiling broadly and holding up a hand. "Easy. You could knock me over with a feather. I'm just learning to keep my balance." He raised and merrily waggled a cane.

†††

On July 10, Theresa Hassler again found herself tending to terrible wounds and dying young men. Patton's invasion of Sicily had begun.

At this moment, in a large tent not far inland, she was cutting away the field jacket and fatigue shirt of a soldier with a chest wound. She was trying to be gentle, but her experience told her that she had few moments to spare.

"Jesus, sweet Jesus," he was muttering angrily through clenched jaws that tasted of his own splattered blood. His back was arching spasmodically. "I made it all the way across North Africa. Here, I don't even make it across the fucking beach." Eyes watering, he gritted his teeth but didn't apologize for his choice of words. Theresa was neither offended nor surprised.

"But," she said calmly, pulling apart the rent, sodden clothing, "you will make it home."

"In a casket?" His tongue flicked over blood-encrusted lips.

Theresa was applying a pressure bandage. "I think the doctor will agree with my assessment." Her bloodied hands were pressing hard against the soldier's upper right chest.

He winced. "That being?"

"When you get back home, you'll still be wearing your dog tags."

His back arched again and he groaned as another wave of pain went shooting through him. He blinked away more pain-induced tears. "I could kiss you."

"If that would help."

"It would."

Theresa leaned down, hands still pushing hard on the bandage, and tenderly touched her lips to his.

"Hassler," he murmured, reading the name stitched to her fatigues. His anger deflated, he said, "I might just remember you." He tried to smile. Theresa looked up and away.

†††

It had been several days since Lea Peiffer had last spoken with Lieutenant Karl Hoffman. Today she was standing where a short street, Rue de la Fraternite, met Place de la Sinne. She saw Hoffman entering the plaza. A few more paces and he spotted her and waved. Lea waved shyly in reply but didn't move. Will Hoffman continue on his way or will he come to me? I don't want to be seen with him in the plaza.

Hoffman hesitated then began walking toward Lea. She smiled.

"Bon jour, Mademoiselle."

"Bon jour, Lieutenant."

"What are you doing standing here?"

"People watching."

"Ah, a favorite pastime of mine as well."

"It's fun to speculate, isn't it? Where are people going? What are they thinking? Are you thinking about home, Lieutenant? About dancing?"

"Actually, I was thinking about the boring report that I must prepare today – every day -- for Captain Oberster. It's nothing more than make-work."

"A pity to use such a glorious day for such routine matters."

"I quite agree," he said. "But Captain Oberster requires the report. I mean, I should mention this conversation with you." Hoffman was wondering whether Lea liked or pitied him. But, he concluded, right now it doesn't much matter. He certainly liked her.

"You would report our conversation?" The mere suggestion worried Lea.

"I should but I won't."

She wanted to trust him but knew that Maurice would scoff at the notion of trusting a German soldier. "Perhaps I could help you change the routine...relieve your boredom."

"Oh, how?"

"With a glass of our best riesling. Or muscadet if you prefer."

Hoffman was taken aback by the invitation, and his face registered his shock. A moment went by, then he smiled, eyes brightening. "That sounds very tempting." He looked at his watch. "I love good riesling."

"Our home and cellars are just a couple minutes from here," said Lea. "Around the corner in Rue des Boulangers."

Hoffman's lips pursed in indecision. Yearning won out. "I will still have time to write the report on time. Lead the way."

†††

"This way," Lea said, entering the alley beside the Peiffer's home. "The stairs are at the rear of our house." She was hoping that no one had seen Lieutenant Hoffman following her. Too late now, though. She had chosen a day – a time – when her mother was upstairs and her father in nearby Riquewihr on business. They should know nothing of this. Guilt was building in her.

At the rear of the house, Lea bent and began pulling up the double doors leading to the cellars. Hoffman reached down and helped. Lea pulled on a cord, and a light switched on. At the bottom of the stairs, Lea said, "This way. Our tasting room is down this aisle."

Hoffman was marveling at the huge barrels and the many rows of racks filled floor to ceiling with bottles of fine wines. "This is amazing, really. I've never been in a wine cellar."

Lea entered the tasting room and switched on another light. "I think we can find riesling you'll like." She stepped around and behind a table. From a rack behind her, she removed a riesling. She set it on the table and picked up a corkscrew.

"Let me," Lieutenant Hoffman said, smiling kindly.

"If you like."

"I don't believe this is happening," Hoffman said, smiling and shaking his head. "I wish I could tell my men. Let them know how friendly you are. But that wouldn't be very wise."

Lea watched Hoffman maneuver the corkscrew into place. He had barely begun his effort when a strong left forearm coiled around his neck and jerked hard. Simultaneously, an even stronger right arm drove a knife into Hoffman's back. His eyes widened and teared. The terror in his eyes caused Lea to avert hers and flinch. In another moment, his throat crushed and the knife blade penetrating deeply, the young German was dead. Maurice Trimbach eased Hoffman's body to the floor.

Two more partisans stepped forward and rolled the body over. Quickly, they placed rags over the knife wound.

"Better that no one sees any blood," Maurice said, "not even your parents." He looked at Lea, pale and shaken. "Will you be all right?" Then Maurice looked at the body at his feet and he shivered. He had never before killed.

Lea felt bile rising in her throat and struggled to gulp it down. "I think so." A pause. "He was nice."

The two partisans carried Hoffman's body to the farthest corner in the cellars. There, they laid him in a grave that already had been dug. A bucket of lime sat beside the grave.

"You go back upstairs," Maurice said to Lea. "You've done well. Saved lives."

"We hope," she murmured, still shaken. "We hope."

"Yes." A pause. "We will cover the body and patch the floor."

Lea nodded. After the partisans finished their work, she knew the plan was to bring the excess earth upstairs in wine casks and place them at the rear of the house. Then later, under cover of darkness, use a wheelbarrow to take the casks to a nearby vineyard and empty them.

Lea left the house and walked to the fountain in Place de la Sinne. She shivered again, bent over and cupped water in her hands. She put her face into the cool water. Then she spread her fingers to let the water drain and straightened. A lone thought occupied her mind: God, please forgive me.

†††

"Do you have any idea where he is?" Captain Gerhard Oberster asked Lieutenant Paul Kohler. Oberster was sitting at his desk in the Hostellerie des Seigneurs de

Ribeaupierrie. A large Nazi flag hung above the hotel's entrance, a daily reminder and irritant for the villagers.

"We've looked everywhere," Kohler replied. "Asked everyone."

"Violence?"

"Here? No, I don't think so. Resentment? Sure, the villagers don't like us being here, but we've never experienced open hostility."

"Has Hoffman said anything unusual lately? Done anything out of the ordinary?"

"Hmm. No. Well, he has been talking about a girl."

"Who?" A lead, Oberster was thinking, a solution to the mystery?

"No one here. Back in Frankfurt. His hometown. He has talked about the girl now and then ever since we got here. And always after home leave. But recently more often. He says they like to go dancing together."

Captain Oberster's right thumb and forefinger rubbed his chin. "It's really hard to imagine Hoffman just up and walking off. Too responsible a soldier."

"I agree."

"Maybe he will return on his own," said Oberster. "But from where?"

"Do you think he could have gotten across the Rhine and to Frankfurt?"

Oberster smiled. "Don't you think you could lie your way past guards at the bridge?"

"I suppose."

"Especially if you had prepared yourself leave papers."

"I see your meaning, Sir. What will we do next?"

"Two things. I think I'll wait until tomorrow. But if Hoffman isn't back by then, I'll really have no choice but to report him as absent from his post without permission. Meanwhile, you and your men keep looking and questioning the villagers. Secondly, I think it's time for me to sit down again with Mayor Javelot. Remind him of certain realities."

"I think he has kept his people under control, " said Lieutenant Kohler.

"So far, yes. But it wouldn't hurt to remind him of the consequences if he were to lose control."

CHAPTER 24

Soldiers, a seemingly endless stream of them, were carrying their duffel bags up the gangplanks. After months of arduous training, the 101st Airborne Division was embarking from New York to England. It was September 5, 1943. The 101st – dubbed the Screaming Eagles for its distinctive unit arm patch -- had been activated on August 16, 1942, at Camp Claiborne, Louisiana. Two months later, its training got underway at Fort Benning, Georgia.

Thousands of New Yorkers were at the bustling port to see the men off. Most didn't know any of the soldiers. It didn't matter. They were pressing cigarettes, cigars, lighters, lighter fluid and candy on the departing troops. Many women and some men hugged the young warriors. A few men had even passed small bottles of whiskey to the soldiers. The civilians stood along side the transports, waving and cheering.

Paul Brecker graciously accepted a box of R.G. Dunn cigars and a bottle of Irish whiskey from a man who, tears welling, was shaking Paul's hand vigorously. "I lost a son on Bataan," the man murmured unsteadily. Paul felt a lump forming in his throat. He pulled his hand away from the man, stepped back and snapped off a salute. Then he put the cigars and whiskey in his duffel bag and started up the gangplank.

Aboard the transport, Paul was recalling fondly the leave he took before entraining for New York. He had headed for Shelby to visit family and friends and to Brecksville to see his brother Tom. The reunions had been joyous affairs, especially the one with Tom.

As their time together was winding down, Tom had spoken movingly to Paul. "Take care of yourself," Tom cautioned him. "I mean it. Don't play hero."

"People keep telling me that."

"You better be listening."

"You mean like you?" Paul said.

"I'm no hero."

"That's not what I'm hearing."

"People exaggerate."

"Uh huh."

†††

In England, their training, to no one's surprise, was intense. The agenda included night fighting, urban warfare, amphibious landings, German equipment familiarization, map reading and, of course, jumping out of airplanes.

After the first two weeks, Paul was sitting in his tent one night and decided it was time to take pen in hand. Using a crate for a desk, he wrote letters to Tom and Jack.

"September 27, 1943

Dear Tom,

Just a few quick words to let you know I'm here and doing fine. After I finish this letter to you, I will jot one to Jack.

I think it will be easy to avoid being a hero. The training here is pretty realistic. It has included some live fire exercises that are intended to teach us to stay low and dig in. It works.

How are you doing? Running any races yet? Tossed away the cane? How is Bridgett doing at my old job at the Salesbook? She probably smells alcohol in her dreams. That's what we use to clean the presses. She's a fine young woman. You've won yourself quite a prize.

Since you got out of the hospital, I'll bet Shelby never looked so good. Am I right? Seen any good movies at the Castamba or the State? Man, what I wouldn't give to see a good cowboy movie and some Popeye cartoons. I know you must be enjoying Mom's home cooking. Chow down!

As always, your loving brother,

Paul"

"September 27, 1943

Dear Jack,

I just finished writing to Tom. Yes, I know, you are the oldest brother and I should write to you first. Forgive me? Ha ha.

When I saw Tom, he told me about you hunting the mountain lion. It's hard to picture my priestly brother with a rifle in his hand much less shooting it. Do Mom and Dad know about it? Father Mac? What the hell – er, heck – will you be doing next? Steer wrestling? Bronc riding? My brother, the cowboy priest. Ha ha.

Things are good here so far. The training is hard, but the food is good, the weather has been nice, mostly sunny, although I'm told that will probably change soon. I haven't seen many of the local people, but the few I have seen have been very polite.

The division has chaplains – Catholic, Protestant, Jewish. But I doubt if any of them have hunted big game like my big brother. Hey, that's what we need – a chaplain who knows how to handle a rifle. We could even teach him to jump out of airplanes. Ha ha.

Has that Arizona sun browned you up yet? Are you looking like a Mexican or an Indian yet? Or just a burnt piece of toast? Ha ha.

Take care, Father Older Brother.
Your loving younger brother,
Paul"

†††

In Cleveland, Lou Boudreau had just finished his second season as player-manager. He had, in fact, saved owner Alva Bradley a salary, but had yet to deliver a championship. The Indians had finished in third place in the American League, winning 82 games and losing 71. Boudreau was disappointed. Back in April, he had thought the Indians, under his leadership, could win the pennant. There was a measure of consolation in knowing that his ace pitcher, Bob Feller, still was serving in the Navy.

†††

In Upper Largo, Scotland, Thaddeus Metz was growing increasingly impatient. He recognized the value of training, but chafed, knowing that each day Hitler's murderers were executing more Poles. That reality – and the images of slaughter that jolted him awake many nights – was tearing at him daily. Three years now had passed since the German invasion. Still, he thought often of his escape and the young woman who had made it possible.

†††

In Warsaw, Bernadeta Gudek continued her war of resistance. She continued to assist with harrowing sabotage missions, and she continued to live in her cramped room and in the dingy church basement. She was thinking of attempting another visit to her family near Zyrardow.

†††

In Ribeauville, no replacement had been sent for Lieutenant Hoffman. No word, no sign of him had been reported. No rumors had been spread. Captain Oberster had loathed having to report Hoffman as absent without permission. He liked Hoffman and his mysterious disappearance was a blot on Oberster's record.

Lea Peiffer thought often of Hoffman. His bright, friendly countenance often occupied her mind. Sometimes sharp stabs of guilt froze her thoughts and actions. She knew, though, that she had to keep struggling to suppress her guilt, to keep up an appearance of normalcy for her parents and her best friend, Marie Kieny. So far, there had been no threats made to Ribeauville's Jewish families, the Steiners and the Somers. Lea was grateful for that. She was even wondering whether the Germans knew yet that Ribeauville was home to two Jewish families. Perhaps no one had informed on them.

†††

Mayor Christian Javelot was sobered by his meeting with Captain Gerhard Oberster. The German's words were not spoken crudely, but they were direct and their meaning unmistakable. "This is war," Oberster said. "Just because your village has been very peaceful doesn't mean my soldiers are not still soldiers. It doesn't mean I can relax my obligations as a German officer. Our army has policies, and it remains my duty to carry them all out to the letter. To the letter."

Though sobered, Javelot was not frightened because he knew he had no reason to be. Almost as soon as the Germans had occupied Ribeauville nearly three and a half years ago, he had urged his fellow villagers to be accommodating, to avoid the vicious reprisals that he knew would follow any harm to German troops or equipment.

"I understand completely," Javelot replied to Oberster's pointed reminder. "I have seen or heard nothing that would give me – or you – cause for concern. I intend to keep it that way."

"Good. Good. I appreciate your reassurance. You may go."

On Javelot's way back to his town hall office, he decided to walk slowly through the streets of Ribeauville. His intent was to share with enough villagers the content of his meeting with Oberster to assure that word spread throughout the community. If Oberster thought a reminder was appropriate for me, Javelot concluded, then one would be appropriate for my people. There is no need for trouble, not now, not after all this time. A few years ago, I saw myself only as a leader and administrator. Now I also see myself as a protector. Oberster was right. It is peaceful, but we still are at war. I wonder when that will change...if it will change.

†††

In Sicily, the fighting had ended on August 17. Theresa Hassler's workload had eased as combat operations had moved across the straits to Italy. She thought often of Hal Walker and occasionally of the young soldier she had kissed back on invasion day. Theresa hoped he was recovering at his home. She had learned that he was from Belvidere, Illinois, and she tried to picture the town as he had described it. She wondered where she would be sent next. She didn't have to wait long for an answer. In November, the 504th Parachute Infantry Regiment of the 82 Airborne Division was detached to prepare to join the fighting in Italy. The rest of the 82nd and the 128th Evacuation Hospital were to be moved from Italy to England. England, Theresa reflected, I almost feel like I'm going home. I'll ask for leave so I can spend some time in my room in Carlisle Lane. Visit St. Thomas. Stroll along side the Thames. Read a book. Write some letters. Mr. Turner will be happy to see me. And I him.

†††

On October 16, 1943, George Patton was on his way to meet with Dwight Eisenhower in Algiers. Relations between the two had been strained since August 13. That was the day Eisenhower had learned that Patton had slapped two hospitalized soldiers, the first on August 3 and the second a few days later. The news had incensed Eisenhower, and he had toyed with firing Patton or at least sending him back to the United States in disgrace. What stopped Eisenhower was a tempering reality; Patton, as politically insensitive a general as existed, was Eisenhower's ablest senior field commander. He knew he would need Patton's bold leadership. For his part, Patton knew he was lucky to have been spared, and he was genuinely grateful.

Chapter 25

"You are doing important work."

"I know that, Bishop."

"Your parishioners in Ajo. The mission Indians. I have received no complaints about you. None. That is remarkable, believe me."

"I appreciate that, Bishop," said Jack. "It's just that I feel I can serve an even higher calling."

"By rights, I could deny your request. And if I were of a mind to grant it, I should get Vatican approval. After all, they sent you here. Moving you from one parish to another, that's my purview. But letting you go, that's a different matter. Very different."

"It would only be temporary," said Jack. "You know I would come back here. I love it here."

"I know that's your intention," said Bishop Metzger. His office was furnished and decorated sparsely, appropriately, he thought, for a mission country church leader. "But events could work out differently."

Jack knew he couldn't argue the point and didn't try. "If you take my request to the Vatican or even the Josephinum, it could mean a lot of time."

Bishop Metzger surprised Jack with an outburst of hearty laughter. "Now there's a diplomatic observation. What you really mean to say is that our church bureaucracy could grind ever so slowly. You could well be right about that. Out here, in mission country, we don't stand so much on paperwork and ceremony. Sometimes the good priests in the eastern big city dioceses and in Rome get caught up in procedure. They have little understanding of our situation."

"Now," said Jack, clearing his throat, "there's a diplomatic observation."

Bishop Metzger laughed again. "Very good, Father Brecker. I can see why you are getting on well with your people. You know," he said somberly, "they will miss you."

"Yes. And I them."

"I don't know how soon we could get a replacement. And near-term, there could be no weekly Masses on the reservation. No one to hear confessions, to minister to the sick, to baptize, to handle funerals. Of course, until we get a new man, I could probably get over there now and then. Yes....Yes, that's a possibility."

Jack looked pensively at the bishop but said nothing.

"You know," Bishop Metzger continued, "that might be good for me. Getting out of Tucson once in awhile. Back to my missionary roots. Tucson has twenty thousand people now, but when I arrived here...Ah well, no need for a history lesson."

Jack smiled. "I think you're talking yourself into this."

"So I seem to be," said the bishop. "Look, since we don't put a premium on red tape out here, maybe the best thing is for me to give you my blessing – and then plead for one from Rome."

"November 15, 1943

Dear Tom,

If you and Bridgett can set a wedding date and soon, I just might be able to do the honors. No, I'm not going to be on leave, not officially, but I am going to be traveling east. I won't be back in Shelby for Thanksgiving, but I think I'll be there by mid-December. I'll explain later, when I have more time. Right now, I have so very much to do before leaving.

How does this sound to you? A December 18 wedding. That's a Saturday. Better check with Bridgett. If she agrees, I suggest you see Father Mac right away. Even though we're talking about the holiday season, if you explain things, I'm betting Father Mac will clear the decks – no pun intended, Seaman Brecker.

Let me know as soon as possible if is going to work out. Say 'Hi' to Mom and Dad for me.

Blessings, Brother

Jack"

†††

Bernadeta Gudek had decided she would try to return to Zyrardow for Christmas. The Nazis had been suppressing the church, but Bernadeta knew they couldn't completely quash the holiday spirit, certainly not in the Gudek household. She knew that no gift could surpass her being at home with her parents and Barbara. That would be true for both her and them. She knew, too, that once again her journey would require night travel and daylight concealment. Once more, her luger would have to remain in Warsaw with Captain Kaz Majos.

†††

In Shelby, in Most Pure Heart of Mary Church on December 18, Jack Brecker stood at the open gate in the ornate white marble Communion rail. Beneath his gold-rimmed glasses, he was grinning. During his student days at the Josephinum, he had anticipated much. But not all. Not saying Mass on his first Christmas as a priest on an Indian reservation. Not tracking and killing a mountain lion. Not performing a wedding for his youngest brother in their hometown.

Tom Brecker made his way from a side entrance to the open gateway. His best man, Sam Tortino, followed. Even walking slowly, neither young veteran could completely obscure evidence of war wounds. Tom was doing well with his prosthesis, and Sam – his knee smashed aboard the Hornet – was determined to minimize his limp during the ceremony. He wanted all attention focused on Tom and his bride. Being asked to travel from Brooklyn to Shelby, Sam couldn't have felt more privileged or honored. Tom's invitation had served as incentive for Sam to push harder on his rehabilitation.

Jack spoke to the congregation. "If you have a camera and you'd like to take pictures during the ceremony, please do. This should be a happy and festive occasion."

Many parishioners were thinking the same thought: how lucky we are to be here today. A hometown priest is about to marry off his war hero brother. And a third brother in England now, getting ready to take on Hitler. They are young men to be proud of.

The previous night, after the rehearsal dinner at the Brickley Hotel, Tom, Jack and Sam had repaired to the bar at the local American Legion post on East Main Street.

"One of the first things I did when I got back from Brecksville was join," Tom had said, referring to his Legion membership. "Lots of good men here. World War One vets. We'll run a tab, and I'll be surprised if someone doesn't pick it up. That's their way."

"I'm sure they're proud of you, Tom," Jack had said. "And all the rest of the Shelby boys who are serving."

"Actually," Tom had said with feeling, "I'm proud of these men. We even have a few members who are Spanish-American War vets."

"When I get back to Brooklyn, I'll have to join," Sam had said. "And," he smiled, "not just for free bar tabs."

They all had laughed.

"In the desert," Jack had observed, "I've learned never to refuse a cold beer. Now, Shelby isn't exactly the desert but tonight is not a night for refusing a beer. And if you'll let me, I'd like to offer a toast."

"Please do, Father," Sam had said.

"Call me Jack, please."

"If you insist."

"I do. Let's raise our glasses. To a future free of war and tyranny, to a future free of war deaths and injuries."

"Here, here," Sam had said.

"Likewise," Tom had added.

The three had drunk deeply of their Johnny Pfeiffers in glasses emblazoned with a red and blue strutting Johnny Pfeiffer caricature of a patriot.

Now, inside the church, the organist had struck up "Here Comes The Bride." In the vestibule, some 150 feet down the aisle from Jack, Tom and Sam, Bridgett Hassler and her father, Joe, arm-in-arm, started toward the sanctuary. Family and friends stood and pivoted to watch. Several took Jack up on his invitation to take pictures. Only one thing could make me happier, Bridgett was thinking, and that would be for Theresa to be here, too. And Paul. That thought did not sadden Bridgett. Too much else was going just as she had hoped. Walking down the aisle with her dad, her eyes riveted on Tom, Bridgett was beaming.

†††

For the third consecutive year, Ribeauville's villagers celebrated Christmas in subdued fashion. Compared to Poles, Russians and other peoples under Hitler's thumb, they knew they were fortunate. All save a few knew they had given their occupiers no cause for reprisals, and the occupiers, under Captain Oberster, had been civil, even kindly. Yet the villagers were not free, and the stark realization that they might not be free for many years, if ever, cast an annual shadow over the holiday season.

Inside the Natzwiller concentration camp, the long shadow hovering over the 1943 holiday season did more than temper spirits. Camp Commandant Josef Kramer saw to that. Kramer had been born in Munich in 1906. Six feet tall, solidly built with broad shoulders the brown-haired Kramer had deep-set dark eyes and a heavy, square jaw. He had joined the Nazi party in 1931. In 1932, he joined the SS or Schutzstaffel. Two years later, he joined the concentration camp service and was appointed a guard at Dachau, Hitler's first concentration camp that was opened in 1933 near Munich.

Kramer advanced quickly through a series of postings and in 1940 was appointed assistant commandant at Auschwitz. In April 1941, he was named commandant at Natzwiller and oversaw the camp's construction.

In 1943 on both Christmas Eve and Christmas Day, Kramer permitted prisoners to rise one hour later than the usual 6 a.m. winter wakeup. On these same two days, inmates had to work only in the mornings. French prisoners – partisans and others – were encouraged to organize something special for Christmas Eve. They decorated a fir tree with garlands and candles provided by Kramer's staff. They sang carols and, most significantly, they were given extra food – potatoes and gravy.

Kramer, however, had more in mind. On Christmas day, as the prisoners were returning to the camp from their quarrying work, they had just passed through the main gate when they were ordered to stop. Kramer, who had been sitting on a chair, stood and walked briskly to the ranks of prisoners. Unexpectedly, he pointed to one and said, "You." Then he took a half-dozen steps and pointed to a second prisoner and said, "You." Shivers of dread began coursing through the men.

Kramer returned to his chair and sat. Then he nodded and Nazi guards approached the two designated prisoners and pulled them from the ranks. They then dragged the hapless men to the nearby gallows and placed nooses around their necks. Another nod from Kramer and the men were hanged – slow hanging, by strangulation. They each took at least two, seemingly interminable minutes to die.

While the men still were twisting, Kramer lit a cigar. He puffed contentedly, watching for reactions among the other prisoners. There were none. Most had closed their eyes. They were trying to concentrate on the extra food they would be eating a few minutes later.

After their meal, the prisoners sang more carols. Hope was hard to execute.

Jack Brecker stayed on in Shelby through Christmas before continuing his journey eastward. He relished his mother's home cooking and loved visiting with childhood friends. He said a Mass each morning at one of the white marble side altars in Most Pure Heart of Mary, and they were well attended by his parents and friends. Father McFadden attended one of them. Jack even enjoyed the cold and snow. He took pictures of the snow and mailed them to Luke Haynes with a note asking him to show them to his fellow Ajo parishioners and the Indians at his missions. Jack missed them. At the same time, it occurred to him that he was feeling freer than at any time since first leaving Shelby for St. Joseph's seminary in 1932. The two weeks in Shelby had the feel of elementary school summer vacations combined with spirited playground games of jailbreak. In those rousing games of youth, the only concern was being caught and confined in an outdoor bin used for storing the coal that heated the church and adjacent school during winter months. And then, inevitably, usually within minutes, freedom would arrive when playmates attempted a jailbreak. Constant shouting and laughter had accompanied that game. Now, in December of 1943, each day provided Jack with many new reasons to laugh and he did so frequently and robustly. He knew this reverie would be ending soon.

Chapter 26

"This training is getting old fast," Thaddeus Metz said to General Sosabowski. "The men are getting bored. They are tired of doing the same things repeatedly."

Sosabowski nodded his understanding. "You know, Captain, that repetition could save their lives. Your life. You might remind the men of that."

"Yes, Sir."

"I think our waiting time might be ending soon. General Patton had dinner with General Eisenhower a few days ago, and yesterday – Saturday, the twenty-ninth – he arrived at Third Army headquarters at Knutsford."

"Knutsford?"

"It's near Manchester where the British airborne is training."

"That's encouraging," said Thaddeus. "I'd like to tell the men."

"That's fine," said Sosabowski. "Patton's whereabouts are always well-known. He sees to that."

Thaddeus chuckled. "Do you care to guess when the invasion might begin?"

"Between you and me? Strictly between us?"

"Yes, Sir."

"I think in the spring, after the Channel weather calms down. We likely will be flying across the Channel and jumping onto the continent. But all the rest – infantry, armored, artillery, motorized cavalry – will be going by ship and making amphibious landings. That simply cannot be done when the Channel waters are like eggs being whipped."

†††

On that same Sunday in Boston, the harbor's waters were choppy and the wind was blowing damp, raw air against Jack Brecker's deeply tanned face. He was wearing Army dress greens, and to his greatcoat were pinned captain's bars and a chaplain's cross. It was close to noon, and he was nearing a neighborhood church when parishioners were exiting after Mass. Jack stood watching, his gloved hands folded across his chest. I'm a long way from Ajo and Charco, he was musing. Or even Shelby and the

Josephinum. And yet everything here seems so familiar. I feel comfortable. Nice church. People dressed nicely. Everything so peaceful.

A family of five – father, mother, two teenage daughters and a younger son – were approaching him. The man spotted Jack's cross insignia. "Hello, Father," he said. "You are a Catholic priest?"

"Yes," Jack smiled, "and hello to you – and to you," he said, nodding to the other family members.

"You're not from here," said the man. "The accent and your complexion say as much."

Jack chuckled. "Dead giveaways that I'm a stranger in your town. No, I'm from Ohio and my parish is in Arizona."

"A long way from home and a bad day to be out strolling," the man observed in an accent that revealed his ethnicity. "What brings you to Boston?"

"I'm in training…to be a chaplain. The school is on Harvard's campus. I just felt like getting away, walking, thinking. After services, Sundays are our day off."

The man looked at his wife. She smiled and nodded. He knew they were thinking the same thing.

"Father," said the man, "we don't want to intrude on your time alone, but would you like to join us for dinner? At our home?"

Before Jack could reply, the woman spoke. "We'll be having baked chicken, dumplings with giblet gravy, rolls, carrots and beans and apple pie."

Jack smiled. He was thinking that the hospitality here was a match for that on the Tohono Reservation. These Bostonians looked and sounded nothing like the Indians, but their hearts were as warm. "That is a very tempting menu, Ma'am. I would be very pleased to join you. Thank you for the invitation." Jack removed his right glove and reached for the man's right hand and they shook. Then Jack shook hands with the other family members.

"It's only about three blocks walk," said the man. "Here in Boston, we have a church every few blocks. I'm Kevin Riley and this is Mary Catherine. Our daughters are Kathleen and Rosemary and our son Sean."

"And I'm Jack Brecker. It was a long walk from Cambridge, Kevin," Jack smiled. "I think I can manage three more blocks."

†††

"Mary Catherine, I want you to know that the food at the Chaplain's School is fine, but this is divine." Jack was just a few exquisite forkfuls into his meal. "I could not have prayed for a more wonderful dinner."

Mary Catherine blushed and the rest of the family was beaming. "You are very kind, Father," she said. "Thank you."

"Believe me," Jack smiled, "the compliment is richly deserved."

The two teenage girls, normally awkward with friends of their parents, were eyeing Jack with a mix of awe and curiosity. He's dreamy, Kathleen was thinking. Tall, bronzed, handsome, funny, nice. Rosemary's thoughts were charting a similar course.

"So," said Kevin, "when you're not on duty, what do you like to do?"

"I like to read and I follow baseball. Pretty closely, actually."

"Your team?" Kevin asked.

"Not your Red Sox, I'm afraid," Jack smiled. "I'm an Indians fan. One of my friends is Lou Boudreau."

"You now Lou Boudreau?" Sean blurted,.

"Yes, Sean, quite well. If I weren't here in Boston, I'd be planning to attend some Indians spring training games in Tucson next month. Lou said he would leave passes for me for all their home exhibition games."

"Oh, my God!" cried Sean. "Oops, I'm sorry."

"No apology needed, Sean. It is pretty exciting to have a friend who is a major leaguer."

"Pretty exciting? Are you kidding, Father? That is totally fantastic."

"'Cool' is the word many young people are using, isn't it?" Jack said.

Cool and dreamy is what Kathleen and Rosemary were thinking about Jack. "Uh huh," said Kathleen. "We're saying it all the time at school. Even one of my teachers."

"Father," said Kevin, "I'm surprised to hear the Chaplain's School is at Harvard. I guess I would have expected it to be at an Army post."

"Until recently, it was," Jack replied. "Fort Benjamin Harrison in Indiana. And I've heard that soon it will be moving to Fort Devens here in Massachusetts. But since Forty-Two, it's been at Harvard. I must say, though, that the building we use there would never be confused with a soaring tribute to our Lord. It's a squatty, stone structure, and I wouldn't be surprised if Harvard never uses it again after the Chaplain's School moves."

"How long is the training?" Mary Catherine asked.

"Eight weeks. Four weeks down, with four to go."

"What does the training include?" Sean asked.

"They assume we all know how to conduct a service," Jack said dryly. Laughter all around the table. "We get into working in field conditions, map reading, combat survival, writing letters and other correspondence, reports and such."

Sean's eyes had grown noticeably wider during Jack's recitation, and Kathleen's and Rosemary's were riveted on Jack's countenance as intently as a hawk's on its prey.

"Where will you go after training?" Kevin asked.

"They could send me anywhere there's a need," said Jack. "But I've requested assignment with an airborne division. If I get that, it will mean Europe."

"If you get that," Kevin observed, "it could mean parachuting."

"It could."

At that, Kathleen and Rosemary were close to swooning, and if someone had suggested to Sean that he genuflect, he would have shoved his chair away from the table and bent his knees on the spot.

"Why airborne?" Kevin asked.

"One of my younger brothers – Paul – is with the One Hundred And First Airborne in England. He joked once in a letter that they could use a chaplain with ...uh, certain experiences. I decided to take his joke seriously."

"Do you have any other brothers or sisters?" Mary Catherine asked.

"Another brother – Tom. He's the youngest of us. I married him and his bride before Christmas. He's home from the Navy now."

"On leave?" Kevin asked.

"No, he was injured in the Pacific and was sent home."

"I hope not too seriously," Mary Catherine said, her concern evident.

"He lost a foot when the Hornet went down and had his leg pretty torn up."

"Oh, my Lord," Mary Catherine gasped. "The poor thing."

"He's going to get along just fine," Jack said. "Don't worry. He's already getting comfortable with a prosthesis, and his leg has just about healed completely. And his morale is very good."

"His bride is no doubt helping in that department," Kevin said wryly.

"Kevin!" Mary Catherine admonished him. "Please."

Kevin reddened and said nothing more. His two daughters blushed along with him.

Jack smiled. "Bridgett – Tom's bride – is a loving, lovely girl. She will stand by him – just as she did for the two years they didn't see each other."

"Are you afraid?" Sean asked quietly, in a nearly prayer-like tone.

"I'm sorry," Jack replied. "Afraid of what?"

"War. Parachuting."

"For sure," Jack smiled. He was being truthful about being afraid of war. He chose not to tell the boy that he was actually hoping to have a chance to leap from an airplane. To Jack, that sounded downright exciting. "I don't think there are very many people who aren't afraid of war."

"But you're going anyway," Kathleen said with a hint of awe and in what was barely more than a whisper. To Mary Catherine, though, her daughter's adulation was as visible as the cross insignia on Jack's dress green jacket.

Jack nodded. "We are told at the school that many young soldiers find comfort in having chaplains around."

"I have a feeling you will be particularly comforting to them," Mary Catherine said. "You seem very understanding and mature."

"Thank you for those kind words. You know…" Jack checked his watch. It was nearing 4 p.m. "I think I'd better be on my way. I need to write a couple letters yet tonight. I can't tell you how much your hospitality means to me. You have been very generous."

"Ah, tis nothing," said Kevin. "It has been our pleasure."

"Same here!" piped up Sean.

"We've not a car," said Kevin, "or I'd offer to drive you back to Cambridge. Can we call you a taxi?"

"Oh, no thanks," said Jack. "With all of Mary Catherine's wonderful food in my belly, my tank is full for the walk back."

"Father," said Mary Catherine, "you said you would be at Harvard for another four weeks. We'd love to have you back again."

"Absolutely," said Kevin.

"That invitation is very easy to accept," said Jack, "and I do."

"That's wonderful," said Mary Catherine, clapping her hands, and the children's eyes told her they shared her sentiment.

Jack stood and shook hands all around. Sean held up Jack's greatcoat so he could slip his arms in. He buttoned up and then pulled on his wool-lined leather gloves and put on his hat. Jack saluted Sean who, grinning, saluted him back.

Kathleen and Rosemary both felt their hearts swelling, and Mary Catherine felt a tear preparing to escape its duct. Kevin cleared emotion from his throat and opened the door.

"Hasta mas tarde," Jack said. "See you again soon."

A chorus of "Goodbyes" sent him walking down the porch steps and onto the sidewalk.

CHAPTER 27

Although the hour wasn't yet late, it was dark and Marie Kieny was walking just short of running through the streets of Ribeauville. Breathing hard from anxiety as much as exertion, she knocked on the door of the Peiffers.

"I'll get it, Mother," Lea said. She moved toward the door and opened it. "Marie." She could see that Marie was agitated. "What's wrong? Are you all right?"

Marie drew in a deep breath and labored to calm herself. "The Steiners and the Somers. The Nazis are going to take them away."

Lea's eyes widened in alarm. "Are you sure? This is not merely a rumor?"

"I'm sure."

"How do you know?"

"One of the German soldiers – a sergeant – told me."

"A German sergeant? When?"

"Just this evening. A few minutes ago."

A long pause followed. Lea looked thoughtfully at her friend. "Marie, why would he tell you that? Are you...involved?"

"I know what you are thinking."

"And are my thoughts accurate?"

"I am not sleeping with him. We are...close."

Lea's lips pursed tightly. She looked hard at her friend. "When are they taking the Steiners and Somers?"

"I don't know. Soon. Someone must have informed on them. I don't know if it was intentional."

"Of course, it was intentional," Lea whispered disgustedly. "Who –"

"Lea, who is there?" called her mother, Sonia.

"It's Marie, Mother."

"Tell her I said hello."

"She heard you."

"Captain Oberster is checking with the authorities," Marie said. "That's what Erich – Sergeant Boehler – said."

Lea nodded grimly. "Why did you come to me?" She was waiting – and hoping not – to hear Marie suggest that she knew of Lea's ties to the Resistance.

"I...I thought you might know what to do. You have such a quick mind. Sergeant Boehler wanted to be with me longer, but I knew I needed to get away."

"What did you tell him?"

"That my mother is sick and I had to get home to help her."

"All right," said Lea, keeping her voice low and as devoid of emotion as she could manage. "First, Marie, stop being so close to the German sergeant. It can only mean trouble. When this war is over, women who were involved with the Nazis could suffer retribution. Severe." Now it was Marie's eyes that were widening. She was frightened, and Lea was glad. "I can see this happening. You, too, if you think about it. Do you promise?"

"Yes."

Even in the darkness, Lea could see as well as hear that Marie meant it. "Second, go home. Straight home. Stay in your home until you hear from me. Don't ask me any questions. Not about this. Not ever. Do you understand?"

"Yes."

"And tell no one – no one – of this conversation. Is that clear?"

"Yes."

"Go." A pause...a thought germinating. "Marie, where is Sergeant Boehler?"

"Now?"

"Yes."

"Probably at the Hostellerie Ribeaupierre or at the winstub next door."

"All right. Now go."

Lea watched Marie leaving Rue des Boulangers and round the corner into Rue de la Fraternite. Lea needed to sort through her thoughts. How much had Marie heard from the German sergeant – or said to him? Whatever, she was in danger already. Simply possessing the knowledge that the Steiners and Somers were to be deported put her at risk. Lea knew she must warn the two Jewish families and immediately. If they were missing when the

Germans came for them, Marie could be in greater danger – were Sergeant Boehler to disclose that Marie had known of the impending arrests. But that same disclosure could endanger the sergeant. What would he say? What would he do? There could be reprisals. Other villagers could be deported or tortured or executed. That was a genuine and fearsome risk. So far, Lea was thinking, Captain Oberster had demonstrated no desire for hostility. But would the Steiners' and Somers' disappearance change that? Would Oberster be pressured – or ordered – to carry out reprisals? Lea had no way of knowing. What she did know was that action must precede additional deliberations.

"Mother," Lea called to Sonia, "I'm walking with Marie." This lie of necessity came easily.

"All right, Dear. Are you dressed warmly?"

Lea reached for a thick sweater hanging from a peg next to a small mirror just inside the house's entrance. "Yes, Mother."

†††

On the way to the Steiners, Lea went a few blocks out of her way to the home of Maurice Trimbach in Rue du Cavalier. When he answered her knock, she gave him no time to speak.

"Come with me, Maurice. It's important. Please. I'll explain on the way."

Maurice didn't question her or object. He grabbed a thick jacket and joined Lea in the street. "Where are we going?"

"To Rue du Lys. The Steiners and the Somers."

During the short walk, she told him what she had heard. She disclosed her source – Marie – and voiced her deep concern for Marie's well-being.

"Any idea who might have informed?" Maurice asked. "We would be well justified to eliminate an informer."

Lea paused before replying. "No." She then told Maurice about an additional idea. He listened attentively. "What do you think?" Lea asked.

They stopped at the entrance to Rue du Lys. "It's risky," Maurice whispered. "For you, for others. But if it works, Marie would be safer. Perhaps others as well."

"I think…I'd like to try," said Lea. "Will you help?"

"All right. Sure." Trimbach's whispered words, as always, conveyed a reassuring calm. You are perfect for the Resistance, Lea was thinking. You are much stronger than I. "You alert the Steiners and Somers," Maurice said. "Give them time to pack a few things – if you can persuade them to leave. While you're with them, I'll round up two or three of our men. They can lead the Steiners and Somers to safety."

"Where will they take them?"

"Castle ruins. There are two or three excellent hiding places there. That will be temporary, of course. If they stayed there permanently, it would be too dangerous smuggling food to them. After things calm down a little, we'll try to get them into Switzerland – perhaps to Basel."

"Good," said Lea. "Shall we then? I mean, go ahead with my idea?"

Maurice smiled, nodded, turned and left her. Lea walked first to the Steiners' house, some 300 years old, and knocked. The door opened.

"Good evening, Mr. Steiner."

"Why, hello, Lea. How nice to see you. And so unexpected."

Lea sensed that it would be most effective to drive right to the heart of the matter. "Mr. Steiner, the Nazis are going to arrest you and Mrs. Steiner very soon and send you away."

"Oh, Lea, I-"

She cut him off. "Mr. Steiner, please. This is no mere rumor. It is not a time for denial. You know me. Would I be here if this was not so? Would I be saying this to you? Would I?"

"Go on."

"You and Mrs. Steiner must leave tonight. I have friends who will help you. Hide you. You must act now. Right now. If you don't...if you don't, you will die."

Lea's words and tone had the desired effect.

"Let me tell Mrs. Steiner. Do we have time to pack some things?"

"Yes, while you are doing that, I will go to the Somers."

"They are being arrested, too?"

"Yes."

With that, Mr. Steiner stepped back inside his home, and Lea walked farther down the street to the Somers. The scene at the Somers repeated the one at the Steiners. Except there were four Somers, including two teenagers, Muriel and her brother Michel. They, too, set to packing.

Lea waited uneasily at the close of the dead-end street. Pacing, tugging at the hem of her sweater, time seemed to have slowed to a maddening crawl. She was half-expecting German soldiers to come marching into the street. About 30 minutes later, she heard footsteps and froze. It was Maurice, entering the short street. She waved, and he went walking toward her. Minutes later, the Steiners and Somers stepped outside their homes. Lea waited while Maurice led them to the street's entrance. There, three partisans were waiting. "They will guide you. Good luck." To his men, Maurice repeated his earlier caution. "Stay off the Grand' Rue." The men nodded, the Steiners and Somers nervously whispered their gratitude, and the group started on their way.

Maurice turned and saw Lea approaching. "Still want to go through with it?"

She pursed her lips and drew in a breath. "Not really, but yes. You know?"

"Yes, I know."

Lea went striding toward the Hostellerie Ribeaupierre. At the entrance, she looked up at the Nazi banner. Garish, she thought, a banner from Satan. Then she stepped into the small reception area and looked at the few chairs and two small tables. No one. She stepped back outside and started next door to the winstub. Her hope was that, after parting with Marie, Sergeant Eric Boehler had decided to have a beer. If not, Lea's night was over.

Lea pushed open the winstub's door. Sergeant Boehler was seated on a stool at the bar, sipping his beer and chatting with the bartender. She quickly surveyed the low-ceilinged, cozy room. Two German soldiers, both privates, were sitting in a booth at one end. They were oblivious to their surroundings, concentrating instead on beer and talk. Lea also saw four village men, sitting at a table. With no further hesitation, she walked to the end of the room opposite the soldiers and slid into another booth. She breathed deeply and rubbed her hands together. When the bartender eyed her, she held up a forefinger. The bartender was curious. He knew Lea – virtually everyone one in Ribeauville knew each other, by face if not by name – but couldn't recall seeing her in the winstub alone. Nevertheless, he nodded, poured a beer from a tap into a stein and carried it to her booth. She paid him immediately.

"Nothing else, Lea?"

She shook her head. "No, thank you."

Seconds later, Sergeant Erich Boehler pivoted on his stool to see the new customer. He vaguely recalled seeing the young woman passing by on the village's narrow, busy streets. He smiled at her. Lea returned his smile with a warm one of her own. Sergeant Boehler dipped his head and shrugged his shoulders forward. Lea mouthed "Yes" and nodded. Sergeant Boehler picked up his stein, slid off the stool and walked to Lea's booth.

"May I?"

Lea motioned to the bench across from hers and Sergeant Boehler sat. "You are a very attractive young woman. What are you doing here alone?"

Lea chose not to answer directly. "I saw you with another woman tonight. It seemed to me your evening ended early."

He smiled easily. "Too early."

"It needn't." Lea could scarcely believe the words she was speaking were her own.

"Oh?"

"End so early."

"Oh." He sipped his beer. Lea did likewise, nervously. Boehler was thinking that being young and handsome and available had its advantages. Why else would this lovely French woman be propositioning a German soldier? "Are you sure?"

Lea lowered her head, then raised it. "When I saw you with the other woman, I envied her. All our young men are away."

"Ah, yes," said the sergeant. "The war. So many dead, imprisoned or in England. And for so long. Did you have a boyfriend?"

"Yes," Lea lied. "I miss him."

"I'm sure you do. I miss my girlfriend back home."

They each took another long sip of beer. Lea was barely tasting hers.

"Would you like to step outside?" Sergeant Boehler asked.

"Yes."

"Come."

"Go ahead and finish your beer," said Lea.

He did and then they slid off the ends of the benches and stood. "I need to pay my bar tab," said Boehler. "You?"

"I've already paid. I'll wait outside." Lea was glad to be leaving separately and first.

Two minutes later, Boehler joined her in front of the winstub. "My room at the hotel?" he asked.

She averted her eyes again and shook her head. "Too many eyes. Too many whispers."

"Yes, I wouldn't want you to be embarrassed." Not that I really care, he was thinking. It's your virtue that's at stake. Mine already is sullied in the minds of these villagers. That's the reality. "You have a suggestion?"

"This way," Lea said and began walking north along the Grand' Rue. As soon as she came to a side street, she crossed Grand' Rue and went walking west on quiet Rue des Baigneurs.

"Trying to be discrete," Sergeant Boehler observed softly.

"Yes," said Lea without looking at him. She was grateful for the darkness. Minutes later, they were in Rue des Boulangers. "My street," she said. "Down this alley." Lea led and Boehler followed.

Behind the Peiffer's house, Lea reached down for the handle on one of the two cellar doors.

"Yours?" Boehler asked.

"Yes." Lea took a step down and switched on a light. Boehler followed. "Close the doors after you," Lea said quietly.

"No bed down here," said Boehler.

"Tables," said Lea. "In our tasting room." She was struggling to control her anxiety. Yet, she knew her nervousness would seem natural to Sergeant Boehler.

"An apt name for the room tonight," Boehler said lightly.

His remark was amusing and, under any other circumstance, Lea would have laughed. But now her stomach was roiling even more fiercely. "This way," she said and switched on a second light. Moments later, she stepped through a doorway and reached to switch on another light. She caught herself. "Perhaps we don't need much light in her."

"Perhaps not," Boehler said. He saw the tasting tables. Lea walked to one and turned to face Boehler. He extended his arms and they embraced. In the dim light, Sergeant Boehler found her lips and they kissed. Gently. Boehler was in no hurry. He saw this as more than casual conquest, rather fulfillment of his need for companionship and intimacy. Boehler's hands moved down Lea's back and slid beneath her buttocks. He grasped them and lifted Lea onto a table. It was his last voluntary movement.

An instant later, Sergeant Erich Boehler felt an arm coil tightly around his neck and squeeze hard. Nearly simultaneously, he felt sharp pain shooting through his torso and exploding in his brain. His hands flew up to grasp the forearm that was crushing his throat, but he found himself helpless. His hands dropped to his side and his chin drooped against the strangling forearm. Maurice left the knife in Boehler's back and eased him to the floor face down.

Lea looked down and began trembling. She bit her lip.

"Just take it easy," Maurice whispered. "This was hard."

"This is not our world," Lea said, barely audible. "Our world is gone." She leaned back against the table and lowered and shook her head. She tried to breathe deeply. "I'll be all right." Several moments passed before her trembling began to subside.

Maurice was waiting patiently. "Did anyone see you with him?" he asked.

"The bartender at the winstub. There were two privates in the winstub, but I don't think they noticed us. Four village men were sitting at a table, but they were busy gabbing. They saw me, but I left alone, while the sergeant was paying his tab."

"Good...Well, perhaps we made it."

"Reprisals?"

"I wouldn't be surprised."

"I told Marie to stay inside until I come for her."

"I think you should do the same. Until I come for you or you hear from me."

"Do you think I should advise my parents to leave Ribeauville? Suggest they tend to business in one of the other villages?"

"If you can do so without providing details, yes. You will arouse their suspicion but, yes, if you can have them out of harm's way for a couple days, that would be good. Just stress to them that they will be better off not questioning you or your motives."

"I will have them leaving at dawn. On their bicycles with wine in the baskets."

†††

"Where in the world is he?" Captain Oberster said to Lieutenant Kohler.

"Not in his room. I checked. Either his bed was not slept in or he made it before going out."

"Probably slept with some girl."

"Maybe. He was seen last night in the winstub, but alone."

"Alone?"

"Yes, Sir. Sitting at the bar. Shortly after dark."

"He could have met someone later."

"Yes, Sir."

"If he isn't back by 10 a.m...."

†††

It was noon and still there was no sign of Sergeant Boehler. Captain Oberster was steaming. First, Lieutenant Hoffman goes missing. Six months later a sergeant. Can it possibly be coincidence? I doubt it. Both men were young. Are young. And except for annual leaves we all have been away from home for a long time. Duty here is boring. A bad combination. I've tried to keep everyone busy...engaged. This will look very bad on my record. Not fit for command. I can see that judgment going into my file. And I can see myself being demoted and reassigned. Probably to the east. Terrible duty, from what I've heard.

Oberster rose from the desk in the hotel room he was using as his office. He opened the door and addressed the corporal who served as his secretary. "Get me Lieutenant Kohler."

"Yes, Sir," and the corporal was up and moving.

Minutes later, Kohler was standing in front of Oberster.

"I'm not waiting any longer for Boehler. Get the mayor over here. Do it yourself."

"Yes, Sir," said Kohler. He descended to the Grand' Rue and walked quickly to the town hall. A few minutes later, Mayor Christian Javelot was following Lieutenant Kohler back to the hotel. They climbed the stairs to Oberster's office. The corporal opened the door for them.

"Bon jour, Captain," said the mayor.

"Sit down, Mayor."

Javelot immediately went on guard. Oberster's dispensing with a formal greeting and his icy tone put the mayor on alert.

"My sergeant has disappeared. No trace. Six months ago, it was one of my lieutenants. Can you possibly explain that," Oberster said coldly.

"Me? I'm afraid not."

"No, I suppose not. These were two professional soldiers. Professional German soldiers do not just disappear. You are mayor. You are the village's senior officer, as it were. I am making you responsible. Personally responsible."

Mayor Javelot felt the sudden chill of fear. He paused before replying, aware that Oberster knew he was frightened, but feeling a strong need to remain composed. "I am sorry your men are missing, but I assure you that it must be coincidental."

Oberster decided to push harder. "I would be well within my rights – well within German national policy – to order reprisals. Two of my men missing. Ten for one. Twenty of your villagers executed. No trial. Summary execution."

Mayor Javelot blinked. He could feel sweat moistening his armpits. He tried to ignore it. Reason and sincerity are my only allies, he was thinking. He swallowed. "Captain Oberster, have you experienced any sabotage here? Any at all? To your equipment? Your supplies?"

Oberster was glaring at Javelot, saying nothing.

Javelot continued. "Have any of your men been injured? Or accosted in any way?"

Still, Oberster remained silent.

"There is no Resistance here," Javelot said evenly and sincerely. "We have no partisans. None."

Javelot saw Oberster sigh. The mayor was uncertain whether to continue or stop. He decided to stop.

Oberster's hands pressed against his eyes and pulled downward across his face. "I have two men missing. You are responsible. You will deputize twenty villagers. They, with my men, will search every room, every corner, every inch of Ribeauville. Then they will search the vineyards. This will begin this afternoon. Do you have any questions?"

"None, Captain."

†††

The search extended through that afternoon and into the next day. It turned up no sign of the missing soldiers, but it did uncover the disappearance of the two Jewish families. Once again, Mayor Javelot was standing before Captain Oberster's desk. Oberster did not invite him to sit.

"The coincidence is too much to accept, don't you agree?" Oberster said to Javelot. "My sergeant goes missing and so do the Jews."

"I don't know how long the Jews have been gone."

"Well, we know they aren't on holiday, don't we?" Oberster's sarcasm was stinging. Mayor Javelot knew full well the restrictions on travel. "And where would they go? Germany? I think not. Paris? Not these days. Switzerland? If the Swiss would let them in, perhaps. I am at the end of my wits, Mayor. And I have a very strong feeling that if I take strong action, these coincidences will end. Do you agree with that?"

Christian Javelot was human; he felt trapped. Cornered. Was there any way out? He would try to find one. "Captain, let me make a proposal." Javelot's mind was churning. "Let me bring together every person in our village. Every single one. We will meet in Place de la Marie in front of our town hall. You and I, we will both address my people. We will tell them in no uncertain words what must happen…what must not happen. We will spell out the consequences in the most precise terms possible."

Oberster was impressed. He admired Javelot's quick, intelligent mind and his courage. But he wasn't satisfied. "Yes, Mayor, we will have your assembly. But the message there will be stronger if first there is action. Two of my men are missing. Six Jews. Eight in all. Your search party has twenty men. Sixteen must die. Two for one. You choose them."

"Captain, please. I implore you. I am trying to be reasonable."

"You are being reasonable. Actually, so am I. I could make it ten for one. But I must be more than that. The requirements of war."

"These men. Most are old. They have done nothing. Nothing."

"Choose the oldest."

†††

Captain Oberster waited in his office while Mayor Javelot went downstairs to meet with the search party in front of the Hostelliere

Ribeaupierre. Then he summoned his corporal and issued orders. Outside with the search party, Javelot related his discussion with Oberster.

"There's no other way?" one of the men, Marie Kieny's father, asked plaintively.

"No. No," said Javelot. "And if you – any of you – try to escape, he – Oberster – will execute you and your family members."

"He said that?"

"No," said Javelot, "but he didn't have to."

"But," said Marie's father, "he has no evidence – at all – that his men are dead or that any of us helped the Jews."

"Correct," Javelot sighed. "But face it. Oberster has reached a point where he feels he had no choice but to do this – if he wants to save his career and perhaps his own life. We know Hitler and his lackeys don't suffer failures easily."

"His life?" said Marie's father.

"He could be transferred to Russia or Poland. Life expectancies there are short," Javelot observed dryly.

"Then I will be one of the sixteen," said Marie's father.

"I appreciate that, but I am the one to choose and I am not choosing you. I am choosing the oldest plus me."

There was muttering, and glances were exchanged, but there were no loud objections. Javelot selected five from the search party. " Leave. Now. Go to your shops or your homes. Please."

The five men self-consciously shuffled their feet and then slowly went walking away. As they did so, Oberster emerged from the hotel. With him were Lieutenant Kohler and 12 soldiers, each armed with a schmeisser machine pistol.

"You've chosen," Oberster observed.

"Yes, Captain, and I am including myself."

The soldiers surrounded the condemned men while Oberster considered. "No," he said, "I will not have you be a martyr. You must select one of the men you've sent away and order him back here."

Unexpectedly, Javelot found himself thinking with remarkable clarity and speed. He realized – was amazed – that all anxiety had evaporated. Instead, he was experiencing an incredible calmness. Indeed, he couldn't ever recall feeling more at peace than he did at that moment. "Captain," he said, "I have a proposal."

"No proposals," Oberster said firmly. "We exhausted our discussion in my office."

Christian Javelot was unruffled by Oberster's abrupt reply. "Captain, you are a reasonable man. I do not in any degree sense you are a man with bloodlust." Javelot watched as Oberster inhaled with impatience. When he exhaled, no words were spoken. Javelot knew he needed to press on. "You could accomplish much more by executing just one man. Me."

The 15 Ribeauville men were stunned and their shock showed plainly. Before they could utter anything, Oberster reacted. "No, Mayor. That is out of the question. Unacceptable. Totally unacceptable. That is final."

"You misunderstand me, Captain. If you execute sixteen villagers and if you report that to your superiors, your action will be regarded as routine. Ordinary. You know that. You will be doing only what is expected of a German officer in your situation. But it needn't be that way." Javelot was expecting to be interrupted at any moment, but Oberster was looking hard and listening intently. "If you execute me alone, you can report that you executed the man – the mayor – who confessed to organizing and leading a new Resistance cell. You can report that I ordered the deaths of two of your men, and that I directed that their bodies be buried in the mountains. Most importantly, Captain, by executing me, you can report that you have nipped this new Resistance unit in the bud. You can show that you were thinking decisively and imaginatively. It would also have more impact locally." Javelot was done. He had nothing more to say, except, "Think it through, Captain."

Oberster drew in another breath. This time, when he exhaled, words were spoken. "I admire you, Mayor. You are a stronger man than I thought. I don't know how much truth there is in your confession, if any, but I know the part about leadership to be true." Oberster looked at the search party members and his soldiers. He pursed his lips and signed audibly. "You men. You have heard your mayor's words. If any of my vehicles or equipment is sabotaged...even slightly...if any of my men disappear or are even accosted or slandered, I will immediately order and carry out the execution of one hundred of your people – fifty men and fifty women. Of that you can be certain. Now, leave. Leave."

There were more shuffling feet and low murmuring, but the search party began to disperse. Javelot stood watching them and nodded. Now it was Oberster's mind that was thinking with speed and clarity that was astonishing him. How best to reinforce my message? How to make it truly memorable? A firing squad here in the town square? Dramatic but too ordinary. It must be more personal. It must clearly demonstrate my resolve.

Several of the departing men looked back – in time to see Captain Oberster remove his luger from its holster, step forward decisively to the left side of Javelot, place the gun's muzzle against the mayor's head and squeeze the trigger. The explosion startled the men as well as dozens of pigeons and a nest of storks on the hotel's roof. Christian Javelot's head spewed blood and brain and bone fragments, and his body crumpled to the cobblestone pavement.

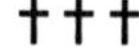

Chapter 28

Theresa Hassler saw the postman coming. She was standing outside the bicycle shop in Carlisle Lane, about to set off for a stroll through the neighborhood. "Hello," she said to the postman.

"Hello, Miss. I do believe I've a letter for you. Yes, here it is."

"Thank you."

"Hope it's good news," he said, stepping inside the bicycle shop.

Theresa used a thumb to break the envelope's seal. A photo was inside with the folded letter. She decided to read the letter before ascending the stairs to her room.

At that moment, the postman exited the shop. "Good day, Miss," he said, continuing on his route.

"February 2, 1944

Dear Theresa,

I must start with an apology. This letter is long overdue – by at least a month. I'm sorry. Since the wedding, time has simply disappeared. Forgive me?

The wedding was everything I wanted it to be! Everything! Happy, happy people! Just look at the picture. Tom, Jack and me!!! Did Tom ever look more handsome? And you can see that Jack was thrilled to be here.

We really couldn't take a honeymoon. Tom isn't ready yet for a lot of walking. We took a train to Cleveland and spent three days and two nights there. We went to the top of the Terminal Tower – you've been there and know how spectacular the views are – and saw a couple movies at the Hippodrome on Euclid Avenue. We also spent a lot of time in bed. Sex is great! I love it!! Details needn't be discussed, right?

Big news! No, I'm not pregnant. Not yet. Or if I am I don't know it yet. But Jack was able to do our wedding because he was on his way to Boston to the Chaplain's School. Yes, Jack has decided to become an Army chaplain, and the school is at Harvard. Harvard! Isn't that neat? He doesn't know where he will be sent, but he told us he would request assignment with an airborne division so that he might be close to Paul. Isn't that something? I hope he gets his wish. If he does, maybe you can see him. Wouldn't that be nifty?

How are you doing? How do you like being back in London? What's next for you? Please write soonest.

Your loving little sister,

Bridgett"

Theresa looked again at the letter. Yes, Bridgett, those are three very happy looking people. You are very fortunate and you know it. That's important. Some people never realize how fortunate they are. Jack. You look so handsome, so utterly at peace with yourself. An Army chaplain. I wonder if you still are wearing the Saint Christopher medal. I can see you in a soldier's uniform now.

Theresa heard the bicycle shop door open behind her and turned.

"Are you all right?" Ronald Turner asked.

"Yes, I am. I was going for a walk – to clear my mind – when the postman handed me this letter. Would you like to see the picture?"

"Certainly."

"My sister Bridgett is the bride. Tom Brecker is the groom. He's the one I told you about – injured in the Pacific. The priest is Tom's brother, Jack. He married them."

"Very nice, indeed," said Mr. Turner. "It was very nice of your sister to send the photograph. Do you actually know the two men?"

"Oh, yes," Theresa smiled. "We are all from Shelby, and it is a very small town. It would probably fit rather easily into this neighborhood. Bridgett, Tom, Jack and I, we are all friends. Although it's been many years since I've seen Jack."

It didn't require heavenly divining for Mr. Turner to discern Theresa's wistfulness. "I see. That's good. You know, I think I've an idea."

"Oh?"

"You said you want to clear your mind. Why not take one of my bicycles? For a little ride around London."

"Oh, I don't know...It's been so long since I've ridden a bike. Years."

"Oh, you'll do fine. I think you would find it terribly relaxing. A cycling tonic, if you will. Look, why don't you go upstairs and change? May I suggest you put on your fatigue uniform? More comfy for riding than a dress or skirt. I'll pick out a lovely bike. All right?"

Theresa smiled and gently rocked her head from side to side in indecision. Mr. Turner's offer was becoming more appealing by the moment. "All right. It's a deal."

"Good! You get yourself upstairs while I select a bike."

†††

The cool London air rushing past Theresa's face as she went peddling the red bike with white striping down Westminster Bridge Road toward the Thames seemed to be serving as a cleansing agent. Purifying, Theresa thought. Bombing debris notwithstanding, her mind seemed to be emptying of concerns, of issues. Traffic wasn't heavy but she had to concentrate on staying to the left side. She smiled. 'Wrong side' of the road, but a wonderful idea, Mr. Turner. It was, as you are fond of saying, spot on. As Theresa neared the bridge, two elderly male pedestrians were eyeing her closely. With dignity, they both snapped off British-style salutes, palms outward. Theresa smiled. Then remembering that she was in uniform, she removed her right hand from the handlebar grip and returned their salute American-style.

Over Westminster Bridge she went, then cut left or west onto Birdcage Walk and on toward Buckingham Palace which, with trees still barren of leaves, she could see in the distance. As she neared the palace grounds, she could see more bomb damage, and her first reaction was sadness – for the palace built in 1703, for the people of London and their nearly four years of hardships. Some 30,000 Londoners already had been killed. But that depressing reflection was replaced almost immediately by thoughts of the remarkable pluck shown by so many Londoners who went on living and working with a resilient, up-tempo attitude. Count Mr. Turner among them. Then, without warning, an image of Hal Walker popped into her mind. She recalled vividly that first time she had been in an airplane, Hal at the controls, taking her out over Lake Erie and over Canada's south shore. One of the best days of my life, she reminded herself, no matter what has happened since. Poor Hal. Are you still alive? Will I see you again? You will always have my love.

At Buckingham Palace, she wheeled right or north onto Green Park and then quickly turned left or west again and pedaled toward Hyde Park Corner. Will anyone be on a soapbox today? Theresa wondered. Proselytizing? Another image formed in Theresa's mind. It was of Jack... Jack the effervescent teenager and dance partner...the serious boy headed off to a seminary. Jack, she mused, I don't know that this was such a good time for me to see that picture of you. You're a priest now, yes, but you also were my first great love. Does a person get over their first love? Do they ever forget the first kiss – even if it was in first grade? Don't think so. I gave you that Saint Christopher medal. Maybe there should be one for lost loves. I could be wearing two of them. Along with my two dog tags.

At Hyde Park Corner, sure enough, a London man, shabbily dressed but clean-shaven, was railing against something. "Churchill shouldn't be..." His audience was small and transitory. Theresa pedaled on, wheeling east into Picadilly. Ahead she could make out Picadilly Circus but without its famed aluminum statue of Eros. Eros, old friend. God of love. Grecian cupid. They had to store you away during the war. Couldn't have love bombed to bits. Not at all proper. Too bad you're in hiding. I wish I could see you any time I want. Maybe sometime, after the war, you can shoot your arrow my way again. Maybe it could be an arrow you used before, one that was right on target.

As Theresa pedaled around the circus and cut south onto Haymarket, a group of five schoolgirls saw her and waved timidly. Gaily, Theresa waved back and blew them a kiss. They giggled and waved more vigorously. Then, on an impulse, Theresa braked, hopped off the bike, lowered the kickstand, ran back to the girls and began hugging each one. They squealed, jumped and hugged Theresa hard. "Theresa," she told the girls, "that's my name. I'm a nurse. Remember me!"

Now she was at Trafalgar Square, and Admiral Nelson atop his 185-foot column was surveying the horizons. At the column's base, four huge bronze lions were on guard and, thought Theresa, probably wishing they could somehow shed the multitudinous pigeons and their droppings. Admiral Nelson, how do you like being shit on every day? I'm curious, Admiral, when you were at sea, did a gull ever shit on you? You know, prepare you for shit-sheathed immortality? At that thought, Theresa tilted her head back and laughed out loud.

She was still smiling as she pedaled down Whitehall, past the Horse Guards parade ground and No. 10 Downing Street, home to British prime ministers since 1732. Keep at it, Mr. Churchill. You've been a savior. As for you, Hitler, you mad sop, you have not defeated these people and you won't. They…we…are coming to get you. It's only a matter of time, and your time is growing short.

Westminster Bridge was coming into view. Almost home, Theresa thought. I've managed to keep Mr. Turner's bike and myself in one piece. Hallelujah! Mr. Turner, you were so right – about riding the bike and how good it would be for me. I need to do this again. Better than a psychiatrist's couch – or a talk with a chaplain. Well, except maybe for a certain chaplain.

†††

If anything, Jack's second visit with the Rileys was more fun than the first. There was no need for getting acquainted. It was like greeting old and dear friends. Conversation erupted immediately and kept flowing as steadily as the nearby Charles River. As that Sunday afternoon was drawing to a close, Mary Catherine walked to an end table, picked up a camera and said, "Father, would you mind if we took a few pictures?"

"Not at all," said Jack. "Any time."

"Now?"

"Now is fine."

"Wonderful!" she said and, with camera in hand, began directing. First, there was Jack with Kevin, then Jack with Kathleen, Rosemary and Sean. Then Mary Catherine handed the camera to Kathleen to take a picture of Jack with her and Kevin. Click. Click. Click.

"Oh, wait," said Mary Catherine. "Let's do each picture again, so I can give a set to you, Father."

"Great!" said Jack. "I'd love to have my own set."

After the second photo of Jack with Mary Catherine and Kevin was taken, Jack said, "Just a minute. I have something for you." He walked to the hall tree where his great coat was hanging. He extracted an envelope from a pocket. Then to each of the five Rileys, he handed a small prayer card, about three by five inches. They were identical. On the front was a color rendering of Jesus, hands folded over his heart. On the reverse was the Lord's Prayer. Above the prayer, on each card, Jack had written, To Kevin, To Mary Catherine, and so on. At the bottom, he had signed the cards, Fr. Jack Brecker, Feb. 1944. "Just a little something to help you remember me."

The Rileys were deeply touched. "This is very thoughtful of you, Father," said Mary Catherine, her throat thickening. "You can be sure we'll remember you. Always."

CHAPTER 29

"I am so sorry to hear about Mayor Javelot," said Mr. Steiner. "A good man."

The windowless room in the castle ruins was cold and cheerless. Only a partially open doorway admitted dim light. The news about the mayor seemed to deepen the room's gloom. As a haven, it had proved safe from prying eyes but was devoid of creature comforts. The danger of smoke being seen from below ruled out warming fires during the day.

"I thought you should know," replied Maurice Trimbach. There were two reasons for Maurice's telling the Steiners and Somers about Javelot's bravery and execution. First, they were fellow villagers and thus deserved to know. Second, he wanted them to understand their jeopardy hadn't been exaggerated.

"Has a new mayor been elected or appointed?" Mr. Somer asked.

"No," said Maurice, "Captain Oberster has made it clear that he alone will rule. And ruthlessly if he considers it necessary."

"We've been here two weeks now," said Mr. Steiner. "Surely, it must be getting more dangerous for you and your friends to visit us...to bring us food."

Maurice nodded. "We should be moving you to a safer place. And warmer."

"But?" Mr. Steiner discerned unease in Maurice's tone if not his words.

"I don't think we can get you to Switzerland. Too far with too many Germans about. I think it would be too dangerous for you – all of you – and our guide."

"I see," Mr. Steiner said pensively. "I think I can speak for all of us." He looked at the others and they nodded their agreement. "I would not want to expose our families or our guide to the Nazis. So we stay here."

"For the time being," said Maurice. He had an alternative in mind but didn't want to voice it before checking its viability.

†††

"I think it could work," said Lea Peiffer.

"You've spoken with your parents?" Maurice asked. "They approve?"

"I wasn't sure if they would," Lea admitted. "But given Mayor Javelot's sacrifice and knowing about the camp at Natzwiller, they said yes."

"And they understand the risk? Fully?"

"Yes."

"All right. Good. We'll get started."

†††

"Who will be first?" Maurice asked.

"Our daughter, Muriel," said Mr. Somer. "We all agree on that."

"All right," said Maurice. "We should leave now. I want to be at the bottom of the mountain before dawn. Ready, Muriel?"

"Yes, Mr. Trimbach."

"Take my hand," said Maurice. "The moon and stars are providing some light but not much and we need to be careful...We need to be quiet and sound carries at night. Germans are patrolling the streets below."

"I understand."

Maurice directed his gaze to the others. "I or one of my men will return tomorrow night. Probably me." The fewer involved in this undertaking the better, he was thinking.

"Our son, Michel, will be next," said Mr. Somer.

"Good," said Maurice.

†††

Slowly, Maurice and Muriel began edging down the steep slope from the castle ruins. Muriel's young eyes adjusted quickly to the dim light and they made good time. At the base of the mountain, at Ribeauville's northern edge, Maurice spoke quietly to the teenage girl. "The Germans are serious about the curfew. They might shoot before asking questions. If we are spotted, we will run to the nearest hillside and up into the vineyards. If one of us is shot – either one – the other must keep running. And we must stay away from the castle."

"I understand." Muriel was feeling a surge of courage and was hoping it wouldn't desert her.

"If you are feeling nervous," said Maurice, "it is natural."

"I'm all right."

"Good." He was impressed by the girl's coolness. "From here on, no words," Maurice cautioned.

Still holding hands and staying close to buildings, they slowly made their way to Rue des Boulangers. Ahead, they saw a cat pad noiselessly across the street. No sign of German soldiers.

A few minutes later, Maurice and Muriel were at the rear of the Peiffers. No signal was necessary. Lea was waiting. She stepped outside to meet them, patted Muriel's hand and raised the doors to the wine cellar. Silently, Maurice descended, not switching on the first light. Muriel followed, then Lea who closed the doors behind them and switched on the light.

Moments later, they were in the tasting room. Muriel surveyed her new surroundings. Six sleeping rolls were lined up against one wall. A chamber pot was in a corner behind the tables. "This is where you and your family will sleep," said Lea. "During the daylight hours, you will live in our attic. I'm sorry it has to be this way," said Lea.

"Don't be," said Muriel. "We know the risk you are taking. I am grateful. We all are."

"We will stay here with you the rest of the night, until curfew lifts," said Maurice. "Then you can go upstairs with Lea. I'll then go to my shop. Business as usual. Then at night I will bring Michel down."

†††

At the moment, Stanislaw Sosabowski and Frederick "Boy" Browning were two very agitated generals. Thaddeus Metz was one very interested observer.

"General," said Browning, "I don't think I could be more reasonable."

"From your viewpoint, perhaps," said Sosabowski. "From mine, your viewpoint is unacceptable."

Careful, General, Thaddeus was thinking. Keep your temper in check, although heaven knows you've every right to show it…to let it boil over a bit.

"General Sosabowski," Browning said, his exasperation leaking from beneath his tight collar, "if you would just agree to make your Poles part of our British command, you would be my equal in rank. You would not be subservient in any way. And please bear in mind, we British have placed ourselves under General Eisenhower's command. In this war, there must be accommodation."

Sosabowski spat his reply heatedly. "Don't try to tell me that Montgomery enjoys serving under Eisenhower. You agreed only because you have no choice."

"Do you?" Browning asked bitingly.

"Our brigade's mission is to jump into Poland, surprise and disperse the Nazi occupiers and free our country. If we agree to become part of British airborne command, that will not happen. You know that as well as I do." Sosabowski could feel the heat in his face.

"General," said Browning, "liberating Poland was your mission in forming your airborne brigade. A most worthy objective. After all, it was Hitler's invasion of your country that caused Britain to declare war on Germany. But do you still believe your goal is achievable? We Allies have not yet invaded the continent, and the Russians are pushing the Nazis back toward Poland and Germany."

Lips pursed tightly, Sosabowski sighed heavily through his nose. "The morale of my men is low. Isn't that right, Captain Metz?" Thaddeus nodded. "They know valuable time is passing by. But they want to stay true to our intended purpose."

"Again, General, do you think that purpose is achievable? Truly achievable?"

"No." It pained Sosabowski to utter that single, definitive word.

"I thought not."

Neither man was taking any pleasure from this contentious exchange. Both wanted it to end, but only on terms both could accept.

"Let me make a proposal," said Sosabowski, willing his blood pressure to begin receding.

"Go ahead, please."

"When the invasion begins and your airborne units suffer casualties, you will have ample replacements available."

"True."

"We Poles will not. Our brigade is our brigade and we have no airborne reserves. When one of my men goes down, there is no one to step in. As you know, the other Poles in England are infantry and armor. The same with the Poles fighting in Italy. If I agree to put our brigade under British control and participate in the invasion, if – when – our casualties rise to twenty-five percent of our strength, you will agree that we can withdraw so we will still have a substantial force for eventual fighting in Poland…for liberating our people. From the Russians, if necessary."

Browning knew what his reply must be but let silence prevail for long moments. He massaged his chin once, twice, a third time. Let Sosabowski sense the response before hearing the words. Then speak those words slowly, sympathetically. "General, I appreciate your effort to find an acceptable alternative. But I'm afraid your proposal is not acceptable. If I were to agree and you did withdraw, it would imperil far too many Allied lives. It would strengthen the Germans' opportunity for a quick counter strike. If you are going to be in, General, you must be all the way in. I'm sorry, but that's the way it must be. Monty agrees."

"Montgomery," Sosabowski growled with contempt. "He wants total control. Your position was predictable, General Browning." Sosabowski forced a small, brief smile.

"And reasonable."

"Understandable."

"Close enough."

"Not quite," said Sosabowski. "I have another alternative in mind."

"Go ahead." Browning already was readying himself to veto Sosabowski's next gambit. Thaddeus could see as much from the way Browning was holding himself, arms folded across his chest.

"We agree – don't we? – that the invasion will be very risky. Eisenhower acknowledges this."

"So he does."

"So on invasion day, I will hold our Polish Brigade in reserve. Just as you will be doing with your British First Airborne Division. If the invasion succeeds, if the Allies gain and keep a foothold in France, then I will commit our Polish brigade to an operation of your choosing. We would be fully committed. Fully."

Browning's arms unfolded and his hands moved downward and rested against his hips. "This alternative has promise, General. Let me offer this amendment. If I agree to your proposal, would you be willing to join with our British First Airborne to serve as the enemy in a pre-invasion rehearsal against our British Sixth Airborne?"

Now it was Sosabowski who was considering. Thaddeus was thinking Browning's counter-proposal to be reasonable and was silently urging Sosabowski to accept. "How realistic will this rehearsal be?" Sosabowski asked.

"Live fire, for the most part," Browning replied. "Some smoke to approximate artillery."

"Such a rehearsal would be good for my men's morale," said Sosabowski. "It would put them in good fighting trim for real combat."

"And our British Sixth will need such a rehearsal before jumping into France. Have we struck a deal, General?"

"We have," said Sosabowski. "Reluctantly but, yes, we have a deal." Thaddeus was glad.

†††

On the second night, under heavy cloud cover and in total darkness, Maurice Trimbach had successfully brought young Michel Somer down from the castle to the Peiffer's wine cellars. The third night, when he brought Mrs. Somer down – Mrs. Steiner had insisted that Mrs. Somer precede her so she could join her children – also proved uneventful.

On the fourth night, thick clouds obscured the moon and most stars as Maurice started down with Mrs. Steiner. Maurice was tired. He had had little sleep since starting the operation. It worried him that he was having to force himself to remain alert. He wondered whether he should have asked another partisan to take over his role. That might have been the wiser choice, he was thinking. Still, they reached the base of the mountain without incident. As they stepped from behind a large boulder, Maurice's grip on Mrs. Steiner's hand tightened. She moved her face to within an inch of Maurice's right ear and whispered, "What is it?" Her stomach already was knotting.

Maurice turned his face to her ear. "I'm not sure. I think I saw a small flash of light." He shook his head and squinted and saw another small circle of reddish orange brighten and then fade in the darkness. "A German smoking a cigarette, I think."

"What do we do?"

"First, let's wait to see any movement." During the next 10 minutes, they both could see the cigarette's flame brighten and fade several times. Afterward, they saw nothing, no sign that the soldier was moving on.

"It seems we have two choices, Mrs. Steiner. Neither is ideal. We could wait here all day for darkness to fall." She shook her head. They were thinking the same thought. Waiting all day in the concealment offered by the boulder was a much too generous invitation to being seen. "Or," Maurice continued, "we could wait for dawn and the curfew to lift at seven-thirty. Wait for people to begin walking the streets to shops, youngsters to school. Then we will stroll into Rue de Boulangers and head for the Peiffers."

"If we are seen," she said, "by Germans? Or recognized by a villager who might inform?"

Maurice's lips pursed, then parted and his tongue flicked his upper lip. "It's a risk. I can't tell you it's not. But at least we will not have to enter the center of the village. We can stay on the outskirts until we reach Rue de Boulangers. If we see a German, if we sense danger, we must not hesitate. We must –"

"Let's go as soon as the curfew is over," Mrs. Steiner said, cutting him off.

An hour later, they emerged from behind the boulder. No soldier to be seen. Together they walked south on Rue de Rampart which curved and became Rue de la Marne. They were sauntering, exchanging an occasional word, as might a husband and wife. A few other pedestrians were taking to the streets, but none as yet near Maurice and Mrs. Steiner on the fringe of the village.

Now they were nearing the west end of Rue des Boulangers. "Almost there," murmured Maurice, glancing at Mrs. Steiner who met his gaze. They both inhaled. "Mrs. Steiner," Maurice whispered, "you remember the alley beside the Peiffers?"

"Yes."

"When we get there, if no one is watching us, just slip into it. Go to the Peiffer's rear door. If no one is there, knock lightly."

"And if someone is watching?"

"We'll keep walking, together, past their house."

"All right."

They turned into Rue des Boulangers. Ahead of them and walking in the same direction were two small groups of children on their way to school. Maurice and Mrs. Steiner could hear the buzz of their subdued chattering. They saw one small boy poke another in the ribs. The second boy poked back and both giggled. No one else was to be seen. Maurice allowed himself the smallest of smiles.

The Peiffer's house was on the north side of Rue des Boulangers, near the other end of the street. Maurice and Mrs. Steiner were about 20 paces into the street when fear struck fast and hard. Two German soldiers, privates, were stepping out of a boulangerie-patisserie about midway down on the south side of the street. One soldier was holding two newly baked croissants in waxed paper, the other a baguette. "Coffee?" one asked.

"Sounds good," replied the second. "That café has excellent coffee." He was gesturing toward a café just two doors away on the same side of the street – in the direction from which Maurice and Mrs. Steiner were approaching.

Fatigue notwithstanding, Maurice's mind had shaken off the rush of fear. It now was clear and quickly processing the situation. "Stay on this side of the street," he whispered. "Keep walking. Take no notice of me."

Immediately, Maurice began angling across the street toward the two soldiers, and Mrs. Steiner continued straight on, fighting off temptation to speed her pace, instead maintaining an unhurried gait.

"French breads and French coffee," one soldier was saying with a smile. "They're reason enough for us to occupy this country."

"They are spoiling us," said the other, "and I hope it doesn't end."

The first soldier chuckled. "It beats being in the East."

"Do you still think we can win the war?" said the second soldier.

"Do you?" His deep skepticism was obvious to his friend. "We've lost in Africa and Italy. We are losing in Russia. Even Lieutenant Hoffman and Sergeant Boehler have disappeared. If the Allies invade Europe..."

Now Maurice was directly in front of them, just steps away. He removed a pack of cigarettes and a lighter from his jacket pocket. The soldiers had looked up and were watching. "After our breads and coffee, a cigarette would taste wonderful," said one soldier.

Maurice put the cigarette between his lips and opened the lighter. Across the street, while Mrs. Steiner proceeded, she was forcing herself to refrain from watching. Maurice rubbed his thumb against the lighter's friction wheel, too lightly to produce a flame. "Damn," he muttered. He was only a few feet from the soldiers.

The soldier holding the croissants spoke. "Need a light?"

Maurice looked up from his lighter at the soldier. "Yes, please. Umm, your breads smell delicious. I should buy one for myself."

The soldier shifted his croissants to his left hand and with his right pulled a lighter from a trouser pocket. He reached forward, holding the lighter under the tip of Maurice's cigarette. The soldier's thumb pulled down on the friction wheel and flame ignited the tobacco as Maurice inhaled. "Ah, I needed that." Across the street, Mrs. Steiner was now three paces past Maurice and the soldiers. She did not look back. "Thank you," Maurice smiled.

"It's nothing," replied the soldier.

"Ah," said Maurice, "a gesture of kindness is always something." He held out his cigarette pack. "Take one. Both of you. Please."

The two soldiers each took one. Maurice bowed his head, stepped around the soldiers and continued walking. "Thank you," both soldiers said. "Nice fellow," said one of them. The second nodded.

Mrs. Steiner had disappeared from the street.

Chapter 30

At the end of their last day of training at Harvard, Jack and the other chaplains in his class were told to report to the Day Room the next morning at 7:30 for their travel orders.

Smiling, Jack said to another young chaplain, "I'm feeling like I'm about to be ordained a second time. One difference, though."

"What's that?"

"If I get sent to Europe, instead of driving west in a used Ford, this time I'll be taking a boat east. And I'll see a little more water on this trip than on my drive across Texas, New Mexico and Arizona."

The other chaplain laughed. "And think about it; you won't have to worry about changing flat tires."

Jack laughed. "Right. And I hope we don't have to dodge German torpedos."

†††

The next morning, the 14 new chaplains – ministers, priests, rabbis – all arrived early for the meeting. Moments later, an Army master sergeant entered, holding a sheaf of papers. "Good morning, Padres," he said, bags still hanging heavily under tired eyes.

"Good morning, Sarge," came the chorus of replies. "Late night?" Jack asked, teasingly.

"Late enough," the sergeant replied wearily, no trace of a smile. He then looked at the name – Captain Ronald Hersh -- at the top of the first sheet of paper, spoke Hersh's name and handed him his orders. Rabbi Hersh saw that he was headed to the 1st Infantry Division. "The Big Red One," he smiled, murmuring the division's nickname that derived from the unit's shoulder patches.

Midway through the sheaf, the sergeant said, "Captain John Brecker."

"Here, Sarge," said Jack, stepping forward and taking his orders. As he stepped back, Jack scanned the order sheet for his destination. Then he saw it: England, 82nd Airborne Division. Not Paul's 101st, he said to himself, but it's airborne and it's England. Maybe I can still see Paul. I'll have to write to him.

†††

"The Jews fought bravely during their uprising in the ghetto," said Bernadeta Gudek.

"Yes," agreed Captain Kaz Majos, "but they were crushed."

"Some escaped and joined us," said Bernadeta. "And they killed three hundred Nazis."

"But at such a price," replied Kaz.

"They would have been deported and murdered anyway," said Bernadeta. "At least they fought hard and died honorably. They should be respected and honored for that."

Bernadeta, Kaz and other partisans in their Home Army cell were gathered in a basement underneath St. Anne's church, a sturdy house of worship built in 1454. Surrounding them were shelves stocked with candles, incense and sacramental wine. A tunnel ran from the basement beneath Krakowskie Przedmiescie street to the rectory on the other side. So far, the Nazis hadn't been eager to probe church basements. Part of their reticence resulted from unease with defiling church property and part – the bigger part – from the inherent danger.

"A second uprising," Kaz considered. "How much damage could we inflict?"

"It would have to be all of Warsaw, all Poles, rising up," said Bernadeta. "Not the few but the many. And it would have to be coordinated."

"We've been stockpiling weapons," Kaz said pensively. "Mostly small arms. A few small field pieces. Which," he smiled wryly, "the Nazis keep hunting for. They keep such meticulous records, you know. It gauls them to no end when something is missing."

Low, brief chuckles were heard in the basement chamber.

"I think more of our people – more and more – are ready to fight back," said Bernadeta. "In the open."

"I think you might be right," Kaz agreed.

Others in the basement murmured or nodded their assents.

"Do you think we could count on help?" Bernadeta asked. "From the Russians?"

"Too early to say," Kaz replied, "but I'm not inclined to trust them any more than the Nazis. Remember, Stalin was more than happy to agree with Hitler to divide our country between them."

"And then Hitler betrayed Stalin."

"Yes," said Kaz, "but could we rely on the word of Stalin?"

†††

Maurice Trimbach's nerves generally were paragons of steadiness, but they had been jangled by the close call that morning with Mrs. Steiner. In the next day's pre-dawn hours, he was back inside the castle ruins with Mr. Steiner and Mr. Somer. When as usual they asked how things had gone the previous night, Maurice already had concluded that one set of frayed nerves would be enough. "No problems," he lied. "We've been lucky," he said truthfully, hoping their luck would endure.

"We've had the benefit of good planning," Mr. Steiner observed gratefully.

Maurice looked at the two men – Nazi prey – with admiration. Perhaps, he thought, their nerves are stronger than mine. "Who's next?" he asked.

"Mr. Somer," said Mr. Steiner. "Same reason. Keeping a family together."

Maurice nodded. "Let's go."

Mr. Somer and Mr. Steiner shook hands. "Good luck," said Mr. Steiner.

†††

"What now?" Kaz said to Bernadeta in the church basement.

"I'm going outside to do a little shopping. Find some onions, bread, cheese. Maybe an apple or two. Want to join me?"

"I just might…Ah, I need to clear up a couple things here first," said Kaz. "You go ahead. I'll catch up."

"If you can find me in the market," she smiled, teasing.

"You are easy to spot," Kaz replied with affection. He was tempted to say: Be careful, Bernadeta, watch your step. But he refrained. She and other Home Army members knew more keenly than most Poles that they always needed to be careful and watch their steps. So Kaz merely touched

Bernadeta's shoulder and brushed his lips against her cheek. She returned his affection with a peck on the cheek.

Upstairs, before exiting the church, Bernadeta dipped her fingers into a holy water font and crossed herself. Then she leaned against a door, slowly creating a narrow crack. She studied the street in both directions. No Nazis. She edged the door open wider and slipped outside. Down the steps she went and then began walking toward a nearby outdoor market. Soon she was strolling among stalls and pushcarts, eyeing baked goods, produce, eggs, cheeses, a few sausages. Merchants were chatting with each other and with customers. The air was raw, but the sun was shining and warmed spirits, all things considered, were a barometer of another arriving spring.

Bernadeta lifted and studied a large potato, rotating it in her right hand. From a few feet away, she heard a voice. "Miss?" She paid no attention. "Miss?" This time the voice carried a measure of insistence. Bernadeta shifted her gaze from the potato to the source of the voice. It was a German lieutenant. She pointed at herself, mouthing "Me?"

The lieutenant stepped around the cart and approached Bernadeta. "You look familiar," he said with simple directness. "Haven't we met?" He was speaking quite good Polish.

"I don't think so." Such a clumsy attempt to get my attention, she thought derisively.

"Are you sure? I just have this feeling..."

Remain polite, Bernadeta was thinking. Don't give him reason for becoming agitated. "I'm sorry, but I don't think so." Her sincerity was convincing because it was genuine.

"Hmmm...Well, perhaps I'm mistaken."

"I think you must be," she said, shrugging.

The lieutenant touched his hand to his billed hat. He turned away, slightly shaking his head in puzzlement. Bernadeta watched him for a long moment. He can't possibly think I would be interested in a Nazi, she thought. Then she returned to her shopping.

The lieutenant had strolled about 40 feet when a memory jarred his senses. The scar. By her mouth. I've seen that scar. When? Where? He pivoted.

Bernadeta had purchased two potatoes that she was carrying in a small cloth bag that she had been carrying in her purse. Now she was standing at a cart stocked with onions.

The lieutenant approached her. "Miss?"

Bernadeta looked up at the sound of the now familiar voice. "Yes?"

The lieutenant stopped an arm's length from her. "What is your name?"

"Bernadeta Gudek."

"You have identification papers?"

"Yes. If you like –"

He cut her off. "Where are you from?"

"I live with friends." True. "Our home was bombed back in Thirty-Nine." False.

The lieutenant shook his head. "No, I mean, where are you from? Your place of birth?"

Bernadeta felt herself growing chilly with anxiety. Being questioned by a Nazi officer in a public setting was trying enough, but adding to her discomfort was dawning recognition – hers and the lieutenant's. Zyrardow...the farm...Of course, she was remembering...Zyrardow...the lieutenant who came to our house, looking for his guards and the prisoners in the cow pen. Bernadeta could almost feel her mind shifting into a higher gear. Back then, she had known instantly that she shouldn't play dumb, so she had lied as convincingly as was possible. Could she do so again? "I was born here in Warsaw. Near the Jewish ghetto. Or what was the ghetto."

"Are you sure?" Lieutenant Blatz asked. His tone was turning hard with growing suspicion. "I could swear I've seen that scar." His right arm extended and his forefinger grazed the scar. "It's the kind of thing a man doesn't forget. Yes, I'm quite positive I've seen it."

Involuntarily, Bernadeta's head rocked backward. His rudeness, his touch, thoroughly disgusted her, but she knew it would be wise to try to mask her revulsion. "I can't imagine where."

He lowered his arm. "I don't think I believe you...about where you're from." He shook his head. "That scar. I think you might be lying. Probably. Actually."

"No," Bernadeta said, hoping she could keep the mounting anxiety from unsteadying her voice.

Lieutenant Blatz reached out and grasped her left arm. "I think you should go with me. For questioning."

You mean for torture, Bernadeta was thinking. Your Nazi version of questioning begins with torture. "I assure you, Sir. This is the first time we've met. I would certainly remember you."

"No," Lieutenant Blatz said firmly. "You might not remember me, but I remember you. From somewhere." Still grasping Bernadeta's arm, his left eye closed and his head nodded in concentration, his memory searching. "Zyrardow...Zyrardow," he murmured, pulling the memory further forward. Bernadeta struggled to avoid a visible reaction. "A farm...a girl at the door. Yes, that's where you're from. That was you." He stared hard, eyes narrowed and drilling into Bernadeta's. He was searching for a confirmation.

"I'm sorry," she said, and now she could hear a quaver in her voice. But she also knew that would be the expected reaction by a Polish woman in the grasp of a suspicious Nazi officer. "I don't know Zyrardow."

"Oh, I think you do," the lieutenant said confidently. His voice had taken on an unmistakable tone of certainty. "I think you are the farm girl who has come to Warsaw. Why? Why Warsaw? Why would you leave a peaceful farm? To join the Resistance? A possibility. A very real possibility. You are a partisan?"

"No." Bernadeta jerked hard and freed her arm.

Lieutenant Blatz reached out quickly and grasped the lapel of her coat. "Stop it," he ordered. "You are coming with me for questioning." He jerked Bernadeta toward him and turned, beginning to pull her along with him. Her mind continued processing thoughts at a furious pace. Where is he taking me? What exactly will questioning entail? What kind of torture? How much? How long? Can I endure it? My papers are excellent forgeries. Will they rape me? How many times? Will they execute me even if they have no proof? They do that every day. No matter what, I must not tell the truth. I must deny anything and everything about Zyrardow. My family would be executed as soon as German soldiers could get to the farm. And Kaz and my friends...

Another voice was speaking, intruding on her thinking. "Lieutenant." Not Lieutenant Blatz's voice, Bernadeta realized, but another man's. "Lieutenant, please, Sir."

Lieutenant Blatz stopped, maintaining his firm grip on Bernadeta's lapel, and turned to look behind him. A man, wearing a dirty gray fedora, was approaching casually, sauntering, hands clasped behind his back. "Yes?" Blatz snapped impatiently. "What is it?" He was of no mind to tolerate either curiosity or impertinence. But then, perhaps this man had useful information about the young woman. Perhaps he wanted to curry favor.

Bernadeta recognized the voice and also turned to look.

The man, now about eight feet from Lieutenant Blatz, calmly unclasped his hands. The right one was holding a luger. Blatz saw it and had no time to speak before the gun spit fire and he felt searing pain. His grip on Bernadeta's lapel loosened and both hands involuntarily went flying to his chest as he spun and fell face down.

Kaz took two quick paces toward Bernadeta. "Let's go. Now," he said urgently. He reached for Bernadeta's hand and began pulling her with him through the tangle of carts, stalls and customers. "Get back to the church," Kaz directed her.

"You?"

"I'll meet you there later."

The merchants and their customers were scattering. That single shot. A German officer lying in the street. No one paused to study him, much less render assistance. This was not an occasion for being a Samaritan. They knew what was coming next. More German soldiers and immediate reprisals.

Tears of pain were leaking from Lieutenant Blatz's eyes. He could feel blood oozing between his fingers and spreading on his uniform and the pavement. He moaned. He also knew he had been right about the farm girl from Zyrardow.

CHAPTER 31

Thaddeus Metz crouched, knees slightly bent, in the open doorway, gazing down at the lush, green countryside. Then he crouched down a little more and leaped from the Dakota. Jumping from 800 feet, Thaddeus knew from experience that he would be on the ground fast. During his descent, he looked back up at the parade of Dakotas and watched other Poles leaping into the void. He and the others were hoping this would be their last practice jump. The real thing couldn't come soon enough. If they couldn't jump into Poland, then jumping into France still would give them the opportunity to fight – to kill – Germans. Kill. I've killed, Thaddeus was reflecting, but I don't see myself as a killer. No. Not at all. But the Germans are murderers...pitiless, remorseless savages, and they must be eradicated. In another few seconds, Thaddeus' boots thudded against earth.

†††

Jack Brecker was in the middle of the "stick" or line of 18 men standing, waiting to jump from the Douglas C-47 transport. It would be his first practice jump, and the other members of the 82nd Airborne aboard the plane had told the young chaplain – at 27, older than every other soldier on the craft – that he should go neither first nor last on his maiden jump. Common sense, Jack had agreed, and hadn't protested.

"You ready, Padre?" It was Captain Walt Hunter's soothing voice.

"As ready as I'll ever be, Captain," Jack replied.

The "go light" flashed on and one-by-one in quick succession, fully equipped and armed young paratroopers began their leaps. When Jack stepped to the doorway, less encumbered than the other soldiers, he used his right thumb to quickly make a small sign of the cross over his heart. With no hesitation, his hands reached out and grasped the edges of the doorway. In the next instant, he propelled himself outward. The rush of air and the jolt that accompanied the billowing of his parachute were far greater than when he had leaped, tethered, from the practice tower. Now, only scant seconds in the air, Jack had a non-religious epiphany: I liked being in that airplane and I liked jumping from it. Imagine that. During his descent, Jack was grinning. A flying desert priest. The Indian elder at Charco might see a heavenly sign in my flight.

†††

Thaddeus and General Sosabowski were standing together, watching the second flight of Dakotas ferry the rest of the Polish Airborne Brigade to their practice jump zone. As with past rehearsals, American crews were piloting the Dakotas.

"I must tell you, General," Thaddeus said, "even after all of our training and all our practice jumps, I still have to pinch myself when I think about this former lancer riding planes instead of horses. I even find it thrilling to watch our men jumping."

General Sosabowski chuckled. "I was a foot soldier so I never rode anything. Nothing with legs and hoofs. Never expected to. But remember this, Captain, after we jump and hit the ground, we all become infantry. Foot soldiers."

As the flight of Dakotas went passing overhead, Thaddeus' head jerked in a quick, involuntary doubletake. "General, look!" Thaddeus cried, pointing skyward.

"Jesus!" Sosabowski implored, "pull up! Pull away!"

"Now!" Thaddeus urged the crews of the Dakotas. "Now!" Two of the troop-carrying planes had drifted far too close to each other. From the ground it seemed as though the nose of the second Dakota was touching the tail of the first. Neither plane seemed to be altering speed or course, and seconds later there was the nauseating sound of metal crunching against metal, and almost instantly two mortally wounded planes were plummeting gracelessly toward earth. Thaddeus and the general both cringed, their faces twisting in anguish.

Because the two planes had been flying at a low, jump altitude, there was no time for any but the first two paratroopers in each plane to leap to safety. The rest of the men were trapped inside by the planes' steep angles of descent and rapidly mounting 'G' forces.

On the ground, Sosabowski, Thaddeus and hundreds of other disbelieving Poles watched in silent horror as the planes carried their friends to certain death. The four soldiers who had parachuted, descending more slowly, watched the two planes go screaming toward the ground.

Two fiery, massive explosions followed impact. To a man, the Poles went running toward the wreckage and the four descending troopers.

At the crash site, amidst the burning debris, there were no intact corpses, just fragments of blackened body parts.

"Oh, my Lord, no," Sosabowski groaned. Around him, many Poles were crying and many more were making the sign of the cross. Thaddeus tugged at the general's sleeve and pointed to where the four parachutists had landed. They and dozens of their comrades went running toward the troopers.

Thaddeus, sprinting hard, was among the first to arrive. The four airborne men were struggling to their feet, beginning to gather their chutes' silk and cords. One of them, Thaddeus saw, was Henryk, one of his cow pen mates. Thaddeus took hold gently of Henryk's arms. "Are you all right? Are you hurt? Let me help you get out of this thing," he said, unbuckling the chute harness. Other Poles were providing the same assistance to the other three parachutists.

"What happened?" Thaddeus asked. Sosabowski, winded, now had caught up to the younger soldiers.

"I don't know," said Henryk. "It all happened so fast. I barely saw the second plane closing on us. I jumped and then came the collision."

"Are you sure you're all right?" Sosabowski asked.

"Yes, Sir. I am...Any other survivors?"

Thaddeus shook his head.

"Piotr was onboard with me," said Henryk, "farther back. He had no chance." He wiped a hand slowly across his moistening eyes.

Thaddeus, too, could feel tears welling, as he recalled Piotr helping to save his life at Dunkirk. Almost four years ago. More than four years since meeting him in the cow pen at Zyrardow. Thaddeus dabbed at his eyes.

"I'm so sorry, Sir," Henryk said mournfully to Thaddeus.

Thaddeus worked to clear his throat. "Do you know...do you know if we lost anyone else from the cow pen?"

Henryk shook his head before replying. "I don't think so. I think they all jumped with you and General Sosabowski on the first practice run." Again he wiped tears from his eyes and cheeks. "Look," he said, pointing. It was Stephan, Marek and Jerzy, tending to one of the parachutists.

"Excuse me, Henryk," said the general, "I need to go check on the other three."

"Yes, Sir, go ahead. You, too, Captain Metz. Go see to the others. I'm all right. Really."

Thaddeus nodded and began following Sosabowski. "We'll probably never know the cause, General." And they wouldn't. They would know only that when the two planes struck earth, eight American crewmen and 26 Poles perished. During the months leading up to the invasion of Europe, deadly incidents were not uncommon. They claimed many lives. On April 27-28, 1944, during a rehearsal of an amphibious landing at Slapton Sands on the South Devon coast, 750 Allied soldiers died and 300 were wounded when German mid-sized cruisers broke through a surprised ring of Allied ships and sank six landing craft and damaged six others.

†††

"Well, Padre, it looks like your guardian angel was hauling silk today," said Captain Hunter. "Nice jump."

"Thanks, Captain," Jack replied. "You couldn't have confused my landing with ballet, but I think all my bones are intact."

"Walt. Call me Walt."

"I think I can manage that."

"Thought you might. You know, you have your own tent, but I'm wondering whether you might be up for a little sharing tonight – good Scotch in my tent. Nicely aged, locally made."

"I think I might be able to manage that, too, Walt. Just so that I don't sleep through reveille."

"I'll take personal responsibility to make sure you don't."

†††

That evening, Jack and Captain Walt Hunter were sitting on a cot and a crate in a tent that also was serving as home to another 82nd Airborne officer, Lieutenant Dale Reiser. Walt stuck his arm deep into his duffel bag, and when it came out it was holding a bottle of Teachers. From another crate serving as a locker, Walt removed three glasses. "Can't stand drinking Scotch from tin cups. Liberated these from a local club." He poured and handed glasses to Jack and Dale. "To staying alive," Walt said.

"And in a state of grace," Jack replied.

"Does Scotch have a place in that state?" Walt asked, eyes twinkling.

"That state's borders are closed to certain practices, but sipping good Scotch isn't one of them. Now, if we had cigars, the good residents of that state might come looking to issue us invitations."

"You like cigars?" Dale Reiser asked.

"It's like this," said Jack. "I tried cigarettes but found them generally tasteless. At the Josephinum – my seminary – I smoked some cigars and enjoyed them. And when one of my mission Indians – an elder – learned that I enjoy cigars, he gave me one nearly every time he saw me. I don't smoke 'em often, but what better way is there to relax with a great taste?"

"Just a minute," Walt said, rising quickly. "I'll be back in a jiff." He exited the tent.

"Latrine call?" Dale speculated.

Jack shrugged and sipped his Scotch.

A few minutes later, Walt pushed open the tent flap. He was grinning triumphantly and holding aloft three White Owl cigars. "I worked a quick deal at the quartermaster's. Another liberation, so to speak."

"Hey, great!" Jack exulted.

"Way to go, Captain," said Lieutenant Reiser.

They lighted the White Owls. Jack took another sip of Scotch and then drew heavily on the cigar. "White Owls are what I smoked at the seminary. If this isn't in the state of grace, I'm going to petition the pope."

Walt and Dale laughed. All three continued sipping and puffing contentedly while the air inside the tent grew deliciously gray and smokey.

"Why airborne, Padre?" Dale asked.

"No reason that you would consider heroic or romantic. My brother Paul is with the Hundred And First. He told me in a letter that good chaplains were needed. We'll soon find out how good I am – if I am needed. And now that I've flown…" he said wistfully.

"It's to your liking, I take it," said Walt.

"Be nice if I had one of those babies," Jack said.

"A C-Forty-Seven?" Walt asked incredulously.

"Not that big a baby," Jack chuckled. "But my own plane would be nice. Be easier to get around Arizona. Easier to get back home."

"A priest with his own plane?" Walt said, still struggling to visualize a priest at flight controls. "You mean you'd fly if you didn't have to?"

"Why not? Put me a little closer to heaven." Jack laughed, and Walt and Dale laughed with him. "Seriously, if I had my own plane, I could visit my missions more often. And it would sure make it easier to visit my family. Or see an Indians game or two when I'm back in Ohio."

"Well, I'll be..." Walt was shaking his head. He drew on his cigar and blew out the smoke forcefully. "I can't say I've known a lot of priests – I'm Lutheran – but you are one very different man of the cloth."

"Did you think we were all cut from the same bolt of cloth?" Jack asked and winked.

"In your case, Padre, certainly not dull, black cloth."

"Black is merely the color of our cassocks. Our robes are quite bright – golds, greens, reds. Colors of joy and celebration."

"I think I'm starting to get this picture," Walt smiled. "Priest, parachutist, pilot, Indian missionary, baseball fan. Cigar smoker. Scotch drinker. Am I missing anything?"

Jack laughed. "You paint with a pretty broad brush. Hmmm...Let's see. I once played catch with Lou Boudreau...I speak passable Spanish... I've shot a mountain lion, and now I'm saying Mass with a jeep hood for an altar."

"You shot a mountain lion?" Dale asked, as incredulously as Walt had on learning of Jack's fondness for flying.

"Well, I pulled the trigger, but a friend made it happen."

"Why?"

"The lion was eating the Indians' sheep – their food, their clothing and blankets."

"A veritable renaissance man," Walt teased, but with his admiration clearly visible.

"Renaissance man...Now there," Jack observed, "is a reference you seldom here from G.I.s."

"Unless," said Walt, "they've done some reading of European history or looked at some works of the masters."

"And you have..."

"University of Virginia," Walt said. "Liberal arts."

"I'm impressed."

"Don't be. At Virginia, I spent darned near as much time carousing as studying."

"Are you from Virginia?" Jack asked.

"Not quite," Walt said, eyes twinkling again. "You and I...we're almost neighbors."

Jack looked questioningly at Walt. "Ohio?"

"Nope. Arizona."

"Arizona!"

"Near Globe."

"In the mountains."

"Yep. About eighty miles east of Tucson. About thirty-eight hundred feet up."

"Well, I'll be," said Jack, marveling at the unlikely coincidence. He digested this news for a moment, then asked, "Why Virginia?"

"Dad thought it would be good for me to see a different part of the country." Walt held up his empty glass. "More?" Jack and Dale both nodded and Walt stood and poured. He put the bottle down and puffed his cigar. "'Course, Dad didn't think I'd get this far east."

"What does your dad do?" Jack asked.

"Works at a mine. Copper."

"That's very hard work," Jack said sympathetically.

"Not so hard for him," Walt replied.

"Why's that?"

"He owns it."

"Oh my," Jack laughed. "Let's see if I've got this picture. I'm in the company of an airborne captain with a liberal arts degree who understands the renaissance...who appreciates good Scotch and cigars and whose father is a mining tycoon with the good sense to see that his son gets educated and broadens his horizons at the same time. I am impressed."

"I feel like I'm in the presence of military royalty," Dale said, bowing with mock reverence. "I can get a blessing and a belt on the same night in the same tent." Laughter all around.

"Actually," Jack said pensively, peering out through a new cloud of smoke, "all in all, we're been pretty lucky. We know that millions have died in Europe and Asia. That millions more are suffering from injuries or starving. May the Lord have mercy on them."

"And on us," said Walt.

"Yes," Jack said softly, "on all of us – who will soon enough be in harm's way. Well, it's time I get back to my tent. Gentlemen, this has been a fine, fine evening. One to be remembered." Jack stood, put his glass down and ground his cigar stub into a mess tin that was serving as a communal ashtray.

Dale cleared his throat. "Father…" Dale's face was reddening. "Would you mind giving a blessing?"

Jack smiled. "Not at all." Dale began to kneel. "That's not necessary," said Jack. Just stand at ease." Walt stood, too. "Lord, thank you for this wonderful night of comradeship. May we have many more like them together. In the name of the Father, the Son and the Holy Spirit."

"Amen."

"Amen."

Chapter 32

Father Jack Brecker's youth, age 27, notwithstanding, he quickly came to be regarded highly by men of the 82nd Airborne. There were other division chaplains, but word had spread rapidly about Jack's fondness for flying, his having played catch with Lou Boudreau and having felled a mountain lion with an M-1, his appreciation of Scotch and cigars, and his two brothers, one with the 101st Airborne and the other home after losing a foot on the Hornet. To the men, all this made him more human, more approachable, and they soon took to approaching him frequently.

In his tent, Jack heard homesick soldiers unburden their loneliness and talk of lost loves. He heard their confessions and wrote letters for those who found it difficult to impossible to express their thoughts and feelings with pen and ink.

Outside the tent, he joined other soldiers in calisthenics and in spare moments could be found playing catch whenever a soldier – or soldiers – arrived at his tent with an extra glove and a ball. Twice he was invited to play in games, and the troopers saw for themselves that Jack Brecker was as adept at hitting, fielding and throwing as he was at counseling troubled G.I.s.

In one of those games, with the score tied at 2-2 in the ninth inning, Jack came to bat. A teammate was on first base with two outs. On the first pitch, Jack lined the ball hard on a low trajectory to the left centerfield gap. He went dashing toward first base and saw the ball rolling and the centerfielder chasing. Jack kicked his running into a higher gear. There was no fence to stop the ball, and Jack sensed an opportunity for a homerun. When Jack was midway between second and third bases, the centerfielder had reached the ball and was hurriedly preparing to launch his throw. Jack kept sprinting, touched third and kept going. The shortstop caught the centerfielder's throw in shallow left centerfield, pivoted and made a strong relay throw to the catcher who applied the tag to a sliding Jack's left hand as it was stretching for the burlap sack that was serving as homeplate.

"You're out!" shouted a master sergeant who was serving as umpire.

From his sitting position, Jack flopped backward and lay flat. Alarmed, several players from both teams came running to see if he was injured. They found Jack grinning broadly. "We won anyway, right?"

"You're right, Padre. The runner from first base scored before you were tagged out."

Jack folded his right hand into a fist and pounded the ground in exultation. "Too bad Lou Boudreau wasn't here today."

Laughter all around.

"Padre," said Walt Hunter who had been watching the game, "Maybe you missed your real calling."

"No," Jack said, chuckling, "I think the Lord called me in the right direction. He knew I should have stopped at third."

†††

It was Good Friday, 1944, and there was no church in the 82nd's camp in which to say the Stations of the Cross. A little after 3 p.m., Jack Brecker was sitting in his tent, on the edge of his cot, meditating. I'm grateful for the sacrifices you made, Lord. They have made it easier for me to see the way...the way in which I can do the most good for the many. My parishioners in Ajo...the reservation Indians...these young soldiers. The sacrifices I make...the ones I will make in the future, they seem paltry compared to yours. I think I am strong enough to make most sacrifices that will confront me. The ultimate one...to give my life for others...the biggest test of my faith...If confronted, I hope I can do that without flinching. Lord, I beseech thee to watch-

"Father Brecker," the voice outside Jack's tent called softly, "you in there? It's me, Walt Hunter. Are you busy?"

Jack looked up and rested his hands on his knees. No, I'm not busy, he thought, but this isn't the best time for visitors. I'd like to finish my prayers. But..."Come in, Walt." Jack stood.

Captain Walt Hunter pulled open the tent flap and stepped inside. Another man followed.

"Hello, Father," Walt said, extending his right hand. Jack took it and they shook. "I hope I'm not disturbing you, Father." Walt sensed this was not an occasion for using the more familiar "Padre" in addressing Jack.

"Not at all, Walt. You know my policy. If I'm not with someone, I'm not too busy to see someone."

Captain Hunter nodded. "Father, I'd like you to meet someone," he said, motioning with his head toward the visitor. "Captain Jack Brecker, this is Captain Thaddeus Metz. Captain Metz, Captain Brecker."

"How do you do, Father," said Thaddeus. "I am very pleased to meet you." He saluted Jack who returned the salute.

"Likewise, Captain Metz."

"Father," said Walt, "Captain Metz is with the Polish Airborne Brigade. They are stationed at Upper Largo in Scotland. North of Edinburgh. Soon they'll be moving south down to Peterborough."

"I see," said Jack. "What brings the two of you here?"

"Staff meeting," said Walt. "A coordination meeting between the various airborne units. Eighty-Second, Hundred And First, British First and Sixth. The Poles. Captain Metz is aide to General Sosabowski, who commands the Poles."

"And to my tent?"

"Let me explain, Father," said Thaddeus. "After the meeting, Captain Hunter and I were talking. He asked me about our needs. I knew he meant material needs, but something – some things – caused me to think of spiritual needs…" A pause.

"Go ahead," said Jack, "please continue."

"As you know, this is Good Friday. Most of us Poles are Catholics. Almost all. We don't have a permanent chaplain. A priest. Sunday is Easter and recently we lost some men in a training accident."

"The plane collision?" Jack asked.

"Yes. We lost twenty-six good men. Men who already had been through a lot. In Poland, in France, at Dunkirk. I thought it would be good for morale if we had a priest visit us. Say a little. Give us a blessing."

"I see," Jack said. "I'd like to help. Your English is excellent, Captain, but I don't speak Polish, you know. Not at all. I speak Spanish but I'm afraid that wouldn't be of much use with your men. I'm guessing very few understand English. Right?"

"Right, Father. I am fortunate. I studied English and French at university. I was planning a career in government or law before the Germans invaded."

"Yes, well, and Upper Largo, that's a long way off."

"I would send a plane for you, Father," said Thaddeus. "If that's all right with you. And English or Spanish, it would make no difference to our men. Just being there and giving them a blessing is what really would matter."

Walt Hunter thought he knew what Jack Brecker was thinking and he was right. A chance to help some soldiers in need and a chance to fly. Twice. Up and back.

"I would be happy to serve you and your men, Captain Metz."

"That is wonderful, Father. Thank you very much."

"Happy to help," said Jack. "When do you propose that I go?"

"Today, if you like, Father. You could fly back with us. Or any time that is convenient for you."

An idea was percolating in Jack's mind. "Captain Metz, what do you think of this? Instead of flying back with you today, how about if I say Mass for your men on Easter?"

"Father...Father, that would be so wonderful." Walt could hear high emotion creeping into Thaddeus' voice and he, a Lutheran, felt his own excitement growing. "My men would be very grateful, more grateful than you can imagine."

Actually, no, Jack was thinking. He was remembering vividly how grateful the Indians had been when he had driven to their reservation to say a Mass on Christmas. "It would be my pleasure, Captain. I will say the Mass in Latin and speak a brief homily in English and perhaps you can translate."

"Yes, Father, I can do that. When do you propose I pick you up?"

"Well," said Jack, "I'm planning to say two Masses on Easter morning. Then mingle with the troops, have lunch with them in the mess tent. How about one o'clock?"

"Perfect," said Thaddeus. "I will tell our men and they will await your arrival with great anticipation. This will be our best Easter since Nineteen Thirty-Nine."

"Very good, Captain." Jack reached out, Thaddeus shook his hand vigorously and then saluted. "See you Sunday, Father."

"See you, Captain."

Thaddeus turned to exit the tent. Walt Hunter smiled at Jack and turned to leave.

"Captain Hunter," said Jack.

"Yes, Father?"

"Thanks."

CHAPTER 33

Easter morning in northern England dawned gray and chilly, but Jack, rising early, felt rested and warm. He eased off his cot, stood and stretched, grunting. He was looking forward to saying Mass for men of the 82nd and, later, for the Polish brigade. Jack stepped outside his tent and began strolling to the latrine. He was hoping for dry weather because he knew that meant he could say Mass outdoors and more men would attend. In the event of rain, his church would be a mess tent. It would accommodate a smaller congregation, and the inside of a drab tent would be less uplifting than a service held under open skies.

Jack got his weather wish – his prayer. After the second Mass, he returned to his tent, removed his vestments, put his Communion wafer box, water and wine cruets, chalice and paten in his footlocker, and then went strolling toward the mess tent. Inside, he gladly filled a mess tray with fried chicken, mashed potatoes, green beans and two slices of bread. He filled a white mug with steaming black coffee. He sat at a table with troopers, accepted their greetings and thanks, and cheerily rehashed the recent baseball game after which word of his diamond exploits had spread quickly throughout the division.

A few minutes before 1 p.m., he stood and picked up his tray and mug.

"Put it down, Father," said one of the troopers. "I'll take it back for you."

Jack almost said, "Thanks but I'll do it" but recognized the offer for what it was and set the tray and mug back on the table. "Thank you, Corporal. I do have another service to conduct." Jack smiled, turned and exited the tent. He stopped abruptly.

Captain Metz was standing there. That didn't surprise Jack. What did surprise him was seeing Captain Walt Hunter there, too. The three captains exchanged salutes.

"Captain Hunter, I wasn't expecting to see you here."

Walt grinned impishly. "After we left your tent on Friday," he said, motioning toward Captain Metz, "we talked about how I might be of assistance today. I'm not Catholic so I can't assist at Mass. But I can do something else." Walt held up a green cloth moneybag with a drawstring pulled tight. "Camera," Walt grinned. "Thought I might capture this Mass for the record. Maybe you could show the pictures to your Indians back in Arizona."

"You say Mass for Indians?" Thaddeus said, his tone suggesting both awe and alarm.

Jack grinned. "They are quite civilized, Captain Metz." He turned to Captain Hunter. "You might be disappointed with your picture taking. Saying Mass from a jeep hood with lots of men around, you're not likely to get much."

"Well, who knows?" Walt replied. "Maybe I'll get lucky and get a decent picture or two."

†††

The small plane was piloted by an American, Lieutenant Calvin Wardell. Jack sat beside Wardell, Thaddeus and Walt behind them. In the air, Thaddeus said, "Father, please tell me about your work with the Indians."

Jack swung his head sideways and spoke loudly, above the din of the engine and roaring of the wind, "There's not much to say, Captain. They live on a large reservation in southern Arizona. Each week I drive to one of their communities to say Mass, hear confessions, visit the sick and infirm. They are good people, and I count them as friends."

Captain Metz smiled. "Today, Father, perhaps we Poles are like your Indians. You fly to our reservation. You say Mass. Perhaps speak with some of our men. Some of us were lancers and rode horses like your Indians."

Jack chuckled. "The Polish Indians of the steppes. Actually, Captain, very few Indians ride horses today. But if your fellow Poles are men of moral strength and character, then the comparison is very appropriate."

"You can judge for yourself," Thaddeus smiled. "I will say only that we have some excellent horsemen who have learned to jump out of airplanes and who are eager to liberate our homeland."

†††

The small plane rolled to a stop on a grassy strip. A jeep with a driver was waiting. "Father, this is Stephan. He doesn't speak English, but he knows who you are and asked to serve as your driver."

Jack extended his hand and Stephan shook it. "Very pleased to meet you, Stephan."

Stephan replied in Polish. "We are very grateful you have come today."

Jack nodded and looked at Thaddeus. "No need to translate that, Captain Metz."

Jack sat in front and again Thaddeus and Walt sat in the rear. "Stephan and I have fought and trained together for five years," said Thaddeus. "He also helped save my life at Dunkirk."

"I'm impressed," said Jack.

†††

A few minutes later, Stephan braked the jeep and Jack was surprised. The surprise wasn't that a throng of hundreds of men were waiting. It was that they were standing at rigid attention. In front of them was General Sosabowski. As Jack swung his legs from the jeep and stood, every Pole raised his right arm in salute. Jack, touched, returned as sharp a salute as he ever had rendered and held it in place for a good three seconds before snapping it off.

"Good day, Captain Brecker," said General Sosabowski. "Please excuse my English. It is not as good as Captain Metz's."

"It's still a good deal better than my Polish," Jack smiled.

"Thank you. First," the general continued, "let me introduce you to my deputy, Lieutenant Colonel Stanislaw Jachnik." He and Jack shook hands. "Second, on behalf of the Polish First Independent Parachute Brigade, I welcome you."

Jack paused and then projected his voice loudly. "Happy Easter! Holy Easter!"

Hundreds of men who didn't understand his words understood his meaning, and a roar of greeting and approval began building. Someone began to clap and others joined and within moments the applause was joyously thunderous.

"This way, Father," said Thaddeus. Men parted as Thaddeus led Jack through the throng. Stephan followed with Jack's vestments and religious accouterments. Walt was right behind with his camera, and then came the general. Many men were reaching out to touch Jack's shoulders as he slowly followed Thaddeus.

At the front edge of the throng, Jack stopped abruptly and gaped. A long moment passed before he closed his mouth. He turned toward Thaddeus who merely shrugged. Walt eased to Jack's side, aimed his camera and depressed the shutter button. "Picture number one, Father Brecker."

"I'll say." Jack shook his head in disbelief.

"You are pleased, Father?" Thaddeus asked.

"Who...who wouldn't be? This is...it's magnificent."

"I...we...all of us are pleased you approve," said Thaddeus. "May I tell our men?"

"By all means, yes, please do," Jack replied.

Thaddeus shouted his translation to the brigade and the men cheered again.

"Well, Father," Walt said dryly, "I don't think you're going to be saying Mass from the hood of a jeep this afternoon."

On Good Friday, after Thaddeus had returned to Upper Largo from his introduction to Father Jack Brecker, he had put things in motion. He had dispatched the brigade's most accomplished scroungers. He had put to work the skilled soldier craftsmen who had built the brigade's jump practice tower. On this Easter Sunday afternoon, Jack was marveling at the results of their efforts with unmitigated awe.

No, today, there would be no jeep-hood-as-altar. The scroungers had confiscated the materials for the craftsmen to build an altar. First, they had built a wood riser 24 inches high, 10 feet long and six feet deep. On top of that they had used more wood to nail together a stout altar 40 inches high and six feet wide. Behind the altar, on the first level of the jump practice tower, they had constructed a simple wood tabernacle. On top of it was affixed a small brass cross.

The scroungers had been creative, operating at their confiscatory best. The altar was covered with clean white bed linens. There were no candles; the scroungers knew they wouldn't stay lighted in brisk afternoon Scottish winds. But they had requisitioned two lovely green potted plants and two bouquets of yellow daffodils. Their vases: two spent artillery shell casings. Their final touch: on either side of the tabernacle, flying from the jump practice tower were the Polish and U.S. flags.

"You are the first American soldier most of our men have seen," Thaddeus observed. "We thought the flags would be appropriate."

"Very appropriate," Jack murmured. "I don't think I've ever seen flags look more fitting."

Jack looked at Stephan and motioned him to accompany him. They walked to the side of the altar where Stephan helped Jack into his brightly colored vestments. The brigade remained hushed. Jack made some quick, small adjustments to his vestments and then he and Stephan stepped onto the riser. Stephan held two boxes. One held Communion wafers, the second a paten, chalice, large missal and two cruets -- one containing wine, the other water. Jack placed these items on the altar and inserted the Communion wafers into the tabernacle. "Would you stay and assist me?" Jack asked Stephan.

Thaddeus quickly translated, and Stephan blushed and smiled. "Yes, but it has been many years since I was an altar boy."

Thaddeus translated for Jack who said, "Not a problem. Just follow my lead. I'll direct you with my hands."

Everybody ready, Jack stood looking at his expectant congregation. First, using both arms, he beckoned the Poles to edge closer to the altar. Then a thought occurred to him. This is a day, he concluded instantly, that calls for an addition to the order of Mass. With no hesitation, Jack turned his back to the altar and the men, looked up and snapped and held a solemn salute to the U.S. flag. Then he turned and did likewise to the Polish flag. Immediately, tears began welling in men's eyes and lumps began forming in their throats. Then Jack turned to face the men, raised his arms and the Mass was underway.

†††

During the Mass and afterward, Walt used all of his black and white film. Jack, he was thinking as he carefully composed picture after picture, these will tell a story you'll long remember. Hmmm…Bet Stars And Stripes would run at least a couple of them.

After the final blessing, Jack shook hands – hundreds of them -- for a good 15 minutes. At the jeep, Henryk, one of the cow pen soldiers, handed Jack a small box. "Please, open it," Henryk said, gesturing clearly. Again, Jack needed no translation. Inside was a crucifix, fashioned from brass, about six inches long both vertically and horizontally. On the horizontal was etched Fr.Brecker and on the vertical Polska.

"Thank you ever so much," Jack said softly. He held the crucifix high over his head for all to see. "I will treasure this always."

Thaddeus then spoke. "This is but a small token of our appreciation. We cannot possibly thank you enough for coming. You have made this Easter truly special for our men. It has done wonders for their morale."

"You have it wrong, Captain Metz. It is I who cannot thank you enough for allowing me to join you and your men. I can see clearly that they are men of great moral strength and character."

"Thank you, Father. If it is all right with you, I will not join you for the return flight."

"Oh, no problem at all," Jack said quickly. "It is quite unnecessary."

Thaddeus smiled. "I am afraid you don't understand, Father."

"Oh?"

"We insist on sending an escort with you. But if it is all right with you, I would like to ask one of my men to perform this role."

"Of course," said Jack.

"This is Marek," Thaddeus said, and Marek stepped forward and extended his hand. Jack took it immediately and shook. "Marek is like Stephan. He, too, has been with me for the last five years. He and I both were injured at Dunkirk. He would consider it a great honor to ride with you in the plane back to the Eighty-Second."

Jack nodded. "Please tell Marek it will be very much my privilege to have such a brave warrior as my escort."

"Marek, Jerzy, Stephan, Henryk, a few others and I and General Sosabowski…We call ourselves the cow pen soldiers," Thaddeus said softly and proudly. "Perhaps some day I will tell you why."

Jack smiled. "Some Indians call me the desert priest. If our paths should cross again, perhaps I'll explain why."

Thaddeus laughed. "Cow pen soldiers and a desert priest. Surely our paths must cross again."

Part 3

Chapter 34

June 5, 1944. The Cleveland Indians were struggling, but player-manager Lou Boudreau was sizzling with his bat. He was hitting well over .300, easily the highest average of his career to date. Despite the daily grind of leading a major league team, long hours of train travel and the stresses of playing shortstop, Boudreau, one of only a handful of college graduates in the major leagues, thought often of teammate Bob Feller, serving in the Navy, and other major leaguers in military service. Occasionally, too, he thought about Father Jack Brecker – wondered where he was and how he was doing. That previous spring, when Jack had not picked up any of the tickets that Boudreau had left for him for Indians' exhibition games in Tucson, Lou had made inquiries and learned of Jack's decision to become a chaplain. Lou found himself including Jack in his prayers, with a daily request to the Lord to bring Jack back for another game of catch. Meanwhile, Lou kept on hitting at a league-leading clip.

†††

June 5, 1944. George Patton was fidgeting, still unable to accept gracefully or fully his role as a decoy. After stirring victories in Africa and Sicily, Patton was itching for more combat. Instead, he had been assigned command of Operation Fortitude and a dummy "army" near Dover – opposite Calais, with the distance between the two towns the narrowest crossing of the English Channel. Patton's "army" consisted of non-existent troops, plywood "tanks," and rubber balloons shaped as trucks and tanks.

Because Hitler and other German leaders expected the Allies to invade near Calais and because of misleading Allies' radio messages seeming to confirm their belief, the ruse worked splendidly. It led Rommel to keep nine of his 11 armored divisions near Calais, far north and east from the beaches of Normandy.

Patton was thoroughly aware of the operation's success and fully understood its importance. Certainly, he knew of the high regard in which he was held by Germany's leaders – they judged him the Allies' best field general by far – and their expectation that Patton would personally lead the invasion of Europe. Still, Patton felt deprived of what he saw as his ultimate opportunity for achieving lasting glory.

In his quarters, he was pacing, slapping his riding crop against his thigh. Goddammit, he was fuming, Ike is off meeting with invasion troops, smiling and boosting their morale, and here I am, boosting the egos of Hitler and his pussy-footing sycophants. At this very moment, that maniacal bastard is probably gloating over reports that are telling him that he has done everything right to stop the invasion. Patton – history's greatest decoy. That's how I'm destined to be remembered. The general who faked Hitler. What it is, goddammit, is history's greatest shame. No one, no general, certainly not Montgomery or Bradley could end this war as fast as I could. Ike has to know that. I know he knows that. Okay, all right, his approach will save lives. At least during the initial phase of the invasion. I'll give him that. But after that, as the war drags on, how many thousand lives will it cost? I should be leading, not sitting. Lord, please don't let this war come to an end before I have my chance to show the world what military leadership is really all about.

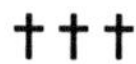

Chapter 35

June 5-6, 1944. "You really don't need to go with us Pathfinders," Captain Walt Hunter said to Father Jack Brecker. "Jumping in the dark is hazardous in the extreme, and you've had just the one practice jump – in daylight." It was about 10 p.m. on June 5, and Captains Hunter and Brecker were standing in a line of men slowly boarding the C-47 transports and the gliders they would be towing across the English Channel to France.

"I appreciate your concern for my safety," Jack replied, "but last I heard chaplains are supposed to demonstrate their faith, not their lack of it."

"Touche, Padre. Let's get onboard."

The Pathfinders included members of the 82nd and 101st Airborne and British 6th Airborne Divisions. Their mission was to jump into Normandy behind the invasion beaches just after midnight. They were to mark out the landing zones that would be used by their comrades from those three divisions beginning about an hour later. Their principal job was to take area bridges and close off possible German escape routes from the beaches.

In the blackness above the Channel, the drone of the engines in the C-47 in which Jack was flying was accompanied only by the hushed rustling of his fingers maneuvering rosary beads. He had begun silently saying the rosary in customary fashion, but after a few minutes realized that his recitation had deviated from Lord's Prayers and Hail Mary's. Dear God, Jack was beseeching, be with these young men tonight. Their mission is one meant to restore freedom to oppressed peoples, to end the tyranny of those who deny you. Please be merciful to them as they go about this holy work. Theirs is a crusade of the highest cause...the noblest order. Bless them, please, and keep them close to you.

As the first in the fleet of 822 husky transports crossed over the French coast, word came from cockpits to make ready. As the 17 men on the C-47 with Jack stood, his right hand motioned a quick blessing. A sergeant opened the fuselage door and cold, bracing air came streaming inside. Jack and the others reached up to fasten their static lines to the overhead anchor cable that ran the length of the troop compartment.

"Ready, Padre?" Walt asked.

Jack nodded and patted Walt's left shoulder. "All set."

Moments later, the "go light" flashed on and the Pathfinders onboard that C-47 and others in the formation began leaping into Hitler's France. Almost immediately, all their training was being tested severely. Beneath the Pathfinders was dense fog, and up through the grayness came arcing tracer bullets. Deceptively entrancing. Deadly. In the rush of air and over his own heavy breathing, Jack heard an anguished scream from below. Just one. But he sensed his first work would be waiting on the ground.

On the way down, Jack concentrated. Keep my knees and feet together. Rotate my torso away from the direction of descent. Keep my chin against my chest. Then another sound. "Ow! Geez!" That shriek, Jack realized, had erupted from his own lips. He felt stinging pain on his left side and wanted to reach across with his right hand and grab the pain's source. He knew, though, that he had to keep his grip on the chute cords. "Oh, man, uh." He could feel blood dripping and spreading beneath his fatigues. Scant seconds later, Jack was thankful when his boots thudded against earth even though, despite focusing on technique, he belly-flopped. He pressed his hands against the ground and pushed himself to a kneeling position.

"You okay, Padre?" It was Walt Hunter's voice.

"Yeah, I think so. I just...There, got it." Jack was referring to his parachute harness buckles. He unfastened them and began pulling the cords and silk toward him and into a tangled bundle. "I heard a scream."

"Over here," said Walt. He led Jack to a young private who was being tended to by a medic. In the darkness, the blood staining the private's face and neck looked black. Jack bent low. The medic looked up. "Nothing I can do, Father," he whispered. "He's yours." For the first time in his young career, Jack Brecker began administering the sacrament of the last rites.

The young soldier died before Jack completed the sacrament. In the darkness, Jack lowered himself so that the lenses of his glasses were almost touching the soldier's name patch: McCreary.

Upon finishing the rites, for the first time, Jack's right hand probed for the source of his own pain and bleeding. He put his hand against his neck and it came away reddened. He felt a second time and realized his extraordinary luck. A bullet, one of those entrancing tracers, had grazed his neck but done no serious damage. "Medic," Jack said calmly, "you should probably put a bandage here – on my neck."

†††

As that night wore on and the first rays of dawn began to brighten the eastern horizon, confusion complicated the airborne's work. Numerous men had missed their assigned landing zones, often bringing them together with men from the other divisions. Compounding their difficulties, about 60 percent of the air-dropped equipment fell into swamps or German hands. Some airborne battalions were so scattered that they took days to sort themselves and reform. The June 6th operation turned out to be the war's last major parachute night drop.

Still, the mixed units managed to work with remarkable effectiveness. They eliminated German artillery and machine gun positions, captured bridges and causeways and closed roads.

Soon after daybreak, Jack and the medic found themselves with a mixed unit that, with Walt Hunter leading, was attempting to knock out a German artillery battery that was pounding Utah Beach, west of Omaha Beach. Stealthily, Hunter's men flanked and surprised the Germans who quickly lost their composure and began fleeing to the east. Jack stood transfixed as American riflemen and machine gunners shot the panicking Germans – all of them, perhaps 20.

After the firing stopped, Jack shook his head sadly and began walking toward the fallen enemy troops.

"Father, wait!" It was Walt Hunter. "Be careful. Some of them might still be alive."

"That's what I'm hoping," Jack murmured. In another minute, he was stepping among the sprawled Germans. Most were dead, but he heard moans coming from four or five. He located a dying German and knelt beside him. Jack could see that his wounds – two rounds had penetrated the soldier's back and torn trough his chest – were mortal. Tears born of pain were moistening the soldier's eyes, and he was coughing blood. His chest was rattling audibly. Jack took the soldier's right hand in his and began administering the last rites.

When he had finished, the medic shouted, "Over here, Padre."

Jack walked hurriedly to the medic who had applied a pressure bandage to a shoulder wound and was injecting morphine. "Bullet tore up his shoulder real bad, but I think he's gonna make it," the medic said. "You're real lucky, Jerry," the corpsman added. "Looks like you'll be a POW instead of a corpse."

Jack knelt beside the young German. In repose, he looked so very small and vulnerable. Only a boy, Jack realized. Can't be more than eighteen. You're a boy in a man's war – or were. Jack pointed to the cross insignia on his helmet, then reached beneath his bloody fatigue shirt and pulled out the St. Christopher medal that Theresa Hassler had given him back in 1932. The young German forced a small smile. "Doc here says you're going to be okay," Jack murmured softly. "Hang in there. No last rites for you. We'll get you medical assistance."

A few of the men were searching German corpses and taking watches and other souvenirs. More were collecting German weapons and ammunition. Still others, including Walt Hunter, were watching the corpsman and Jack go about their work.

Jack heard more moaning. He stood and followed the sound to another downed German. This one, too, Jack felt had a chance to survive. "Doc," Jack called out, "this one should be next. Stay awake, young man," Jack said comfortingly. "I think you will live to see peace."

As the medic came half-running toward him, another man was approaching from behind. "Jack?" he asked.

Jack looked back and up over his left shoulder and blinked. Looking down at him was a face heavily smudged and partially obscured by a helmet that was sitting low over the man's eyebrows. Still, there was no mistaking the man's identity. "Paul! Paul!" Jack stood and the brothers locked arms in bear hugs. "I can't believe it. It's you."

On the ground, the wounded German looked up in puzzlement. Two soldiers hugging on the battlefield? These Americans are strange. They try to kill me then they help me. Then they embrace each other. Strange.

"Yes, big brother, it's me." Paul half-chuckled. "If nothing else it looks like all the confusion produced an unplanned reunion." Paul saw the stained bandage on Jack's neck. "You okay."

"Just a nick. Where've you been?"

"That's what we" -- Paul pointed behind him toward two other members of the 101st – "have been trying to figure out. We dropped into a creek and never did hook up with our company. We've been wandering around all night. We heard shots and decided to have a look. Nice to be with the Eighty-Second, if only temporarily."

"Glad to have you with us," said Jack.

"Oh, hey," said Paul, "this is Roscoe Remlinger and Gary Vanutti. I think they've already figured out who you are."

Jack stuck out his right arm and shook hands with both men. "Nice to meet you."

Before Jack could say anything more, the medic called to him. "Over here, Padre. Another customer. Alive, but needs last rites."

"Okay." Jack turned toward the injured German. "Coming."

"I'll go with you," said Paul. "Nasty business."

"Yeah. I wasn't expecting it to be this nasty. Naïve, I guess."

"Like the rest of us."

†††

"Do you have time to talk a little?" Jack asked Paul

"I guess so. Now that it's daylight, we want to keep trying to find our company – or at least some unit of the Hundred And First."

"Maybe our radio man can help."

"Good idea. You just might make a good soldier." Paul smiled tiredly and then walked to confer with the radioman. Moments later, he returned to Jack's side.

"How long we been in France?" Jack asked. "Six hours? Maybe seven? I've already seen more suffering than in all my life. And gruesome. Look at some of those wounds. Men torn apart. God's creatures made in his image."

"I know. And it's only the beginning. I've been lucky so far. The creek we landed in was shallow. Barely a trickle. We'd been told the Germans were flooding low-lying areas but obviously not that creek. Lucky ducks." Then Paul patted his M-1. "I haven't fired a shot. Wonder how long that will last?"

Jack smiled. "Not long enough." A troubled expression clouded Jack's eyes. "We shot them in the back, Paul."

"They were running away, Jack. Not surrendering. They would've fought again."

"I know."

"There will be more of this, much more. Look around. Some of these men – ours – will be killed. It's bound to happen." A pause. "Could you stand changing subjects?" Paul asked.

"Go ahead."

"Have you been in touch with Theresa? I guess I'm thinking of her because of all this, and she's a nurse. Both of you…In England, I thought you might have talked with her."

"No. And to be honest, I can't say I even thought about her after I got to England. Too busy with training and ministering."

Paul smiled, lovingly. "That's my brother. Nose to the old priestly grindstone." Jack smiled. "You know, big brother, she's always had a thing for you."

"A thing?"

"Yes, a thing." Paul chuckled. "You mean you never even suspected it?"

"Well…we liked each other. Danced a little back in our school days. But we were just kids."

"Kids or not, Jack, you were blind. If you hadn't gone off to seminary… She loved you, man. We all could see it. Knew it."

Jack shook his head and, mouth closed, blew out a breath through his nose. "Maybe it's better that I was blind."

"Yeah. Maybe."

"Do you know where she is now?" Jack asked.

"Not for sure. But if she's not in France now, she'll probably be here soon. I'm sure they'll be setting up aid stations and evac hospitals damn soon, if they haven't already."

"Her boyfriend. The pilot…"

"No word on him in four years," said Paul. "Probably dead or in a POW camp."

"Poor man. Lord have mercy. Poor Theresa." Jack rubbed his chin with his right hand. Then he fingered the St. Christopher medal.

Paul smiled. "You may never see her again, but she made sure you won't forget her, huh?"

"No. No, I won't." A long, mildly strained pause. "Well, come what may, I hope she finds peace and happiness."

"She deserves it," said Paul. "Well, brother, I should check with your radioman. See if he's learned anything."

"Right. Look, Paul, take care of yourself. If you never have to fire that rifle, don't let it get to you. Count yourself lucky. If the war comes to you, that's one thing. But don't go looking for trouble."

"That's three of you," Paul grinned.

"Three?"

"A pressman at the Salesbook – a World War One vet -- Tom and you have all told me the same thing -- keep my head down."

"I hope you're taking it to heart."

"I'll promise you this much. I'll do what I need to do. That's all. I'm not looking for medals."

"Good. Tom's got all the medals this family needs."

"Amen."

Jack smiled. "Amen, little brother."

†††

June 6, 1944. In Warsaw, two hours ahead of Normandy, in her tiny room, Bernadeta Gudek was awake early. She lay on her small bed, staring at the ceiling. She was feeling ambivalent. Cheering her was the knowledge that the Russian Army was continuing to push back the hated Germans. In fact, the Russians, once on the brink of collapse, now were proving relentless in attacking and defeating Germans. Tempering Bernadeta's optimism was the knowledge that Stalin couldn't be trusted. He had been happy enough to agree with Hitler to partition Poland on August 23, 1939 or more than a week before Germany invaded us. Now, if the Russians succeed in pushing the Wehrmacht back into Germany, will Stalin be satisfied with liberating Poland or, Bernadeta was wondering, will he occupy us? Perhaps permanently? Perhaps as ruthlessly as the Nazis? Will I ever again experience life like I lived it before the Germans invaded? Will I ever be able to return openly to the farm? To live a life of peace? Be a wife and mother?

America. A name that can inspire hope, Bernadeta mused. I keep hearing that the Americans will invade western Europe, but I've been hearing that for two years. Will they really come? And if they do, can they push the Germans back like the Russians are doing? Kaz points out that the Russians had an advantage. They started their push on their own ground. Their homeland. They did not have to cross an ocean. They did not have to organize, equip and train for amphibious landings which is what Kaz says the Americans would need to do to invade western Europe, just like they did in Africa, Sicily and Italy. And they – the Russians – have genuine hatred – an unquenchable zeal for revenge – to motivate them. The Americans…I can see why they would hate Japan and want to take revenge. But Europe…Hitler…Would American soldiers fight as hard against the Germans? Bernadeta rocked her head back and forth on the pillow. Perhaps it is better I don't have the answer – especially if the answer is, No, they won't.

That morning, Bernadeta, as usual, ate little. Some bread, a little cheese, some ersatz coffee. She knew her strength and stamina had diminished. She tried not to worry about what the poor diet might be doing to her health. She had lost weight but wasn't certain how much. Finding a scales and weighing herself hadn't been a priority in Warsaw.

The weather that morning was sunny and mild. The stroll from her cramped room to St. Anne's would be pleasant, but Bernadeta knew the church's basement would be cool so she carried a blue sweater over her arm. She was wondering what news this day might bring.

†††

June 6, 1944. "How reliable is your source?" Captain Gerhard Oberster asked Lieutenant Paul Kohler.

"I'm not sure. She's not the same one who told us about the Jewish families. That much I know."

"Hmmm…And now this other woman is telling us that she thinks a local family is buying more food than they can consume. Pretty flimsy evidence."

"Agreed," said Kohler, "but perhaps worth investigating."

"Why is she informing?"

"She says it's because she thinks they might be helping the Jews, but I think it might be some sort of petty jealousy. Perhaps both."

Oberster shook his head in dismay. “Hate and jealousy. Twisted motives.” He rolled his eyes upward. “This family she suspects, they are wine merchants?”

“Yes,” Kohler replied. “They have their own vineyards, make their own wines. They sell them here and in nearby villages. They ship some to Colmar and Strasbourg for sale there.”

“So,” said Captain Oberster, “they likely entertain at their home.”

“Probably.”

“Yes. Quite likely, if they are good business people.” Oberster sighed. “All right, I suppose we should have a look. Take some men and pay them a visit. Search their home. Ask questions. Be polite.”

“Yes, Sir. This morning?”

“Why not? This is proving to be just another ordinary day in an occupation that has seen too many ordinary days. Boring days.” A pause. “Don’t tell the men I said that.”

“With all due respect, Sir, the men have been saying the same thing for a long time. Some of them still think boredom is behind the disappearances of Hoffman and Boehler.”

“Even after I executed Mayor Javelot?”

“I’m afraid so, Sir.”

“I know the men aren’t stupid, but it was just too much of a coincidence for both Hoffman and Boehler to disappear without a trace. I have to believe something happened to them. Something drastic.”

†††

Paying for the food to feed the Steiners and Somers had not been a problem. The Peiffers could afford to buy extra food and so could Maurice Trimbach. The Steiners and Somers were contributing the cash they had taken with them when they had fled their homes for the castle ruins. Unfortunately, they couldn’t withdraw any cash from their bank accounts or arrange for the Peiffers or Maurice to do it for them without arousing suspicion and risking more Nazi investigation. Logistics – shopping for the extra food and getting it inside the Peiffers’ home – were trickier. Sonia and Lea Peiffer and Maurice took care to buy food in ordinary quantities but at different shops and with no set schedule. Maurice had continued to violate the curfew frequently and skillfully. He knew well the Germans’ patrol routines which had become more regular than militarily wise but were the result of understandable complacency.

Lieutenant Kohler took a corporal and five privates and began walking toward Rue des Boulangers. It was a little after 8 a.m. From the window in his office at the Hostellerie de Ribeaupierre, Captain Oberster watched the squad as they proceeded north on the Grand'Rue. Sometimes, he thought, I almost wish I shared Hitler's maniacal hatred of the Jews. It's irrational. Jews. They work like we do, live and laugh like we do. To declare them sub-human, to be evil incarnate, it's something out of the Dark Ages. But is Hitler rational? He invades Poland and France and other countries and we win easily. But Russia. The first lesson of military history, one we all heard, is Don't invade Russia. Then he declares war on America. Foolish. Some of my family – aunts, uncles, cousins -- have emigrated there. In their letters before the war, they talked of what a wonderful country America is. Full of hope and energy. Even during their Great Depression, they didn't abandon hope. It's too bad I can't receive letters from them now. We've already seen America's military strength in Africa, Sicily and Italy. Can France be far behind? The Jews. If Kohler finds them, I'll have no choice. Deport them immediately. To almost certain death. And, yes, execute their keepers. Their protectors. Immediately. I would have no choice. A bad business.

Oberster's phone rang and he picked up the receiver. "You are quite sure?" he asked. "I see. Well, it was only a matter of time...Yes, Sir, we will carry on. Heil Hitler." Oberster put the receiver back in its cradle. "Corporal," he called to his aide outside the office. "Come here, please."

†††

Lieutenant Kohler and his men rounded the corner into Rue des Boulangers. At the Peiffer's home, he knocked firmly. Klaus Peiffer answered. "Yes?"

"We are here to search your premises."

"What? Why?"

"That's our business," Kohler replied sharply. Politeness, he reminded himself, didn't preclude firmness. He stepped past Klaus and motioned his men to follow. Sonia and Lea appeared in the hallway. "Where is the entrance to your cellars?"

"In back," Sonia replied, fear quickly gripping her.

"Lead these two men," Kohler ordered. "Show them everything."

"Yes, Sir," Sonia replied meekly. I know they can see my fear, she told herself. Try to stay calm.

"You two," Kohler ordered, "search this floor. Thoroughly. You two," he said to the remaining soldiers, "follow me upstairs. Come with us," he said to Lea who, like her mother, was struggling to conceal her fright.

Klaus watched uneasily as the seven soldiers separated to begin searching.

Two soldiers let Sonia lift one of the two cellar doors, and then one of them reached down and raised the second door. Sonia switched on a light and down the stairs they went. She switched on a second light and let the soldiers step in front of her.

"So much wine," one soldier remarked. "I've never seen so much."

"Maybe we should pay a return visit," the second joked. Sonia said nothing. The soldiers walked between rows of racks as they moved farther into the cellar's reaches. One came to a doorway. "What's this?" he asked.

"Our tasting room."

"Lights?"

"The switch is just inside," said Sonia.

The soldier switched on the light. He saw more racks of wine, tables, buckets, a corkscrew. Nothing else. Sonia took care each morning to roll up the sleeping mats and conceal them and the emptied chamber pot in a large aging barrel into which a side portal had been cut – the side away from any light.

"Any other rooms down here?" A soldier asked Sonia.

"No."

The two soldiers looked cursorily between the most distant rows of racks. Sonia didn't offer to switch on more lights and they didn't ask. They paid no attention to the floor in the cellar's darkest corners.

"Let's go back up," said one. Outside again, they lowered the two cellar doors. "Not locked?" one asked Sonia.

"There has been no need."

†††

"If I knew what you were looking for," Lea said timidly, "I could tell you if we have it."

"How very helpful," Lieutenant Kohler said with cutting sarcasm. "I'm sure you would tell us if you were harboring Jews."

"Jews?!"

"Oh, please," Kohler said disgustedly, "everyone in Ribeauville knows the Jewish families disappeared."

"Yes," said Lea, "but-"

"But," Kohler cut her off, "you think we deported them."

"Yes," said Lea, "it is what we've heard." Lea felt her racing pulse beginning to slow. Her acting seemed to be having a calming effect.

"Nothing on this floor, Sir," said one of the privates.

"There is another floor," said Kohler. "Let's go up. You, too," he said to Lea.

"I have nothing personal against Jews," Lea said evenly, "but I would never have one actually living in our house."

"Is that so?" said Kohler. "Why?"

"They're different, aren't they?" Lea replied.

"Oh, yes," said Kohler, "very different."

"Nothing here, Sir," one of the privates reported.

"Your attic…" said Kohler.

"There's nothing there."

"Why"

"No entrance."

"No? Why?" Kohler asked.

"I don't know," said Lea. "Our house is very old. I've never heard Father or Mother talk about it."

Above Lieutenant Kohler's and Lea's heads, in the attic, the Steiners and Somers, all six of them, were straining to hear the conversation below. They couldn't make out the words, but they knew they were hearing a German accent and that was enough to cause fright.

"I'm not sure I should believe you," said Kohler. "Go fetch your father. We'll wait – and keep looking. You," Kohler said to one of the privates, "go with her."

Lea turned and walked down the stairs to the floor below, the private trailing behind. As she moved to descend to the ground floor, Captain Oberster's aide was climbing the steps hurriedly. "Look out," he said to Lea and the private who stepped aside to let him pass. "Lieutenant!" the corporal called out.

From the floor above came a shouted reply. "Yes?"

"Lieutenant, Captain Oberster wants to see you."

"After we have completed our search," said Kohler, still shouting as the aide climbed the stairs to the third level.

A trifle winded, the aide said, "The captain said it was urgent."

"Urgent?"

"Yes, Sir. He is expecting you to come now."

Kohler sighed, then growled to the remaining soldier. "All right. Let's go. Let's see what's so urgent. Do you know what it is?"

"With all due respect, Sir, I think you should hear it from Captain Oberster."

On the ground floor, Kohler spoke. "Anything in the cellar?"

"Just wine, Sir. Lots of wine."

"All right," said Kohler, "let's get back to the hotel. The corporal here says Captain Oberster has something urgent to share." To Klaus Peiffer, he said, "For your sake, I hope you had nothing to do with the Jews' disappearance." Kohler was thinking that, later, he would have sharp words with his informant: Bring me reliable information or keep quiet. I have no stomach for embarrassing myself before the captain. He and I are friends, well as friendly as one can be with a superior officer, and I don't want to lose his respect because of flawed intelligence.

†††

June 6, 1944. Over the BBC, Theresa Hassler and the other nurses were listening raptly to the stirring words of Prime Minister Winston Churchill. The Allies' forces had invaded France, and the great crusade of liberation from Hitler's oppression was underway.

"When do we go?" Theresa asked Lieutenant Colonel Marilyn Carter.

"Four days, I'm told."

"That long?"

"To be honest," said Carter, "I think that's because the troops need to gain a foothold and no one is quite sure when that will happen – if it will happen."

"Churchill just said –"

"Would he say anything else? Anything less? Certainly he wouldn't betray any doubts. That would hurt morale and give Hitler juicy propaganda ammunition to motivate his troops."

"Meanwhile, the injured…Men are being shot…"

"Yes," said Colonel Carter, "no doubt they are, even as we speak. Our corpsmen will have to make do as best they can. And men wounded on the beaches, boats should still be there to take them on, bring them back to England."

"If…When our troops begin to push inland –"

"Precisely," Colonel Carter cut in, "that's when we'll be needed. No boats handy. They'll need aid stations and evacs. Don't worry," she said, smiling kindly, "I have a feeling there will be plenty for us to do."

"Maybe too much," Theresa said somberly.

"Very likely," said the colonel, "very likely."

†††

"Yes, Sir, what is it?" Lieutenant Kohler said upon entering Captain Oberster's office and saluting.

"Sit down, Kohler," Oberster said, motioning toward one of the two chairs across from his desk. "The news isn't good."

"Oh?"

"The Allies have invaded France."

"When, Sir? Where?" Kohler spluttered. The alarm on his face was visible immediately.

"This morning. Normandy."

"Normandy? Not Calais?"

"Normandy. They seem to be coming ashore along a broad front."

"Can we stop them?" Kohler asked.

"I don't know. Oh, I'm sure Rommel will try to push them back into the sea. But can we?"

"Our defenses are strong," said Kohler.

Oberster smiled wryly. "Is that a statement of your belief or a question?"

Kohler smiled nervously in return. "I'm not sure, Sir." A brief pause. "The French also had strong, fixed defenses and they did little good. What do you think this means for us?"

"Well, this morning only one thing is certain; we have more questions than answers. I will tell you this. I think we should be flexible. I don't think we should be surprised if we are ordered to leave here to join a front-line combat unit. In Normandy…or on the Eastern Front."

Kohler nodded. "I think Normandy would be preferable."

"The way things are going in the east, I agree."

"I should tell the men about this."

"Yes, no need to try to keep it a secret. They'll be hearing rumors soon enough anyway."

"Right, Sir."

"Kohler?"

"How was the search? Turn up anything?"

Kohler had to refocus his thoughts. He reddened. "Nothing, Sir. An empty house. A full wine cellar."

"Hmmm…your informant?"

"I will have words with her. No information is better than bad information. Now the whole village will know about the search. She needs to know that – and will. In the strongest possible terms."

"It may be too late," Oberster observed.

"I know, Sir. I'm sorry." The apology was not easy for Kohler to articulate, but common sense was telling him it was the most effective way to avoid creating lasting friction between him and Oberster. And should Oberster have any say about the course of Kohler's next military assignment, he didn't want lingering animosity influencing Oberster's decision. "This is embarrassing and possibly damaging and it will not happen again."

"Very good," Oberster said evenly, "but don't make promises you might not be able to keep."

"No, Sir. Will that be all, Sir?"

"Yes," Oberster said, somewhat distractedly, "you may leave."

Kohler stood, saluted and turned to exit.

"Lieutenant."

"Yes, Sir?"

"Some secrets are best kept. Minimizes risks."

"Yes, Sir."

"Sometimes, though, a man still feels compelled to reveal…to share a secret."

"I understand, Sir."

"I'm not a Nazi…Not a party member."

"You needn't worry, Sir. Your secret's safe. I'm not either."

"Thank you."

Kohler saluted again and left. Slowly, Oberster rose to his feet, turned and looked out the window onto the Grand' Rue. Losing this war, he was thinking, might not be the worst thing – if we live through the defeat.

Chapter 36

In the days following the Allies' invasion at Normandy, Lea Peiffers' emotions were fluctuating between elation and consternation. News of the invasion sent spirits soaring among the people of Ribeauville. For some villagers, it was a struggle to conceal their joy from Captain Oberster and his occupation contingent.

The local German soldiers were less concerned about the villagers' increasing optimism than their own potential fates. All now were anticipating new assignments, and all expected them to be more challenging – and far more dangerous – than the environment in Ribeauville.

Lea's consternation was resulting from a decision made by her good friend, Maurice Trimbach. Upon learning that the Natzwiller concentration camp was receiving large numbers of transfers from death camps in Poland and from French jails, Maurice and leaders of other Resistance cells throughout the Alsace had decided to try attacking and freeing the prisoners at Natzwiller. The camp's population was in the process of soaring from 4,000 to 7,000. Lea knew the partisans' mission was fraught with peril. It was why Maurice had flatly forbidden Lea to join the operation. "Don't even think about it," he had said, and his eyes and tone made it clear that he would brook no debate on the matter. At that moment, what neither Maurice nor Lea knew was that an informant had cost the Resistance its advantage of surprise.

Upon being alerted that an attack was in the making, Natzwiller's Commandant Josef Kramer immediately made three decisions. First, he halted daily labor routines outside the camp and instead put prisoners to work digging a deep trench around the camp's perimeter. Second, he had quickly decided to machine gun prisoners if the camp were attacked. Third, Kramer alerted the Schutzstaffel (SS) which began organizing a determined hunt for partisans in the area.

The SS initiative was successful. Within days, trucks carrying captured partisans – men and women – were entering Natzwiller's main gate, and their executions began immediately. Some were hanged, some shot, some injected with poisons, all cremated.

When word of Kramer's atrocities reached Lea, she agonized over whether to share this development with the Steiners and Somers. Eventually, she decided to tell them all she knew – good news and bad. Lea reasoned that the more her Jewish friends knew, the more time they would spend worrying about the plight of others and the less about their own ongoing predicament.

The SS roundup of partisans and Kramer's defensive preparations gutted the planned attack on Natzwiller. Still, there were groups of partisans on the loose, with most trying to evade capture and return to their towns and villages. Some, though, still hadn't begun their retreat and remained in the camp's vicinity. Maurice found himself in such a group.

One night, from the crest of a hill near Natzwiller, Maurice and a group of seven partisans could hear gunshots and see the chimneys of the camp's crematorium burning red. Then Maurice and the others heard another sound, and it sent shivers of terror up and down their spines. It was the agitated barking of SS dogs.

The initial reaction of the partisans was to flee immediately. "Wait," Maurice said, holding his arms up, palms pointed outward, "wait." The other partisans paused. "Listen, listen carefully. Let's try to determine how many dogs they have." Maurice and the other partisans listened intently to the barking. "Three, I think," Maurice said.

Another partisan murmured, "I think you are right."

Maurice nodded his agreement. "We have a choice. We can split up and make a run for our villages. Any of us is free to do that. Without recrimination. We've already lost too many of our people in this operation. Or, we can try to kill the dogs and the Nazis." Maurice paused.

"Go on," a fellow partisan said calmly.

"Three dogs. If we are right, I'm guessing no more than a dozen or so Nazis. That's more than we have. But the Nazis would be expecting their prey to flee. What if their prey attacked."

"We are well-armed," a partisan observed, patting his captured schmeisser machine pistol. In fact, all seven in the group had machine pistols as well as lugers and mausers. Four also were carrying German grenades.

"Yes," said Maurice, "and even though we no longer have surprise on our side to attack the camp, we do have it to attack the Nazi hunting party."

"Your plan?"

"It's pretty simple," said Maurice. "We don't have the men or the time for anything complicated." The others nodded. "You three," he said, pointing at three of his companions, "circle to the left of the barking. You three go to the right. I will wait right here. When the barking gets closer, I will make a noise. Shout. When the Nazis close in, I will throw these." He pointed to two German hand grenades hanging from his belt. "Then you all open fire. If the grenades haven't killed the dogs, aim for them first."

"What will you shout?" a fellow partisan asked Maurice.

"I'm not sure. Anything. You'll know it's me."

"Why not shout, 'I give up. Don't shoot. Please'?"

"Good idea," said Maurice. "Sound cowardly."

"First in French, then in German."

"Even better," Maurice acknowledged. "We French," he said wryly, "we are a creative sort, aren't we? Except, of course, for certain of our government officials and generals." The other partisans permitted themselves small chuckles.

"Maurice, what if we fail?" a partisan asked.

Maurice pointed toward the camp and its glowing chimneys. Everyone understood. "I don't plan to be taken alive," Maurice said solemnly. Then he gestured twice with his left arm and the other six partisans divided and began moving among the trees to flank their oncoming predators.

The barking was growing louder. Maurice looked around for the thickest tree trunk. He stepped behind it, put his machine pistol on the ground, and detached the grenades from his belt. He slowly sucked in a deep breath and held it for five full seconds before exhaling. Now, over the barking he could hear the German boots scuffling on the forest floor. Then a German voice. "The dogs are pulling harder. We must be closing in."

"Agreed, " a second voice said loudly to be heard over the canine cacophony. Then the voice shouted, "We know you are there. Come out where we can see you. Put down your weapons. It's no use to resist. We will not hurt you."

Maurice's eyes rolled upward cynically. What utter bullshit, he was thinking derisively. Surely you don't think we believe that. Then he called out, "We are coming out. Don't shoot, please. And please keep the dogs away." Maurice peaked from behind the tree and saw that the dogs and the soldiers were now about 75 feet away, advancing slowly among the trees. Three dogs, German shepherds, each straining furiously at a short leash. Fourteen Germans, all advancing cautiously, weapons at the ready. Maurice edged from behind the tree, arms dangling at his sides.

One handler immediately released a dog that came charging angrily toward Maurice. With a graceful motion, Maurice swung his arms backward and forward releasing the grenades on a low trajectory. Then he stooped quickly to pick up his machine pistol. Scant moments later the grenades exploded. The blasts detonated behind the lead dog who kept charging. Maurice squeezed the trigger and a hail of bullets went tearing through the air; one smashed into the mouth of the dog who collapsed and rolled over, whimpering.

In that same instant, gunfire erupted. The partisans quickly dispatched the other two dogs. The startled German soldiers began shooting blindly in the darkness. The fire erupting from their gun muzzles provided excellent targets for the partisans. In a minute – no more – the firing ceased. Slowly, cautiously, Maurice and the partisans moved toward the downed Germans and their dogs. Four soldiers and one dog were still alive. One German was on his hands and knees, attempting to rise. A second was curled into a fetal position. Another was sitting, bloodied hands covering a gaping abdominal wound, pleading for mercy and medical attention.

"Everyone all right?" Maurice said to his comrades. A couple replied with murmured affirmatives. The others nodded. "Good," said Maurice. He then removed his luger from its holster and walked to the German trying to stand, put the gun to the soldier's left temple and squeezed the trigger. The force of the bullet's impact sent the German sprawling. Maurice was feeling neither pity nor remorse. Then he walked to the whimpering dog and shot it through an ear. One of Maurice's comrades walked to the sitting German and shot him through an eye. Two more partisans executed the remaining pair of wounded Germans.

"That's it," one partisan said grimly.

"We can expect more Germans soon," Maurice said. "We need to move on. It's been my privilege to work with you, Gentlemen. Let's return to our villages. And let's hope the Allies reach this area soon. Liberate the camp." The men nodded. "One more thing," Maurice said, "let's hope our paths cross again after liberation. It would be nice to toast life instead of death."

The seven men shook hands, glanced briefly at their slain enemies, and slipped away into the darkness in varying directions.

Chapter 37

On July 30, George Patton's troops brushed aside light resistance and captured Avranches and its key road junction at the base of the Cotentin Peninsula and southwest of Normandy's beaches.

On August 1, his 3rd Army was officially activated. "Now we'll begin showing our real stuff," Patton boasted to his chief aide, Colonel Charles Codman. "No more of that phoney baloney with rubber tanks and trucks. Look at these men. Trained splendidly. Excellent equipment. Raring to go. Nothing can stop them. Certainly no worn-out sonsabitchin' Nazis. We are going to end this war and damned fast. We'll leave Monty in our dust – again, just like we did in Sicily."

Within 24 hours, while Allied air power and armor held open a five-mile gap at Avranches, Patton pushed four divisions through the town and onto the roads of France. By August 8, 3rd Army had sped 85 miles southeast to LeMans where it outflanked and destroyed a German panzer division. In all, during 3rd Army's first 11 days on the march, it would advance 160 miles, putting it within 50 miles southwest of Paris.

Patton was euphoric. Victory and glory were accruing in his soldierly account.

†††

Some 1,000 miles farther east on the night of July 31 in Warsaw, emotions also were running high, but no one would mistake the prevailing feeling for euphoria. Hope, determination and fear all were present in large measures.

"Tomorrow it begins," Kaz Majos said to Bernadeta Gudek and the other 30 partisans gathered in a basement room of St. Anne's church. "Our long wait is over. All over Warsaw, our fellow citizens are ready to rise up. We now have arms. Ammunition. We want to inflict as much death and pain on the Nazis as possible. Drive them from Warsaw if we can. We will hold nothing back. Nothing in reserve. We must capture the spirit of the Jews who fought so bravely in their ghetto. The ones who escaped and joined us will fight to the death." Kaz could feel the tide of his emotions rising fast and threatening to roll over him. He paused to gather himself.

He lowered his voice and spoke more slowly. "Sleep will be hard to come by tonight, but try to rest and be fresh in the morning. This is our time to show the Nazis – all the world – that we Poles have not given up the dream of regaining our freedom." Kaz surveyed his comrades' faces drawn tight by intensity. "It is likely that some of us will not survive this battle. I want you to know you all will be in my prayers tonight." Another pause, a briefer one. "Does anyone have any questions? Is everyone clear on their roles for tomorrow?"

"Kaz." The voice spoke his name softly.

"Yes, Bernadeta?"

"The Russians. They have been promising us aid and now they are not far away on the other side of the Vistula. Do they know our uprising begins tomorrow?"

"Yes," said Kaz, "they do."

"Do you think they will honor their promise? Do you think they will push hard to Warsaw to help us?"

Kaz sighed and scanned the faces of his fellow partisans, now among his closest friends. "You said it yourself once before," Kaz said mildly. "You don't trust Stalin. I want to in this case but I don't either. If the Russians drive to help us, I will be ecstatic. If they don't, I will not be surprised." Kaz closed his eyes, intertwined his fingers and squeezed them. Eyes open again, he continued. "I think Stalin will be more than happy to let us kill as many Germans as we can…to let us spare Russian lives. And he has no love for Poles. I hope I am wrong, but I don't want any of us to begin this uprising with false optimism."

†††

In a corner of a room in the church basement that they had come to think of as theirs, Bernadeta and Kaz laid out blankets on the floor. They eased themselves down and reclined, side by side. All candles in the basement were extinguished but one. For long minutes, nothing was said. Then Bernadeta whispered, "What are you thinking?"

"Actually," Kaz murmured, "I was praying."

"For our success? For our safety? For God's blessing?"

"Yes. All of that. But also that this won't be our last night together."

"It won't be."

In the near darkness, Kaz grinned. "I'm glad you are so certain."

Bernadeta smiled in return, her eyes searching his. She draped her left arm over Kaz's shoulders and pulled herself closer to him. "One of us has to be."

Early the next morning, the 32 members of the Home Army cell in St. Anne's basement were awake early, checking weapons and ammunition, reviewing their plan one final time. Other partisan cells around Warsaw were doing likewise. A few minutes before 7:30 a.m., Kaz and his comrades climbed the steps from the basement to the church and made their way to the front door. Kaz eased the door open and surveyed the street. The curfew still in effect for a couple more minutes, the street was empty. Kaz looked at his watch, turned to the group behind him and nodded.

Kaz and Bernadeta walked down the church steps and crossed the street. The temperature already was climbing, promising a hot, humid day in the Polish capital. Kaz wore a white short sleeve shirt, Bernadeta a yellow short sleeve blouse. In her right hand she carried a woven shopping basket with a blue cloth visible inside. Kaz hooked Bernadeta's left arm with his right and they began chatting as might a long-married couple. A few steps behind them, similarly dressed, was another couple from the cell. Like Bernadeta, the second woman also carried a shopping basket.

The other 28 members of the cell waited until the lead couples had proceeded about 50 yards, and then they began exiting the church. In twos and threes, staying on the church side of the street, they followed in the same direction. Unlike the lead couples, though, they all had sweaters or raincoats draped over their shoulders or arms. The women also carried cloth shopping bags or woven baskets.

At the first major intersection, Kaz and Bernadeta rounded the corner to the right. The second couple followed. About 60 yards down the street on the right was the entrance to a hotel that was serving as a billet for some 150 German soldiers. As Kaz and Bernadeta neared the hotel entrance, a German emerged, removing a cigarette from a pack. Kaz and Bernadeta did not break stride.

Back at the intersection, the 28 cell members were dividing, some crossing the street, others remaining behind and milling in a group.

As the German raised a lighter to his cigarette, Bernadeta shifted the basket to her left arm. Kaz reached into it and slid his hand beneath the blue cloth. When his hand reappeared, it was holding a luger. As he and Bernadeta passed in front of the German, Kaz extended his right arm and squeezed the trigger. The explosion echoed up and down the street, as the bullet tore through the German's abdomen, separating him from his cigarette and sending him staggering and groaning backward into the hotel entrance.

The second man removed a luger from his companion's basket. He and Kaz simultaneously used the guns' butts as clubs to smash hotel windows. As they were doing so, Bernadeta and the other woman also were reaching into their baskets. In their hands now were a pair of grenades. They pulled the pins and tossed the grenades through the broken windows. Even before the explosions, the two couples were running down the street, away from the intersection.

The pair of explosions sent shards of glass and smoke into the street. The two couples, breathing hard, reached an alley and ducked into it.

Moments later, German soldiers began stumbling from the hotel, some armed, others not. They were coughing, trying to clear smoke from their lungs and eyes. Three of them bore evidence of the flying grenade and window fragments; blood was staining their torn uniforms and gashed faces. When about 30 Germans were in the street, the 28 cell members now were standing and kneeling in a long line across the intersection. One opened fire and the rest followed. Germans began screaming and falling. Some began to return fire. One of the partisans was hit, spun and fell on her back, eyes open in death.

Another dozen Germans came running out of the hotel and five were hit almost immediately. At that moment, six Germans began running in the opposite direction – toward the alley. One was hit, shot in the right buttock, staggered and fell. The other five, including Lieutenant Blatz, reached the alley and braked themselves hard. When they rounded the corner, they were startled to see Kaz, Bernadeta and the other couple all on one knee, right arms extended.

For Lieutenant Blatz, recognition this time came instantly. The farm girl from Zyrardow. Hair dark instead of light but her without doubt. Kneeling there, too, was the partisan who had shot him by the market carts.

The four partisans squeezed their triggers, fire erupted from the muzzles and Germans began falling. Two of the five, including Blatz, got off shots while going down, and Kaz Majos screamed, twisted and fell. In another moment, the five Germans were lying on the alley's cobblestones. Three were dead, two wounded.

Bernadeta and the other woman walked cautiously to the wounded Germans. Blatz looked up at Bernadeta and spoke haltingly – and accusingly -- through his pain. "You lied to me. At the farm, you lied." Almost imperceptibly, Bernadetta nodded. Blatz, grimacing and trying to blink away pain, croaked, "You cannot win."

Bernadeta's reply was hushed. "Nor can you – and what's more, you don't deserve to." She then extended her right arm and shot Blatz in his upper right chest.

The other woman shot the remaining German in the back of his neck and muttered, "Just like you executed Poles."

Then the two women ran back to join the man who was kneeling beside Kaz.

In the street, in front of the hotel, the shooting had stopped.

†††

That morning, similar scenes were playing out across the city. For the first time, many German soldiers in Warsaw were feeling terror. Most never had been under attack, certainly not in the confines of a city where every window, doorway, corner and pile of rubble could erupt instantly with the instruments of maiming or death.

Despite their surprise at the uprising, German senior officers foresaw its quick suppression. They were wrong. Not only did the fighting continue, the spirited Poles at first seized large parts of the city.

Soon, though, Germans began to mount counterattacks, relying heavily on planes and tanks. The Poles held on stubbornly, but Kaz's thinking about Stalin and the nearby Russians proved sadly prophetic. They were content to slow their offensive while Poles and Germans went about killing each other.

Word of the uprising spread rapidly outside Warsaw. When it reached a farm near Zyrardow, Jszef and Tosia and their daughter Barbara reacted not with joy but alarm. They sensed immediately that Bernadeta was in the worst of the combat, if not dead or captured, and they became sick with worry.

"Where are you going?" Tosia asked Barbara as she walked toward the front door of the farmhouse.

"Out."

"Out where?"

"Just out." A pause, then Barbara turned back toward her mother. "I know what you are thinking. Don't worry. I'm not going to try going to Warsaw. I know I would never make it alive. Not now." And then Barbara stepped outside into the heat of an August afternoon on the Polish plains. Her arms folded themselves across her chest and her head drooped. Bernadeta, will I ever see you again? Will we ever laugh together again? Share secrets and dreams? Barbara's arms dropped to her sides and she raised her head skyward. Eyes closed, she let the sun warm her face. Then she turned and walked slowly toward the nearby woods. Minutes later, she was standing where the cow pen soldiers had buried the two German guards. Five years, Barbara reflected. Next month it will be five years since Hitler sent his army against us. Barbara stared down at the burial site, covered with forest undergrowth. Then she spat.

Chapter 38

August 1944 saw the Allies tightening a noose around German forces in France. On August 15, the Allies succeeded with an amphibious landing on France's south coast between Cannes and Toulon. The U.S. 7th Army and French 1st Army met little resistance as they began rolling up the Rhone Valley. Within a month, they would be joining Patton's 3rd Army at Epinal, just 35 miles west of Ribeauville.

On August 19, as American and French forces neared Paris, excitement – and organized resistance – were nearing a crescendo. The Paris police, little more than puppets during four years of German control, sent a clear message to their Nazi occupiers by going on strike. More unsettling to the Nazis, on that same day, 3,000 armed French police seized the city's prefecture building – Paris' political nerve center.

On August 20, Hitler concluded that, were his troops to lose Paris, there should be nothing left for the liberators or the city's residents to celebrate. He ordered his new commander-in-chief in Paris, General Dietrich von Choltitz, to burn the city. Hitler wanted nothing left "but a pile of ruins." The order appalled von Choltitz. He knew he had neither the number – about 20,000 -- nor quality of troops to withstand a determined Allied push into the city. He delayed, playing for time. He ordered explosive charges wired to all major buildings and bridges but stipulated that none be detonated without his express, written orders.

As the Allies began penetrating the Paris suburbs, some 900 miles to the east, Hitler was convening a senior staff meeting. When he learned that Allied troops were advancing on the city's center, he began screaming, "Is Paris burning?" He looked angrily around the meeting table. When no reply was forthcoming, Hitler ordered Field Marshall Alfred Jodl, chief of his general staff, to personally phone von Choltitz. "Jodl," Hitler bellowed, "I want to know. Is Paris burning? Is Paris burning right now, Jodl?"

On August 25, the French 2nd Armored Division, driving American-built Sherman tanks, went rumbling into central Paris. Delirium erupted. Celebrants clogged city streets and parks. Parisian women who had cohabited with Nazis had their heads shaved and swastikas painted on their foreheads. They were then paraded amidst mass derision.

Following close behind the French was the U.S. 4th Infantry Division which had stepped aside to let French soldiers lead the liberation. The American troops, in their fatigues, went marching soberly down the Champs Elysees in pursuit of the Germans east of the city. In fact, they saw action that afternoon.

At about noon that day, French fireman Captain Sarniguet outraced two French soldiers up the 1,750 steps to the top of the Eiffel Tower where he hoisted a French tri-color to the pinnacle of the flagpole. Sarniguet had fashioned his homemade flag from three old military bedsheets – died pink, washed-out blue and tattletale gray.

Meanwhile, although some Germans were surrendering quickly, others were resisting fiercely, and many Paris streets remained avenues of death. At Nazi headquarters in the lobby of the posh Hotel Meurice on the Rue de Rivoli, just down the street from the Louvre, von Choltitz was negotiating a surrender that enabled him to withdraw his occupying garrison while leaving the City of Light intact. At about 1:30 p.m. on the 25th, von Choltitz himself capitulated meekly to French troops. He wanted to surrender with proper military protocol, presenting his weapon to his conquerors. But he had no weapon of his own and so borrowed a pistol from one of his staff. In the hotel lobby, before a French officer, von Choltitz solemnly laid the pistol on a table.

Although Paris was some 250 miles west of the Rhine, the city's liberation reverberated throughout France, including the Alsace. Germany's high command declared the concentration camp at Natzwiller to be in a war zone. Commandant Josef Kramer wasted little time complying with the order. He began organizing an evacuation. While he and his staff made plans, they continued to receive trainloads of French prisoners from the jails in Epinal, Nancy, Belfort, Rennes and other towns. Arriving prisoners told inmates of the military situation – the Allies pushing east from Paris, the Russians driving to the west. Some inmates began to hope for a quick liberation. Their hopes would be crushed.

On August 31, in the hours leading up to the start of the evacuation on September 1, SS trucks arrived with more captured French partisans. Kramer ordered many of them, men and women alike, murdered immediately, shot in the nape and cremated.

†††

"I feel so absolutely helpless," Maurice Trimbach said sadly to Lea Peiffer. His anguish was both audible and visible. He and Lea were in the Peiffer's sitting room. Three levels above, the Steiners and Somers were silently eating their evening meal. Soon they would be descending to the wine cellar's tasting room to remove their sleeping mats from the huge aging barrel, unroll them and try to sleep away another fitful night.

"You've done so much," Lea replied, trying to buoy Maurice's sagging spirits. She couldn't recall ever before seeing him depressed. She also reminded herself that, strong though he was, he was human and had his limits.

"But I keep thinking about our countrymen at Natzwiller. About their suffering. About their fates. If only the Americans could get here faster."

"They have made amazing progress," Lea observed. "You have said so yourself. I'm hearing their General Patton is advancing so rapidly, the Americans cannot keep him supplied with petrol."

"Yes, I hear the same," Maurice said dispiritedly. He rubbed his eyes and sniffled. "Still, there must be more we can do."

"Perhaps you will think of something." Lea wasn't at all certain of that but was hoping to say something to lift her great good friend's morale. "Maybe there will be another opportunity."

†††

"I'm afraid our party is over" Captain Gerhard Oberster said to Lieutenant Paul Kohler. They were in Oberster's office at the Hostellerie Ribeaupierre.

"We are being ordered elsewhere?"

"North to Metz," Oberster replied. "To help strengthen the fortifications there."

Kohler nodded. "It could be worse."

"I suppose. Instead of trying to stop the Russians, we'll be trying to stop Patton."

"Yes," said Kohler, "but I'm hearing that the Americans are not the merciless thugs that the Russians are."

"I hope your information is accurate because we might well have a chance to test it."

"When do we leave?" Kohler asked.

"Tomorrow morning"

"I'll tell the men."

"Yes. Good."

"Captain?"

"Yes?"

"We've been lucky so far," Kohler observed. "Perhaps our luck will hold."

"Perhaps," Oberster smiled, brightening slightly. "Do you have some dice?"

"No. But I'm sure I can get some."

"Maybe you should," Oberster said, still smiling. "Just be sure they have been proved lucky ones."

"I will do a thorough background check on them," Kohler joked softly. "To be sure they are fit for Wehrmacht duty."

†††

At 10 p.m. on the 31st, the first evacuation started from Natzwiller. Of the 7,000 prisoners, some 2,000 started down the mountain on foot. Guarding them were both SS and Wehrmacht troops, many with police dogs. Most of the prisoners were without shoes. Some wore clogs. Kramer, smoking a cigar, watched this procession get underway from the porch of his quarters.

Later that night at the bottom of the mountain, Kramer arrived in his chauffeured car. He got out and ordered everyone back up the mountain. There was a train waiting at the Natzwiller station, but it had no engine, and Kramer would not chance any prisoners escaping during a long, nighttime wait.

At 5 a.m., the same 2,000 prisoners were again assembled. This time they were loaded into cattle trucks, about 65 men and women in each. Down the mountain they went again. At 10 a.m., they were loaded onto the train. The locomotive's whistle blew twice. The Natzwiller evacuees, eventually all 7,000 of them, would be passing through Strasbourg, Radstadt, Stuttgart, Augsburg. Destination: Dachau. There, liberation by the U.S. 7th Army would arrive but not until April 29, 1945. By then, most of the Natzwiller evacuees would perish.

†††

At 9 a.m. on September 1, a staff car and two troop trucks were parked on the Grand' Rue in front of the Hostellerie Ribeaupierre. Amidst only a low buzz of chatter, Captain Oberster and his men were loading their belongings into the vehicles. Watching motionless from building entrances and windows were a goodly number of Ribeauville's citizens. Word of the Germans' departure had spread rapidly through the village, and some had guessed correctly the route Oberster's men would be taking. A few minutes later, the small convoy headed north on the Grand' Rue. They would be passing through Selestadt, Strasbourg and St. Avold on the way to Metz. It wasn't the most direct route, but it had the advantage of avoiding having to traverse the dangerously climbing, dipping and twisting road through the Vosges Mountains to Nancy and then north to Metz.

†††

As the convoy left Ribeauville, on the third level of the Peiffer's house, Lea pulled a small rug away from in front of a large cupboard and then tugged to pull the cupboard away from an interior wall. She slipped through the opening and climbed steep, narrow stairs. She knocked gently on the door and pushed it open. Inside the attic, the Steiners and Somers all were standing, tensed. They saw Lea's face and relaxed.

"The Germans are leaving Ribeauville," Lea said, smiling kindly. "Permanently. The Allies are closing in. You can come down."

The six Jews hesitated, looking at each other and then at Lea. "Is it safe," Mrs. Steiner asked. "Truly safe?"

"I think so."

"Our homes," said Mrs. Somer, "do you think we can return to them?"

Lea shrugged. "I think so."

"We'll never be able to thank you enough," said Mr. Steiner, brushing away a tear. "You saved our lives." He stepped forward and embraced Lea. "Bless you, Dear, Bless you."

She tried to reply, but her thickening throat limited her to a modest nod.

†††

The road from Ribeauville wound past the mountain atop which sat the St. Ulrich castle ruins that had provided a haven for the Steiners and Somers. As the small convoy rounded a curve, a large, downed tree blocked its way.

Captain Oberster's military instincts kicked in and he reacted immediately. "Out of the trucks!" he shouted. "Now! Now! Everyone out now and take cover."

As his men began leaping from the rear of the two trucks, gunfire erupted. Bullets tore through the windshield of his open staff car. Oberster's driver – the corporal who had served as his aide at the hotel – was hit immediately, blood spurting from his left eye socket and neck.

From both sides of the road, Maurice and his six fellow partisans poured fire among the Germans. Oberster himself dove for cover at the road's edge. He rolled onto his back, raised himself slightly and began shouting. "Men from the first truck, to the right! Men from the second truck, to the left! Get down and stay down! Look for muzzle flashes! Return fire!"

Maurice and his men were impressed by Oberster's poise and the discipline of his men. As the Germans' return fire began tearing at the partisans, Maurice reacted equally decisively. "Fall back! Into the woods! Now!" He and his men on the west side of the road began climbing through the forest that covered the castle-topped mountain. His three men on the east side of the road slipped away into vineyards.

"Cease firing!" Oberster shouted. "Lieutenant Kohler, check the men. Then move this tree off the road. The rest stand guard. If you see movement – even the slightest movement – shoot."

As Oberster's men went about their work, above them on the mountain, from his vantage point, Maurice looked down through his binoculars. He could see now what Oberster already knew. Three Germans lay dead. Four more were wounded; all would survive.

"What do you think?" a partisan asked Maurice.

"We killed some Nazis. Not enough."

"But some..."

"Yes, better than none," Maurice agreed with no hint of enthusiasm or triumph.

Far below, while men were dragging the tree from the road, Lieutenant Kohler stepped to Captain Oberster's side. "Partisans from Ribeauville?"

"Of course," Oberster half-snarled, "where else? They are the ones that Mayor Javelot said didn't exist."

"Shall we return? Impose reprisals?"

"I'd like to, but I think the price would be more of our own lives. That price seems too rich. We'll keep moving toward Metz."

Minutes later, Oberster's men loaded the dead onto the first truck and their wounded aboard the second truck. Then the convoy got underway, continuing north.

From the castle ramparts, Maurice and thee partisans were watching. "Good decision, Oberster," Maurice murmured. "Very wise."

Chapter 39

The idea was British General Bernard Law Montgomery's. Employ the largest Allied airdrop of the war. From bases in England, use 1,500 planes and gliders to parachute 30,000 men and equipment from the 101st and 82nd U.S. Airbornes, British 1st Airborne, and the Polish Airborne Brigade. Their mission: behind German lines, along a 60-mile stretch of a single road running north through The Netherlands, capture and hold six bridges, the last at Arnhem over the Rhine. Driving up that road would be 5,000 men from British XXX Corp's armor and infantry units.

Montgomery's vision: cross the bridge at Arnhem in force into Germany's industrial heartland, bypass the more difficult terrain to the south, and end the war before Christmas. Eisenhower was uneasy with Montgomery's plan, and Patton detested it. Montgomery, with his dogged personality, prevailed and Operation Market Garden was scheduled to get underway on September 17, 1944.

†††

"How did your meeting go?" Captain Thaddeus Metz asked General Stanislaw Sosabowski.

The general's reply was a disgusted growl. "General Urquhart is skeptical, as I am. So is the American general Gavin. We are to be dropped behind German lines in landing zones that are too far from a single road – a raised road – that will make our men and vehicles handy targets for the Germans. Then we are to capture and hold both ends of several bridges while Thirty Corps covers sixty miles in two days. Two days! Montgomery must think the Germans will turn tail at the first glimpse of tanks and infantry. He is a fool. An egotistical fool."

Thaddeus couldn't help smiling inwardly. His beloved Sosabowski, calling Montgomery egotistical, was very much like the pot calling the kettle black. Thaddeus kept his expression blank and merely asked, "But still we go ahead?"

"General Browning, quoting Montgomery in every other sentence, brushes aside all questions and concerns. He is nothing more than Montgomery's puppet."

"The men will be pleased to see action."

"If they aren't massacred," Sosabowski snapped. "I told Browning I should write a letter, saying we were coerced into participating in this madness."

"Will you? Write such a letter?"

"No. If we are massacred, what difference will it make?"

"I will tell the men to make ready," said Thaddeus.

"Yes," said Sosabowski, "and tell them this is a dangerous mission." A pause. "But you needn't tell them of my disagreement with Browning. Bad for morale."

†††

In Warsaw, the uprising was nearing the end of its seventh week. Poles still were fighting desperately, but superior German troop strength and firepower were re-taking parts of the city lost back in the first week of August. Warsaw was being reduced to piles of rubble by German bombs and artillery shells. The Russians still were east of the Vistula River, biding their time. Stalin's pledge to help the Poles was long forgotten.

In the basement of St. Anne's, Bernadeta was finding it difficult to ward off a crushing sadness. She looked down on a church pew that had been ripped loose from the floor above and lowered to the basement. The figure reclining on it, covered with two blankets looked shrunken. In the dim, candle lit basement, his pallid stillness could have had him mistaken for a corpse. Kaz Majos was alive but not yet recovered. Behind his closed eyelids, he sensed a presence. Eyes opening slowly, his tongue flicked across his lips.

"Water?" Bernadeta asked.

Kaz nodded. "So dry. Still so weak. I seem to do nothing but sleep."

"Your body needs it," Bernadeta whispered. "Just a minute." She left their corner and in seconds returned with a small glass of water. She held it, and he took it from her and sipped. He took another sip and returned the glass. Then he began struggling – groaning lowly – to a sitting position. Bernadeta reached down to assist and steady him.

"Smile," he said softly. "I need to see a smile."

Bernadeta responded with a small smile that seemed to push lower the scar that ran downward from the left corner of her lip.

Kaz's smile widened. "I think my scar will be bigger than yours. And much more noticeable." He reached up and fingered tenderly the wound that ran from the outside edge of his right eye back across his temple. "Now all I have to do is get used to seeing with one eye." Bernadeta felt her throat thickening. "Do you think I should take to wearing a patch," Kaz asked playfully.

Bernadeta forced a swallow before speaking. "It would make you far too dashing. You couldn't hope to escape the clutches of every woman in the Home Army."

Kaz chuckled. "Maybe I don't want to escape their clutches. Well, maybe I don't want to escape the clutches of one in particular."

†††

"We'll be following behind Thirty Corps," Lieutenant Colonel Marilyn Carter told the assembled nurses. "We'll have British nurses with us. British doctors will be working with ours. It's a joint operation from A to Z. And by now you all know the dangers, so be careful." By war's end, 201 U.S. Army nurses would die. At Anzio alone, six had been killed in German bombings. "We'll be setting up our evac hospital just south of Eindhoven."

Theresa and her nursing colleagues had seen little rest since landing in Normandy on June 10. Her biggest worry was making a mistake that could be fatal to a wounded soldier. She was depending more and more on caffeine and nicotine to keep up the torrid pace. Other nurses were doing likewise. She was longing for a respite from the carnage – the broken, burned and disfigured men and their pain and depression – but knew that rest could be a long time arriving.

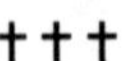

In Boston, dawn had not yet arrived. Mary Catherine Riley lay staring up through the darkness to the ceiling. Beside her, she felt Kevin stirring. "Awake?" she whispered.

"I think so," he said groggily. "Can't sleep?"

"It's been a bad night."

"Hmmm...Worried?"

"I...I just have this sense of dread...this sense that Father Brecker is in danger. Mortal danger."

"It's your Irish instincts playing the devil," Kevin teased. Then, seriously, he said, "I'm sure God is looking out for him."

"Do you really think so?"

"Yes," Kevin said with greater certainty than he actually was feeling. Thousands of other fine young men, he knew, had been under God's watch but still had perished. "I think he will make it through."

Mary Catherine snuggled closer to Kevin. "I so hope you are right." A long pause. "Do you think we'll ever see him again?"

With this reply, Kevin was thinking, I should be truer to my feelings. "I don't know, Dear. You can pray for that but pray harder for his survival."

"Yes, well, if we're going to stay awake, Husband, we can go to the five-thirty Mass."

"We can do that, Wife. And we also can make love."

"That we can."

†††

Corporal Paul Brecker was thankful that this jump, his first since the early hours of June 6 – D-Day – would be taking place in daylight. Although September 17 was a Sunday, there had been no Mass. Inside the C-47, Paul was praying silently and sensed that others were, too. Just get me on the ground in one piece, Lord. Don't let me be shot in the air. That's all I'm asking this day. After that, I'll take what comes.

The 101st Airborne was to land near Eindhoven, the southern most town along the 60-mile stretch of road leading to Arnhem and the bridge over the Rhine.

Below, in a Belgian village, a priest was saying Mass. Part way through the liturgy, he and his parishioners began hearing the steady drone of planes. One parishioner, a boy of 12, rose, exited his pew and began walking toward the church doors. Another boy followed, and then the rest of the congregation did likewise. The priest shrugged and motioned for his two altar boys to follow the crowd as did he. Outside, above them, was the largest armada of aircraft they ever had witnessed. 1,500 planes and gliders. To a person, all stared upward in muted awe. A few had the presence of mind to pray for the men in the sky.

†††

Jack Brecker and others in the 82nd Airborne would be jumping between Grave and Nijmegen, two towns farther north, about 12 miles south of Arnhem along the single, raised road. The British 1st Airborne would be jumping into open fields even closer to Arnhem. The mission of the British was to rush to Arnhem and the bridge over the Rhine, seize both ends and hold on for 48 hours until the arrival of XXX Corps.

General Sosabowski, Thaddeus Metz and the Polish Airborne were scheduled to jump on Day Three, September 19, near Arnhem to reinforce the British.

†††

From a jump altitude of only 700 feet, Paul Brecker made it to earth in one, unscathed piece. So did his buddy, Roscoe Remlinger. Silently, Paul offered a short prayer of gratitude. Thanks, God, I guess it doesn't hurt having a brother for a priest. I'm sure he talks to you when I forget. I know that gives me an edge.

Pathfinders had landed an hour earlier and done an excellent job of marking landing zones. The Germans were surprised. Market Garden seemed to be getting off to a promising start. Encountering little resistance, Paul was among 101st troops that captured the bridge at Veghel. Together, the 101st and XXX Corps liberated several Dutch towns and repulsed several early German counterattacks.

Later that Sunday, near the village of Uden, just north of Veghel, Paul and Roscoe were among a squad scouting the countryside. Ahead was a house and barn on the left side of the road.

"What do you think?" Paul whispered to Roscoe.

"Farms look peaceful. This one looks too peaceful."

The squad approached cautiously, half on either side of the road and widely spaced. A rectangle of white cloth was dangling from the barn's loft doorway. Thirty yards from the barn, Lieutenant Billy Clawson was leading the American squad. He turned and used his hands to direct his men to fan out. Paul was nearing a waist-high stone fence surrounding the barnyard. Inside, three milk cows were munching contentedly on a haystack. In front of the barn and near the house, several chickens were clucking. Paul could see no sign of human activity. He checked his watch. Any time now, a farmer should be coming to milk the cows. He and other soldiers began easing over the fence. Then Paul saw a grenade come sailing out from the loft doorway. He shouted a warning, "Grenade! Down!" As he scrambled back over the fence, the grenade exploded and a fragment struck his right hand, separating it from his M-1 rifle which fell on the barnyard side of the fence. Paul winced as blood streamed from the back of his hand.

"You all right?" Roscoe called. "Paul?"

"Yeah, I'm okay."

German rifle fire poured from the loft doorway and the main barn door below. The cows were panicking, lowing madly and banging into each other.

"We have to clear out the barn," Lieutenant Clawson shouted above the din to his men. "Harrison!"

"Yes, Sir."

"You and I are going to give the Germans a taste of their own – grenades for chow. You put one through the barn door. I'll try to put one into the loft. If I miss, hug the ground. The rest of you provide covering fire. Ready?"

Paul, he and his rifle on opposite sides of the fence, felt useless. Clawson's men nodded and he shouted, "Now!"

Clawson's squad began shooting rapidly, concentrating their fire on the open barn door and loft doorway. As they did so, Clawson and Harrison vaulted the stone fence and went sprinting toward the barn. Clawson had to sidestep one of the frenzied cows. The other two followed Harrison toward the barn door. Harrison flattened himself against the barn wall and, with his left hand, reached out and tossed his grenade through the door. Nearly simultaneously, Lieutenant Clawson was throwing his grenade up toward the loft doorway. His aim was good. Two detonations sent fiery blasts ripping up through and out from the barn's apertures and cracks in its siding.

As Harrison and Clawson pivoted to retreat to the fence, a rifle shot sent Harrison sprawling in the muddy barnyard. One of the panicked cows went running toward the stone fence. Instinctively, Paul ducked low. The cow didn't slow in the slightest. The crash stunned the animal, causing it to collapse among falling stones.

Paul leaped back over the fence to retrieve his M-1 but found it wedged beneath the downed cow. His right hand grabbed the rifle's muzzle and tugged but futilely. Meanwhile, intense German rifle fire was coming from both sides of the haystack. One bullet sent a sharp chip from the stone fence slicing across Roscoe's left cheek. His adrenalin coursing strongly, R didn't feel the wound or notice the blood running down his face and off his chin.

In frustration, Paul loosened a grenade from his belt and lobbed it at the haystack. The explosion sent two Germans stumbling from behind it, smoke momentarily obscuring their vision. One was coughing. R riddled the German on the right. Simultaneously, Paul went sprinting toward the German on the left. During those adrenalin-charged seconds, it didn't occur to Paul that he was reneging on his pledge to Jack, Tom and the Salesbook pressman to do nothing more than was required. The German saw Paul and raised his rifle to fire. Paul lunged and grabbed the German's bayonet with his left hand, forcing it down. The German twisted and pulled the bayonet, and Paul half-screamed a curse as the sharp edges sliced into his palm and fingers. Through the pain, he tried not to lose his grip but failed. On his knees and hands, Paul looked up in time to see the grim-faced German preparing to thrust the bayonet. In that fleeting instant, Paul could see death coming.

Then something caused the German to straighten and rock backward. A round, reddening hole in the German's forehead provided the explanation. The soldier dropped his rifle and fell at Paul's side. Still on his knees and hands, Paul pushed himself up and looked back. R, his face grim and blood-covered, was sending Paul a thumb-up sign. Paul nodded, and then his head and torso began to shiver from the trauma of his near death moment. Paul knew what was happening to his body and thought he might pass out. He remained kneeling calmly until the trembling ceased. Then he rose slowly to his feet and went trudging back to the fence, blood dripping from both hands. The cow, too, had regained its footing, and Paul picked up his mud-caked M-1. Blood from his hands began mixing with the mud.

R approached. "You okay, Paul? You look a little shaky."

"Close call but nothing serious. Thanks."

"Forget it."

"What about your face?"

"Huh?"

"It's bleeding."

R then saw on his uniform the blood that was dripping off his face. Tenderly, he reached up to his cheek. "Ouch. Ricochet?"

Paul shrugged. "Could be. We need to get you patched up."

"You, too," R said, pointing to Paul's bleeding hands.

Lieutenant Clawson was checking on Private Ralph Harrison. Dead from a bullet through his neck. Clawson gulped and breathed deeply. "Anyone else hurt?" Paul and R joined a chorus of "No, Sirs."

"What about the barn?" Clawson asked.

"Three dead Jerries," a private informed him. "Four more hightailing it down the road to Uden."

So much for a good start, Paul was thinking. I wonder what's next.

From the farmhouse emerged a man in overalls and rubber boots. Following were his wife and four young children. "You are Americans?" the man said in halting English.

"Yes," Clawson said wearily.

The farmer tentatively extended his right hand and Clawson took it. "Thank you," the farmer said, "thank you. The Germans ordered us to stay inside. The white cloth was their idea."

"It's all right," Clawson replied.

"We will cover your man," the farmer said, pointing to Private Harrison's body, "and take him to our wood shed."

Clawson nodded. "Thanks."

The farmer's wife saw Paul's bloodied hands and R's torn face and walked toward them. "Please give me your weapon," she said to Paul. "I will clean your hands and bandage them." Paul nodded. Grimacing, he removed the ammunition clip, jerked back the bolt to eject a chambered bullet and handed her the M-1. She then handed the empty rifle to her oldest child who appeared to be about 12. "Clean the mud from this. Be careful." Then, looking intently at R, she said, "I will clean and patch your face." Then the woman took Paul's right arm and led him and R toward the house. R watched them go inside first, his face not hinting at the question that kept jabbing at his thoughts: How in the world will we ever get through this war?

†††

On Day Three, the Poles' first contingent, including General Sosabowski and Thaddeus Metz, took off from England. Their mission was to land at Arnhem, join British Lieutenant Colonel John Frost and his men in defense of the Arnhem bridge, and wait for XXX Corps.

The jump and the landing went badly. The Germans no longer were surprised; several Poles were shot before landing. A few Poles managed to fight their way into Arnhem, but the group was battered badly. The rest of that first contingent, including General Sosabowski and Thaddeus, were pinned against the river. Their plight was symptomatic of the entire operation. Market Garden was unraveling as quickly and inartistically as a ball of string under attack by a litter of frisky kittens. Many British radios were equipped with the wrong crystals, disrupting communications and coordination. Fog was delaying flights of airborne units, including the rest of the Polish Brigade. German resistance was much stiffer than anticipated by General Browning who was so intent on furthering Montgomery's grand plan that he had pooh-poohed reconnaissance photos showing large concentrations of German armor near Arnhem. He had deemed them dummies and non-operational. Attempts to airdrop ammunition and supplies to the airborne troops were failing; most of the parachuted loads were falling into the hands of Germans who had taken control of landing zones. In Arnhem, Lieutenant Colonel Frost and his men already were trying to husband ammunition. They held only one end of the bridge, and the two days they had been told to hold it were now stretching into four.

Frost was feisty. When a German officer under a white flag crossed the bridge on foot to Frost's side to question him about surrendering, Frost's muttered reply was, "Tell them to go to hell." His second-in-command replied more imaginatively, "We'd like to take you all prisoner but we haven't the proper facilities. Sorry."

On the evening of Day Three, Jack Brecker was sitting on the ground near the river at Nijmegen with other members of the 82nd. Nijmegen was the northern most town south of Arnhem, only 10 miles distant. Its long bridge was the last crucial link separating XXX Corps' armor from Lieutenant Colonel Frost's trapped and bloodied men in Arnhem.

Jack looked up to see Major Julian Cook of the 82nd walking among his lounging soldiers. Cook asked for their attention. Jack and the others got to their feet.

"What is it, Sir?"

"Well," Cook said laconically, "we've just been given a doozy of a mission. A real nightmare. We're going to be crossing the river. Taking the far end of the bridge. Our British friends will be taking this end."

"How, Sir?"

"Small boats. British-built. I'd like to think they're worthy of the Royal Navy, but these are army boats, so all bets are off."

A scattering of low chuckles were heard.

"When do we go?" Jack asked.

"As soon as the boats arrive."

"Any idea when that will be?"

"Tonight. Tomorrow morning. As soon as they get here – if they get here. I suggest you all try to get a little rest."

"Anything else, Major?" Jack asked.

"Only that the Rhine is wide and the current strong. If I receive any other cheery information, I'll be only too happy to share it."

Major Cook began walking away. "Sir," Jack said.

Cook stopped and turned. "Yes, Padre?"

Jack sighed. "You called it a nightmare mission and I've no doubt about that. If you'd stay another minute, I'd like to pull the men together for a prayer. Offer a blessing. No sermon, I promise. It might just make their night a little easier."

"Good idea, Padre."

Jack and Captain Walt Hunter called the men together. Major Cook stood by. "Men," Jack said, looking out over the hushed assembly, "during the last three months your sacrifices have been many and great. You have shown tremendous courage and great compassion – for each other and for the people you've liberated. I am certain the Lord is pleased with your efforts. May he please be with you in this next endeavor. Your efforts will put us one step closer to ending this war and bringing peace and setting us on the road home…a road we all look forward to taking. May the good

Lord bless us all. In the name of the Father and of the Son and the Holy Spirit. Amen."

"Amen," came a murmured chorus.

†††

"Theresa?"

She looked inquiringly at the soldier with his bandaged hands. He was standing at the hospital tent entrance, almost 10 feet away. "Paul? Paul!" Her eyes widened in surprise and delight. "Oh, Paul." She quickly closed the gap between them, grasping his arms, then releasing and gently hugging him. "How are you?"

"Embarrassed."

"Embarrassed? Why?"

As Theresa disengaged, Paul extended his arms. "I've seen wounds a lot worse than these and men weren't evac'd."

"Oh, Paul. No one should be embarrassed by war wounds. They can become infected. Damage internal organs. Better to be safe than sorry. We have lost too many men unnecessarily."

"I don't doubt that," Paul said. "But I think I'm here just because Lieutenant Clawson felt I could use a break – and because the Hundred And First has been ordered back south to protect our southern flank from being cut off."

"Lieutenant Clawson strikes me as an officer with good judgment," Theresa smiled.

"Maybe so," Paul acknowledged grudgingly.

"Let me get these bandages off and look at your hands," Theresa said. "Sit."

Paul sat on the edge of a cot. "You're bossy," he teased, "in a nice sort of way."

"Bull-headed soldiers have made me that way," she joked. As Theresa unwound the bandages, she murmured, "It's so good to see someone from back home. From Shelby. It's been so long."

"I think Jack's here, too," Paul replied softly.

Theresa looked up. "In Holland? As part of Market Garden?"

Paul nodded. "He's with the Eighty-Second, and they're having a rough time of it. Rougher than the Hundred And First. They're farther north, closer to Arnhem, and I'm hearing German resistance there is stiffer."

Theresa said nothing, but Paul could see the light in her eyes dimming.

"Your medic did a very good job on your hands," Theresa said. "There will be stiffness for awhile, but they eventually should be as good as new. I'll change the bandages."

"Theresa," Paul murmured, "I think Jack will be okay. I really do."

He saw her eyes moistening. He stood and wrapped his damaged hands around her. "If the Lord is looking over anyone, it's gotta be Jack."

"And how about you, Paul?"

"I've got myself a certified guardian angel," Paul said cheerily.

"Oh?"

"His name is Roscoe."

†††

It wasn't until the afternoon of Day Four that British trucks arrived with the boats. They had been delayed by traffic snarls on the single road and by German artillery. One of the trucks and the boats it was carrying were destroyed. As the first truck appeared, Major Cook shouted, "Let's go! Let's go!"

Men scrambled to their feet, slung rifles over their shoulders and went rushing up an embankment to the raised road to unload the trucks. When Jack helped a group of men pull one of the first boats off, they were astounded at their flimsiness – coated canvass with thin wood struts. A long moment's hesitation followed. Major Cook ended it with a brusque challenge. "What did you expect? Battleships? Let's go."

His men immediately resumed pulling the boats onto the ground and locking in place the struts that gave a semblance of stability to the craft.

"Okay, let's get them into the river," Cook shouted. "Go! Go!"

At that moment, XXX Corps British tanks on the road began firing smoke shells to the river's far bank to provide a screen for Cook's men. Jack grabbed the side of a boat with other men and began dragging it to the river.

"Father." At the sound of his title, Jack looked up. It was Major Cook. "You don't have to go, Father."

Jack's reply was a hard stare.

"Okay," said Cook, "I know you will."

"I'm going in your boat," Jack said.

Some 250 men pushed 26 small boats into the swiftly moving Rhine. "Row! Row!" shouted Cook. "If you don't have an oar, use your rifle butt."

With no rifle, Jack wielded an oar.

Less than halfway across the river, Jack felt a breeze strengthening and he knew that meant trouble. The smoke screen began to thin. Almost immediately, German mortars and machine gun fire began targeting the tiny armada. Nearly simultaneously, XXX Corps' tanks began to respond by firing rounds at German positions. The exploding shells hurled dirt and more smoke into the air, again providing cover for the oncoming boats.

Meanwhile, near the Nijmegen bridge, a German general and an engineer captain stood ready to blow the span should the British and American forces succeed with their efforts.

Back in the river, Cook's men were straining, rowing as fast and as hard as they could. To the right of Jack's boat, a mortar round scored a direct hit, sending 10 soldiers into the water. Farther to the right, machine gun fire raked another boat. Three soldiers in the front were hit, screamed and slumped. One slipped overboard. Men were thrashing in the water, screaming for help.

"Row! Row!" Cook demanded, shouting above the tumult. "Keep rowing!"

Men were drowning and dying from wounds, and Jack desperately wanted to help them. Instead, he muttered, "Lord, have mercy, please. Have mercy," and kept rowing. The far shore was nearing and still XXX Corps tanks were sending covering shells.

Behind Jack's boat and to the left, he heard more screams and turned. A soldier in the front of the boat was clutching his shoulder. Another mortar exploded near enough to a fourth boat to injure most of the occupants and send them falling into shallow water near shore.

Now, Major Cook leaped from his boat and began rushing ashore, firing his rifle. Jack jumped from the boat and followed. Behind him, at the water's edge, he could hear a fallen soldier pleading softly, "Help me. Help me." Jack kept running. Men from other boats were throwing grenades at German machine gun, rifle and mortar positions and fixing bayonets as they charged ashore. Jack watched horrified as several soldiers overran a squad of German riflemen, bayoneting them. Witnessing their deaths was awful, made more so when Jack saw that the enemy troops were boys, barely into their teens.

Cook and his men made it to a road paralleling the river and immediately began running toward the bridge. Back on the other side of the river, British troops also were nearing the bridge.

The German general and captain were watching. "Are you ready, Captain? It looks certain that the bridge will be taken."

"Yes, Sir."

"We'll wait until their first tanks begin to cross and then blow the bridge."

"Yes, Sir."

"Then, Captain, try to escape or surrender. Don't sacrifice yourself. Despite our Fuhrer's protestations, this war is lost."

"Yes, General."

German soldiers were running toward both ends of the bridge to try to secure it. German snipers were positioned high in the bridge's steel framework. Gun emplacements were at both ends.

As Cook and his men closed in, enemy firing intensified. A German grenade detonated, and Cook's men went diving for cover. As they stood to continue their assault, two were hit, one screaming, the other uttering no sound. Jack rushed to the side of the man who had screamed. Another grenade detonated and the explosion sent Cook and his men sprawling. "You'll make it," Jack said to the wounded soldier. Then, as he looked toward the soldier who had fallen silently, Jack saw a German rising from behind a mound of earth and taking aim at Cook. "Major!" Jack shouted. "Get down!" Cook was oblivious to the warning, instead intent on pushing the attack on the bridge. Scarcely hesitating, Jack picked up the fallen soldier's M-1, jammed the butt against his right shoulder and quickly squeezed off two shots. The bullets tore by Cook's left ear and knocked the helmet off the German's head. Startled, Cook looked in Jack's direction and, for the briefest instant, his face showed his surprise at seeing a weapon in the chaplain's hands. Jack was equally surprised.

Cook and his men again resumed their assault. Jack stood and watched. Moments before Cook and his men reached their end of the bridge, British troops were storming the other end. The British and the Americans were pushing German troops back onto the span and firing effectively on the snipers. The Germans began raising their arms in surrender. Seconds later, the lead tank of XXX Corps began crossing the bridge.

"Now!" shouted the German general, and the captain responded by forcing down the plunger on the detonator. Nothing. "Again!" screamed the general and again the captain plunged the detonator handle. Nothing. Immediately, he tried a third time. Nothing. "Shit," the general seethed. "They're across." He didn't know about, much less care about, all that had been going wrong for the Allies. "Nothing can stop them now. Nothing." He was wrong.

Jack watched the procession of XXX Corps tanks clanking across the bridge but felt no elation or satisfaction. He was drained. Still holding the M-1, sweat streaming down his face, his glasses smudged, he walked slowly toward the German he had shot. He saw the soldier lying supine, eyes open, arms outstretched. Jack knelt. He saw a bullet high on the soldier's forehead. Jack put the fingers of his right hand against the soldier's neck as he had seen corpsmen do so often. No pulse. He looked at the rifle in his left hand and gently laid it down. Then he began saying the last rites.

†††

XXX Corps tanks began rolling through Nijmegen toward Arnhem. On Day Five, about a mile south of the town, German resistance was unyielding, and XXX Corps' lead tank commander halted his column. He had been ordered to advance no farther without accompanying infantry, and the infantry was hours behind him. This delay spelled the end for Lieutenant Colonel Frost and his men. They were out of ammunition and preparing to surrender.

†††

Later on Day Five, another flight of C-47s was nearing a drop zone near Arnhem. The planes were carrying the remainder of General Sosabowski's

Polish Airborne Brigade. The drop was successful, and the brigade was preparing to board a ferry to cross the river and come to the aid of General Roy Urquhart and other members of the British 1st Airborne who were trapped in a pocket south of Arnhem. As the Poles began to board, well-aimed German artillery hit and sank the ferry.

Sosabowski was stuck. Lieutenant Colonel Jachnik, Thaddeus and the men were frustrated. This was to have been their first opportunity to strike back at the Germans since fighting them in France in 1940.

"What now, Sir?" Thaddeus asked Sosabowski who was sitting at a rickety table in a small warehouse.

"We will probably be ordered to retreat south," the general replied. "We are of no use here at all. None."

"So..."

"So for now we wait," Sosabowski fumed, shaking his head in disgust.

†††

To the Poles, Day Six, September 22, came to be remembered as Black Friday.

"General," Thaddeus said, "we have a visitor." The sun had set and darkness was closing in. Thaddeus held open the door and a bare-chested British 1st Airborne soldier stepped inside the small warehouse that Sosabowski was using as a command post. The soldier was soaked, water still dripping from his ears and chin. The soldier saluted Sosabowski who returned the salute but remained seated. "Yes, young man?"

"Sir," he said, still laboring for breath, "I come from General Urquhart with a message."

"How did you manage that? Did you swim?"

"Yes, Sir, I swam the Rhine." He gulped a breath. "The general asks if you'll get your men across...We've been holding out for six days. Any help you could provide, any help at all, would be of considerable assistance."

"Will you swim back with my reply?"

"Yes, Sir."

"Well, we can't swim," said Sosabowski. "Not with equipment." Thaddeus was biting his tongue. He had an idea and was staring hard at the general.

"I agree," said the swimmer.

Sosabowski glanced at Thaddeus who mouthed a single word. Sosabowski turned back to the swimmer. "We have small rubber rafts. That's all."

"They do sound a bit flimsy for crossing the Rhine, Sir."

Sosabowski nodded. As much as he detested General Montgomery and despite his disputes with General Browning over control and use of the Polish brigade, Sosabowski had grown to respect and like General Roy Urquhart. "Tell the general we are coming. Tell him we are coming tonight."

†††

"Are you sure?" Jack Brecker asked Captain Walt Hunter. They were standing in front of Jack's pup tent south of Nijmegen.

"I'm sure," said Walt. "We've finally got some of our radios working. Word from the British First is that the Poles are going to try to get through to them tonight. Using small rafts – rubber ones – to cross the Rhine."

Thoughts of the recent, harrowing crossing by Cook's men flooded Jack's mind. He could hear the mortar explosions and the screams of dying men. "That could be disastrous."

"Right," said Walt. "A slaughter if the Germans detect them."

A pregnant pause ensued. The noises of the camp seemed to fade.

"I'm going," said Jack.

"What?"

"They – the Poles – don't have a chaplain. I won't be able to save any lives, but maybe I can bring some comfort. Don't you know? That's why the Army is paying me this princely salary."

Walt grinned despite himself. "Jack – Father – you've already been through a lot. Too much, some would say. Some like me."

"I hear you," Jack replied, "but I'm also listening to my conscience. Get me there, Walt."

†††

"Get in," Walt said, patting the jeep's empty passenger seat.

"I can drive," Jack said. "You've been through every bit as much as I have."

Walt laughed. "You want to get there tonight, don't you? Get in." Jack hesitated. "You're not the only one with a conscience talking to him," Walt said wryly. "Mine's speaking rather loudly."

Walt drove north, maneuvering the jeep briskly on the river road. When he found the Poles, they already had rigged a cable with pulleys across the Rhine. No chaplain, Jack mused, but engineers they have – good ones. Soldiers were inflating and preparing the first rafts. Jack and Walt exited the jeep.

"Where is Captain Metz?" Jack asked a soldier, hoping he understood English.

"Metz?" the soldier replied.

"Thaddeus Metz," Jack said slowly, hoping his American accent wasn't rendering useless his careful enunciation.

A second Pole heard Jack and stepped forward. "Father Brecker?" It was Jerzy, one of the cow pen soldiers Jack had met back at the Poles' camp on Easter.

Jack dispensed with a salute and took Jerzy's hand. "Good to see you again, Jerzy," Jack smiled. "You remember Captain Hunter." Walt reached out for Jerzy's hand and they shook.

"Come this way," Jerzy said in Polish and gesturing effectively. "I will take you to Captain Metz."

Seconds later, Captains Metz, Brecker and Hunter were exchanging heart-felt handshakes. "It is so good to see you, Father," said Thaddeus. "I am most surprised."

Jack chuckled heartily, his rich bass voice pleasing to the ear. "The last time you came looking for me. This time I thought I would come looking for you." Thaddeus laughed. Jack continued. "I heard what you are doing tonight. I now know more about river crossings than I care to. I thought you and your men might like another blessing."

Thaddeus nodded. "Yes, of course. Thank you. Let me gather the men. We must do it quietly. We are trying to make no noise."

"I understand," said Jack.

Thaddeus, Jerzy and Stephan brought the men together with General Sosabowski. All were surprised and pleased to see Jack. Knowing the need for quiet, they crowded tightly around him. Walt stayed on the outside perimeter of the group, reflecting. I might remember nights like this – and the Easter Mass – longer than any firefight.

"Will you please translate?" Jack asked Thaddeus.

"Yes, of course."

"Dear Lord, these brave men are about to undertake their own special crusade. To help release their homeland from the unjust grip of the Nazis and return it to free Poles. Please be with them." Silently, Jack elevated his right arm and made a sweeping sign of the cross. "Amen."

"Amen" came a whispered chorus, which included Walt.

"Thank you very much," Thaddeus said. "First Easter, now tonight. We are twice blessed by your presence, and we will remember you always."

Thaddeus and Jack shook hands warmly.

"I would like to go with you," Jack said softly.

Walt's left eyebrow shot up in surprise and alarm.

"I'm sorry, Father," Thaddeus replied, his mind racing. "We would like to have you with us, but you don't speak Polish, and I am afraid that will be a necessity tonight."

Listen to him for God's sake, Walt was pleading silently. If you go, I'll have to go with you, and I think we've already pushed our luck way too far. That Saint Christopher medal of yours can only bring so much safe travel.

Jack nodded slowly. "All right." He bit his lip pensively. "But I expect to see you again."

"I'm sure you will, Father," said Thaddeus. "Somewhere."

Thaddeus turned away and walked to the river's edge. General Sosabowski stepped into the first raft with Thaddeus and three of the cow pen soldiers – Jerzy, Marek and Henryk – plus two more soldiers.

On the other side of the Rhine, a team of Poles had completed assembling a system that combined pulleys and a long loop of rope that now spanned the river. They began pulling on the rope, trying to be as silent as possible. The men in the first raft and others helped by pulling on the rope, and the rafts began their agonizingly slow crossing.

The first two rafts made it across without incident. The men quickly climbed out and removed weapons and gear. Then they began helping the team pulling on the rope. Eight more rafts made it across, and then a German flare lit the sky above. Poles on both sides of the river – as well as

Jack Brecker and Walt Hunter – froze and held their breaths. Long, quiet seconds passed, and then the silence was shattered. German machine gun bullets began pocking the water's surface and ripping into the rafts and the men inside them. General Sosabowski and Thaddeus began pulling madly on the rope and shouting at the men to pull harder and faster. In the river, Stephan and other men in the rafts started pulling furiously on the rope. Then began their screams of anguish, heard above the terrifying gunfire. Rafts and men were foundering. On the far side, no more rafts were put into the water.

As the crossing deteriorated into disaster, Jack felt tears welling. He removed his glasses and rubbed his eyes. A crushing futility was weighing him down. He sank to one knee. Walt stood behind him, watching and feeling equally helpless. My God, what a price, Jack was praying. Too steep. Too much to ask of anyone. For freedom, for anything. Please have mercy on their souls.

Only 52 Poles made it across the Rhine that night. On Day Seven, 150 more would manage to cross. They weren't nearly enough to relieve General Urquhart's besieged men.

There was nothing left for Jack and Walt to do. They drove south back to Nijmegen, as silent and sad a ride as either man had ever taken.

On Day Nine, the last day of Market Garden, the order to withdraw reached Roy Urquhart and Stanislaw Sosabowski. Poles on both sides of the river helped to cover the retreat of the remnants of the British 1st Airborne back across the Rhine – still another crossing in small boats. The British 1st had gone in with 10,000 men. They came out with 2,000 – 8,000 were dead, wounded, captured or missing. The Polish Airborne Brigade lost 378 men killed in action, with many more wounded or missing. Stephan, one of the cow pen soldiers, was among the missing, presumed drowned in the Rhine.

Chapter 40

"We can't win," Bernadeta said resignedly in the basement of St. Anne's in Warsaw.

"No," said Kaz, "it is only a question of how many of us will die...how many will survive."

It was the morning of September 26, the day after Operation Market Garden had ended in The Netherlands, and death was much on the minds of Poles both there and in Warsaw. Back at General Browning's command post, Generals Urquhart and Sosabowski listened in astonishment as Browning reported General Montgomery's assessment of Market Garden. "Monty thinks it was a ninety percent success," said Browning.

"A success," Urquhart spluttered. "He can't be serious. I lose eighty percent of my men, fail to take our objective and he calls it a success. He's bloody bananas."

"Nevertheless," Browning said evenly, "that's how Monty sees it. You tied up thousands of German troops for nine days and allowed thousands more of ours to push further across France and closer to Germany."

"At what price?!" Urquhart fumed. "What do you think? Personally?"

"Well, actually," Browning acknowledged blithely, "I've always thought we were trying to go a bridge too far."

There followed a long moment of silence and then General Sosabowski spoke through clenched jaws. "General Montgomery is an asshole," he seethed. "He is like the emperor with no clothes. A fool. A complete fool. If he is smart, then I am stupid. Hopelessly stupid."

"Now, hold on," Browning protested.

"No," Sosabowski cut him off, "you hold on. I sent my men – brave, intelligent, motivated Polish warriors – on a suicide mission. Why? Because Montgomery can't stand the thought of Patton beating him into Germany. Sixty miles behind enemy lines. A single, raised road. Only a week to plan. Reconnaissance reports ignored. Botched radios. General Montgomery is no General Patton."

†††

In Warsaw, Sosabowski's countrymen saw their situation with stark, unblinking reality. It was now September 28. Kaz Majos' cell in the church basement had shrunk from 32 members to 24, and the survivors were weakened for want of food, water and rest. The sturdy church above them was crumbling gradually, part of the roof already collapsed, from strikes by German artillery and small arms fire. Its basement now was bathed in a thick coat of dust as were its occupants. Coughing and sneezing were endemic.

"The Germans have retaken almost the entire city," Kaz said to his fellow partisans. "They are closing in on us."

"We will continue to fight, won't we," Bernadeta said with a mix of hopefulness and forlornness.

"Our Homeland Army leaders have been begging the Russians for help," said Kaz. "They are receiving no encouragement...and they are talking about surrendering."

"No!" Bernadeta protested. "That can't be. Surrender will mean the destruction of Warsaw and annihilation of our people. They must know that."

"Yes, I think they know that," Kaz said dejectedly. He fingered the scarring on his face and temple. "But I think they are facing reality. As you said yourself, Bernadeta, we can't win. I think our leaders are hoping that surrender might buy us time."

"For what?" Bernadeta snapped. "Time for what?"

"Liberation," Kaz said, "by the Russians or the Americans."

"The Russians? Rescuers? That's a joke, right?" Bernadeta said cynically. "And the Americans. Only now are they nearing Germany. My map shows that Warsaw is a long way from the Rhine." She slammed a balled right fist into her left palm. "We have only ourselves to count on."

"And," said Kaz, his sightless eye not yet covered by a patch, "we are not enough."

Her venting dissipated, Bernadeta now felt as deflated as a pricked balloon. And as lifeless. "We tried," she murmured, "we tried so hard."

Kaz rose. "Come with me," he said to Bernadeta and headed for the stairs up to the church.

†††

In Cleveland, acute ambivalence defined Lou Boudreau's disposition. As a manager, he felt humbled. His Indians, who had finished in third place in 1943, had slipped to sixth in 1944. As an individual player, though, Boudreau had reason to feel proud. He had led the American League in hitting with an average of .327. Playing 150 of a possible 154 games, he had 191 hits plus 73 bases on balls an struck out only 39 times. Only age 27, Boudreau saw himself excelling as a player for several more years. In fact, a few years later, he would hit .355. Although disappointed with his managerial effectiveness to date, he still expected to succeed. With the war seemingly going America's way, he was looking forward to the return of star pitcher Bob Feller from Navy service. He also was looking forward to reuniting with his friend, Father Brecker.

†††

After the months Tom Brecker had spent recuperating from his war wounds and learning to walk with a prosthesis in the Veterans Administration hospital in Brecksville, Ohio, the thought of walking into Shelby Memorial Hospital – even as a visitor – was unsettling to the point of feeling ill. His stomach seemed in incipient rebellion, and he felt slightly feverish.

Tom took a deep breath and told himself he needed to be calm. Steady. I have to be steady. The last thing Bridgett needs is for me to seem scared or nervous. Which I am. Plenty. I never expected this.

Tom helped Bridgett from the 1937 Chevrolet that Bridgett's parents had given the couple. Although the car had seen better days, they were grateful – because they had little money and because Detroit had not been producing new cars during the war, thus driving up the prices of used cars. Tom took Bridgett's left arm in his left hand and wrapped his right arm around the small of her back. "It'll be all right," he said soothingly. "Everything's going to be fine."

"I hope so," Bridgett murmured anxiously.

"I know so," Tom said with a certainty that belied his anxiety. "Doctor Kingsboro will take good care of you. The nurses, too."

† † †

Nine hours later, Tom had quit counting the cups of coffee he had drunk. The caffeine, combined with anxiety, had his stomach juices gurgling noisily. He couldn't sit and when he stood, he felt compelled to pace.

The sight of Dr. Wilson Kingsboro walking into the waiting room startled Tom. The doctor was drying his hands with a white cloth. "Do you have names picked out?" he asked.

"Four," said Tom. "Two each for boys and girls. Which will we be using?"

"One of each," the doctor said, reaching to shake Tom's hand. "They – and Bridgett – are all doing fine."

Tom's knees nearly buckled before he located a chair behind him. He and Bridgett had been shocked when told to expect twins, but the reality of their birth still sent his mind reeling. He shook his head to clear his thoughts. "When can I see Bridg?"

"In a little while," Dr. Kingsboro smiled. "Delivering two is an ordeal. The nurses are helping her freshen up. Let her rest a bit."

"The babies?"

"The nurses are cleaning them up, too. In a few minutes, you can get your first look. Your first look at your children, Tom. How does that sound?"

"Fantastic," Tom answered. "Thank you, Doctor." Another thought was occurring to Tom. On the Hornet, if someone had said I would soon be a husband and father, I would have told him to take a long swim in the Pacific. What's happening today is not much short of a miracle.

"You are entirely welcome," said Dr. Kingsboro. "I think you and Bridgett will make excellent parents." The doctor meant that. He believed what Tom and Bridgett had endured would give them deeper maturity and better parenting skills.

"Thanks," Tom said. As Dr. Kingsboro exited the waiting room, Tom's thoughts returned to the burning Hornet and men who had not escaped the horrors of combat. The memories were vivid and horrifying. When will it end? How many more must die? How many more must lose legs and arms and their sight? How many will never become husbands and fathers? How many must lose hope?"

†††

Hope among the Poles in Warsaw had been vanquished. It was late the night – about 9 p.m. – of October 2, and the only light to be seen came from the fires consuming Warsaw's buildings. The number of partisans in Kaz's cell now was down to 19. That night, to escape the choking dust in the basement, they had ascended into the church. Debris from the collapsing roof made walking treacherous. There Kaz told them what they dreaded hearing. "Tomorrow," he said, "the Home Army will surrender to the Nazis. We will be laying down our arms."

"Will you?" a partisan asked. "Will you lay down your arms?" Though posed as a question, the query clearly was more of a challenge.

Kaz recognized it as such and replied deliberately. "I don't want to. You know that. But if we don't, the Nazis have said they will begin executing those who do."

"They might do that anyway," Kaz's fellow partisan muttered darkly.

"They might," Kaz agreed. "Look, I'm not ordering you or anyone to turn in your weapons. It's your choice. But me? I will comply. Think it over. The surrender is to take effect when we leaders meet with the Nazis. If we don't surrender, then death will be a certainty for many, if not all, still in Warsaw."

"In Warsaw…I might try to escape," said the partisan. "To the countryside."

"Then you should leave now," Kaz said evenly, "while it's still dark."

Bernadeta was sitting beside Kaz on the step in front of the church's marble Communion rail. She turned to him and whispered, "I'm leaving now." Kaz's good eye stared hard into hers. "Yes," she continued, "I know the dangers. But who knows better than I Warsaw's sewers and streets? And, Kaz, if the Nazis don't execute us, if they send us to a camp, I have a feeling I'll never see my family again. I can't stand that thought."

"Bernadeta, if you are caught…"

"I know. The Nazis will murder me on the spot. Leave my body to rot."

Kaz sighed and looked away. "Then you had better leave now, too."

Bernadeta's left hand reached out and touched Kaz's chin, turning it toward her. "I love you," she whispered tenderly. "I always will."

Kaz felt tears forming, tears born of the belief that these were their last moments together. "I love you, too." A pause. "I'm glad you told me."

"I think you knew."

He sniffled and tried to force a small smile. "The words are important."

The partisan who had spoken of leaving stood and stepped from a church pew. Solemnly, he shook hands all around and walked outside. Two others stood, hesitated -- and followed. Kaz watched them and then asked Bernadeta, "Will you be joining them?"

She shook her head. "I think I should go alone. That's what I'm used to doing. I know the way out of Warsaw to Zyrardow. The bends in the road, the forests, the hiding places." She blinked away tears and stood.

Kaz stood and faced her. "You know I want to go with you."

"I know."

"But I have to stay."

"I know." She reached out and touched the scarring along the right side of his face and head. She smiled. "You were right. Yours is worse than mine."

Kaz, tears trickling down his face, reached out and touched the scar running down from the lower left corner of Bernadeta's mouth. "I'm glad about that."

They embraced, then drew apart and kissed lightly. Then Bernadeta turned and began walking down the long aisle, stepping around and over debris, to the church's entrance. Now, the tears streaming from her eyes were falling in a torrent.

†††

After the Home Army's surrender on October 3, the Germans evacuated the entire population of Warsaw's left bank or everyone on the west side of the Vistula River. They then set about systematically demolishing most of what remained of Warsaw. In all, 85 percent of the city's buildings were destroyed. During the uprising, some 250,000 Poles died. Afterward, the Nazis dispatched 600,000 residents, virtually the entire surviving population, to concentrations camps. Kaz Majos was among them.

Chapter 41

On October 3, the same day that the Home Army was surrendering to the Germans, George Patton's forces were making their first assault on the forts at Metz. It was unsuccessful. Patton wasted no time pulling together his senior officers, and he minced no words. "These are fixed fortifications," he seethed. "No fixed fortifications should be able to withstand a modern army. Not a well-trained, well-armed and well-led army. I know for a fact that our Third Army is well trained and well armed. The question – the obvious question – is whether it is well led. By all that is holy," he was thundering now, "you will take Metz or I will fire all of you and replace you on the spot with your subordinates, and we'll see if they can lead. I will not be seen as another Montgomery. Getting bogged down. Offering up lame excuses. Too timid. Too by-the-book. You will be creative and you will take Metz, or I'll keep firing and promoting until I find leaders who will lead, not flail. Is that perfectly clear?"

After his harangue, alone in his office with Colonel Codman, Patton did something very un-Patton-like: he expressed self-doubt. "Damn it all to hell, Charlie, I can't help wondering how much the leadership failure is mine. Maybe I should have been closer to the front."

"General," Codman replied with his customary blend of deference and honesty, "I worry sometimes that you get too close to the front. Starting with Hitler, the Germans would like nothing more than to see you get knocked off."

"They would, wouldn't they?" Patton grinned cheesily. "The sonsabitches would love to provide pallbearers for my funeral."

"That they would, Sir. But, General, there is another point to consider. No one can argue that your presence with front-line troops hasn't paid handsome dividends. The men -- officers and enlisted alike -- respond to your leadership. They recognize and appreciate the risks you take. They see you as a soldier's general."

"You're right, Charlie – as usual. By God, I've got to get closer to the front again – right away."

On October 12, Patton moved his base to Nancy, just 30 miles south of Metz. For a headquarters, he took over the home of a local coalmine owner.

Upon entering for the first time with Colonel Codman, Patton took in the dull, greenish brown and purple tapestries. Pointing at them, he observed, "They look as foreboding and uninspiring as his mines no doubt do." Then he took note of three-foot high gilded angels and a cherub suspended from the ceiling. Looking up, Patton chuckled and remarked, "By God, that's more like it. We can use all the celestial help we can round up." A pause. "That reminds me, Charlie. I want you to get me the warrior priest."

"Who?"

"You know, the priest who knocked off a kraut at Nijmegen. I want him with us. With my troops."

"Well, Sir," said Codman, "I believe I read where he's with the Eighty-Second."

"I know that. But one phone call from you and he'll be on his way here."

"Sir," said Codman, "it's highly likely the Eighty-Second will be in this area in the not too distant future." Codman was hoping to forestall depriving the 82nd of a needed chaplain to satisfy his boss' fancy, but as soon as those words had passed between the colonel's lips, he knew he'd made a mistake. He braced himself for a pointed rejoinder.

"Now, look here, Charlie. 'In the not too distant future' kind of thinking is the problem up at Metz. I want that warrior priest with us and I want him pronto."

† † †

Theresa Hassler's evacuation hospital was steadily moving east, following the advancing Allied forces. In late October near Metz, she heard her name shouted at mail call. Theresa stepped forward, reached out and was handed an envelope. She saw the return address and felt her pulse quicken. She took several paces away through gummy, ankle-deep mud and then carefully opened the envelope.

"Oct. 1, 1944

Dear Theresa,

I am very tired but still am positively thrilled to be writing you this letter. I have a surprise. I am a mother. No, that's not the surprise. You already knew that was going to happen. What I hadn't told you was that I was going to be a mother twice! Twins!! Yes, I have given birth to twins. We are so thrilled! Tom and I. Both our parents.

The little darlings are just perfect. You can see that in the picture!! A boy and a girl, and the girl arrived first by a few minutes. Imagine the teasing that will happen in a few years.

Are you curious about their names? Well, Tom and I decided they should have names that really mean something, names that are truly special. So we decided to name them after a special aunt and uncle. So, Aunt Theresa, look at this picture and meet little Theresa and little Jack. Well, on the birth certificate he is John, but you know everyone will call him after his Uncle Jack!

We are so happy!! I hope the war ends soon so you can come home and hold our little darlings. You will just love holding your namesake!

I'm running out of energy, and I still need to nurse them before I take a nap. Please be careful. I love you and I miss you.

Your faithful sister,

Bridgett"

Theresa, holding the letter in her left hand and the picture in her right, sighed longingly and looked skyward, eyes squeezed shut.

"Are you all right?"

Theresa looked to her left and saw Lieutenant Colonel Marilyn Carter. "I guess so."

"Guess?"

Theresa handed the picture to Colonel Carter. "It's my first niece and nephew," Theresa said wistfully. "They named the niece after me. The baby boy is her twin. He's named after..." Theresa forced a swallow and blinked back tears. "After an uncle...a friend." There followed a long pause that Colonel Carter felt it inappropriate to break. "Since I came to

Europe, I haven't felt homesick very often. But right now, home is where my heart is…or where I wish it was."

"You're lucky," Carter said. Theresa looked at her questioningly. "You've been here longer than I have, but I feel homesick a lot. Yes, I've been in the Army a long time but never outside the states. Never so far from family and friends."

"Thanks."

"It's true," Carter said, handing the picture back to Theresa. "Anyway, the babies are beautiful." Then Carter looked around and saw that no one was paying attention to her and Theresa. She stepped closer to Theresa and embraced her, patting her on the back. "Not precisely a military gesture," Colonel Carter murmured, "but sometimes a salute just won't do."

Theresa, still holding the letter and picture, returned the hug. "It's nice to be reminded that you're more than a colonel."

†††

"Come in," General Patton said, eyes shining, smiling warmly.

Captain Jack Brecker stepped forward and saluted.

Standing behind his desk, Patton returned the salute. "I'm pleased to meet you, Chaplain. Sit down. Can I tempt you with a drink?"

Jack paused before replying. "As long as it's something besides altar wine," he said dryly.

Patton laughed. "My inventory of altar wine is on the short side, but my stock of good Scotch whiskey has been replenished. That okay?"

"That'll be fine, Sir."

The general poured generous drinks and handed one to Jack. "No ice handy."

"Straight up is the way I like it," Jack said.

"Same here." Patton extended his glass toward Jack's and Jack responded in kind, and they both sipped.

"Hits the spot, especially in this weather."

"Good." Patton took a second sip. "Curious, Chaplain?"

"I am, Sir. You have a chaplain on staff. And frankly, I'm needed with the Eighty-Second."

"No doubt you are. Look, you'll soon be back with the Eighty-Second. Consider this temporary duty."

"And what duty might that be, Sir?"

"Satisfying my zeal for history."

"Would you care to elaborate, General?"

Patton laughed again, heartily. "You don't seem intimidated, Chaplain. I like that."

"We are all children of God, General."

"So we are…So we are. I heard about you shooting that German. Are you aware that made history?"

"If I did, it's history that I'm not particularly proud of."

"Well," Patton said stubbornly, "you should be. You saved a life. Maybe more than one."

"And took one to do it. That's not my calling."

"Be that as it may," Patton said, "when I heard about it, I was proud that one of our men of the cloth knew how to use a rifle and knew when to use it. I also asked my aide to do a little research."

"Research?"

"Into the history of chaplains. Do you know it?"

Jack shook his head. "It wasn't covered at the Chaplain's School."

"Maybe it should be. In military history, warrior chaplains were plentiful," Patton said. "At the Battle of Hastings in Ten Sixty-Six, William The Conqueror's half-brother was a bishop who fought with a mace. In colonial America, chaplains ministered to neighbors in the militias – and fought with them. Back in the Sixteen Hundreds, a minister advised our colonial ancestors on God's chosen route for attacking the natives. And the natives were defeated. During the Revolutionary War, clergy often raised fighting units from their own congregations and led them into battle. Warrior chaplains. They served and some were killed and wounded and imprisoned. They carried ranks from captain to colonel. So far in this war, twenty chaplains have been killed. Forty-seven wounded, twelve missing. One a POW."

"Your aide was impressively thorough in his work," Jack observed sincerely.

"Yes, he was," Patton smiled. "But he and my staff know I require much, including thoroughness. At any rate, things changed and chaplains now are not allowed to bear arms. A mistake, perhaps."

"I think not, General. I'd rather we be seen as men of mercy, and bearing arms would distort that perception. Destroy it."

"Hmmm…I'm not so sure, Chaplain. I doubt very much that you've lost respect after taking up that M-1. But look, we can continue our debate another time. Tell me, where did you learn to handle an M-1. Not at Chaplain's School."

Jack sipped his Scotch and smiled. "On an Indian reservation in Arizona." Patton's face registered surprise then curiosity. With a wave, he gestured Jack to continue. "A friend taught me how to fire an M-1. The only time I ever shot it – before Nijmegen – was when I used it to shoot a mountain lion that was killing the Indians' sheep."

Patton slapped his thigh with his hand. "By the Lord, Chaplain, I just might have to write to the Chaplain's School and recommend they add riflery to the curriculum."

"You're joking, Sir."

"Yes, I am." Patton sipped his Scotch. "I have many faults – very adequately documented as you no doubt know. Selfishness is one of them. I was selfish to bring you here. I know that. But I really did want to meet and shake hands with a man who made history. Will you shake my hand, Chaplain?"

Jack leaned forward, extended his right hand and Patton shook it vigorously.

"Good," said Patton.

"How long is temporary duty?" Jack asked.

"I'll have you back with the Eighty-Second soon enough." Patton drained his Scotch. "Come with me, Chaplain. We'll do a thing or two before you depart."

†††

"I'm not particularly welcome here," Patton said ruefully. "They don't exactly roll out a red carpet for me."

"A man can gain strength by facing up to his mistakes," Jack observed.

"If that's true," Patton said, smiling widely, "then I've got a lot of potential for strengthening my character."

Jack chuckled, and the two men, along with Patton's aide, Colonel Codman, entered the 128th evacuation hospital tent. "I'll be on my best behavior," Patton whispered to them. "No repeat of the incidents in Sicily." Patton was alluding to two occasions when he had slapped soldiers hospitalized with battle fatigue. His behavior had nearly cost him his career, a reality he was acutely aware of.

The hospital staff – doctors, nurses, orderlies – stood at attention.

"At ease, everyone," Patton said. "Please. I'm just here to salute these brave young soldiers and you fine people who are tending to their needs." Patton then shook hands with the senior surgeon, said a few words and began slowly making his way down the narrow aisle between the two rows of cots. Patton's warmth was sincere; he possessed genuine, deep affection for his troops.

About 20 feet away, Theresa Hassler was watching the general. She saw the two men behind him, but Patton was obscuring her vision.

Behind Patton, a recovering soldier said, "Chaplain, could I talk with you?"

Jack stepped to the side of the cot and knelt on one knee. "Certainly, what is it?"

Theresa saw the cross insignia on the chaplain's helmet and then returned her gaze to Patton. Then she saw the chaplain remove his helmet and involuntarily she sucked in a quick breath. Oh, my God, she thought, and felt her heart begin to race and pound.

After spending a minute with the soldier, Jack blessed him with the sign of the cross.

"Thank you, Father," the young soldier said.

"You are very welcome. And may the Lord be at your side."

Patton shook hands with Lieutenant Colonel Marilyn Carter and then with Theresa. Taller than the average woman, Patton was thinking about the 5'7" nurse. Colonel Codman still was a step behind the general and then followed Jack. Patton and Codman moved by, and Jack shook hands with Colonel Carter. Then he heard his name – "Jack" – spoken softly. He looked at Theresa, uncertain for a moment. Then Father Jack Brecker was thunderstruck.

"Theresa!" There was nothing soft about his greeting. It was full of shock and exuberance.

Patton stopped and pivoted. “You know each other...”

“Friends,” Jack said. “From the same town. Since childhood.” Jack shook his head and then shook hands with Theresa who was standing mute, her emotions building like a volcanic dome under pressure.

It was Lieutenant Colonel Carter who immediately sensed an opportunity and seized it. “Why don’t the two of you step outside and visit. I’m sure the general won’t mind.” She was thinking that this unexpected reunion would either ease Theresa’s pangs of homesickness or worsen them. She was hoping fervently for the former.

“Mind? Not at all,” Patton boomed. “Go ahead. We’ll catch up.”

Jack, still holding Theresa’s hand, led her back down the aisle toward the evac hospital’s entrance. Wounded soldiers and staff watched with fascination, some smiling.

Outside the large tent, Jack released Theresa’s hand and placed his hands on his hips. “Theresa, what a marvelous surprise. I knew you were in Europe. Paul told me back in

Normandy. But I didn’t know where, and I certainly never expected to see you. This is wonderful.”

“I saw Paul, too, last month during Market Garden,” she said, her pulse rate mercifully slowing.

“You did? In a hospital?” She nodded. “Is he okay?” Jack asked worriedly.

“His hands were cut pretty badly, but he’s fine. Really. Don’t worry.”

Jack nodded. “Okay, I won’t. Not too much anyway. Now, how are you? You look terrific.” He looked her up and down and laughed. “Well, given the circumstances.” Jack gestured to their mud-covered boots and splattered fatigue pants, and Theresa forced a small laugh.

“I’m all right,” Theresa said. “I’m...Sometimes...” She saw the questioning look in Jack’s eyes and stopped herself. The last thing he needs is to hear about my dark moments, she thought. “Have you seen a picture of the twins?”

Before Jack could reply, Theresa could see from the blankness of his expression that the news hadn’t reached him. “Twins?”

“Bridgett and Tom had twins. Last month.”

"Wow! Oh my. I've been on the move and General Patton summoned me. I'm sure the mail boys just haven't been able to catch up with me."

"I just got the letter and picture."

"Show me!" Jack said exultantly.

"Okay," said Theresa, "come with me." Across the muddy compound, she led Jack to the nurse's tent. "In here. Don't worry, all the nurses are on duty or seeing General Patton." She pushed the tent flap aside and stepped inside with Jack following. From a footlocker, she removed an envelope and handed it to Jack. She watched as he opened the envelope, unfolded the letter and looked at the black and white picture of two tiny newborns. "Oh my," he said with awe. "Oh my."

Theresa's emotions again were on the verge of overwhelming her. Long-suppressed desires to show – and receive – affection were storming her senses. She struggled to calm them.

"What are they?" Jack asked. "I mean, boys or girls or both?"

"Both," Theresa smiled. "That's the girl," she said, pointing to the baby to Jack's left.

"What are their names?"

That question, or rather her pending answer, was causing a surge of heat to redden her face. "Bridgett said…Wait, read her letter."

"Okay," Jack said. He returned the picture to Theresa and began reading.

Theresa was watching him intently. When he shook his head, she knew he'd reached Bridgett's news on the names.

"Well, to say that this day has brought with it more than its fair share of surprises wouldn't offend a Brit's finely honed sense of understatement. Agreed?"

"Agreed."

"How long has it been, Theresa?"

She didn't ask him to clarify or elaborate on his question. "Since you left for the seminary."

"Oh my. Nineteen Thirty-Two. Whew. Well, let me say if you've changed it's only been for the better. Even," gesturing again toward her muddied boots and fatigues, "dressed this way, you look terrific."

"You look good, too, Jack. Most of all, I'm glad you're okay."

He smiled broadly. “Thanks to this,” he said, reaching beneath his field jacket and fatigue shirt and removing the St. Christopher medal. “Remember it?” She nodded, feeling her chest beginning to swell again. “Remember when you gave it to me?”

“The train station.”

“Right! It’s covered a lot of miles with me. Arizona. The desert and mountains. England. France. Holland.”

“Holland…Market Garden.”

“Yes,” Jack smiled, “I was there with the Eighty-Second. And with the Poles.”

“I thought so.”

“How did you know?”

“When I saw Paul near Eindhoven, he told me you were with the Eighty-Second and probably with them up north.”

“That’s right. At Nijmegen.”

A jarring thought hit Theresa. “Jack, you’re not…You’re not…”

“The chaplain who shot a German?” She nodded. Jack sighed heavily. “I’m afraid so. It uh…it happened so fast. I just reacted.”

“That’s okay,” she murmured. “Really.”

Jack sighed again and shook his head. “It’s why I’m here with Patton. He heard about it and called for me. Speaking of which, I guess I’d better get back to the hospital before he sends Colonel Codman hunting for me.”

In that moment, Theresa quit resisting the impulse that had been pushing its way to the surface. She leaned forward and put her face against Jack’s chest and the St. Christopher medal. She placed her hands on his upper arms.

Jack, still holding the letter, felt her affection, raised his arms and placed his hands on her shoulders.

After a long moment, Theresa pulled her face away from Jack’s chest and looked into his eyes. “I’m sorry if I upset you.”

“Surprised me, yes. Upset, no.” Jack, feeling a surge of warming affection, leaned forward and kissed Theresa on her forehead. No more words were spoken. They each released their holds. Jack put the letter on Theresa’s cot and then turned and exited the tent. Theresa followed.

As they were crossing the compound, General Patton and Colonel Codman were exiting the hospital tent. The senior surgeon and Lieutenant Colonel Carter followed.

"Well," Patton said, smiling widely, "did the two of you cover the hometown news?"

"Yes, Sir," Jack replied. "And big news. My brother and his wife – Lieutenant Hassler's sister," he gestured toward Theresa, "had twins last month. A boy and a girl."

"Marvelous!" Patton said. "This visit has worked out even better than expected." He climbed into the jeep and Colonel Codman did likewise, behind the steering wheel.

Jack looked at Theresa. "It was great to see you. Thanks for sharing the picture and the letter."

"You're welcome."

"I'll have to write to Tom and Bridgett."

"Take care, Jack."

"I think this," he said, smiling and tucking the St. Christopher medal beneath his jacket and shirt, "has been doing a good job of taking care of me, and I'm pretty sure it will continue to." He climbed into the jeep's rear seat.

"Ready, General?" Codman asked.

"Let's roll."

CHAPTER 42

It had been a difficult transition for Bernadeta, but gradually she again was becoming accustomed to the rhythm of life on the farm.

In escaping from Warsaw, she had relied heavily on experience gained during her two visits to Zyrardow. She knew Warsaw's rubble-strewn streets and, walking southwest to the farm, she knew the road and its bends. She knew where there would be patches of forest and barns for concealment. To her surprise and benefit, the road had been less trafficked than she had expected. There was one thing different about this third journey homeward; this time she had taken the schmeisser and the luger.

Her parents, Jszef and Tosia, and younger sister Barbara, having heard about the uprising and knowing about Theresa's work with the Home Army, had feared the worst. When she arrived at the farmhouse door, they were both stunned and overjoyed.

During Bernadeta's first week home, her parents had exercised restraint, refraining from asking about details of her life in Warsaw that she didn't volunteer. Barbara's restraint was shorter-lived. On Bernadeta's third afternoon home, Barbara asked her if she would like to come to the barn and join in milking the two cows and feeding them and the ox. Bernadeta agreed without hesitation, if not with enthusiasm.

"Captain Majos," Barbara said tentatively when they were inside the cow pen, "do you know what happened to him?"

Bernadeta looked at her sister and shrugged. "He was planning to surrender. He was probably sent to a camp."

"Do you love him?"

"Yes."

"Does he know that?"

"Yes."

"Do you think you might get married?"

"You mean if we both survive the war? I don't know. We care for each other...very much. We both have seen so much suffering, so much death. I don't know if marriage for us would be best. Do you understand?"

"I'm not sure," Barbara replied. "You have been through ordeals I can only imagine. I don't know how they would affect the future. I do know one thing, though."

"What's that?"

"I love you and I'm glad you're home."

"Same here, younger sister."

"Mother and Father can hardly believe you're here. They thought you might be dead or in a camp."

"I've been lucky. Death was everywhere. Still is."

"Did you kill any Germans?" Barbara blurted.

"Yes. But I'd rather not talk about it. Not now."

"I think I understand that," Barbara said, "but I'm glad you killed some. They are evil, unspeakably evil. God should strike them down. Every one of them."

"I don't disagree."

Barbara's curiosity was intense, and she was bent on satisfying it – as long as Bernadeta didn't object. "Bernadeta, are you still a virgin?"

"No."

"Captain Majos?"

"Yes."

"Good. I'm glad for you. I'm still a virgin."

"Good. Your time – with the right man – will come. You will like it."

Barbara now was sitting on the milking stool. "Did you ever hear anything about the soldiers that you helped escape from here?"

"No. Nothing. They could be alive…or not. They were going to try to escape to the west. It would have been a long and dangerous journey."

"Do you ever think of that young soldier? Metz, I think his name was."

"You really are very nosy today, aren't you?" Bernadeta spoke not with irritation but affection.

"You have given me much to be nosy about, don't you think?" Barbara smiled impishly.

Bernadeta laughed. It was something she hadn't done often during the past five years, and it sounded and felt good. "I guess I have."

"Well, do you? Think about Metz?"

"Thaddeus Metz. From time to time, yes. I'm not sure why. It was just one evening and it's been five years."

"Maybe it was love at first sight."

"Maybe it was," Bernadeta agreed wistfully.

"Could you love both men – Metz and Majos?" Bernadeta smiled and shook her head. "Now, that is definitely more complicated than I want to contemplate."

"I can hardly believe everything you've seen and done. My sister, the soldier."

"Your sister, a farmer – and glad of it." She began laughing again, and Barbara joined in.

Chapter 43

Beginning on November 8, 1944, the Battle of Huertgen Forest near Metz lasted three weeks and led to 35,000 Allies killed, wounded, captured or missing. Still, the forts at Metz remained in German hands.

On a late November morning, southeast of Nancy, Paul Brecker was traveling with a platoon from the 101st Airborne. It was Thursday, Thanksgiving in the United States. He was riding in one of three two-and-a-half-ton trucks – deuce and a half's, the paratroopers called them – that were following a jeep southeast into the Vosges Mountains. Driving the jeep was a corporal; his passengers were Lieutenant Billy Clawson, a sergeant and a bi-lingual French partisan serving as guide.

On that same morning, Lea Peiffer, Maurice Trimbach and six other partisans from Ribeauville were making their way northwest in a delivery truck owned by Lea's father. Maurice was driving. All were armed with captured German machine pistols, sidearms and grenades.

†††

"Do you think it's true?" Roscoe Remlinger asked Paul.

"How many rumors have you heard over the last year?"

"Can't count 'em all," said R.

"Exactly," Paul said. "How many were true?"

"Count 'em on one hand."

"Right. A few. So," Paul said, "we'll find out soon enough." He smiled wryly. As the truck wound through the mountains, Paul studied his hands. The scarring still was reddish, but the pain had largely disappeared. Just minor discomfort remained. Theresa had been right in predicting that stiffness would linger. That was particularly true as to his left hand where the bayonet had sliced into his palm and fingers.

"Thank you for letting me come along," Lea said to Maurice.

"Did I have a choice?" he smiled wryly. "After all, the truck is your father's."

"Well, at least you didn't make me fight you to go."

Maurice chuckled. "I think that's a fight I would have lost." He was thinking something else, too. If what he'd heard was accurate, the danger should be less than on recent missions, especially the aborted attack on Natzwiller and the ambush of Captain Oberster's convoy.

Lea smiled. "Your idea is a good one," she said. "No one should ever forget. Not ever."

Although the small, German occupation garrison had left Ribeauville and some other area villages, the Alsace still was under Nazi control, especially to the south and east of Ribeauville. In fact, a sizable occupation force remained in place in Colmar, just 10 miles south of Ribeauville, 10 miles west of the Rhine, and the largest town between Strasbourg and Mulhouse. The Allies already were referring to the area as the Colmar Pocket.

Even though Maurice was driving in the opposite direction, he was proceeding alertly. At the first sign of German troops, he and Lea and the other partisans were prepared to immediately abandon the truck and dash into the forests coating the mountainsides.

†††

In the jeep, the guide said to Lieutenant Clawson in fluent English, "We should be getting close."

"How close?" Clawson asked.

"There. See the sign. Three kilometers."

Clawson nodded and then spoke to the driver, "Go two more kilometers and then stop."

"Yes, Sir."

†††

Maurice braked the delivery truck. "I know what we've heard, but I don't think we should chance driving any closer. From here, let's continue on foot, half on each side of the road. We'll skirt the village and move up through the forest. It's slower but safer."

†††

At the base of a mountain, the partisan guide spoke to Lieutenant Clawson. "The village is to our left," he pointed, "the camp up this road to the right."

Clawson nodded. "Corporal, pick five men and stay here at the base of the mountain with our vehicles. Everyone else divide up on either side of the road. Keep plenty of space between you. R, you take the point on the left. I'll take it on the right. Sarge, you and Brecker bring up the rear. Let's go."

The platoon began walking, arms at the ready. The road wound steeply up the mountain.

†††

Near the top of the mountain, Maurice, Lea and the other six partisans emerged from the woods. As they had heard, the Natzwiller camp was abandoned. It also was intact, so much so that it looked like a well-tended outdoor museum. They walked toward the front gate that stood open.

"No scavengers yet," Lea observed. "Perhaps the villagers are still afraid to come here."

"Who can blame them?" said Maurice. "They knew what was going on here. They could hear gunshots, see smoke. Maybe some of them were murdered here."

"We'll need to speak with the villagers," Lea said, "if we are going to keep scavengers away and preserve the camp as a memorial."

"We will do that very thing," Maurice replied. "We'll also leave four of our group here today as insurance. Then we'll recruit other partisans in the area to take guard rotations to see that the camp remains intact."

"I'll be happy to be one of the first four," Lea said.

"Good," said Maurice.

Three other partisans volunteered and then one spoke, "Listen."

All became quiet. They could hear, faintly, the sound of boots scuffing the surface of the earthen road that wound up the mountain.

"It must be a large group," Maurice said. "Not villagers. Soldiers likely. Germans. Let's get into the woods on both sides of the road. When enough of them are in sight, shoot to kill. If they outnumber us by too much, we'll disappear deeper into the woods. Quickly, quietly, let's get into position. Wait for me to fire the first shot."

The eight partisans split and took cover behind trees where the clearing around the camp met the forest.

A couple minutes later, Lieutenant Billy Clawson and Roscoe Remlinger rounded the last bend in the road before reaching the summit. Ahead, they could see the gates of the camp. Clawson raised his left hand and the platoon stopped.

Through the trees, Maurice was able to see only glimpses of uniforms. Why are they stopping? he wondered. That doesn't make sense.

With his left arm, Clawson motioned for the platoon to continue its climb. The partisan guide moved to Clawson's side. "The camp looks abandoned."

Clawson nodded. "Maybe." He waited until the distance between him and Remlinger and the sergeant and Paul Brecker at the rear had closed a little, and then he and R resumed walking – slowly, alertly.

Why are they being so tentative, so cautious? Maurice wondered. It's their camp. He steadied himself, preparing to open fire. The other partisans did likewise.

"Maurice."

The voice Maurice heard was a whisper that carried with it a tone of urgency. He turned to look for its source.

Lea gave a small wave to get his attention. "Look at their helmets." Maurice turned away from Lea, his machine pistol at the ready. "Their helmets are not German," Lea whispered again.

Then as Clawson and R came closer, Maurice saw, too, that neither the uniforms nor the boots were German. He turned back toward Lea and silently mouthed one word: "Americans?"

She shrugged. Neither she nor Maurice had ever seen an American soldier. Nor had any of their partisan colleagues.

Maurice was torn. If the soldiers were enemy, he felt a strong obligation to shoot and kill as many as possible. If they were Allies, he surely didn't want to greet them with a volley of deadly fire. Then Maurice saw a single civilian, carrying a German machine pistol and walking behind the lead soldiers. Maurice decided to take another in his long series of risks. He knew it would mean losing the element of surprise. "Stop!" he shouted in French. "If you are not Germans, who are you?"

"Down!" shouted Lieutenant Clawson. "Everybody down!" Then, to the guide, Clawson said, "What did he say?"

The guide translated.

"If he is French," said Clawson, "tell him we are Americans and to come out where I can see him."

Again, the guide translated. Moments later, Maurice, holding his machine pistol muzzle pointed toward the ground, emerged from the trees onto the road.

Clawson was on one knee. "Are you alone?"

"No," Maurice replied.

"Tell the others to come out," Clawson instructed.

Maurice complied. Lea and the other six partisans all stepped from the woods onto the road.

There was no spontaneous commingling. Uncertainty, suspicion and caution still prevailed.

"What are you doing here?" Clawson asked. The guide continued translating for him and Maurice.

"We knew the Nazis abandoned this camp," Maurice explained, "and we came here to check it out. We want to preserve it as a memorial to the thousands who were murdered here."

"When did the Nazis leave?" Clawson asked. By now, other platoon members had advanced far enough to witness this meeting.

"In early September. After Paris was liberated," Maurice said. "Before the Nazis evacuated the camp, we and other partisans in the area tried to attack it to liberate our people. But an informant had alerted the Nazis and our attack failed. Many of our fellow partisans were hunted down, brought here and executed. We managed to kill a few Nazis before escaping back to our villages."

Clawson stood and walked closer to Maurice. The guide and R followed.

"We heard about the camp from partisans near Nancy," said Clawson. "We didn't know it had been evacuated." Clawson then stepped still closer to Maurice and extended his right arm. Maurice responded in kind and the two leaders shook hands warmly. “My name is Lieutenant Billy Clawson. We are with the United States Hundred And First Airborne Division.”

“My name is Maurice Trimbach and we are from the village of Ribeauville.”

“What is your plan?” Clawson asked.

“I am leaving four of my people here to guard the camp against scavengers. The rest of us are going to nearby villages to recruit other partisans to assist us in guarding the camp.”

Clawson nodded his understanding. “Perhaps we can help. I could leave a couple of my men here for a day or two. Our guide, too.”

“That is very generous, Lieutenant,” said Maurice. “We accept your offer.”

“Good. The rest of us will be leaving now. Our vehicles are parked a kilometer from the base of the mountain.”

“We, too, have a vehicle nearby,” said Maurice. “In a couple days, after we have recruited more partisans to help here, we will use our truck to return your men and guide to you.”

“Very good,” Clawson said. “Now I’d like to get my men back to our camp. In the United States, today is a holiday – our Thanksgiving we call it – and I want to get our men back to camp before nightfall for a proper meal.”

Maurice nodded and said, “Just a minute, Lieutenant.” Then Maurice huddled with Lea and the other partisans. They conferred and reached quick agreement and then Maurice turned and spoke. “We have a suggestion, Lieutenant. Actually an invitation. We are honored to meet you. And we are certain the people in the village below – Natzwiller – would be thrilled to meet you – and feed your men a proper holiday feast. This is your Thanksgiving. It can be ours as well.”

Clawson was touched by Maurice’s offer and was tempted to accept on the spot. Instead, he said, “Please give us a moment.” Then he walked back among his men. “What do you think? A turkey dinner back at camp or I’m not sure what with these partisans and local villagers?”

Paul Brecker spoke up. “Lieutenant, I’m not sure what we’d be eating here, but I’ll bet we’d drinking some fine wine. That won’t be the case back at camp. Speaking only for myself, I’d like us to accept his invitation.”

"Me, too," said R in his soft drawl. "A bottle of French wine and a relaxing evening sound pretty darn good to me. Better than another bumpy truck ride today. We can see if French hospitality matches southern hospitality." Laughter all around.

Clawson nodded. "Okay. R and Brecker. You and our guide will stay here a couple days." Then Clawson spoke to the platoon radioman, "Get hold of HQ and tell them we won't be home for dinner."

†††

Maurice had been right. The Natzwiller villagers below the camp, alerted by Clawsons's guide and one of the partisans, welcomed the Americans with unbounded joy and gratitude. As the Americans walked into Natzwiller, the villagers thronged them, handing them flowers, fruit and wine, shaking their hands, patting their shoulders and bestowing more than a few kisses on blushing 101st Airborne cheeks and lips. Then the women of the village, when told of the American holiday, set about preparing a feast.

†††

The village's two restaurants were turned into banquet halls for Lieutenant Clawson and his platoon and Maurice Trimbach and his partisans. Paul Brecker and R and the guide were sharing a table with Lea Peiffer, one of her fellow partisans and two of the local villagers.

When all were seated at tables in the two restaurants, the first wines were poured. Then salads and freshly baked breads were placed on the tables. The sight and aroma sent American and French salivary glands alike into overdrive. Onion tarte flambees followed. Then came fish freshly caught in nearby mountain streams along with potatoes and cabbage.

"This isn't exactly turkey with all the trimmings," Paul said, smiling, "but I've never enjoyed a meal more." He looked at his table companions and said solemnly, "Thank you." The guide's translation was greeted by warm smiles and replies that didn't require translating.

"Please tell them," R said softly, "that where I come from in America hospitality is a very important part of our culture and that their hospitality is easily the equal of any that I've ever experienced."

"Well said, R," Paul complimented his friend.

Throughout the dinner, no wine glass remained empty for long. Then village women arrived at each table with freshly baked apple pies.

"I think if my brother the chaplain was here," Paul smiled, "he would agree we are getting a preview of heaven."

The guide's translation resulted in a warm chorus of Oohs and Aahs.

Lea spoke for the first time. "Your brother is a man of God?"

"Yes," Paul said, after hearing her question translated, "a Catholic priest. He is with here with our Army. Eighty-Second Airborne Division."

"Do you know where?" Lea asked.

"No, just probably somewhere in France."

"Two brothers here in France. We are very grateful for the sacrifices you are making," said Lea.

"You are welcome," Paul said, looking closely at the young woman. "From what I've been hearing, you and your people also have made many sacrifices."

"Yes, but we really had no choice. France is our country. These villages are our homes, don't you see?"

"Yes," said Paul, "I do." A pause. "Are Germans still occupying your village?"

"They left after Paris was liberated," said Lea.

"Did you have troubles with them?" Paul asked.

"Yes. They executed our mayor."

Given the Nazis' widespread ferocity, her answer shouldn't have surprised Paul. He knew that. But he was stunned nonetheless, perhaps by Lea's matter-of-fact reply. "Why?"

"The German officer in charge suspected our villagers in the disappearance of two of his men and our two Jewish families. They were going to be arrested and deported. He was going to execute sixteen of our men, but our mayor volunteered to take their place."

"A brave man," Paul said with visible admiration.

"Yes."

"Were you involved in those disappearances?" Paul asked gently. "The Nazis and the Jewish families?"

"Yes," said Lea. "Maurice, too, and our comrades."

Paul looked at Roscoe who said, "Whew, I'm gettin' an epidemic of goosebumps."

"Goosebumps?" the guide asked.

Roscoe rubbed his arm vigorously and shivered exaggeratedly.

"Ah, yes, I understand," said the guide who translated. Lea's lips showed only the trace of a smile.

"What is your name?" Paul asked.

"Lea Peiffer. And yours?"

"Paul Brecker. This is my friend, Roscoe Remlinger. He is a big man but we call him by a short name -- R." Smiles and chuckles around the table.

The mayor of Natzwiller tapped his wine glass with a spoon and asked for attention. "Our new and great friends from afar – America – and near – Ribeauville – it has been our great pleasure to share our food and wine with you tonight. We will be grateful eternally for your arrival. I have spoken with the Lieutenant Clawson. He has accepted our offer to provide all of you soldiers with real beds tonight. Rest easy and sleep well, please." He poured wine in his glass and raised it. "A toast." All glasses were elevated. "To freedom."

Then the mayor excused himself and dashed across the street to the other restaurant to repeat his toast. After he had done so, the group in the first restaurant could hear clearly the second group's shouted reply to the mayor's toast: "Liberte! Freedom!"

†††

Paul and R were sharing a bed in one of the village's two hotels. "What a day," said R. "This is gonna make some letter home."

Paul chuckled. "Your folks back home in Georgia might think you've fallen into the lap of luxury."

"Nah, I'll be sure to include that I had to double up in bed with a G.I. and a Yankee one at that."

"Maybe I should censor your letter," Paul joked.

Staring up through the darkness toward the ceiling, R said softly, "I think that girl – Lea – has eyes for you, Paul."

"Ah, come on. She was just being courteous."

"Uh huh. Maybe. Ya' gotta admit, though, she's one unusual young woman. Not pretty in a soft way, but striking. And smart and tough. She'd rank right high as a classic southern belle."

"Yeah," Paul said contemplatively, "except you'd have to broaden the definition of southern belle. Include women in plain dresses who carry machine pistols and help make Nazis disappear."

R laughed softly. "Not bad, Paul. You know, I think you're gonna be glad Lieutenant Clawson assigned you an' me to stick around here a couple days."

"Uh huh…Goodnight, R."

"Good night, Paul."

†††

The next day at mid-morning, Paul and Lea left the village and started walking slowly up the mountain road toward the abandoned camp. R, the guide and the other Ribeauville partisans stayed behind and later would be providing relief in shifts. Four Natzwiller villagers also volunteered to take shifts. Paul was carrying his M-1, Lea her machine pistol and a luger. Paul was thinking that, while the unexpected had become routine, walking up a mountain side-by-side with an armed female partisan still qualified as rich irony. He looked at Lea and smiled.

The air atop the mountain was cold, but the exertion from climbing the road and the late November sun had Paul and Lea feeling comfortably warm.

"Come," said Paul, pointing toward the camp's main gate, "let's have a look around. Okay?"

"Okay," Lea said, correctly interpreting Paul's gesture and words.

Inside the camp they saw scattered about shovels, picks, wheelbarrows and carts and, near one cabin, cigar butts. They looked up at the guard towers and the perimeter fence – electrified barbed wire. Then they saw the hanging gallows, and Lea stopped. Paul was watching her. I think I might know what you're thinking. They resumed their tour and soon arrived at the gas chamber. Again, Lea stopped. She brushed away a tear. Paul could feel a lump forming in his throat.

They moved on and soon came to the crematorium ovens. It was too easy to imagine the bodies of thousands of innocents being incinerated. Paul shook his head and cursed the Nazis as fucking animals to be corralled and butchered. By now, tears were trickling steadily down Lea's cheeks. I don't think I could speak now if I wanted to, Paul thought. The evil done here is just too much for hearts to handle.

As they turned away from the ovens, Paul gently grasped Lea's left arm and guided her in turning to look away from the mountaintop camp. The contrast between the camp's grim interior and the majesty of the nearby mountains was as sharp as that between black ice and sun-kissed cherry blossoms. Paul, knowing that Lea couldn't understand his words, kept looking out to the mountains and began speaking aloud from the heart. "This area is the most beautiful place I've ever seen. All the suffering and death that went on inside this camp doesn't change that for me. And you are part of its beauty. The courage you've shown…amazing. R was right. I am glad the lieutenant had me stick around. I'll be going in a day or two and who knows what's next?" Paul laughed a short, rueful laugh and shifted his gaze from the mountains to Lea. "I don't think it would take much for me to fall in love with you. And, boy, would that ever make for a letter home. Small town American boy meets French village girl and takes a tumble into romance." Paul shook his head and redirected his gaze to the mountains. "Maybe it's a good thing you can't understand me."

"You are a long way from home and your family," were Lea's first spoken words since entering the camp. Paul looked at her but she kept her gaze on the mountains. "Fighting for another country. That is much to ask for a young man. Any young man. I respect you and your fellow soldiers. You are all nicer than I would have thought. I kept thinking that when Americans came, they would be harsh. Hardened from war and killing. I thought we in the village might be in danger from you." Lea turned her eyes toward Paul. "But now I can see your kindness. I can see why you are defeating our enemy. When you leave, I will miss you. But I will remember you always. Just as you are at this moment. On a mountaintop in my country. Bringing freedom and a future."

Lea brushed away another tear and began walking back toward the camp's main gate. Paul paused several moments before he began following. He looked at his watch. Relief should be arriving soon.

Not long after Paul and Lea arrived at the gate, they saw Roscoe and one of the Ribeauville partisans approaching.

"Hey Paul!" R called out. "How's it goin'?"

"Just fine, R."

Perhaps, thought Lea, feeling her spirits beginning to buoy, I should begin learning English. She greeted her fellow partisan. Then the four shook hands.

"Been inside?" R asked Paul.

"Pretty much everywhere. You'd better brace youself, R. Inside has gotta be something like hell on earth. It's like nothing you've ever seen. Or will want to see again."

"That bad?"

"It takes some special doing to kill thousands of innocent people and dispose of their bodies."

"Thanks for the warning."

"No problem."

"Well," said R, "why don't the two of you start back down? You might not have much appetite after seeing this place, but the village ladies are preparing one heck of a lunch for you."

"Okay, thanks."

With his left hand, Paul gestured to Lea to begin their descent.

Late that afternoon, Paul and Lea's second trek up the mountain together passed silently. Lunch had been everything R had indicated it would be. The ladies had served them tomato bisque – and Paul had wondered how they had managed that in November – fresh bread, a salad, foie gras, cheese, an apple and riesling. They also served Paul what he regarded as a small miracle. It was an eight-ounce bottle of Coca Cola.

"They know Americans like Coca Cola," the guide had explained to Paul, "and they were determined to find some and surprise you. They also gave a bottle to your friend, R."

"Please tell them that their thoughtfulness – and their resourcefulness – is deeply appreciated. I will thoroughly enjoy every swallow." And he did. The crisply carbonated beverage seemed to cut through months of accumulated grit, far more effectively than a toothbrush.

Lea had enjoyed the lunch and had enjoyed watching Paul enjoy it.

"Do you French eat like this all the time?" Paul had asked the guide. "This is terrific."

"We do take our food and our wines very seriously" the guide had replied, smiling. "And we like talking while we eat nearly as much as the food. Perhaps more," the guide laughed.

Walking up the mountain, Paul and Lea wanted to talk with each other, but the language gap was inhibiting them.

Inside the camp again, they slowly walked the perimeter near the fence. As they completed their circuit, the sun was dropping close to the distant summits. Paul had an idea and spoke. "Come with me." He gently took hold of Lea's left arm and began walking toward the main gate. Outside, he surveyed the terrain and saw a cluster of boulders near the edge of the mountaintop. He led Lea to them and said, "Let's sit and watch the sun set." He pointed to the sun, rested his M-1 against a boulder and then sat on top on top of the huge rock. He pointed to the adjacent boulder.

Lea smiled. "This is an excellent idea." She unslung her machine pistol and sat, facing the sinking sun. "I like you. Do you mind if I call you Paul?"

His spoken name was the only word he understood, but that was enough for him to say, "Do you mind if I call you Lea?"

"That's fine with me," she said. So, she thought, perhaps this is how ancients learned to communicate with each other.

After a minute of silence – silence that seemed less strained than during their earlier times together – Paul looked at Lea and spoke again. "Lea, the last thing I expected was to meet a girl I really care about. Not during this war. I've been concentrating mostly on just staying alive. And helping friends like R stay alive. I don't know when this war is going to end. The sooner, the better. For sure. At least we're closing in on the Rhine. Tomorrow R and I will be heading back to join our platoon. I'm going to miss you. A lot. And I can't help thinking that we'll never see each other again. That's sad. Very sad."

Lea waited to hear whether Paul would say more. When his gaze shifted back toward the western sun, now beginning to dip behind a summit, Lea began speaking. "It's funny. Growing up in a small village here in the Alsace, I had no contact with Americans. Oh, a few might have passed through. Tourists. But I would have had no occasion to speak with them. Now I am spending time with one – a younger one – and he is a soldier coming to help free us from the Germans. You are carrying a gun and probably have shot it at Germans and perhaps killed some. Yet you are thoughtful and kind. I wish we had more time to learn more about each other. When you leave, I know I will miss you." She paused and then laughed softly. "I will always remember this as the conversation between strangers speaking strange tongues." She smiled.

Paul looked at his watch. "Our relief will be coming soon." He slipped off the boulder and rotated his head and shoulders to ease the stiffness. Then he bent down and picked up his M-1.

Lea stood, too, and picked up her machine pistol. "We will have one more shift together before you leave," she said. "I think we should have another conversation in our two strange tongues."

"I would like to kiss you," Paul replied. "Right here and now. But the last thing I want is for you to think I'm taking advantage. The American cowboy riding to the damsel's rescue. Although from what I'm gathering, you don't need much rescuing. Your country, yes. But you specifically, I'm not so sure. You are a very impressive girl. It's hard for me to not reach out and take you in my arms."

They began strolling toward the road to await their relief. "Paul, I think I know what you are thinking. I think I see the words in your eyes. So I will chance that I'm right." Lea stopped and touched Paul's arm. When he turned toward her, she stepped closer, elevated her five-foot three-inch self onto her toes, and kissed him lightly on his lips.

And then they heard the boots of their relief.

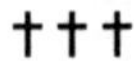

Chapter 44

"That doesn't sound very Christian, Padre," General George Patton observed dryly.

"It could save lives – lots of them," Father Jack Brecker replied, "on both sides. What could be more Christian than that?"

"Touche!" Patton smiled appreciatively. "You're a man of God for the ages."

"Perhaps only for today."

"Well, Padre, if you can stand being a little loose with the truth, by God, socan I."

"There is a kernel of truth to it."

"Ah, Padre, a small kernel," Patton teased.

It was early December and Patton and Jack were near Metz whose German-manned forts were still stubbornly resisting the American onslaught. The Germans' resolve was slowing the Americans' advance and adding to the casualty total. After another staff meeting during which Patton had vented his mounting exasperation in particularly colorful language, Jack had lingered.

"Yes, Padre?" Patton had said, eyeing Jack with evident suspicion and simmering impatience. "If you are going to critique my choice of vocabulary, this might not be the most propitious occasion."

"Actually, General, it's your vocabulary that got me to thinking. If you'll indulge me for just a moment...To me, it seems the key to taking Metz might be words, not guns."

Patton's facial expression had changed, suspicion and irritation giving way to curiosity born of respect for the warrior chaplain. "Go on, Padre."

Jack had then articulated his thoughts. When he had finished, Patton chuckled and said, "You heard a calling and it led you to altars and pulpits. If you had heard that voice differently, you might be wearing a bird or a star instead of a cross on your helmet. That's damned creative military strategy. We'll give it a try."

"Thank you, General."

"Now, I've got to pick someone to go."

"I'll go."

"What?"

"It should be me, General."

"With all due respect for you and your idea, Padre, this is a job for one of my line officers."

"Will he be armed?"

"A sidearm. With a small escort."

"General, if you don't mind me taking the idea a step further, I think that would defeat the purpose – and effect – of the idea."

"Hmmm…All right, Padre, let's hear the rest of your thinking."

†††

"Ready?" Jack asked Staff Sergeant Jerry Parma.

"Ready, Chaplain."

"No one ordered you to go with me?"

"I volunteered, Chaplain. Really."

"You understand why you can't go armed?"

"Yes. I do."

The two men climbed into a jeep, Parma behind the steering wheel. Patton, Colonel Codman and other senior staff members were there to see them off.

"Good luck, Padre," Patton said. "You might want to rub that Saint Christopher medal a time or two."

"Will do, General."

"And, Sergeant," Patton said to Parma, "don't take any risks on that washboard excuse for a road. I want both of you back in one piece."

"Yes, Sir," Parma said, snapping off a salute that Patton returned.

Sergeant Parma put the jeep in gear and headed north, the vehicle bouncing along the frozen, wickedly rutted road. "A bladder buster, wouldn't you say, Chaplain?" Parma said.

"It's a good thing we're not carrying explosives," Jack replied, smiling ruefully.

Soon thereafter, Parma and Jack were passing through the Allies' front lines. Along the way, soldiers waved and saluted. Moments later, Jack reached behind him for two items. In his left hand, he held upright a six-foot pole to which was affixed a large section of a white bed sheet. In his right hand, he held aloft the small brass crucifix that the Poles had given him after he had said Easter Mass for them. Not exactly the armament of a Polish lancer or a paratrooper, Jack was thinking, but hopefully it will carry the day.

Sergeant Parma glanced at Jack and smiled slightly. "I've seen and done a lot during the last six months," he said, "but I never imagined a sight like this."

"Let's hope it has the desired effect."

"You mean, pray it does?"

"That, too."

†††

As the jeep neared the German line of fortifications, Parma slowed it to a virtual crawl. The reduced speed was meant to provide the Germans with a long look at the oncoming jeep, its occupants and their symbols. It also eased the jarring ride.

A couple minutes later, a German soldier appeared on the road. He was holding aloft a large square of white cloth.

"So far so good," Sergeant Parma murmured.

"Let's stop and get out," Jack replied.

Parma braked and Jack stepped out, still holding aloft the white flag and crucifix. He sensed thousands of pairs of German eyes watching in puzzlement. He began walking toward the German. Sergeant Parma was walking at Jack's left. They stopped about six feet from the German who lowered his white flag. Jack did likewise, handing the flagpole to Parma and shifting the crucifix to his left hand.

"You are?" the German said in passable English.

"I am Chaplain Brecker, Jack Brecker. This is Sergeant Jerry Parma."

"You are a captain," the German observed. He and his superiors had been watching the jeep's approach through binoculars.

"As are you," Jack replied.

"Captain Gerhard Oberster," replied the German. "What is your purpose? Surely it is not to propose your surrender."

Jack smiled at the captain's wit. "Actually, Captain, I am here on behalf of General Patton." Oberster nodded his understanding. "First,

Captain, General Patton has asked me to convey his admiration for your defense of Metz. You and your fellow soldiers have fought valiantly and are to be commended."

"Thank you," Captain Oberster said. "General Patton is an excellent field commander and his compliment is well received."

"Secondly," Jack continued, "he deplores the loss of life that both sides are suffering. He is going to bring that to an end. You will have a choice in determining how he does that."

"Please proceed, Captain," Oberster said.

"The garrison at Metz can surrender to General Patton and his Third Army front-line soldiers," Jack said. "That is your first choice and, if you elect it, you must do so immediately. If you do not, then your second choice is to watch General Patton and his front-line troops bypass Metz. We will surround your fortifications and deny you supplies. Your men will grow hungry and starve. Eventually, you will surrender but your surrender will not be to combat soldiers. Instead, you will lay down your arms to Third Army cooks and clerks, to supply personnel and couriers. Many of them are Negroes. Those are your choices."

Captain Oberster's face had remained expressionless until hearing Jack's last three sentences. At those, Oberster's veneer reflected a hint of distaste if not outright disgust. His reply was somber and militarily correct. "I will carry your message to my superior officers. They will consider the choices you have presented and decide whether to accept either one of them or to offer a counter-proposal."

"I understand your position, Captain," Jack said. "Of course, you must consult. But I must tell you in the clearest possible words that General Patton absolutely insists that he will entertain no counterproposal. If we do not have your reply to one of the two choices I have presented by morning, General Patton will immediately begin his bypass of Metz. Do you understand, Captain? Fully understand?"

"Yes, Captain."

"Good."

Jack saluted Oberster who responded with a German Army salute, not the exaggerated Heil Hitler. Oberster pivoted and began walking back toward Metz. Jack and Sergeant Parma returned to the jeep.

"What do you think, Father?"

"I'm not sure. We know the Germans have a great deal of military pride. We'll find out soon how proud – and sensible – they are. One more thing, Sergeant."

"Yes, Chaplain?"

"What I said about cooks and clerks and Negroes. I'd appreciate it if you didn't spread that around. It might be true but I hated saying it."

"Understood."

†††

Word of the Germans' choice wasn't long in coming. Three of Metz's forts surrendered immediately. Within days, the others did likewise. One of the German soldiers most relieved by the choice made was Captain Gerhard Oberster. He was tired of fighting and killing, of seeing others killed. Too often for his peace of mind, he still had dreams – nightmares – about his execution of Mayor Javelot. Though he was proud to be a German soldier, a disciplined warrior, he was glad his war was ending.

Chapter 45

"I wanted to tell you before I tell the rest of the staff and our men."

"I can't believe it," Thaddeus said despondently. "It makes no sense. None."

"It makes perfect sense to Montgomery and Browning," General Sosabowski said. "Since the English people are seeing Market Garden for what it was – an embarrassing defeat – they need a scapegoat."

"But why you?"

"Who is there to protest? The British people will not be upset. A Polish general…To them I am nobody."

"But to relieve you…It's wrong," Thaddeus said. "It's humiliating." December 9 was rapidly becoming Thaddeus' bleakest day in the more than two months since Operation Market Garden.

"Yes, it is that," said Sosabowski. "They say I objected too strenuously to Market Garden. They say we Poles did not enter the battle soon enough or fight hard enough."

"That's insane!" Thaddeus exploded. "Those are lies! We couldn't go in any sooner because of the fog. Our men fought hard and too many died. We lost almost half…The river crossings…I have lost all respect for Montgomery and Browning. They are spineless."

"General Urquhart sent his condolences," Sosabowski said. "He telephoned me yesterday."

"A good man," Thaddeus said, his temper moderating, albeit only slightly. "But Montgomery and Browning, they bring shame on themselves and the British military. And whose fault was it that their radios were bad or that so much equipment was damaged in the drops? Or that we even tried to take Arnhem with only a single road and all those bridges to take and hold? And who was it that misjudged German strength? It was stupidity! Sheer stupidity! Our men will protest this strongly. They will –"

"Stop," Sosabowski said forcefully. "The men will be upset."

"Angry. Furious."

"Angry, too. But you and the other senior staff must see that they do nothing stupid…nothing that brings dishonor to Poland."

"Who will lead us?"

"Lieutenant Colonel Jachnik. At least temporarily."

"Well, he is your deputy," Thaddeus observed, "so you know his capabilities."

"He is an able man," Sosabowski said. "He deserves your respect – and the men's"

"What about you?" Thaddeus asked, pursing his lips in disgust.

"I am to be inspector of salvage and disposal."

The utter disbelief that Thaddeus was feeling was etched clearly in his features. "That is an insult," he muttered. "A profound insult to you and our brigade."

The insult had been in the works for weeks. After Market Garden, General Montgomery, despite his proclamation that Market Garden had been a ninety percent success, had written to Sir Alan Brooke, chief of the Imperial General Staff (CIGS) – head of the British Army – that the "Polish forces fought very badly and showed no keenness to fight if it meant risking their own lives. I do not want this brigade here and possibly you may like to send them to join other Poles in Italy."

General Browning had followed up Montgomery's letter with one to the Deputy CIGS, recommending that General Sosabowski be relieved of his command "and that a younger, more flexibly minded and co-operative officer be made available to succeed him."

General Urquhart, now in command of the British 1st Airborne, was aghast at the treachery. He admired Sosabowski and the men of the Polish Airborne Brigade. Urquhart, the Poles believed, was not only physically bigger and braver than the runty Montgomery and the delicately built "Boy" Browning – Urquhart stood six-feet two inches and weighed 200 pounds – but they also endorsed the British airborne soldiers' view of Urquhart as "a bloody general who didn't mind doing the work of a sergeant."

"It hurts," Sosabowski said. "I will not pretend it doesn't."

Thaddeus was searching his mind for additional words that might provide some meaningful consolation to his general, mentor and friend. He spoke the only remaining words that seemed appropriate. "I am sorry, very sorry, General."

"Thank you."

A pause. "Sir, if you don't mind, could I ask you a question?"

"Of course."

"Do you know what is next for our brigade?"

"Nothing certain," Sosabowski replied softly. "I have heard rumors that when the fighting is over, we...you will be sent to Germany as part of the occupation force."

"Germany! Not Poland?"

"That is what I've heard. Nothing confirmed. Thaddeus, listen to me. The war will not go on much longer. That much is certain. The end for Hitler becomes closer every day. You have done your part...in Poland, France, Holland. Be proud of yourself and your achievements. Just as I am proud of you."

Thaddeus' throat was thickening. He swallowed, twice. "You should feel the same pride, General." Thaddeus' voice caught, and he paused before trying to continue. "You led us with intelligence and courage. I would not have wanted to serve with any other general."

"Except perhaps Urquhart," Sosabowski said teasingly, trying to lighten the mood.

Thaddeus smiled, too. "After the war, General, we can continue to see each other in Poland."

"Perhaps, perhaps not."

"What does that mean?"

"I've been thinking. If the Russians are occupying Poland, that might not be a healthy situation for a Polish ex-general."

"Do you really think? –"

"We know that the Russians and the Germans have not hesitated to execute Polish officers and political officials. And the Russians have their gulag..."

"So..."

"I haven't decided yet, but I might remain in England. Make a new life there."

"I see..."

"Do what you feel you must, Thaddeus. Build your own life where you feel you must...where your heart takes you."

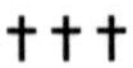

Chapter 46

"Thank you, Sir. I'm glad you have a minute for me," Jack said upon entering Patton's office.

Patton smiled wryly as the two men saluted each other. "I think I would be well advised to make time for a chaplain with your range of talent and connections. Are you here to offer up more brilliant military strategy? I can always use some."

"No, General. I think I've exhausted my limited supply of military strategizing. Spiritual matters are what I have in mind. My temporary duty with you is feeling more like permanent. With your concurrence, I'll be leaving to get back with the Eighty-Second."

"I have no objection whatever to your doing that very thing," Patton replied. "But at this moment, that might be problematic, Chaplain." It was December 16, 1944. "The Germans have launched a massive counterattack in the Ardennes. North of here. We've been hearing rumblings the Nazis might try something big. They've been maintaining radio silence, and our recon aircraft have spotted them moving bridging equipment to the front lines. But our forces were still surprised. Frankly, Chaplain, our front line is collapsing, and so far we haven't figured out how to respond. But I think I can say with certainty that traveling north to where your Eighty-Second is would be out of the question."

"I see... " Jack's right thumb and forefinger were rubbing his chin. "I don't think any words from me would be too likely to persuade the Germans to surrender."

"Not this time, Chaplain. I think this is Hitler's last gasp. The mad bastard thinks he still can win the war. He's delusional but determined and desperate, and that means more men will be dying. Hitler could care less."

Jack shook his head slightly. "I will tell you something I've told no one – and trust you not to pass it on." Patton nodded his assent. "Hitler and his evil have tested my faith." Jack sighed and Patton said nothing, remaining stone-faced. "I am having difficulty reconciling a caring God with all this death and suffering," Jack said in what was amounting to his personal confession. "I keep praying for an end to the carnage, but each day brings more. I'm thinking there is a limit to my faith and maybe I've reached it."

Patton exhaled audibly. "Chaplain, I am certain that many – Germans and Americans alike, certainly the Brits – regard me as a heartless son-of-a-bitch. A wanton killer. They might be right. An egotistical prima donna. They are right about that. But I am not Godless or faithless. I am certain that God is on the side of right, and that is our side. Your side. I believe He is hearing your prayers and His divine intervention saved thousands of lives at Metz. You were His instrument. So keep the faith, Chaplain. You keep praying, and the end will arrive sooner rather than later."

Jack uttered a small hint of a grateful chuckle. "Sir, you have made an outstanding general, and you just might make an excellent bishop."

Patton laughed heartily. "God in His most liberal moment surely would have to deny me a bishop's mitre."

†††

On December 17, the 101st Airborne Division was ordered north to reinforce U.S. troops at Bastogne, a Belgian town that was a major road hub and considered vital by both Hitler and the Allies. Lieutenant Billy Clawson, Paul Brecker and Roscoe Remlinger were in a truck that was one of the first American vehicles to arrive at the town. Paul couldn't help thinking about the contrast between a peaceful Alsatian mountaintop and this newest hell of crashing artillery shells and exploding buildings, vehicles and men. Commanding Allied troops at Bastogne was Brigadier General Anthony McAuliffe. His stubbornness in the face of the seemingly unstoppable German onslaught soon would become legendary.

†††

On December 18, fast-moving German forces encircled Bastogne and the nearby countryside. Caught in the encirclement was the 128th Evacuation Hospital. As American casualties mounted, the work of the doctors, nurses and orderlies became non-stop. The intensity of her labors notwithstanding, Lieutenant Theresa Hassler realized with certainty that enemy shelling was much closer to their cluster of hospital tents than she ever had previously experienced. The explosions were causing moments of high anxiety, but they passed quickly as she concentrated on the men she was working to save and comfort.

†††

In a senior staff meeting near Metz, American and British generals were discussing the massive German counterstrike and the fate of American troops at Bastogne – the entire 101st Airborne Division plus combat command soldiers from the U.S. 9th and 10th Armored Divisions. General and after general voiced pessimism ranging from severe doubt to hopelessness that anything could be done to spare the trapped American forces from having to surrender into Nazi captivity.

Patton had been listening, remaining uncustomarily silent. After everyone else around the large, oval table had expressed themselves moribundly, Patton spoke up. "My Third Army can get through."

"Impossible," spluttered a British general. "Your men have been fighting continuously at Metz. They are exhausted. It is a good hundred and twenty-five miles to Bastogne. Even Monty would recognize the cruel folly of such an undertaking."

"No doubt," Patton said, smiling congenially, "Monty would be content to remain in place and let events unfold." The British general bristled, but Patton ignored him and continued. "My men can make it to Bastogne and we can do it in forty-eight hours." Patton knew he was exaggerating but deemed his hubris essential to winning permission to proceed.

"Really," the British general replied contemptuously, "that is beyond the pale. Your men need rest, not a forced march."

"My men will do precisely what I order them to," Patton said, no longer exaggerating. "Not because they love me but because they fear me and because they know that I will personally lead them." Patton decided to plunge ahead with his assertions, not to wait for permission. "We will move out immediately. We will march and fight straight through the night, and we will break through to Bastogne in two days."

Patton firmly believed he would succeed. Not in two days but succeed nonetheless. Others, including Dwight Eisenhower, believed Patton would betasting defeat for the first time in his remarkable career.

†††

In a surgery tent, Lieutenant Colonel Marilyn Carter, Lieutenant Theresa Hassler and other nurses were assisting doctors operating on six wounded American soldiers. German shelling was continuing to come closer, ominously. Each new explosion saw the medical staff flinching involuntarily.

The next explosion hit just north of the hospital compound. "Someone get on the horn," the chief surgeon barked. "Tell division HQ to get planes in the air to knock out the Germans' artillery or we'll be the next casualties."

Colonel Carter looked around the tent. "Lieutenant Hassler, get to our radioman."

"Yes, Ma'am." Theresa quickly pulled off surgical gloves, left the tent and went running across the snow-covered compound, her brown hair flying behind her. Two more shells landed near the compound's perimeter and shook the ground. Inside a small tent, she found the radioman, a corporal, sitting nervously at a field desk.

"Corporal," said Theresa, standing over him, "this shelling has to stop. Call HQ and -"

"I already have," he interrupted. "They say it's too foggy to send planes up. Sorry."

"But this is a hospital. We don't have trenches and bunkers."

"You're telling me?" the corporal said edgily.

"Try again," Theresa commanded. "Now. Call HQ."

"If you say so." The radioman reached a captain with the 101st Airborne in Bastogne.

"Give me your headset," Theresa said. The corporal complied. "Captain," said Theresa, "I'm a colonel here with the Evac." Her lie momentarily startled the corporal who quickly grew to admire the deception. "Colonel Carter. German shells are falling all around us. Getting too damned close. Fog or no fog, you need to figure out a way to end this shelling. Now! If you don't, you will have more blood on your hands than you could put in a forty-gallon drum. You yourself might have need of our services, Captain. I hope not but if you do, it would be to your benefit if there was still a hospital here."

The captain nearly cut her off curtly, but something – Theresa's words, her tone, her situation, her rank – caused him to reconsider. "I'll do what I can. Believe me, I will."

"Thank you, Captain. If this shelling doesn't stop in twenty minutes, I'll be talking to your superior officer – if I'm still in one piece." Theresa removed the headset and handed it to the corporal. "Thank you, too."

Theresa glanced down at him, almost smiled and then stepped outside. At that moment, a shell exploded between her and the surgery tent. Dirt, stones and steel fragments went rocketing across the compound.

†††

In Bastogne, a colonel approached General McAuliffe. "The Germans are proposing surrender terms. They say we have no chance and to delay surrendering means certain defeat and many more casualties. Shall I call our senior staff together?"

"There will be no need for that." McAuliffe said grimly.

"What is our reply? Do we tell them we will surrender? I hate that thought," the colonel said, "and so will the men."

"Tell the Germans," McAuliffe instructed, "nuts."

"Nuts?"

"That's right. Nuts."

†††

"That's what he said?" Patton asked Colonel Codman.

"Yes. Nuts."

"Splendid!" Patton exulted. "By God, General McAuliffe is my kind of warrior leader. You tell him to hold on, that we are coming."

"Yes, Sir."

Slowly, Theresa pushed herself to her feet. Her helmet lay on the dirty snow. She reached down and groaned in pain that was the most excruciating she had ever felt. Still doubled over at the waist, she began to examine herself. She saw dark blood staining her right hip and realized that was the source of the searing pain. Her eyes were watering, and her fatigue pants were ripped and singed at the point of the bleeding. Tenderly, Theresa fingered the wound. No shrapnel inside, she thought, but I think it sliced bone on the way through. I'll need stitches. Maybe surgery. She rubbed her bloodied hand on her pants. Then she looked up and across the compound to the surgery tent. Between her and the tent was a large crater. She saw several gashes in the tent's canvass.

Theresa's first impulse was to run. She took one step and collapsed to her hands and knees. She tried to will away the pain – unsuccessfully. Slowly, she regained her feet and went staggering toward the tent. She pushed her way inside. Some of the staff were crouching beside surgery tables, others were standing. All were stunned and silent. One surgery table had overturned, and the anesthetized patient was lying on the wooden floor. Then Theresa saw a second body lying supine on the floor. Tentatively, Theresa limped closer and slowly knelt. She put her fingers on the bloodied neck. No pulse. She wasn't surprised. So much blood…severed artery… no chance. It was Lieutenant Colonel Marilyn Carter.

†††

Patton's 3rd Army had to traverse 125 miles to reach Bastogne. His men were making good progress, but the going wasn't easy. Germans were continually harassing his units with artillery fire, snipers and trees felled across roads. Patton was growing ever more frustrated. He knew strong air support would expedite progress, but persistent fog was continuing to keep Allies' planes grounded.

"Where's Chaplain Brecker?" Patton asked Colonel Codman. They were standing on crusted snow beside Patton's jeep. Men went trudging by, flanking rumbling vehicles.

"I don't know, Sir, but I'll get him."

Minutes later, Codman returned. "Sir, it seems Chaplain Brecker has gone on ahead with a scouting patrol."

Patton grimaced and shook his head. "How soon can you get him here?"

"An hour," the colonel replied. "There abouts. Can't be certain."

†††

Jack Brecker could see the four stars mounted on the jeep's hood. He bounded from the jeep in which he was riding and went striding across the crunching snow to the oncoming vehicle. He stopped beside it and saluted. "You wanted to see me, Sir."

"Yes," Patton said, returning the salute. "Get in. I need a prayer. A special prayer."

"For what, Sir?"

"Good weather. Clear skies, so we can get some close air support. If we don't move faster, Bastogne will fall."

"Hmmm…"

"I think I know what you're thinking," Patton said. "It might be a trifle much to ask of the Lord. But this is a damned difficult situation, and we're losing men on the way to relieve other men who are dying. Prayer couldn't hurt, Chaplain, and it might help. A little faith," Patton smiled. "Right?"

Jack grinned. "Yes, Sir, a little faith."

"In the interest of full disclosure," Patton smiled wryly, "when I wasn't sure how soon they could get you here, I gave the same assignment to another chaplain."

"Tag-teaming the Lord," Jack smiled teasingly.

"Think he'll mind?" Patton asked.

"If our Lord can be flattered," Jack said, "He probably is."

"Can you write me this prayer within an hour? I'd like to read it to my staff this evening and then have them spread it among the men."

"Thirty minutes, General."

"Excellent!"

†††

Patton looked at the prayers written by the two chaplains. I don't see much difference, he thought. Similar words. Similar in tone. But I'm using Chaplain Brecker's. I have more faith in the warrior priest.

Theresa Hassler, despite her crushing workload, was grieving hard over the death of Colonel Carter. In the operating tent, Theresa had to force herself to purge her mind of thoughts of the colonel. In the nurses' tent, when she tried to nap, she thought of no one else. Marilyn Carter had been an extraordinary leader, unflappable, an outstanding nurse, an understanding superior, a mentor and a friend. I miss you terribly, Theresa repeatedly said in her thoughts, and I will remember you forever in my daily prayers. I pledge that before God. Marilyn Carter. Hal Walker. Dear God, I now have lost two friends who were so very close to me. Please bring this war to an end. Please.

†††

On the morning of December 23, George Patton was in high spirits. "Look at that," he said to Colonel Codman and Jack Brecker. Patton was pointing to a clear sky that was becoming rapidly bluer. Already, American planes were roaring by at low altitudes, strafing and dropping their bombs on enemy units. "Chaplain, I trust you've put aside any and all doubts about your faith. Clearly, our Lord listened to your prayer. I'm going to decorate you for this."

"That's not necessary, General. But if you insist, decorate the other chaplain, too. I don't think the Lord would want you playing favorites with his messengers."

"Not mere messengers," Patton grinned, "but angels of the Third Army."

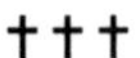

CHAPTER 47

Bernadeta Gudek stepped down on the top edge of the shovel, forcing it into the hard ground. She then removed the shovel and dumped the upturned earth into the wheelbarrow. With a second shovel, her younger sister Barbara followed suit.

The calendar, lowering temperatures, falling snow and cutting winds all were heralding the arrival of winter on the plains of Poland.

The sisters continued digging in a corner inside the barn. The two milk cows and the ox were watching passively.

"Do you think Father is worrying too much?" Barbara asked. "Do you think he is being too cautious?"

"No," Bernadeta replied. "When the Russians cross the Vistula, I don't expect the Germans will be gentle in their retreat. And from what we've been hearing, the Russians aren't proving to be the most civilized of liberators."

"So you believe the rumors of rape and murder?" Barbara asked.

"Considering what I saw in Warsaw these past five years, I know that man is perfectly capable of inflicting the worst cruelties."

The sisters kept digging, gradually filling the wheelbarrow.

"I'll take the first load of dirt to the forest," Barbara said.

"As my younger sister," Bernadeta replied dryly, "you should do more than your share."

Barbara laughed. "You always have been the bossy big sister." She then departed with the first load of excavated earth.

Minutes later, when Barbara returned to the barn with the empty wheelbarrow, she and Bernadeta resumed their digging.

"I hope we never need to use this hiding place," said Barbara. "I think it would be very claustrophobic. And dirty. And cold."

Bernadeta chuckled. "If we have to use this hole, perspiration and dirty hair will be the least of your worries. After all the time I spent in that church basement, I sometimes wondered if I ever would feel clean again. And free. But I survived and right now I don't know that I could ask for much more."

"You've become much wiser," Barbara murmured admiringly.

"The inevitable result of experience," Bernadeta smiled.

"I wish we were making this hiding place big enough to hold Father and Mother as well," said Barbara. "But I understand Father's reasoning."

"Good," Bernadeta said, "because he's right. If either German or Russian soldiers visit our farm and they find no one, they will believe it deserted and are more likely to take whatever they see and destroy it. If they come and see Father and Mother...well, they still will be in danger but they and the farm might be saved."

"Bernadeta, let's still make this hole big enough for three. Big enough for us and Mother. I can't stand the thought of her being raped. Father could say he is a widower. What do you think?"

"I think he's already thought of that, but he might listen to us," said Bernadeta. "Of course, we will have to persuade Mother as well. She is so worried about us she might refuse to worry about herself."

"Nothing new about that."

"No, not a thing."

"Will you try?" Barbara asked. "To persuade them I mean?"

"Yes. Now, let's keep digging. Remember, we have to be able to fit our clothes in here, too. We can't leave signs of ourselves in the house."

Despite the cold, the sisters were sweating. The hole was growing deeper and wider. Their plan was to cover the completed hole with a flat sheet of wood planking, with cracks wide enough to admit air. They then would spread straw over the planking. Lastly, they would pile tools in that corner. Later, if they needed to use the hiding place, the sisters would lower themselves in, and their father would disguise it with the straw and tools.

"When the war is over," Barbara said wistfully, "my dream is for love and happiness. No fear, no evil, just love and happiness. Do you think that's too childish?"

"No. It's a good dream," Bernadeta smiled. "Do you mind sharing it with me?"

†††

"Merry Christmas! Merry Christmas! We're nearly there. Merry Christmas. The Lord is smiling on us today. Merry Christmas." Each word of each greeting was accompanied by crystallized breath. On this as on the other mornings during the hard drive north, General George Patton was up and out early, visiting men in all combat units of his 3rd Army. With him were Colonel Codman and Jack Brecker. There wasn't enough time for Jack to say multiple Masses, but at each stop he gave a blessing and distributed Holy Communion to all soldiers desiring it. He was sure he had placed Communion wafers on the tongues of some non-Catholics, and it bothered him not at all. The term ecumenism hadn't become popular, but Jack Brecker was an early and avid practitioner. His renown as the airborne warrior priest made him a welcome visitor for Catholics, Protestants and Jews alike. Patton watched his favorite chaplain with paternal pride.

The breakthrough came the next day, December 26. At 6:45 p.m., 3rd Army units reached the German perimeter around Bastogne. Patton's daring initiative had taken longer than two days – seven, in fact – and many of his men were exhausted to the point of debilitation. Nevertheless, Patton didn't hesitate. He gave the green light for combat units to begin penetrating the weakened German lines. Supply trucks followed quickly. The relief of General McAuliffe and the besieged 101st Airborne was under way.

Jack Brecker was one of the first Americans to reach the center of the battered town. He eased from a jeep driven by Jerry Parma, promoted to Sergeant First Class after Metz. Jack, hands on hips, surveyed his new mission. Burning fires silhouetted the skeletons of buildings. Jeep and truck headlights provided the only other illumination. Through his mind's eye, Charco had never looked so good -- like paradise compared with Bastogne. I've never seen a town so utterly destroyed.

"Can I help you, Chaplain?" The voice speaking the words was softly southern.

Jack turned to his right and saw a soldier approaching through the dim light. His face was blackened from smoke and soot, and his uniform was caked with accumulated filth. "Made out the cross on your helmet," the soldier said.

Jack leaned closer and squinted at the name patch on the soldier's field jacket: Remlinger.

"Your name looks familiar," said Jack. "Aren't you my brother's friend?"

Roscoe Remlinger eyed the name patch on Jack's field jacket. "Aren't you my friend's brother?"

Jack extended his right hand and Roscoe shook it. "You've covered some miles since we met on D-Day."

"That we have, Chaplain, and for a southern boy like me this cold and snow makes each of those miles seem a lot longer."

Jack smiled. "Looks like the Hundred And First has had it pretty rough here," he observed. "Casualties?"

"Bad but I expected worse. We're better – and faster – at diggin' in than we were a few months ago. 'Course diggin' in this half-frozen Belgian ground takes some determined doin'."

Jack nodded. "Where's Paul? Is he okay?"

"He's fine, Chaplain. Should be back soon. We had a couple guys dinged up this afternoon, and he volunteered to help get them to the evac hospital."

Puzzlement showed on Jack's face. "Where is the evac?"

"About where you'd normally expect to find an aid station," Roscoe said, smiling tiredly. "The Germans created their bulge so fast that some of our rear echelon units got themselves trapped. Evac was one."

"Been there?"

"No, but I hear they took some hits. Lost a nurse. Got some folks hurt."

"Names?"

R shook his head. "Sorry, Chaplain. You know someone there?"

"Maybe. I have a friend who's a nurse."

"Maybe Paul can fill you in."

†††

"How is she, Paul?"

"A piece of shrapnel did a pretty nasty job on her hip. Cut it pretty bad, muscle and bone. She's in a lot of pain and she's limping but says she's going to be okay. I believe her. She knows her stuff, Jack. And she's tough. Been through a lot. But she still can smile in a way that helps G.I.s through some tough times."

"I'm glad to hear that."

"You should go see her. She told me you guys finally met down near Metz."

"Maybe I will. Tomorrow."

Paul nodded. "Could you use a drink?"

"Yeah...You hear anything about Walt Hunter?"

"Captain Hunter? Your friend?" Jack nodded. "Nope. Nothing. But I'll ask around. Eighty-Second's not too far away."

"Thanks."

They and Billy Clawson's platoon were squeezed together amidst the basement rubble of a burned out building. Sergeant Parma also was with them.

"Gets pretty cold down here at night," Paul said. "Fortunately, we've had plenty of wine to help fortify us."

"Some hard stuff, too," R said, holding up a bottle of vodka. "This has a little more bite than wine. Keeps my southern blood properly heated."

Jack smiled and nodded. "I think I'd like a shot of what you're selling, R."

"I'm not selling measly shots," R said. He picked up a tin coffee mug, turned it over and tapped its bottom. "Figure vodka should kill any germs inside." Then he turned the mug right side up and poured vodka nearly to its brim. "Not exactly sippin' whiskey but we're all used to makin' sacrifices. You get my special sale price, Chaplain."

Jack accepted the mug. "Thanks, R." He took a large sip and felt his eyes begin to water and his throat to burn. He cleared his throat. "Bite is right," he coughed.

R chuckled lowly. "I didn't promise smooth, just heat."

"Drink up and sleep well," said Paul.

†††

The next afternoon, Jack borrowed Jerry Parma's jeep and headed for the evacuation hospital. His thinking was tortured. I'm sure I can be of some help there, but should I really be going? I want to see her, but is it for the right reason? I've only seen her once in, what, twelve years? And then I think her emotions got the best of her. Her boyfriend – almost a fiancée – lost, maybe dead. Me, an old friend. A familiar face. The moment just overwhelmed her. It won't happen again. I won't let it happen again. But what if it does? Maybe I should just turn around and head back to Bastogne. I can hardly believe I'm even thinking like this. I'm glad thoughts are private. Well, private except for the Lord. Hope he's not eavesdropping on my thoughts -- and my soul.

Jack was barely aware of the passing devastation. Demolished buildings, splintered trees and fences, dead and bloated livestock, deep craters and forlorn Belgians trying to pick up the pieces of shattered lives.

Upon entering the hospital compound, Jack braked the jeep and switched off the engine. He sat behind the steering wheel, surveying the compound. Smudged and torn tents. Dirty snow. Hustling personnel.

An orderly approached. "Help you out, Chaplain?"

"I'm looking for a friend, Lieutenant Hassler."

"I think she's in surgery," the orderly said, pointing toward the large operating tent.

"Thanks."

"Didn't you pay a visit to our hospital with General Patton back near Metz?"

"Yes."

"Thought so. Glad to have you around again. Want some coffee? Mess tent's right over there."

"Sounds good."

"Come with me," the orderly said. "I'll make sure they put some fresh on for you."

"Thanks."

"No problem. Glad you're here, Chaplain. Been kinda bleak."

"Your own chaplain…You have one, don't you?"

"Yes, Sir. But he's in recovery. Got hit during a shelling. A concussion and cuts. He'll be okay, I think, but the docs are insisting he get some bed rest. Won't be moving around much for awhile."

"Thank you. I'll go pay my respects to him. See what I can do to help."

"Why don't you get your coffee first, Chaplain? You look like you could uses some warming up."

"I think you're right," Jack smiled kindly. "Okay."

†††

With his left hand, Jack rubbed the back of his neck. He was standing at the mess tent entrance, sipping fresh, steaming coffee. Black. With each exhalation, he could see his breath crystallizing instantly in the frigid air. *I hope this was the right thing to do. She's only maybe a hundred feet away, but right now I feel like I'm on another planet. Alone. Looking down at Shelby, at the Josephinum, at Charco, at Boston. All those people, my family and friends. They seem so far away.* Jack's eyes were taking in the hectic movement of military men and women across the compound. For them, every day brought life defining moments. *I don't think I ever realized how possible it is to be around so many people and still feel so apart and alone. It's not something I like.* Again, he raised the mug to his lips.

A few minutes later, he saw a doctor and two nurses emerge from the surgery tent. They were walking very slowly, almost shuffling. And then Jack could see why. The doctor and one of the nurses were making sure to maintain a pace slow enough for the second nurse who was limping badly.

Jack felt something unfamiliar – his chest swelling. He knew the cause – the sight of a friend – a woman – who had been injured and who might never experience complete recovery and who was nevertheless carrying on with her mission. How much of his swelling chest, he wondered, was resulting from sympathy and how much from affection? How much did the difference matter? *I'm in strange territory,* Jack mused.

As the three neared the mess tent, Jack made no effort to move. They looked and saw the cross on his helmet.

"Hello, Chaplain," the doctor said.

"Hello, Doctor."

Then the limping nurse gasped and screamed, "Jack!" She stepped awkwardly past the startled doctor and her nurse colleague and extended her arms toward Jack. He, too, was startled as his widened eyes attested. He extended his right hand, the one holding the coffee mug, off to the side and wrapped his left arm around Theresa's back and realized immediately that affection more than sympathy had caused the swelling in his chest.

Theresa disengaged, beaming. "You're making a habit of this, showing up at our evac."

"I'll try to cure myself," Jack smiled.

"No, don't. It's a good habit." Then, face reddening, Theresa said, "Oh, geez. Let me make introductions. Oh, wait. You've already met

– when Jack and General Patton came calling. Where is my brain today? Is Patton here, too?"

"No."

The doctor – a young surgeon – smiled and said, "Look why don't you two share a table inside and catch up? We" nodding to the other nurse "can stand each other's company at another table."

"Okay, good," said Theresa.

"The coffee's fresh," said Jack. "Let's all get inside."

After they all had filled their mugs, the doctor and the other nurse began walking to a table at the opposite end of the mess tent from Theresa and Jack. "What do you think?" whispered the doctor.

"I'm not sure," the nurse replied. "He sure brightens her spirits and Lord knows she could use that."

"That all?"

"I'm just not sure."

"Time will tell."

†††

For a long moment, Theresa and Jack just sat looking at each other across a table in a corner of the tent.

Then Theresa spoke. "How long have you been here?"

"Not long. Maybe half an hour."

"Did you come to…"

"See you? Yes. Last evening, Roscoe – Paul's friend in Bastogne – told me your evac was here…and that a nurse had been injured." Jack sipped his coffee and then blew out a breath. "And then later, Paul told me you were here… and that you were the injured nurse. I'm sorry about that – and I'm sorry about Colonel Carter."

"That was hard, Jack. So hard. To see her lying there…She meant so much to me."

"I pray that she's resting in peace. In fact, I'm sure she is."

"I'm glad you came. So glad. We go years without seeing each other, then twice in a matter of weeks. But the first time was so brief. Stay longer this time."

"All right. After we finish our coffee, I'll visit your chaplain in recovery, and then we can talk."

Theresa sipped her coffee but barely tasted it. Her eyes were focused exclusively on Jack but her thoughts were swirling with the speed and force of a spring tornado. Jack Brecker in the here and now. Hal Walker a poignant memory. A wonderful man. Lost for so long. Jack the boy I loved. The man I still do. How does he feel about me? Can he even dare to allow himself to think of me that way? What does God think about all this? Is he damning me right now? Am I sinning for thinking about Jack and love? Calm down, Theresa Hassler, you're no love-struck adolescent. You're a nurse...a veteran Army nurse in a combat zone. Get a grip on yourself.

"Have you heard anything more from Tom or Bridgett?" she asked.

"Nothing. But like I said back at Metz, we've not been in one place long enough for the mail to catch up to us. How about you?"

"No. But then the Germans haven't been of a mind to let our mail trucks through their lines."

Jack laughed quietly. "That should be changing right about now."

"I hope so."

Jack put his mug on the table. "I think I'll head for recovery. Coming?"

"I'll wait here for awhile," Theresa said. "Go ahead. Take your time."

†††

Later, when Jack exited the recovery tent, Theresa, despite the cold, was waiting outside. She was wearing a fatigue cap, her brown hair hanging down from underneath, and her hands were jammed into the pockets of her field jacket.

"Coffeed out?" Jack said.

"Guess so." Thankfully, she was feeling much calmer than when she had been sitting with him in the mess tent.

"Where now?"

"Come with me," Theresa said. She turned and, hands still in jacket pockets, led Jack across the snowy compound to a tent, Colonel Carter's, not yet reoccupied. They entered. Inside the windowless canvass, the light was dim. Theresa turned and faced Jack. "I've been thinking. Reminiscing. Do you remember the first time I kissed you?"

Her opening question surprised Jack but did nothing to cloud his memory. "St. Mary's. First grade." To his discomfort, Jack felt himself beginning to blush.

Theresa's eyes brightened. "You do remember."

"Some things," Jack smiled self-consciously, "you do remember."

Theresa smiled, a little trembly at first, then more confidently. Her eyes locked on to Jack's, seemingly boring into them. They had seen a lot, Jack was thinking, and he was wondering what they were seeing now. Theresa reached out and grasped his arms, then pulled her face close to his, closed her eyes and kissed Jack warmly. He didn't respond but he didn't resist. After a long moment, Theresa pulled away slightly and looked at Jack. His eyes were open and wide with surprise and anxiety.

"Close your eyes," Theresa said and Jack complied. She then closed hers and kissed him again. This time she could feel Jack returning the kiss. Both took to making cozy little noises.

When they parted, Jack blinked several times and swallowed hard. "I think I'll remember that one, too."

"I want you to, and I want you to stay with me."

"Stay..."

"The night. It's getting dark. It's cold. I'm feeling very alone. Please stay with me, Jack."

"I can't."

"Are you worried about what people might think?"

"Yes."

"Are you worried about what God might think?"

"Yes."

"Score two for honesty. You're a good man, Jack. I love you. There, I said it."

"Theresa..."

"You love me, too, I think."

"I...This is not easy for me. Do you understand?"

Theresa ignored his plea. "If you won't stay the night, at least stay longer. There's no General Patton waiting for you."

"How long?"

"Long enough..."

†††

Darkness had blanketed the compound when Jack and Theresa stepped outside Colonel Carter's tent. Slowly, contemplatively, they walked across the frozen earth. Before getting into the jeep, Jack looked up at the sky. He was grateful to see stars and a half-moon. He knew he couldn't use headlights on the drive back into Bastogne, but the night sky would provide enough illumination, if he drove slowly. And driving slowly would provide another advantage; it would give him more time to think. To consider the last few hours and what they meant and might mean. He climbed into the jeep, then held out his left hand. Theresa took it in hers and squeezed tenderly. She felt Jack's hand flex in response. She released her grip, and Jack withdrew his hand and turned the ignition key. In the darkness, he turned to Theresa and smiled. In that moment in the starlight, Jack saw in her face the serenity he always associated with the Theresa Hassler of their teenage years. Then Jack put the jeep in gear and drove away. Theresa turned and began limping back toward the nurses' tent.

Chapter 48

As 1944 came to a close, two companies of the Polish Airborne Brigade were protesting the firing of General Sosabowski with a hunger strike. But the general had been right; British military leaders, political officials and civilians didn't know him well enough or care sufficiently to cause anyone to act on the protest and reinstate him.

The general entered the office of his former deputy, Lieutenant Colonel Stanislaw Jachnik. Thaddeus Metz was there, too. They saluted each other.

"You must tell the men that I am deeply touched by their protest," Sosabowski said without preamble. "But you must make them understand that it will achieve nothing, except endangering their own health. That's a mistake and we must not let it happen."

"It won't be easy, Sir," said Colonel Jachnik. "They know a grave injustice has been done – and by British generals who should be grateful for your leadership."

"I appreciate that, Colonel. Truly. But you must persuade them. Please promise me that."

"Yes, Sir."

"Thank you." Sosabowski saluted and turned to leave.

"General, wait," said Colonel Jachnik. "Would you please join us in a drink? A belated toast, if you will."

"We would appreciate it if you joined us in making toasts," said Thaddeus.

"All right," Sosabowski said, his gravelly voice still strong.

From a desk drawer, Jachnik produced Scotch and three glasses. "A taste acquired at Upper Largo," he grinned. He poured and the three men stood together.

"To you, General," Jachnik said, "and the sacrifices you have made in leading us." They sipped.

"Thank you," the general murmured.

"To the men – our friends – that we've lost," said Thaddeus. "To their dedication and bravery." The three men raised their glasses.

"To our country," said Sosabowski. "Polska. That she might one day see the light of freedom and taste the nectar of democracy."

†††

On January 11, 1945, Poland began experiencing the repression of Soviet Russia. That was the day when Russian forces crossed the Vistula and entered Warsaw. What greeted them was a city largely reduced to rubble and a smattering of Poles who had managed to escape the forced evacuation of the city after the uprising and had stayed on. There was precious little for Russian soldiers to ravage or loot. For Poles outside Warsaw, the central question became: Who would exact the harsher toll? Retreating Germans or advancing Russians? Both possibilities were unnerving.

Despite Poland's devastated infrastructure, word of the Russian crossing of the Vistula spread with the speed of a summer brushfire on the steppes. By the afternoon of January 12, the Russians' success was the focal point of conversation in the Gudek's home.

"Some of our neighbors are already fleeing," said Bernadeta. "More are preparing to go."

"Who can blame them?" said Tosia. "We know how evil the Nazis are, and the rumors about the Russians are very frightening."

"I am afraid, too," said Jszef. "But I think each of us should think about this question: Do we want to become refugees?"

"If we do," said Barbara, "where will we go?"

"To nowhere, I'm afraid," said Jszef. "We would be trying to stay ahead of the Russians and out of the way of the Germans. I don't know that we would have a destination. It is inconceivable to me that Hitler would allow Polish refugees into Germany. We aren't Jewish, but Hitler and his minions consider all Slavs to be inferior. If only Hitler could look in a mirror and see past his silly mustache."

Bernadeta smiled slightly and nodded. "Father, you asked if we want to become refugees. I think the more important question is how do we best stay alive? If we run, my fear is that we couldn't return to our farm...that the Russians might conclude it is vacated and claim it for one of their own. Just give it to some officer."

"You are right," said Jszef. "And if we leave, as I said a few weeks ago, I think we invite the retreating Germans or the Russians to destroy our farm."

"We should stay," Barbara said firmly. "There will be danger but maybe no more than if we were on the run."

"Mother?" Jszef asked.

"Stay. I think. I…I wish we knew more." She shrugged.

"Bernadeta?"

"Stay. But, Father, if Germans come, I think we should make our farm appear deserted. I know that risks destruction. But still, I think it better to make it seem like all the others that are being abandoned. Draw no attention to it. And pray."

"And Russians?" he said.

'The same," she said pensively. "But after the first wave of Russians have passed by, we come out of hiding. Maybe that way we can protect ourselves and save our farm from being confiscated by their senior officers. What do you think?"

Jszef smiled the smile of a proud parent. "I think your work in the Home Army has taught you some valuable lessons."

"The chickens?" Barbara asked.

Jszef pursed his lips. "Too noisy. We need to kill them now." He made the decision quickly but not cavalierly. The chickens' death would mean the end of egg production.

"Father," said Barbara, "it's very cold. After we kill them, we could gut and bleed them and then hang them up in the barn. They would freeze. If we're lucky, after the danger passes, we could eat them. What we don't eat now, we could stew and preserve in jars – just like we do fruits and vegetables."

"Good thinking, Barbara," said Jszef. "We'll try it." He looked at his daughters. "I'm proud of you both."

†††

About noon on January 13, Barbara came bursting into the farmhouse. She was breathing hard. "A German convoy is coming. A long one."

"Did anyone see you?" Bernadeta asked.

"No Germans. Only the refugees who told me."

"All right," said Jszef. "I will douse the fire in the fireplace. You three go to the barn and get into the hole. Hurry. I'll be there in a minute or two."

The three women walked quickly from the house to the barn. Thank God, Bernadeta was thinking, there is no snow on the ground. No tracks to betray us. They moved the tools aside from the corner where the hole was located and pulled the sheet of planking away. Barbara dropped in first with Bernadeta following. Then the two sisters reached up, grasped Tosia's arms and eased her down.

"Just a minute," said Bernadeta. She hoisted herself back out of the hole, walked to the ladder and climbed up to the loft. While she was there, Jszef entered the barn and walked to the hole. He saw his wife and Barbara and could hear Bernadeta above him. Moments later, she descended and walked to the edge of the hole.

"Do you think that is wise?" Jszef asked.

"If the barn is searched, I didn't want the Germans to find them." Bernadeta was holding her schmeisser machine pistol and luger. "They would execute you immediately."

Jszef nodded, and Bernadeta handed him the guns. Then, with her mother and sister reaching up to provide support, Bernadeta dropped back into the hole. Jszef handed her the weapons and went to work, disguising the hole.

Half an hour later, the German convoy was approaching the Gudek's farm. A pair of staff cars carrying senior officers led the way. Then came a long line of trucks. Sharing the cab's seat in the first truck along with the driver was a captain and a lieutenant.

"What do you think?" said the lieutenant, pointing toward the Gudek's farm.

"It looks like the rest," the captain replied. "Empty. Abandoned."

From inside the barn, Jszef Gudek was peaking nervously through a crack in the siding. Silently, he said a quick prayer for deliverance.

"Maybe we should have a look," the lieutenant said. "To be sure."

"Has anything of value been found on the other farms we've checked?"

"No, nothing of value."

"Right. Look at these refugees. They are carrying what they can and I don't see much that I covet. Do you?"

"No, Sir."

"Tell you what, Lieutenant. If you want to take some men and check it out, go ahead. But we won't wait again and hold up the rest of the convoy. I don't know about you, but the more distance we put between us and the Russians the better I like our prospects."

"Agreed," said the lieutenant. "These people," he said, gesturing toward the migrating refugees, "who do you think they fear the most? Us or the Russians?"

"Well," the captain replied, "they hate us. We know that. We've been hard on them. But they've lived with us for five years. They know us. So, the Russians, I think."

"These Poles don't have much actual knowledge of them," the lieutenant said pensively, "but I'm sure they're hearing lots of scary rumors."

"Exactly," the captain said, "and uncertainty breeds fear. Panic."

The convoy continued to move west. On either side of the road, men, women and children were walking slowly, carrying bundles and guiding the open ox-drawn carts that were jammed with household goods and food. On this frigid day, theirs was a trail of vapor, reinforced by each exhalation of the refugees and their livestock.

†††

As darkness closed in early on the evening of the 13th, the Gudeks felt the situation safe enough to return to their house. Jszef started a fire. "Barbara," he said, "go outside and walk to the road. See if you can see any smoke from the chimney."

"Yes, Father." She left the house and jogged to the road. A few minutes later, she returned. "Nothing, Father. It's too cloudy tonight to see anything from the road."

"Good. Thank you." A pause. "Bernadeta, your thoughts?"

"I hope most of the Russians go north of Zyrardow. They should. It's the most direct route to Berlin. But we need to be prepared. Some likely will be headed south to Cracow. I think the Russians are more likely to be curious than the Germans."

"Why?" Barbara asked.

"I'll bet Father can answer that," said Bernadeta.

Jszef smiled. "The Russians have long supply lines. I'm sure they've had to do much living off the land. They'll be chasing the Germans, but they'll also be looking for food and other provisions. Scavenging. Looting."

"So do you think we should do anything differently?" Barbara asked.

"Remember," said Jszef, "what Bernadeta pointed out; the most important thing is to stay alive. To do that, we need food. I think we should take steps to protect our food supply."

"The hole?" Barbara asked.

"Yes," said Jszef.

"But I think we can do more," Bernadeta said.

†††

Early the next morning, Bernadeta and Barbara went to the barn to milk the cows. Bernadeta used the stool and Barbara squatted down. While they were rhythmically squeezing and pulling the cows' teats, Jszef entered and took down the gutted chickens that were hanging from a beam. He put them in a large burlap sack and tied if off. The sisters took the milk pails to the house and quickly returned to the barn. They opened the two pens.

"Ready?" Jszef asked.

"Ready," Bernadeta replied.

With two lengths of rope, Bernadeta led the two docile cows from the barn and headed toward the forest. Barbara followed, leading the ox. Jszef brought up the rear, carrying the burlap bag over his shoulder. Bernadeta led the slow procession deep into the forest. "I think this is about midway," she said.

They tethered the animals to the trunks of young trees, and Jszef suspended the bag from a sturdy tree limb.

"You stay for one hour, Barbara," said Bernadeta. "Then I'll come to relieve you."

"Good."

"If the Russians come to the farm," said Bernadeta, "two of us will hide in the hole and the third will come to alert the one who is with the animals."

"I understand," said Barbara. A pause. "Bernadeta?"

"Yes?"

"Is this the way it was in Warsaw?"

Bernadeta nodded. "Often, yes. We would make preparations. Hide. Listen. Hope. Not knowing when something might happen. That was probably the worst. It's natural to be nervous. To be afraid. If we did nothing, it would be worse for our nerves."

†††

During the walk back through the woods to the farm, Bernadeta spoke first. "Father, I think you should take the luger – and the extra ammunition."

"I agree. It would be better if we both were armed."

"I don't want to fight any more."

"And," he smiled, "I don't want to start again."

"But if we must..."

"To protect your mother and sister, yes, I will."

†††

"What is this?" Jerzy asked. "Well, I can see it's money but what kind?"

"American," Thaddeus replied.

Jerzy had just entered the tent he shared with Thaddeus, who was sitting on the edge of his cot. It was a cold mid-afternoon.

"Is it a lot?" Jerzy asked.

"Fifty dollars," said Thaddeus. "Yes, I think that's a lot."

"Where did you get it?" Jerzy asked.

"I'll explain later. For now, I want you to take this money and buy as much brandy and cognac as you can."

†††

Two hours later, Jerzy returned to the tent, carrying a wooden ammunition box. He put it down on the small table. "Brandy and cognac – and a bottle of Scotch."

"Good choice," Thaddeus smiled.

"Now what?"

"Go find the cow pen soldiers and bring them here."

"General Sosabowski, too?"

"Of course."

†††

Within 30 minutes, the remaining cow pen soldiers were gathered in the tent with Thaddeus and Jerzy.

"Why do you want to see us?" Henryk asked.

"To celebrate," Thaddeus answered.

"Celebrate what?"

"Being alive. Being together. Being thought of." Thaddeus squatted and reached under his cot. He pulled out a large cardboard carton, lifted and placed it on his cot.

"What is it?" Marek asked.

"The Americans call it a care package," Thaddeus said, unfolding the flaps of the carton. The eyes of the cow pen soldiers widened, General Sosabowski's included, as Thaddeus began removing the carton's contents and placing them on his cot. Cigars. Canned sardines. Saltine crackers. Salted, roasted peanuts in their shells. Cookies – oatmeal, peanut butter and sugar. Popcorn that served as the packing material. "There was also money in the carton that Henryk used to buy this," Thaddeus said, pointing to the brandy, cognac and Scotch.

"But," said Henryk, "who sent it to you?"

"There was a letter, too," Thaddeus said, picking up the envelope from his cot. He unfolded the letter and began to read, translating to Polish:

"December 10, 1944

Dear Captain Metz,

It gives us great pleasure to prepare this package for you and your friends. From experience, we are quite sure that the package won't arrive before Christmas, but maybe you can use it to celebrate the new year – a new year that we hope and pray will bring an end to this war and freedom to your country.

Our son tells us that you and your friends are very brave and thoughtful and have made many difficult sacrifices. He is very impressed by all of you and proud to have met you. He considers you his friends.

He told us that this package would be his way of saying thank you for giving him a wonderful Easter. He said it is the one he will remember the rest of his life.

We hope you enjoy the food and cigars. Please use the enclosed money to buy something good to drink with the food.

You and your friends are in our thoughts and prayers every day.

Very sincerely,

Anthony and Virginia Brecker

Shelby, Ohio USA"

Thaddeus slowly folded the letter and looked around the tent. His friends' faces were variously reflecting semi-shock, awe and deep gratitude. General Sosabowski was visibly touched. "We must write to them and express our thanks," he said. "This is most kind of Father Brecker and his parents. I will long remember this moment."

"Yes, agreed," the other cow pen soldiers echoed.

"Of course," said Thaddeus, "I will write such a letter. In the morning. And I would like all of you to sign it."

"I will be proud to sign," Marek said, amidst concurring nods from his friends.

"Likewise," said the general.

"Good," said Thaddeus. "Meanwhile, though, shall we?" And soon the tent was filling with relaxed conversation, laughter and a thick cloud of aromatic blue-gray smoke. After awhile, Thaddeus said, "Gentlemen, I am guilty of a gross oversight. We need to raise our glasses – or mugs – to the world's best chaplain and his parents. Ready? To Captain Jack Brecker. May our paths cross once more. To his dear mother and father. May you feel the eternal gratitude of the cow pen soldiers. And, finally, Gentlemen, to a Poland for Poles."

†††

"How soon do you think we will catch the Germans?" the lieutenant asked.

"Soon enough," Captain Zanskov said. "Why are you so eager to fight Germans again? It seems like that's all we've been doing since Moscow."

"It's not so much that I really want to fight them again. What I want is for them to surrender."

"Ha. Hitler will never let them. Do not retreat one centimeter. Fight to the last man, that's what he orders." Zanskov snorted. "A military genius he isn't."

Captain Zanskov was leading an advance company of Russian infantry along the road that ran southwest from Warsaw to Zyrardow and beyond to Cracow in the south. As Bernadeta had predicted, most Russian forces were farther north, driving due west and on a line toward Berlin.

"But when we get to Berlin?" the lieutenant asked. "Then what?"

"If Hitler still is alive, the fighting will be fierce. Maybe the worst we've seen. Street by street. House by house. Hitler will never allow himself to fall into our hands. You can imagine what would happen. Our men would tear him to shreds. Literally. And rejoice in every piece of Hitler."

"So?"

"So," Captain Zanskov speculated, "Hitler might try to escape to the mountains. Or kill himself."

"Do you think he might surrender to the Americans?"

Zanskov shook his head. "No chance. Not to a country with Negro soldiers and a president named Roosevelt."

"Jewish?"

"I don't think so, but it sounds Jewish, and Hitler has nothing but contempt for Roosevelt and Stalin."

It was mid-afternoon. From the barn's loft doorway, Bernadeta could see the Russians coming into view, walking down the road. The oncoming soldiers were dirty and unshaven, but they had the look of victors. Their strides were long and strong, their postures erect. Bernadeta hurried down the ladder. Her years of experience in the Home Army notwithstanding, anxiety was tightening her chest. "They are coming. Russian infantry."

"How many?" Jszef asked.

"More than a hundred."

"A company," said Jszef. He breathed deeply and expelled slowly in an effort to calm his nerves. "All right, Tosia, you and Bernadeta into the hole. I will go into the woods to stay with Barbara."

"Be careful," Tosia said. "Please take no chances."

Jszef nodded, acknowledging his wife's concern and love.

"Try not to worry, Mother," said Bernadeta. "Just pray for all of us."

Bernadeta dropped into the hole with athletic grace. She then reached up and grasped her mother about the hips, while Jszef steadied his wife by gripping her armpits. Down she went. Then Jszef quickly disguised the hole, slipped out the barn's narrow rear door and made his way into the forest.

"Another deserted farm," the Russian lieutenant said. "Let's have a look. Maybe they left some food behind. Or other supplies."

"Doubtful," Captain Zanskov said, "but let's check it out. And lieutenant…"

"Yes, Sir?"

"Keep our men under control. If we find any people here, I want no repeat of what happened earlier."

"The men were frustrated, Captain. They were angry. They still are. They had needs. They still do."

Zanskov's reply was firm. "We are here to liberate, not violate. Tell them to save their anger for Germans. Their needs can wait. We are professional soldiers, not an undisciplined mob of barbarians." Captain Zanskov wanted to believe that about his men, but he had born witness to their rage and lust for revenge. Disconcertingly, they were becoming less discriminating in targeting their victims. During the long, hard push across the steppes of Russia and eastern Poland, initially Russian troops had saved their worst for German military personnel and Russians thought to have collaborated with the invaders.

Later, though, some Russian soldiers had taken to raping Russian women and girls and occasionally murdering their husbands and families. Some of those troops were summarily court-martialed and executed. Others, though, had escaped justice.

Since driving into central Poland and then crossing the Vistula into Warsaw, atrocities had continued. Captain Zanskov was determined that his company not engage in wanton behavior. My chief regret, he reflected, is that I wasn't harsher in disciplining those men who committed criminal acts after entering Poland. Looting for necessities I can tolerate. After all, staying alive is necessary for reaching Berlin and crushing Nazism. But if any of my men rape or murder again, I am determined to react as a professional officer should. I will immediately court-martial and execute any transgressor. Of course, that could mean my own death. I believe I have the respect of my men. But I also know my control over them isn't absolute. They have been through hell together, and they could turn on me. Not a comforting thought. But for now, I have to put it aside."

"I'll take a dozen men with me," Captain Zanskov said. "You stay here with the others. Tell them to rest."

"Yes, Sir," the lieutenant replied.

Captain Zanskov and his men went walking slowly but confidently up the path to the farm, weapons at the ready. He turned to a sergeant and said, "You and five others check out the house, chicken coop and privy. We'll check the barn."

Zanskov motioned to three men to circle to the barn's rear. He and the others waited patiently. Then as those three bulled their way through the narrow rear door, Zanskov and his men charged in through the wider front door. Weapons poised, they looked around but saw nothing of interest. Zanskov motioned to two privates to climb the ladder to the loft. Moments later, they walked to the loft's edge and shook their heads. "Nothing, Sir."

In the hole, Tosia and Bernadeta were tensing. This was Tosia's first taste of paralyzing terror, and she closed her eyes and balled her hands into fists to try to contain her body's urge to shake. Bernadeta slipped her left arm around her mother's waist and squeezed. For her, close spaces and lurking danger were familiar companions. Not welcome but not mind-strangling. What to do if discovered? Try using the schmeisser? I might kill a couple Russians but Mother and I would be sure to die in a hail of bullets. Would that bring Father from the forest? Or would he stay with Barbara? The latter, I hope. Or should we beg? Plead for mercy? Would my plea be granted? Or would the Russians scoff, drag us from the hole, rape us in the barn? Leave us violated and humiliated? Shoot us? Would they go searching in the forest? As slowly and noiselessly as possible, Bernadeta drew in a breath of the musty air.

Captian Zanskov looked in the cow pen. No fresh manure. No other sign of recent activity. He looked on the dirt floor beneath a beam. Dried blood, he could see. Looked fairly new but no way to actually determine its origin or age. He inhaled deeply. Not unlike the barn on the farm he grew up on in Russia. A childhood that seemed a lifetime ago. But, in fact, not so long; I'm only twenty-four. I feel older and at this moment I no doubt look older. With a gesture of his head, Zanskov directed his men to exit the barn.

Outside, they could see other soldiers exiting the house. Three were holding up jars of preserved food they had found. A fourth was holding a blue woolen blanket. These were items that the Gudeks purposely had left behind, hoping that if either Germans or Russians found them they would conclude that all else had been taken with the fleeing refugees.

Zanskov and his men now were walking away from the barn toward the other men.

In the hole, Bernadeta wanted to say something to comfort her mother. Instead, she reached over and pressed her fore and middle fingers against Tosia's lips. Still too soon to make a sound.

"Bundle the jars in the blanket," Captain Zanskov instructed. "We'll share it with the other men tonight." He paused and then spoke to the sergeant. "I think I'll use the privy."

"They beat you to it, Sir," the sergeant replied, pointing to two men entering the outhouse.

"I'll use the barn," Zanskov said. "You and the men can head back to the road."

The sergeant nodded, and Zanskov walked back toward the barn. Bernadeta and Tosia heard him approaching and tensed again. Inside, he walked to the cow pen, leaned his machine pistol against the barn's wall, opened his fly and urinated onto the straw. A small pleasure, he was thinking, to be able to piss in private. Finished, he turned and began walking toward the barn's main door.

Tosia sneezed.

Captain Zanskov froze.

Bernadeta tried inhaling as her heart muscles tightened.

Zanskov pivoted, saw no one. No soldier. "Who's there? Where are you?"

Bernadeta and Tosia knew no Russian, but they could understand the meaning of the captain's questions. Again, Bernadeta pressed her fingers against her mother's lips.

Zanskov saw the tools piled in the corner. Senses alerted, he strode to the corner and pulled a couple tools away, tossing them behind him. He looked down at the straw and, using a boot, brushed some aside. Not earth but wood. Rapidly, his mind was processing the situation. He looked behind him. Still no soldiers. "Come out," he said, not loudly but with urgency.

I could fire up through this wood, Bernadeta was thinking clearly, and perhaps kill this Russian. Perhaps. In any event, death for us would come quickly. Maybe that is better. No rape or torture. Just a sudden end. Her right hand reached out for the schmeisser, fingered it, then withdrew.

Above, holding his machine pistol in one hand, Zanskov removed the remaining tools. Again he said, "Come out."

Bernadeta reached up, pushed against the planking and began to shove it aside. Tosia reached up to help. As light came pouring into the hole, it was silhouetting a Russian officer pointing a machine pistol at them.

"Get out," Zanskov commanded, motioning with his machine pistol.

Bernadeta placed her hands on the lip of the hole, jumped up and then used her arms to climb over the hole's edge.

Zanskov stepped back and gestured to Bernadeta to pull her mother out. Zanskov had not seen the schmeisser resting against the near wall of the hole. Now he stood looking at the two disheveled Polish women. Both were attractive but not sisters, he thought. Mother and daughter probably. He noticed the scar running down from the left corner of Bernadeta's mouth. Zanskov looked back over his shoulder. Bernadeta and Tosia were watching him for a sign – any sign – of his intention. Zanskov could see the fear in their eyes. Understandable. He raised his left hand in a sign that said stay where you are. He backed away from them to the edge of the barn door and peered outside. The two soldiers who had used the outhouse had finished and were walking down the path to rejoin their comrades on the road. There, many of the men were eyeing the food jars from the house.

Zanskov stepped back toward the women. "Are you alone?" he spoke quietly. "Where are your men? Dead? Alive? Hiding? In the woods perhaps? We are not your enemy. I wish you could understand. I know you are afraid. You have good reason to be. This has been a cruel war. Can you understand anything I am saying? No, I suppose not."

"Captain!" It was the sergeant's voice. "You all right?"

Zanskov raised a finger to his lips and whispered, "Hush." Then he backed away again from Bernadeta and Tosia. They were both thinking similar thoughts. What is this man doing? Is he their leader? He does not seem vicious. Before reaching the door, Zanskov shouted, "I'll be there in a minute." Then, again speaking to Bernadeta and Tosia, he said, "You might not know it, but you should be thankful it was me who found you. If it had been my men, I really don't know what they might have done." Bernadeta and Tosia, peering hard at Zanskov, were both wishing they could understand the young Russian's words. "If they had decided to rape you, I don't know if I could have stopped them. Not without shooting." Zanskov stepped closer and both women tensed visibly and shrank from him. "Please," said Zanskov, "don't be afraid of me." He pointed to the hole, shook his head and said, "No. You needn't get back in. Just stay here." He reinforced his words by smiling and gesturing with his left hand. "Just stay here until we are gone." Then Zanskov reached out and lightly touched Bernadeta on her forearm. She looked into his eyes and saw kindness. She looked at her mother who was seeing the same thing. Captain Zanskov saw their faces relaxing. He smiled again, nodded, turned and went walking out of the barn.

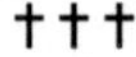

Chapter 49

"When do you think it will happen?" Lea Peiffer asked Maurice Trimbach.

"I think Colmar will be liberated soon. The only questions are how much the Germans will resist and how much damage the city will suffer."

"I hope little. Colmar is such a beautiful town. The Unterlinden. The Koifhus. Maisson des Tetes. The Church of the Dominicans and its cloisters. All such lovely buildings. And so old and historic."

Maurice and Lea were sitting in the kitchen in the Peiffer's home in Rue des Boulangers in Ribeauville. They were sipping wine with Klaus and Sonia Peiffer.

"The Americans have stopped the Germans' counteroffensive," Lea observed. "They are calling it The Battle of the Bulge. They have taken many Germans prisoner."

"More than a hundred thousand," Maurice said. "Plus, the Germans lost another hundred thousand killed and wounded."

"So many," Sonia murmured. "I hope this awful war ends soon – for everyone's sake."

"How are the Steiners and Somers doing?" Maurice asked.

"Good," said Lea. "They are still worried that Nazi troops might return – and that someone might inform again. But they are glad to be out of the cellars and the attic and back in their homes and going about their business. The Somers' children are back in school. A little nervous, too."

Maurice nodded. "I will visit them. Try to reassure them. If the Germans return – which I doubt – we will not hesitate to take them into hiding again." He sipped the wine.

There was one subject no one had raised – that of the two corpses buried under the floor of the Peiffer's wine cellars. Everyone understood that it was too soon yet to consider removing them.

†††

"I didn't think you would mind," Lieutenant Billy Clawson said.

"Well, it makes sense," Paul Brecker replied, "and that's not always the case with command decisions. We've been in the region before and know our way around."

Clawson chuckled. "That's not what I was referring to."

"What do you mean?"

Clawson cleared his throat. "R told me about you and the Resistance woman."

"Oh," Paul reddened.

"Says you took a serious liking to her," Clawson related. "Says it might be love."

"Yeah."

"Been a couple months. Still feel that way?"

"Yeah." Paul sighed heavily. "Of course, I have no idea – not even the slightest – if she still feels that way."

"Be nice to find out."

"Yeah."

"Colmar…The Colmar Pocket has to be rid of Germans. Someone at division remembered our foray to Natzwiller and decided our platoon would make a fine scouting party."

"I see," said Paul. "And I take it that on the way we'll pass through Ribeauville. Or close by."

"If we don't," Clawson grinned, "you will."

"I think I'd better find a French-English dictionary," Paul said pensively.

"A few key words wouldn't hurt," Clawson said. "Good luck."

†††

In central Poland, the Russians had replaced the Germans as occupiers. And as under the Germans, the Gudek's farm was not proving a hub of occupation activity. Late one afternoon toward the end of January, Bernadeta and Barbara were milking the two cows. Outside, a large-flaked snow was falling. Inside, the sound of milk squirting into the metal pails carried with it a rhythm that was familiar and comforting.

"Bernadeta?"

"Yes."

"I just want you to know that I am praying for Captain Majos every day...that he is surviving."

Bernadeta sighed. "I appreciate that."

"Do you think about him often?"

"Every day...and also about the others in our cell. They were...are... such good people. They made so many sacrifices for our country."

"And the cow pen soldier?"

"Thaddeus Metz...Yes, him, too, but not so often any more."

"More than five years..."

"Yes," Bernadeta said wistfully. "You know, it's hard for me now to picture his face. Or remember his voice."

"I think if he walked into our barn, you would recognize him."

"I think you're right. I think it all would come back to me."

"I wonder if he remembers you."

"I don't know...Maybe. I hope so. If he's still alive. It's nice to be remembered."

"Bernadeta?"

"Yes?"

Barbara flicked still-warm milk in Bernadeta's face. She squealed and flicked milk back at Barbara. Then both sisters fell to giggling happily.

"You will always remember me," Barbara said, laughing merrily. "Your little sister, the milkmaid."

In Shelby, Tom and Bridget's twins were growing fast. At six months old, they also were well along to being spoiled by two sets of doting grandparents. Near daily visits by Eleanor Hassler and Virginia Brecker were part of Bridget's routine. It was a part she appreciated. Neither woman was overbearing and both were quite willing to pitch in on sterilizing bottles and laundering diapers. Thankfully, thought Bridget, the two grandmothers were avoiding competing with each other for time with Bridget and the twins.

†††

General George Patton, his aide, Colonel Charles Codman, and staff were boarding a C-47. It was February 13, 1945, and Patton had concluded that he and his staff were in dire need of rest and recreation. They had not had a leave since October 1942. Their destination was Paris, and Patton had arranged for them all to stay in the posh George V Hotel. While there, Patton unwound by playing tennis.

†††

In Tucson, Lou Boudreau was reveling in the optimism that perennially accompanied the early days of spring training. Players had arrived rested and ready for teasing and tomfoolery as much as conditioning and re-sharpening skills dulled during the winter months. As player-manager, albeit still a very young one, Boudreau felt obligated to abstain from most of the players' antics. If nothing else, he knew that during the coming months he would have to demote, trade or release players, some of them his friends.

As usual, Boudreau spent much of his spare time reading and thinking about the war's end and aftermath and how returning warrior players would affect his team and others. He expected that players coming home from the horrors of combat would bring with them a detectable gravitas. He would welcome that.

†††

In the Allies' drive east on Germany, they received a break – perhaps their biggest – when they arrived at Remagen on March 7 and found the Ludendorff Bridge over the Rhine intact. Germans defended the railroad span furiously against an American crossing but attempts to detonate explosives wired to the bridge and bomb it from the air failed. Luck was running against the Germans at Remagen. A stray bullet had cut the wire leading to the charges.

Supported by armor, some very skilled and brave American infantrymen crossed the span and then quickly fanned out, creating a strong foothold in central Germany. A few days afterward, units of Patton's 3rd Army crossed the Rhine to the south, and then three Allied armies went sweeping across to the north. The rout was on.

†††

By early April, the Russians were ready for their final drive on Berlin from the east. For this initiative, they had assembled four million troops.

†††

On April 17, Patton again flew to Paris, this time to visit his son-in-law, Lieutenant Colonel John Waters, who was recovering in a hospital from severe war wounds suffered two years before. Patton found the young man, about whom he cared deeply, improving.

Later that day, Patton squeezed in another tennis match. The next day he was back with 3rd Army units which were driving hard into Czechoslovakia, still controlled by German units.

†††

On April 22, the Russians reached the suburbs of Berlin. Germans not fighting were cowering in cellars or trying to cross the Elbe River, escape to the west and surrender to the Americans. Panicking German soldiers pushed old women out of small boats. Some soldiers swam the river, climbed its banks and walked straight into Allied prisoner cages.

Still, the carnage was horrific. Some 125,000 Berlin civilians were killed, as were between 150,000 and 200,000 German soldiers. The attacking Russians suffered no less, incurring 300,000 casualties. Many Russian troops raped and looted at will. Captain Zanskov managed to keep his company in check.

†††

In late April, Gestapo chief Heinrich Himmler tried to negotiate a peace with the U.S. and Great Britain. Their response: German troops must surrender unconditionally on all fronts.

On April 28, Italian partisans captured Benito Mussolini and his mistress, who had been trying to escape north to Switzerland. They were stood against a wall and shot.

On April 30, Hitler committed suicide by shooting himself in the mouth. On that same day, Paul Brecker and others with the 101st Airborne were in a speeding convoy on their way to capture Hitler's lair at Berchtesgaden. The

Allies were reacting to rumors that Hitler and thousands of his most loyal troops would retreat into the Alps, create a virtually impenetrable redoubt and carry on a guerilla war indefinitely. On their way into the mountains, Paul and his colleagues were operating from one fundamental rule of thumb: if a place was defended and resisted, blast it; if it surrendered, let it be and press on.

In some towns and villages, Paul and R and their brethren were greeted and hailed as longed-for rescuers. The adulation seemed genuine. But their experiences during the last 11 months had taught them another rule of thumb: remain ever alert.

One of the hamlets they were passing through was little more than a bend in the road straddled by a handful of buildings. Paul and R were riding in the rear of an open two-and-half-ton truck – a deuce and a half. It was the last truck in the convoy. With no warning, bullets came tearing at them. One round struck the truck's rail between Paul and R's heads. Instinctively, they ducked. A second bullet grazed R's helmet with enough force to knock it off his head, over the rail and to the ground.

The truck's driver braked hard and pulled the vehicle to the roadside. Paul, R and the other G.I.'s leaped from the truck and dove to the ground. Immediately, they identified the source of the incoming fire – an ancient stone barn on the left or north side of the road. Snipers.

Ahead, other trucks in the convoy had stopped. Lieutenant Billy Clawson came running back to the fire zone. He dropped to his belly beside Paul and Roscoe. Clawson shouted his first words to them and the other men nearby: "No fucking heroics today! Got that?" Because Clawson cursed infrequently, his words today carried a message that all understood. "We've got this war won so our primary objective now is saving our skins. Who's got smoke grenades?"

"Over here," shouted a nearby soldier.

"Me, too," called another.

"Okay," Clawson said, "on my count of three, we all open covering fire on every window and door we can see in that barn plus on the roof. I don't want one fucking German bullet coming this way. Not one. A German sticks his head out and he's dead. Okay, you two get those smoke grenades into the barn and then run like hell. If the snipers come out holding their weapons, kill 'em. If they come out unarmed..." Momentarily, Clawson was tempted to say Kill them, too…"cut 'em a break and let 'em surrender. If they don't come out, stand by while I get a flamethrower and a couple bazookas back here."

Moments later, from prone positions, the G.I.'s were pouring fire at the barn. They paused just long enough for the two soldiers with smoke grenades to get close enough to the barn to heave the explosives inside. Within seconds, four German soldiers went running from the barn's rear door. They were armed, and they were cut down instantly. No one went to check on them. No one even suggested it.

R picked up his helmet, studied the damage and climbed back into the truck. "Close one, Paul."

"Too close, Friend, especially since I've got other plans in mind for you."

"Huh?"

"You'll see. In time."

Chapter 50

On May 2, the end grew nearer still for the Nazis when Berlin surrendered to the Russians, and German forces in Italy laid down their arms.

On May 7, Colonel General Alfred Jodl, the German chief of staff, and Admiral Hans Georg von Friedeburg were escorted into Supreme Allied Commander General Dwight Eisenhower's newest headquarters, a red school building in Reims, about 75 miles east of Paris. There, at 2:41 a.m., on behalf of Germany, Jodl and von Friedeburg signed the documents that stipulated unconditional surrender. Eisenhower chose not to dignify the Germans with his presence, instead waiting in a nearby office.

After signing, Jodl, choking with emotion, said, "With this signature, the German people and armed forces are, for better or worse, delivered into the victors' hands." He and von Friedeburg then were conducted down a hall to Eisenhower's office.

Eisenhower said nothing in the way of a greeting. "Do you understand what you've just signed?" he asked coldly.

"Yes," answered Jodl.

"You will get details of instructions at a later date," Eisenhower continued. "And you will be expected to carry them out faithfully." He did not shake hands with or salute them. They saluted him and left.

On May 8, at the Russians' insistence, this ceremony was repeated in Berlin. That formality sparked what Winston Churchill called "the signal for the greatest outburst of joy in the history of mankind."

V-E Day. War still was raging in the Pacific and Asia, with V-J Day still more than three months away. But that reality did little if anything to cast a pall over explosions of emotion in Paris, Shelby, London, Zyrardow, New York, Ajo, Charco, Moscow, the Josephinum, the Cleveland Indians locker room, and countless other venues throughout much of the western world which all bore witness to scenes of unrestrained glee. In Red Square, a Russian officer, laughing and waving, was held aloft by an adoring crowd. In Shelby, Tom Brecker, standing in front of his house, saluted the American flag and pumped his fists above his head. In Brooklyn, Sam Tortino, Tom's fellow fireman aboard the Hornet, went walking down to the Verrazano Narrows to salute passing ships – and then wept for long minutes. In London, near the House of Commons, Winston Churchill was wearing his bowler, right hand flashing his trademark 'V' for victory sign, surrounded and looking out on a deliriously jubilant throng. Outside a farmhouse near Zyrardow, a husband and wife and their two daughters, all holding hands, danced uninhibitedly in endless circles, happily singing any song that came to mind. In an evacuation hospital, Theresa Hassler sank to her knees, sobbing in cathartic relief; a wounded soldier rose from his cot to comfort her. In Charco, a dignified, graying elder slowly raised his arms to the eastern sun – and then shouted boyishly. A former Polish lancer moved solemnly from one airborne comrade to another, shaking hands, kissing their cheeks, weeping. An American airborne soldier at Berchtesgaden stood on a mountaintop, looking westward, thinking and hoping. A bespectacled chaplain offered a prayer of gratitude, then accepted a fresh cigar and a foaming beer from an 82nd Airborne trooper. In Ribeauville, a young woman, her fellow Resistance fighter and two Jewish families were among a crowd gathered in the town hall plaza on the Grand' Rue, quaffing champagne and new wine in decidedly indecorous fashion.

†††

Days later, Thaddeus Metz went to see General Sosabowski. "You were right, Sir," he said. "They are sending our brigade to Germany for occupation duty."

"How long will you be there?" General Sosabowski asked.

"One year, maybe two. No one seems sure now. The men are angry – and very disappointed."

"At least you will be closer to home."

"You?"

"I've made my choice. I'm staying in England…Making a new life… Putting all things military behind me. Well, almost," Sosabowski grinned semi-sheepishly. "General Urquhart has said I must learn to play golf – his passion."

Thaddeus laughed quietly. "I don't know golf, but if an infantryman could learn to jump out of fast airplanes, I'm sure you can learn to hit a little white ball that is not moving."

Sosabowski's gravelly laughter shifted from semi-shamed to delighted. "Ah, yes but one must hit that little white ball into holes that are somewhat smaller than parachute landing zones."

"You might not be the only Pole learning to play golf in Britain."

"Oh?"

"Some of the men – quite a large number actually – are talking about returning to England after our occupation duty ends."

"Women?"

Thaddeus nodded. "Ones they met in Scotland and England. Plus many hate the idea of returning to a Poland controlled by the Soviets."

Sosabowski sighed. "Very understandable sentiment. And you?"

"I still think Poland is where I belong."

Sosabowski nodded. "You will be careful?"

"I won't advertise that I was a Polish officer or went to university. At least not if the Russians still are persecuting Polish officers and intellectuals, although I hardly consider myself intellectual."

"You speak three languages. To the Soviets that probably defines you as an intellectual."

"Well, then, I might try crossing the border as something quite ordinary...maybe as an itinerant merchant. Nothing to draw unwanted attention."

"Good," said Sosabowski. "And, Thaddeus, I hope you can find that farm girl."

†††

Lieutenant Colonel Carter's tent had been reoccupied by her successor, but the other nurses had vacated their tent, migrating to the mess tent, to give Theresa and Jack privacy.

Inside, Theresa and Jack were standing toe-to-toe, arms around the small of each other's back.

"I wasn't sure if I'd see you again," Theresa said softly.

"Same here."

"I'm glad you decided to come." She leaned forward and their lips touched, melded and finally parted. It was a kiss with the potential to unravel resolve. "Have you got this figured out yet?"

"I wish. I truly wish. I know I love you – there, now I've said it, too. But I'm not sure about the rest of it."

From scant inches away, Theresa's eyes were boring into his. Her lips formed only a trace of a smile. "Giving up the priesthood…"

"Yes."

Her gaze remained unblinking. "You worked hard – hard and long – for it. And there is no higher calling. I'll concede that without question. If I have to be second – and I hope I don't – being second to God is quite a consolation. But, Jack Brecker" – with those words, Theresa moved her nose to within an inch of Jack's – "that doesn't mean I'll actually like it. Not one tiny bit." Then her nose touched Jack's and their lips met in another lingering kiss.

When they parted, Jack said, "I've never thought of myself as indecisive."

Theresa smiled, eyes glittering. "But this is no ordinary decision."

"No. My stomach has been tied into one large and painful knot."

"Good," Theresa said spunkily.

"You know," Jack said, smiling ruefully, "if someone years ago…had told me it was possible to want…really want…two things as much as I do, I…" Jack shook his head in incredulity, "I would have dismissed it as so much foolishness. But now I know it's not foolishness, or fantasy."

"When I gave you that Saint Christopher medal, I gave up all hope for our love. Then after you had to leave Saint Joseph's, I began to hope again. You never knew that, did you?" Jack shook his head. "But then Father Mac got you into the Josephinum, and I knew I had to put you out of my mind. And I did after I met Hal…And then there's now. Well, you'll have time to think it through…sort things out. And you're the only one who can do it, Jack. Maybe I'm the foolish one…thinking I can compete with God. Maybe God already has condemned me for trying. But…" Theresa stopped herself and asked simply, "When do you leave for occupation duty?"

"Soon. They're sending the Eighty-Second to Berlin any day now."

"Do I have to ask you to stay a little longer?" Theresa asked.

"Not this time."

CHAPTER 51

"I'm not very comfortable with this," General Jimmy Doolittle said. "Not comfortable at all." This wasn't the first time that Doolittle felt such discomfort. After his daring raid on Tokyo and subsequent, harrowing escape from China, he had been awarded the Congressional Medal of Honor. But for all his self-confidence and many achievements, he still felt uneasy in the public spotlight. " But this is right down your alley, George."

"Oh, you'll enjoy it," General Patton said. "The American people want to say thank you. Hell, they need to say it."

Their plane was in its final descent to Boston's Logan Airport. It was June 7, 1945.

"The fighting in the Pacific is still going hot and heavy," Doolittle said somberly. "We've got thousands of men fighting and dying at Okinawa and it's not over yet. This all seems premature."

"Nonsense, Jimmy. We need to give our fellow citizens a chance to see their heroes. Keep their morale pumped up to keep turning out planes and buying bonds while our boys in the Pacific keep kicking the shit out of the Japs and making a goddamned hero out of MacArthur."

"You can be a royal pain, George."

Patton grinned. "Hell, I know that...but you like me anyway."

"Heaven knows why."

†††

Along the parade route from the waterfront airport into downtown, some 750,000 Bostonians were gathering. Their mood was jubilant. They were primed for a blow-your-socks-off celebration.

"I think this is a good spot," said Kevin Riley. "Let's watch from here."

"Just think," his son Sean exulted, "we'll get to see the general who raided Tokyo and the general who relieved Bastogne. Wow!"

"You mean the general who is a friend of Father Brecker," his sister Kathleen corrected him.

"That, too," Sean acknowledged less enthusiastically.

"I could hardly believe it when Father Brecker wrote to us about working with General Patton," said Kevin.

"He wasn't really altogether clear on why General Patton wanted him," said Mary Catherine. "He did say they visited some hospitals together. But something tells me there's more to it than that. I wonder if we'll ever learn the whole story."

"Does it matter?" asked Rosemary.

"Not really. You're right," her mother conceded readily. "What matters is that the general and Father Brecker both survived the killing."

"Do you think Father Brecker will really visit us?" Kathleen asked.

"He wrote that he would," Mary Catherine replied.

"And," said Kevin, "we know he's a man of his word."

†††

From Boston, Doolittle and Patton flew to Los Angeles. There, on June 9, 130,000 cheering people jammed into the Los Angeles Colisseum. Patton visibly relished every moment of the adulation. He was at his flamboyant, charming best. Just as visibly, the shorter, inestimably more modest Doolittle struggled to appear comfortable with the rousing outpouring of acclaim. Patton's waves to the crowd were sweeping and all-embracing; Doolittle's were tentative, elbow bent timidly.

†††

The two generals separated after Los Angeles, with Patton back east in Washington, D.C. on June 13 to discuss occupation policy. On July 4, Patton was back in Paris. The next three months passed as tranquilly as any Patton had experienced in years. Then, on October 1, a hammer dropped; he was relieved of command of the 3rd Army. Instead, he was given command of the 15th Army which Patton derided as a "paper clip army." Its stated purpose was to study "the lessons of the war just ended." To his aide, Patton grumbled that serving as a decoy as he had during the D-Day buildup had been vastly more stimulating. "At least then," he grumbled, "I had the Germans jumping. Now I could take a long nap every afternoon and who would notice? Or care? The biggest goddamn lesson from the war just ended is a lesson that has been ignored for millennia. Let politicians – or politically minded generals – call the shots, and wars last longer and more men die. If the newsboys were here, I'd let 'em quote me on that."

Patton celebrated his 60th birthday on November 11, and soon after his spirits were buoyed again. The occasion was a November 27th reunion in Sweden with his pentathlon competitors from the 1912 Stockholm Olympics. Patton had finished fifth but at this reunion was treated as though he had been the gold medallist. He luxuriated in the attention.

On Sunday, December 7, in Germany, Patton once again was in high spirits. "Ready, Willie?" he said to his white bull terrier. "We're going to shoot us some pheasants today."

Willie, Patton and his driver settled into a Cadillac. About 11:45 a.m., they were on an autobahn about 40 miles south of Frankfurt near Mannheim.

"Beautiful morning for tramping through forest," Patton observed. "Blue sky. Cold air."

The driver braked for a passing train, and Patton waited patiently.

Approaching from the opposite direction was a jeep driven by an American soldier, T/5 Robert Thompson. His mind was wandering, daydreaming about his return to the U.S. As the train was clearing the crossing and the Cadillac began moving again, Thompson's jeep suddenly swerved to the left. "Look out!" Patton called out. His driver jerked the steering wheel. Not fast enough. The steel versus steel impact between the two vehicles wasn't heavy, but it was enough to send the Cadillac careening down a steep embankment. Patton was thrown to the floor. "This is bad," he mumbled. Willie was whimpering.

†††

Patton was taken from the accident site to a hospital in Heidelberg, about 20 miles to the southeast. Upon arriving, Patton was in shock. His pulse was weak, his blood pressure extremely low, his hands and feet cold and his face pallid. With his whispered permission, medical staff cut his clothes away. They found that his third cervical vertebra had been fractured and the fourth dislocated against the fifth. Patton was paralyzed.

"Doesn't look good, does it, Bea?" he murmured to Beatrice, his wife of 35 years. "Hell of a way to bring down the curtain. As dramatic endings go, this doesn't quite measure up with Stonewall Jackson or Julius Caesar.

It took bullets and knives to finish them off. No goddamn accident. What a lousy way to die."

"Take it easy, George," she said. "Please. You need to rest. For just once in your life, listen to your doctors. And me."

"Ha," Patton said, grinning with mock wickedness, "I've always listened to you, Bea. You just couldn't hear my answers."

"George..."

"Bea, I have a favor to ask."

"Anything. Anything at all."

†††

"Chaplain. Thanks for coming," Patton said weakly.

"No problem, General," Jack replied. "I would've come anyway once I heard about your condition."

"They don't want me to die in Germany," Patton grumbled lowly. "Not a politically correct move on my part. So they tell me."

"Who's they?"

"The politicos in Washington. Truman and his White House cronies. Goddamn it, you know what's next?" Jack shook his head. "They're going to encase me in plaster of Paris for the trip back to the U.S. The motherfucking sonsabitches. Excuse me again, Chaplain. My tongue keeps running away with me. Look, I'd rather be buried right with my men. You understand?"

Jack nodded. "I understand."

"I knew you would. Look, I don't see myself lasting long enough to start the trip much less making it all the way to Washington." Again, Jack nodded. "Hell, I can feel myself dying." A pause. "I'm not Catholic, Chaplain. You know that."

"Doesn't matter," Jack murmured, looking into Patton's slate-blue eyes.

"I knew you'd feel that way. And, by God, I figure you've got more pull with the man upstairs than any other man of the cloth I know."

"I don't know about that."

"Faith, Jack," Patton smiled. "I've got complete and utter faith in you and your heavenly connections."

Jack uttered a small laugh. A pause. "You'd like me to do the last rites?"

"Sort of," Patton said. "Yes, do your normal prayer but add an amendment."

"That being?"

"I don't want the politicos to get their way. No, Sir. I want my war to end here with my men, not with a fancy, schmancy ceremony at a stateside cemetery."

"General –"

"Jack, I'm gonna deal in something I don't like. Semantics. Hate 'em normally, but this isn't normally. Agreed?"

"Agreed."

"Good. Look, I'm not asking you to pray for me to die. I know you wouldn't agree to that. But I am asking you to pray to the Lord for mercy for me."

"For the man who gave me a history lesson on the Chaplain Corps," Jack smiled affectionately, "that's not a problem. And truth be told, General, I could agree to pray for you to die…to die here with dignity."

Patton's eyes brightened and widened. "You've learned a lot about yourself over here, Jack. I happen to think they've been good lessons."

"So do I."

†††

The next day, Sunday, December 21, George Patton passed away in that Heidelberg hospital. His dying prayer – and Jack's for him – was answered. General Patton was buried at Hamm, Luxembourg with 9,000 of this 3rd Army troops. His grave was marked by a plain cross identical to the others, in one of the long rows, not set apart in any way.

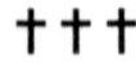

Chapter 52

"How ya' doin', Big Brother?"

"Paul!"

It was the morning of December 23, 1945. The phone connection was clear. "I've been trying to track you down."

"Been with General Patton."

"So I've been told. Our best general, if you ask me."

"You'll get no argument from me on that score."

"Too bad he had to go that way," Paul said.

"Not the way he wanted to."

"Bet you've got some stories to tell."

"Some day...perhaps."

"I want to run something by you," said Paul. "Kind of a long shot."

"Let's hear it."

†††

Scented pine boughs and lighted candles gave the small church a cozy glow. Jack and Paul were standing side-by-side in the sanctuary. It was Christmas morning, and the church was filling quickly with citizens of Ribeauville. Anticipation was running high.

"Glad you could make it, Big Brother. Any trouble getting away?"

"Being a chaplain gives me a certain degree of leeway."

"Especially if you've just come from being with Patton."

"That helped, too."

Behind Jack and Paul was the church's pastor. Standing nearby was Paul's best man, Roscoe Remlinger. Both Paul and R were wearing fatigues but cleaned and pressed and with black neckties. Their scuffed combat boots had been re-heeled and shined as brightly as possible. Dressed the same and ushering in arriving guests were Lieutenant Billy Clawson and Captain Walt Hunter. Neither spoke French beyond "Bon Jour," and on this occasion that was adequate. Their warm greetings were met with wide, beaming smiles. Paul hadn't asked Hunter to participate but, when the captain learned of the occasion from Jack, it didn't require much effort to wangle an invitation. As Hunter had pointed out, as a Methodist he had attended a Catholic Easter Mass, so why not a Catholic wedding Mass? Then Jack suggested to Paul that he ask Walt to usher and the deal was sealed.

The third usher was Maurice Trimbach. He escorted Sonia Peiffer to a front-row pew.

"Hard to believe," said Paul.

Jack smiled. "Guess that French-English dictionary you got came in handy."

"It did. Got me lots of laughs, too, when I came to Ribeauville and began putting it to use. Back at Natzwiller, I'd never seen Lea giggle. Now she can barely help herself when I try speaking French. She's doing far better in English, believe me. By the way, last night she surprised me with a wedding present. Two, actually."

"Is that a local custom?" Jack asked softly. "I mean for the bride to give presents to a groom?"

"No," Paul smiled, "they were special. A sweater she knitted – blue with red trim – and a bottle of her family's riesling."

"I take it there's a story behind this," Jack whispered.

"Yeah. She tells me that when Japan attacked Pearl Harbor, she thought America would never enter the war in Europe. But when Hitler declared war on the U.S., she knew Americans would come and right then and there she decided to knit a sweater and give it and a bottle of the Peiffer's riesling to the first American soldier she saw."

"You've been lucky twice over."

"You got that right."

"Look," said Jack.

Paul shifted his gaze to the church's rear. There, standing radiantly in white was Lea Peiffer. At her side was her father, Klaus. Immediately behind them was Lea's maid of honor, her friend since early childhood, Marie Kieny.

"Isn't she beautiful?" Paul murmured.

"Very much so," Jack replied.

"I am so glad you could get here to marry us. It was important to Lea to be married here with family and friends, and you being here brings me a touch of Shelby."

"Which is where you intend to take Lea."

"Yeah. She's okay with that – as long as she can come back here every once in awhile. And her parents can afford to visit us, too. That helps."

"Sounds like you've got yourself a bride who is more than just beautiful."

"Amen to that, Brother. She's like no other girl I've ever met. Been through so much. You wouldn't believe."

"Actually, I think I could. These last eighteen months have opened my eyes to a lot. You wouldn't believe." The two brothers eyed each other and smiled warmly. "Let's get started," Jack said. He nodded and, with his right arm, beckoned the bride and her father.

As they started slowly down the aisle, it was Marie Kieny whose emotions were churning. She was grateful, doubly so. She was thrilled to be serving her best friend as maid of honor. She was relieved -- massively – that no one had ever learned her dreadful secret – her having informed on the Steiners and Somers. For two years, she had been excoriating herself for her treachery, committed during a moment of inexplicable weakness. She had harbored no deep hatred for the Steiners and Somers yet, in that moment, had fallen victim to some urge she still couldn't fully understand. Almost immediately, she had regretted her disloyalty. And her pain born of regret hadn't lessened when someone else – whose identity she didn't know – later had propagated the rumor that the Peiffers were sheltering the two Jewish families.

During the two years since informing, Marie had confided in no one – not her parents or her priest, certainly not Lea. Marie wondered often whether the Steiners and Somers ever suspected her. Desperately, she hoped not. It would be hard enough living with her secret in a small village. She couldn't imagine staying in Ribeauville were she found out. Seeing the two Jewish families now -- among Lea's wedding guests – Marie raised her eyes and again asked God's forgiveness.

In the sanctuary, Jack put everyone at ease when, with Lea serving as translator, he smiled widely and said, "I am a simple priest from a small town in America. This is the first wedding I have conducted in more than two years. And the very first one in Europe…in France. The last wedding I conducted was for Paul's brother Tom and his bride in my hometown. It was on my way to Europe. I speak good Spanish but, alas, no French. Still, I am going to try to read the ceremony's words in French." He paused.

"And I know I will make more mistakes than a student who hasn't studied for an exam." Among the guests there was quiet, friendly laughter. "Your own priest will help me, thank God. These two young people" – he pointed to Lea and Paul – "have only my best wishes for a long and happy life together. They deserve that. I know you feel the same way. After all, you are here and I am honored to be here with you." Jack bowed. At first, the ensuing applause was scattered and tentative. Then it spread and built throughout the church.

Chapter 53

On January 3, 1946, the 82nd Airborne Division began returning to its new permanent base at Fort Bragg, North Carolina. The 101st Airborne would be following soon after. Jack would be returning with the first contingent of the 82nd and then resigning his commission and heading back to Arizona. Not directly, though.

After processing out at Fort Bragg, Jack first traveled north by train to keep his word. It was a long ride but relaxing. The rhythm of the steel wheels on the steel rails was conducive to reflecting, analyzing and resting. He dozed several times.

After disembarking, he went to the station's taxi stand and waited in a short line for a cab. Following a brief ride, he was standing on the porch of a familiar, modest house. He knocked on the door. Kathleen Riley pulled open the door – and shrieked – a wholly unintelligible shriek. Her sister Rosemary came running to the door, shrieked similarly and began jumping up and down. Jack couldn't refrain from grinning widely. In another few moments, he was squished in the center of a massive group hug with the two sisters, their brother Sean and Mary Catherine and Kevin Riley.

Two days later, Jack arrived in Cleveland's Union Station beneath the soaring Terminal Tower, at that time the tallest building between New York and Chicago. He ached to see Theresa – she had told him of her intent to return there – but she would not be departing Europe until the end of the month. Jack switched trains for the 90-minute ride to Shelby. His homecoming there didn't feature the same piercing shrieks that had greeted his arrival at the Rileys, but the joy among his family and friends was nonetheless noisily manifested and heartfelt. For Jack, a special moment came when he rang the doorbell at the rectory of Most Pure Heart of Mary. Father Michael McFadden answered, took one look and exulted, "Jack! Jack! Please come in." The two men shook hands and then hugged. "This is such a wonderful treat. It's been so long. How are you?"

"I'm fine, Father. It's good to be home."

"Yes, yes, I'm sure it is. Your parents must be thrilled. You know, next month I'm going home myself. To Ireland. For a visit. I've not done so since before the war."

"That's wonderful," Jack said. "I'm sure everyone there is dying to see you."

"And I them."

"I think my timing is good, Father. I mean coming home and coming to see you when I did. Do you have time to talk? To listen?"

†††

In Tucson, Arizona, during the first week of February 1946, German prisoners of war were preparing to decamp for the long journey back to their homeland. They all were well enough informed to be experiencing ambivalence. Yes, they were glad to be gaining their freedom and returning to their families. But they were well aware of the deprivation that awaited them and of the bleakness of their immediate futures. Those returning to Germany's eastern region knew they would be living under repressive communist rule.

By contrast, prisoner of war Captain Gerhard Oberster considered himself lucky three times over. First, he had surrendered to Americans and not brutish Russians. Second, his American relatives – aunts, uncles, cousins – had learned of his captivity in Arizona and had traveled to visit with him. Third, his hometown was Frankfurt in the American zone of occupation. He would miss Arizona's heat and scenic beauty, but his heart was longing to return to a homeland at peace.

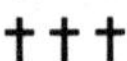

"Thaddeus."

"Yes."

"Colonel Jachnik wants to see you," said Henryk.

"Very good." It was early February and cold and Thaddeus had been discussing Poland's lot under the communists and enjoying hot coffee – real, not ersatz – with fellow cow pen soldiers in the mess hall. These frequent coffee klatches were welcome diversions from the boredom of occupation duty in a Germany where poverty and hunger had replaced prewar exuberance and prosperity.

"I'd like to come with you," Henryk said, his sober countenance masking any knowledge or emotion.

Moments later, Thaddeus and Henryk entered Lieutenant Colonel Jachnik's office, previously for many years the office of a Nazi colonel. Thaddeus saluted. "You wanted to see me, Sir."

Jachnik stepped from behind his desk and spoke with unusual curtness, "Come with me," and exited his office.

Thaddeus shrugged and glanced at Henryk for a clue. None was forthcoming.

Outside, Henryk slipped behind a jeep's steering wheel. "Get in," Jachnik ordered Thaddeus. "In front."

"What?"

"You ride in front," Jachnik said coldly. "I'll ride in back."

"I don't understand."

"I know but today it is appropriate. Let's go, Henryk."

"Would you please mind -?"

"Yes, I would," Jachnik cut him off roughly. "Just keep quiet and wait."

Henryk put the jeep in gear and went roaring away. Minutes later, the jeep was tearing through the German countryside. Riding in the uncovered jeep was cold, the windshield doing little to protect the occupants from the frosty, rushing air.

Henryk saw a barn and turned to Colonel Jachnik. "That the one, Sir?"

"That's it."

Thaddeus eyed both men. "You wouldn't be ready to let me know what's going on, would you?"

"Not yet," said Jachnik.

"Henryk?"

"Captain, there are times when it is best not to answer questions."

Thaddeus nodded questioning assent.

Henryk braked the jeep and bounced out energetically. "Out, Captain – if you please."

"Nice to hear a touch of military courtesy," Thaddeus remarked caustically.

Henryk ignored the jibe.

Thaddeus stepped from the jeep and Jachnik followed. "This way," said Jachnik, who led Thaddeus and Henryk to a wooden fence that enclosed an acre of grass.

"Now what?" Thaddeus asked.

"You are much too curious," Henryk said, the first faint signs of a smile showing.

Jachnik reached into his jacket pocket and extracted an envelope. From the envelope, he removed and unfolded a letter. Before beginning to read, he pointed to the pasture. A horse – brown, somewhat gaunt – was grazing contentedly, not at all interested in the interlopers. Thaddeus shrugged. Jachnik cleared his throat theatrically and began to read:

> *"Dear Thaddeus,*
>
> *It has been more than six years since a Polish lancer and an infantry general found themselves together in a cow pen. From that first day, I knew you were a special soldier, a special man. You demonstrated that every day during our time together.*
>
> *As you know, I have chosen to remain in the west. This is best for me. Unless you have had a change of heart, I know that you are planning to go back to our precious homeland. If you do, to me it seems only appropriate that a Polish lancer should make his return astride a mount. You became a paratrooper, but I know your heart remains that of a lancer.*
>
> *Even if you return as a merchant, well, it is not uncommon for merchants to ride horses.*
>
> *I have asked Colonel Jachnik to locate suitable transportation for you.*
>
> *Captain Metz, it has been my distinct honor and privilege to have served with you. In the years ahead, may our Lord God ride at your side.*
>
> *Yours very truly,*
>
> *Stanislaw Sosabowski, General, Retired, Polish First Independent Parachute Brigade"*

Lieutenant Colonel Jachnik inserted the letter in its envelope and handed it to Thaddeus. Thaddeus sniffled and dabbed at his eyes with the back of his hand. Now, Jachnik and Henryk were both smiling conspiratorially. Thaddeus worked hard at swallowing and shrinking the lump in his throat.

"He's not even here for me to thank," Thaddeus murmured.

"He made me promise to say nothing until I found a horse," Jachnik explained. "He gave me money to buy a horse and care for it. It took awhile to find a horse that wasn't lame, injured or severely malnourished. As you can see, this one isn't in the best of condition."

"Doesn't matter."

"No, I didn't think it would," Jachnik smiled. "I've no doubt than an experienced lancer will know how to nurse the horse back to good health."

Thaddeus nodded. "Do you mind?" he asked.

"Of course not," said Jachnik. "The saddle is in the barn. Take all the time you want. We are in no hurry at all."

Thaddeus climbed and bounded over the fence with grace and strode into the barn. He exited carrying a blanket, saddle and bridle. The horse saw Thaddeus approaching and stood waiting patiently, showing no unease.

"I'm sure you have a name, boy," said Thaddeus, "but I think you need a new one." He put the saddle and bridle on the grass and placed the blanket on the horse's back. Then he picked up and positioned the saddle and bridle. He patted the horse's snout. "How about General? I think that would be fitting. Don't you? Of course, it's going to take awhile to get you looking like a general, but we'll manage."

Thaddeus inserted his left foot in the stirrup and swung easily onto the saddle. "We'll take it nice and easy today, General. Just a couple circuits around the perimeter to give you a little exercise and improve your appetite." Thaddeus clicked his tongue twice and General broke into a slow canter.

Jachnik and Henryk were leaning against the fence.

"They look like a natural fit together, don't they?" said Jachnik.

"Like they were meant for each other all along," Henryk answered.

"We've come a long way," Jachnik observed, "a long way."

"Yes, Colonel, we have," Henryk replied pensively. "But we – and our country – still have a long way to go."

†††

Chapter 54

In Tucson, after a pleasant meeting in the morning with Bishop Metzger, Jack drove south to Green Valley for a reunion with his Josephinum buddy, Mark Hood. As with the Rileys in Boston, Jack didn't alert Mark to his homecoming. Mark's reaction when he heard the door bell chimes and opened the rectory door was more restrained than that of the Riley sisters, but he still emitted a very loud, "Jack!" Whereupon he grabbed Jack by the shoulders, pulled him close and then clapped him vigorously on the back.

"You rascal! You should have phoned ahead. You could have given me an early heart attack. Maybe you did. I'd better check." Mark pressed his fingers against his chest and probed. "Still beating."

Jack laughed heartily. "I'm glad some things haven't changed."

"Hey, I think even the Lord must have a sense of humor. Wow, over two years," Mark marveled. "You look great. Boy, have we got a lot to catch up on."

"More than you can imagine."

†††

Later in the afternoon, after more catching up, the two young priests sat in rocking chairs on the rectory porch, sipping cold beer in mugs that Mark had cooled in his refrigerator.

"I worried about you a lot. The more your letters said don't worry the more I did. I can't tell you how good it is to have you back, Jack."

"Pouring me a beer in a chilled glass says plenty. You don't know how good it feels to be drinking cold beer when cold is what I'm craving. In Germany, it's still the dead of winter. If I were there now, I'd have my hands wrapped around a mug of steaming coffee. Brrr...I get cold just thinking about winter there."

"Winter here, too," Mark smiled wryly, "but just a mite milder."

"I'm Buckeye bred, Mark, but being here in Arizona feels like being home."

"How long do you expect to stay?"

"Not sure." Jack pursed his lips, closed his eyes and shook his head.

"Did you tell Bishop Metzger about Theresa?" Mark asked, nearly whispering.

Jack shook his head. "You and Father McFadden are the only ones who know, and I spared him the details, including her name. Had to tell someone everything. Lucky you."

"Glad I was handy. I mean, I'm not kidding you, I have to admit I'm shocked. But I'm glad you felt like you could tell me. What did Father McFadden say?"

"Not much really. No scathing condemnation. Not that I expected one. I'm sure he was hurt, but all he told me was to think things through very carefully. Remember my vows but don't try to kid God or myself."

"Pretty wise counsel."

Jack scratched the back of his head and took another sip of beer. "I can't help wondering what God must be thinking about me. I'm not one of his prizes. I break one of his commandments and one of my vows, and I'm still wearing a collar."

"I think He's okay with your shooting the German," Mark observed.

"Theresa?"

Mark shrugged. "Not so sure about that one."

"Yeah. Neither am I."

"Want me to hear your confession?"

"Wouldn't hurt. Just go easy on the penance."

"As in don't prescribe any that you might not be able to keep?"

"You're a good priest, Mark – and maybe a better friend."

"Thanks." A pause. "Hey, I've got an idea."

"Yeah?"

"Well, we're drinking beer and it's February and spring training has started. What do you say we go see Lou Boudreau up in Tucson and take in a game? He might even play catch with you again."

"Sounds good," Jack said, brightening. "Real good, in fact. I guess I can put off getting back to Ajo for another day or two."

† † †

Jack felt refreshed. Lou Boudreau was nothing short of elated to see Jack and Mark, and he talked both of them into playing catch before an exhibition game between the Indians and the Chicago Cubs.

"Go easy on me," Mark pleaded. "I am not a baseball player – as will be perfectly evident."

Boudreau asked third baseman Ken Keltner to play a little soft toss with Father Hood. Then Boudreau and Jack did some hard throwing. "This is terrific therapy, Lou, believe me. The smack of this ball in a glove, it's like a tonic."

"Heard you had some tough times," Lou replied. "Word gets around. Thought about you a lot. Prayed, too."

"I think the Lord might have been listening."

"Well, you're here and in one piece and playing catch in Arizona."

"That I am."

†††

Driving west across the desert on Route 86, Jack knew he would stop in Charco on the way to Ajo, and he knew the first person he wanted to see.

"Come with me," said the graying elder.

"Okay."

The two men were walking in a comfortable silence. Then Jack stopped abruptly, and his lower jaw slackened.

The slightest smile creased the elder's face. "We've been busy."

"I'll say. It's beautiful. Absolutely beautiful."

"We figured if we built it you would return to us. Maybe that's not the way God thinks, but sometimes our way of thinking can help."

Jack shook his head in stunned admiration. The dilapidated garage-as-mission chapel was no more. In its place was a handsome, gleaming white-stucco structure with a red-tiled roof and a hammered copper crucifix atop the small bell tower. "It's magnificent. The crucifix is a work of art. I am certain the Lord is proud of you and your people."

"He should be. We worked very hard."

"Thank you," said Jack, "thank you very much."

"When you are ready," said the elder, "we would like you to join us to dedicate our new chapel. To celebrate."

Jack shook the old man's hand. "Would a week from Sunday give you enough time to make your plans?"

"Yes."

†††

For the dedication, the chapel was packed – and with more than the elder and his people. To Jack's surprise and utter delight, Bishop Metzger and Mark Hood were there. So, too, were Lou Boudreau and four other Cleveland Indians.

"Smoke signals?" Jack teasingly asked the elder before the dedication Mass began.

"Something like that," the elder replied. "We did have wings spreading our message."

"Wings?"

"In time you will see."

†††

"May the peace of the Lord be with you always," Bishop Metzger intoned. After his final blessing, he and Jack and Mark slowly began making their way up the aisle. Hands were reaching out to shake Jack's hand and he reciprocated. At the chapel doors, another surprise awaited Jack. "Luke!"

"Howdy, Padre," Luke Haynes replied, grinning slyly, his six-foot four-inch frame as lean as ever. "Word has it that that lesson with the M-1 saved something more than sheep."

Jack took Luke's hand and clasped his shoulder. "Great to see you. But I hope you're not here to give me another lesson."

"Nope. I'm here to provide wheels."

"Wheels?"

"You'll see."

Outside the chapel, under a large tent, the assemblage enjoyed a festive and hearty picnic-style lunch. The reservation Indians were ecstatic; when Mark Hood had asked the elder how he felt about Mark's inviting Bishop Metzger and the Cleveland Indians, the elder welcomed the suggestion but considered it unlikely that all would actually make their way to Charco. He was glad to have been wrong. It was the elder himself who had invited Luke.

As the picnic was winding down, a pickup truck rolled to a stop near the tent. No one got out of the vehicle. Instead, Mark Hood said to Jack,

"Come with me," and began leading him to the pickup. Following close behind were the elder, Bishop Metzger, Lou Boudreau, Luke Haynes and the rest of the large gathering. Boudreau, Bishop Metzger, Luke and the elder eyed each other, and Boudreau winked conspiratorially. The other three smiled knowingly.

As Jack neared the truck, the door opened and out stepped a strapping young man. Again, Jack's jaw slackened. Then he recovered. "Walt! What the?"

Walt Hunter stepped toward Jack. "Captain Brecker, Captain Hunter reporting." Walt snapped off a crisp salute that Jack returned smartly before grasping Walt's hand in both of his own.

"What in the world is going on here?" Jack asked with a mix of bewilderment and suspicion. He looked around. "Does anyone have any more surprises up their sleeves?" He shook his head. "If you do, I might need first aide and a chaplain."

Laughter all around.

"Let's get this convoy rolling," Walt said. "Jack, you ride with me. We'll take the point."

"Convoy? Convoy to where?" Jack's arched eyebrow reflected his dubiousness.

"Way, way too many questions, Jack." Walt put the truck in gear and pulled away. The mission Indians waved their goodbyes, and Jack returned their farewell.

Following Walt's truck was Luke's with the elder as his passenger. Then came Mark driving Bishop Metzger in Mark's car. Bringing up the rear was a car carrying the Cleveland Indians with Lou Boudreau driving. The convoy headed northwest toward Ajo, about 15 miles distant. About 30 minutes later, Ajo's modest airport came into view. It consisted of two hangars and an airstrip and was used mostly by area copper mine operators and their business visitors. Walt didn't slow the truck until braking it behind one of the hangars.

"All right, Walt, let's end the mystery and the games. What's this all about?" Jack was trying to sound stern, but Walt wasn't fazed.

In fact, he ignored Jack's question. "Get out, Jack."

Behind them, the rest of the convoy came to a halt. Everyone exited the vehicles and came walking toward Jack and Walt. When they were all together, Walt said, "This way," and led them around to the front of the hangar. There stood a man leaning casually against the fuselage of a yellow and blue-trimmed Luscombe two-seater. The man straightened and took a step toward the oncoming group.

"Jack," said Walt, "this is Gabe Millerchip. Gabe, this is your student, Father Jack Brecker."

Gabe extended his hand. "Nice to meet you, Father."

Jack took the proffered hand and said, "Student?"

"Flight pupil," said Gabe.

Behind Jack, Mark Hood tried and failed to suppress a giggle. That triggered a round of muffled chuckles and snorts that soon gave way to laughter. Jack looked back at his friends, and his genuine puzzlement turned the laughter into guffaws.

"Come on, Jack, don't you remember?" Walt asked through his own laughter.

"Remember what?"

"When we were getting ready for your first practice jump, you said you'd like to have one of these babies. Remember?"

The faded words came surging forward in Jack's memory. "Yeah…I guess I do remember."

"Well," said Walt, "this is one of those babies and it's yours."

"Mine?"

"Courtesy of my dad," said Walt.

"What? I've never even met your dad."

"No, but he's heard plenty about you. And believe me, he wants you to have this plane."

"A gift?" Jack's perplexity was delicious to behold, a sweet picnic dessert, and his friends again were laughing lustily. "But why?"

"Because you are who you are, Jack, and when I told Dad, he didn't hesitate. I showed him those pictures of you doing the Easter Mass for the Poles. Told him we had to fly you there. He said you needed this plane. I'm not fibbing" – Walt quickly crossed his heart – "or even stretching the truth. Dad said, 'That priest needs wings.' These," he said, pointing to the plane, "are your wings. And Gabe is your instructor – when he's not flying for Dad."

"I…I don't know what to say," Jack stammered. "This is so…I mean, I'm grateful, Walt. Very grateful. Thank you – and your dad – very much. But…Bishop, what about my vow of poverty?"

Bishop Metzger blinked away laugh tears and chuckled. "I don't think you will be using that plane to obtain wealth. Do you?"

"No. I guess not."

"No," said the bishop, "and I don't think your vow ruled out fast transportation."

"I guess not…Walt, uh…well, please tell your dad how much I appreciate his kindness and generosity. This is going to take some getting used to. My own plane…Tell him I will say a Mass in his honor."

"Will do. Although as a Methodist, the significance might be lost on him. But right now, let's get you started."

"Started?"

"Gabe's not here just to rub shoulders with the bishop and major leaguers," said Walt.

"Father," said Gabe, "let's get you up for lesson number one."

"Now?"

"Right now."

Jack looked at the assemblage. To a man, they were grinning affectionately. Jack didn't try to suppress his own grin. "Okay, I'm game. Let's go."

With Jack at his side, Gabe started the Luscombe and taxied to the end of the runway. Then he pivoted the plane in a tight arc and accelerated. Seconds later, the Luscombe was lifting above the brown floor of the western Arizona desert. When Jack looked down, his friends were looking up and waving. Not smoke signals, Jack was thinking, but something like that. He waved back.

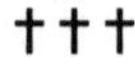

CHAPTER 55

Jack proved an eager and adept student. He and Gabe were in the air virtually every day. Jack delighted in every moment of every lesson. He loved the sharpened sense of tranquility and freedom that flying provided. "I think I'm living a dream," Jack said to Gabe one afternoon.

"Mr. Hunter has a way of making dreams come true," Gabe replied. "Where do you think the Indians got the money for their new chapel?"

Jack swung his head to face Gabe. "Mr. Hunter?"

Gabe nodded. "Right. And, as you know, he's not Catholic. The Indians had saved up some money, but Mr. Hunter put them over the top."

"Well, I'll be. How many people know about this?"

"Not many. Mr. Hunter's wife, Me, Walt, the elder, a banker, you. Doubt if anyone else will ever know. Look," Gabe explained, "Mr. Hunter thinks the world of his son. One word from Walt and things start happening. And speaking of happening, it's time for you to drive this baby."

"Now?"

"I'll sit her down. Then we'll switch seats and you put her back in the air."

"You think I'm ready?"

Gabe grinned. "Seeing as how I'd like to fly a few more years before trying on angel wings..."

Jack chuckled. "I get your drift."

"Thought you would."

†††

Scant weeks later, Gabe was standing on the tarmac, watching Jack take his first solo flight. As Jack drove the Luscombe down the runway and lifted off smoothly, Gabe was thinking, Father, you've got the knack. Most folks don't have the hand-eye coordination -- or the self-confidence – to fly a plane. You're making a dandy pilot.

†††

In early April, Jack flew the Luscombe to Tucson to meet with Bishop Metzger and other diocesan priests about the need for new parishes. As soldiers came flocking backing to the United States from Europe and Asia, many were headed for sunny Arizona, and the state's population was experiencing the early waves of its post-war boom. Bishop Metzger could see that more people meant more Catholics and the need for more churches.

After returning to Ajo, Jack got into his car and drove to Charco. Minutes after arriving he had a passenger – the elder – and he was driving back to Ajo. He headed straight for the airport. After parking, Jack led the elder to the Luscombe. He helped him in and buckled him up. Then Jack got in, settled himself, checked the dials and ignited the engine. "Ready?" he asked.

The elder nodded. "No need for smoke signals today," he smiled wryly.

Jack steered the Luscombe to the end of the runway and the plane began picking up speed.

Soon the elder was seeing his reservation and surrounding territory as never before. "I don't know if I have the proper words, Father. I never dreamed to see my land like the eagles see it."

"I figured it was time you did. I owe you a favor."

"Why?"

"Why? Because you and your people have taught me things I never would have learned somewhere else. I'm grateful."

The elder shook his head emphatically in self-deprecation. "Father, you are a better student than I am a teacher. And I am grateful to you. Now my land seems even more precious. It also – from up here – seems more fragile. I am not sure why."

"Perhaps," said Jack, "it's because from up here you can see the scars more clearly." He was pointing down to one of the gaping craters created by a surface copper mine.

"You might be right. It is an ugly scar, and it is one that seems only to grow. It may never heal. But," the elder observed, "it is also the source of Mr. Hunter's wealth, and he seems to be using it generously and wisely.

After he gave us money for our new chapel, he offered mining jobs to my people. Some have accepted his offer. I hope more will."

"I want to show you a scar that is a thing of beauty…a scar that nature has created," Jack said. He flew north and landed the Luscombe at Flagstaff to refuel. Then he continued flying farther north. In less than an hour, he tipped the plane to give the elder a better view.

"I have seen pictures of this scar," the elder said, "but I never dreamed it to be so beautiful. I think it must be God's perfect scar."

Jack smiled. "Maybe that's how you and I will think about it. As God's scar instead of the Grand Canyon."

Chapter 56

Jack couldn't help grinning. His previous journeys across the country had been ground bound. Now, in his Luscombe, he was cruising above the mountains, bluffs, rivers, prairies, forests and farm fields that make up the continental quilt. All the pieces seemed to have been stitched together randomly but nonetheless artfully. He was thoroughly captivated – and grateful. More than once he found himself giving thanks to Walt Hunter and his dad.

Spread open on the seat beside Jack was a map of the United States. Circled in red ink were the towns that Gabe Millerchip had recommended as refueling stops. Occasionally, Jack glanced at the map. His self-confidence and clear weather were making it easy for him to match landmarks with the map. Above Arizona, New Mexico, Texas, Oklahoma, Kansas, Missouri, Illinois, Indiana and Ohio...He had ample time and inclination to reflect and did so. God and Theresa occupied most of his thoughts, but there also were long moments when images of – and conversations with – others evoked a range of memories and emotions. His brothers Paul and Tom and their wives Lea and Bridgett and his first niece and nephew. George Patton, a roughly textured general with immense faith in God if not in man. Thaddeus Metz, a man who had lost much and was willing to risk all to free his homeland. The German soldier he had killed, God rest his soul.

In Shelby, Jack chose not to land at its small airport. Instead he decided to put the Luscombe down in a meadow on the expansive acreage of the Sacred Heart Seminary that had been built just a few miles south of town. The Sacred Heart order was training its seminarians to serve as missionaries, chiefly in Latin America and Africa. The staff there was expecting Jack and had told him they would gladly give him a ride into Shelby.

Jack spent two days in Shelby and while there phoned Lou Boudreau.

"Of course, Father, I'd love to see you. We all would. Come on up. I'll pick you up personally at the airport. You can stay with me and my family. Take in a couple games as my guest."

†††

Once again, Jack put the Luscombe into the sky, this time heading north to Cleveland's Hopkins Airport.

Lou as chauffeur and his gracious wife as hostess provided Jack with warm hospitality. When Lou escorted Jack into the Indians' clubhouse in the bowels of Cleveland's cavernous Municipal Stadium, the greeting was noisy and good-natured, replete with ribbing.

"You ready to trade your collar and beads for a glove and bat, Father," one Indian joshed him.

"We could use you to intercede with the umpires," teased a second player.

"How about coaching third base for us?" a third kidded him. "The other teams wouldn't dare to steal your signs."

Jack laughed and the Indians laughed with him.

That night, after the game, Jack made another phone call. The next afternoon, gently declining Mrs.Boudreau's offer of a ride, Jack took a taxi to the Cleveland Museum of Art. He paid the driver and then sat on the stone steps. Beside him, he put down a small paper bag that Mrs. Boudreau had given him. Inside the bag was a wooden box that Mrs. Boudreau had wrapped for him. Jack looked out over the museum's lagoon and at the waterfowl swimming slowly in its placid waters. He inhaled deeply and exhaled forcefully. Lord, he thought, please be with me always. Forgive me my sins and shortcomings and remember that I'm a man as well as your servant. Not a perfect one, as you well know. Not always as strong as you no doubt would prefer. Following your path, well, I know that I've gotten sidetracked more than once.

Jack's silent petitioning was interrupted when he saw a familiar figure approaching. She was limping, perhaps a little less so than when Jack had last seen her. He stood, picked up the bag and descended the steps to greet her. They reached out for each other and hugged tightly. They drew apart and kissed, tenderly.

"You look wonderful – just like I knew you would," said Jack.

"You look good, too, Jack. That desert sun is really browning you up."

Jack laughed. "Yeah, I expect I'll soon be looking like the Indians and not the Cleveland ones. Do you want to sit here or walk?"

"Walk."

"You're not tired?"

"No. Like I told you on the phone, Mount Sinai is just a short distance from here. Let's stroll around the lagoon."

"Your hip?"

"Okay. Probably as good as it's ever going to be. I've learned to live with the limp. I know people stare, but I've gotten used to that, too."

"That's good."

"You're not wearing your black suit and collar. Hold my hand." Jack took her hand. "Does anyone know you're here?"

"No one in Shelby. And here, not even the Boudreaus. I'm staying with them. Oh, the folks in Shelby know I'm in Cleveland, but I didn't say anything about seeing you."

"Probably wise. No one else?"

"Mark Hood."

"Who?"

"My Josephinum buddy."

"Oh, the one who's in Arizona with you." Jack nodded. "I was surprised to get your call, Jack."

"Surprised? Why?"

"Because I thought we'd seen the last of each other in Europe."

"I see."

"How did you get here?"

"Taxi." Theresa's face showed mock exasperation. "Oh," Jack said apologetically, "you mean from Arizona."

Theresa nodded. "It's a long way..."

"I flew."

"Really? What airline?" Theresa was thinking perhaps American, Hal Walker's airline.

"Brecker Airways."

"What?"

"A friend's father...You remember me mentioning Walt Hunter?"

"Yes."

"Well, Walt mentioned to his dad that I'd like a plane, and the next thing you know I've got a plane. Of course, that meant I had to learn how to fly."

Theresa laughed and shook her head. "Wow! I'm impressed, Jack. Way to go. The airborne chaplain stays airborne. That doesn't seem altogether priestly, though," she teased.

"Well, the war's over, and I figured I might as well give this Saint Christopher medal more to do."

Theresa smiled, her eyes brightening. "Fourteen years. That's how long it's been since I gave it to you. It's been quite a journey."

"For both of us. And in more ways than one." Theresa nodded her understanding. "Would you like to fly with me?" Jack asked.

Theresa looked at him. "I don't think so."

"Never flown?"

"No. I've flown. With Hal."

"Oh. I'm sorry."

"That's okay, Jack. I know he's gone and probably has been since his last flight. That's what I believe and I've accepted it."

"You're a remarkable woman. A strong woman."

"Are you going to make me prove that again?" Her question – seemingly oblique yet painfully pointed – jarred Jack. He stopped walking and Theresa, still holding his hand, turned to face him. "Well? You have made up your mind, haven't you?"

"Yes."

"That's what I thought." She looked down at the path.

"I do love you."

"I know."

"Do you still love me?"

Theresa paused before replying, breathing in and out. "Maybe you'd like me to say no. That might make it easier for you. But I'm not that strong, Jack. Yes, I still love you. I've never stopped since way back when." She squeezed his hand. "I'm not mad, Jack. How could I be mad at you for choosing God? But it hurts. It really hurts, and if you don't mind I'm going to cry."

As tears began trickling from her eyes, Jack felt helpless, miserable and evil. Then he reached into his pocket and removed a kerchief. Theresa accepted it and dabbed. They were still holding hands. She sniffled and tried to laugh. "The priest and his paramour. The world – at least the world as Shelby sees it – would have been aghast."

Theresa's pain was causing Jack's eyes to well. She handed the kerchief back to him and he dabbed.

"What will you do?" Jack asked. "Stay here?"

Theresa sniffled again and Jack handed the kerchief back to her. "This kerchief is going to get soaked," Theresa managed to smile. "We'll have to wring it out. If you had surprised me and said, 'Let's get married,' I'd go with you anywhere. Disapprovals and disavowals be damned. But that's not what I expected so I've been doing lots of thinking. I'm going back to London."

Jack almost blurted, "What? London? Why?" but he swallowed those words before they could escape and instead said, "It feels more like home?"

"Exactly. I spent the better part of five years there. Eventful years. I care very much for my friends there, and they care about me. I just feel comfortable there."

"More than in Cleveland or Shelby?"

"Yes. My family, especially Mom and Dad, will be upset. Bridgett, too. But right now, I feel like I've got to live for myself. I know that sounds selfish, but that's the way I feel. Maybe some day I'll feel differently."

Jack sighed. "Well, since you are about to start on another journey, I have something for you that seems even more appropriate."

"What?" She rubbed her eyes.

Jack reached down and picked up the paper bag. He released Theresa's hand and removed the package from the bag. "Here."

Puzzled, Theresa carefully removed the wrapping paper to expose the wooden box. "What is it?"

"Go ahead," Jack said, "open it."

Theresa did so. "It's beautiful," she said. "I think I might start to cry again." She looked up at Jack and then gazed lovingly at the small, brass crucifix.

"I wanted you to have something special, something to remember me by that you could keep on display and not have to answer awkward questions."

"That's very thoughtful, Jack. And just like you."

"It's very special, Theresa. The Polish airborne troops gave it to me when I said Easter Mass for them in forty-four. Just like this Saint Christopher medal, it's been through a lot."

"Oh, Jack, are you sure you want me to keep it permanently?" He arched an eyebrow in mock exasperation. "Okay, okay, silly question. I will treasure it always. Do you think you'll ever see your Polish friends again?"

"I don't know. Maybe some day I'll try."

"Or maybe some day," said Theresa, "they'll try to find you." Then she stood on her toes and kissed Jack, catching him by surprise. "Just like in first grade at Saint Mary's, huh, Jack? A surprise kiss."

Jack laughed. "Yes and just as memorable."

"I've changed my mind, Jack."

"Huh?"

"Take me flying in your new plane."

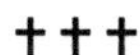

EPILOGUE 1

"Hassler!"

The voice was male and the hail sharply spoken. Outside the entrance to St. Thomas Hospital, Theresa looked around for the voice's source. About 30 feet away on the sidewalk, she saw a man. He looked to be about six-feet tall and trim. He was wearing a raincoat but no hat.

"Hassler," he said again.

Theresa was baffled. Who was this stranger? Why was he calling to her? And what of his accent? Not British.

Slowly, though with no hint of tentativeness, the man began walking toward her. He didn't seem to pose a threat, and Theresa was feeling no fear. This was London, her town and her neighborhood. Dusk had yet to set in. She just stood, watching.

"Lieutenant Hassler."

"Yes. Used to be. Should I know you?"

"You kissed me once."

"What?"

"Just once, but I thought if I found you, you might let me kiss you again." He kept closing the distance.

"Is this a joke?" Theresa asked sternly. "Did someone put you up to this? One of my nurse friends?"

The man laughed, a merry baritone laugh. "Sicily." He was now only about six feet from her, and he was smiling kindly. "You've never heard me laugh before."

Slowly at first, images began forming in Theresa's mind. Memories began to bubble up, recognition to take shape. "Oh my," she murmured.

"That's right," he said. "Sicily. The surgery tent. A kiss with the power of magic, of life."

"Oh my," she repeated. "How?...Who?"

He laughed again. "I thought if I found you, you might agree to join me for dinner. If you agreed to that, maybe you'd let me kiss you again. And if you did that, then maybe you would marry me."

"Marry?" She shook her head in disbelief. "You can't be serious. I...I don't even know your name."

"That's because my name patch was soaked with blood, and you cut open my jacket and shirt and pulled them away from my wound. No name patch visible. So," he smiled wryly, "it's your fault."

Now it was Theresa's turn to smile. She was shedding incredulity and felt her confidence returning. "You're not wearing a name patch now. That's your fault."

He laughed. "So it is. But," he said, reaching inside his raincoat and extracting his passport, "I have this." He handed it to her.

Theresa opened it, read the name and said, "Dean Morton. Belvidere, Illinois." She handed back the passport. "Mr. Morton, you've caught me off guard. How did you find me?"

"Took a little digging. My dad helped. He's a congressman. Some phone calls to the Pentagon, the Army Nurse Corps, St. Thomas Hospital. Of course, after I got some facts, it still took me awhile before I felt up to doing any traveling. But I figured with you still in the Army, or just recently out, I stood a good chance of finding you. Oh, and please call me Dean."

"Okay, Dean."

"Before they hauled me out of that evac, I asked you where you're from."

"What did I say?"

"A little town in northern Ohio."

"Oh."

"So then I put on my most pained expression – which wasn't hard because of the pain – and said, 'Do I have to pry it out of you?'"

Theresa smiled. "Well, did you? Pry it out?"

"Shelby," said Dean Morton, "is a very attractive little town."

"You've been there?" Her surprise was bordering on shock. "Did you talk to anyone? My family?"

Dean shook his head. "I just stopped off on my trip to New York. Just drove around a little. Just enough to get a feel. Dad's research and mine said you weren't married, so I didn't feel a need to ask anyone that. I crossed my fingers that that was still the case." He looked at her left hand and saw no ring. "Looks like my luck is still holding."

"You're amazing," Theresa said, feeling a sense of lightness that she hadn't experienced since her first days after returning to London.

"Determined is more like it. Actually," said Dean, "I've concluded you're the amazing one. I'm just glad to be whole and able to be here."

"Your wound…"

"Healed," he said. "Left a nasty scar and I lost a little motion in my right chest and shoulder. I consider myself lucky. How about you? That limp?"

"Shrapnel. Near Bastogne. There's no pain anymore, just some internal scar tissue and surface scarring."

"Two pretty lucky vets, I'd say."

"I won't disagree with you about that. Well, Dean-"

He cut her off. "Will you have dinner with me, Theresa? Tonight?"

She smiled. "I, uh…"

Dean Morton saluted her, then reached out and took her right hand. "Lieutenant Theresa Hassler, Captain Dean Morton has traveled a goodly distance to track you down. He is hungry, and he requests the pleasure of your company at dinner tonight. He suggests Simpsons-In-The-Strand. He's told the fare is plentiful and tasty, and the bread pudding supposedly is exquisite."

"That does sound tempting, Captain Morton. More so than what I had planned with my humble hotplate."

"You live near here?"

"Just a few minutes walking. A room in Carlisle Lane."

"May I please escort you? I'll wait outside while you freshen up and change."

"I live upstairs, over a bicycle shop. You are welcome to escort me to my humble quarters."

"All right. But then I'll go downstairs while you're dressing to hail a taxi."

"That sounds very much like a plan, Captain Morton."

"Or the beginning of one."

Epilogue 2

As a military unit, the First Independent Polish Airborne Brigade never returned to Poland. The Soviet Union's repressive occupation precluded that. Instead, the brigade remained in Germany until 1947 when it was returned to England and disbanded. Most, though not all, of its men chose to remain in England. Most who stayed married Scottish or English women they had met during training at Upper Largo and Peterborough.

Many of the men took jobs in the brickfields around Peterborough, about two hours drive north of London, where the brigade was stationed during the last months leading up to D-Day.

General Stanislaw Sosabowski did, in fact, remain in England where he became a shopkeeper and factory worker. After his death on September 25, 1967 at age 75, his body was returned to Warsaw where it was given a hero's burial. In attendance were a former Polish lancer and a former farm girl from Zyrardow.

EPILOGUE 3

The evacuation of the Natzwiller concentration camp in eastern France in early September 1944 did no harm to the Nazi career of Commandant Josef Kramer. Afterward, he immediately was appointed commandant of the Auschwitz death camp in southwestern Poland. He remained there until, at the approach of Russian forces, Auschwitz was evacuated on December 2, 1944 and its operations transferred to Bergen-Belsen, with Kramer continuing as commandant.

Kramer still was at the camp when British forces liberated it on April 15, 1945. He was arrested immediately and was among the first Nazis to be tried for war crimes. Because Bergen-Belsen was liberated by the British, Kramer was among the defendants tried by a British-controlled court.

In a touch of irony, Kramer was commandant of the only Nazi concentration camp in France and, later, the only concentration camp liberated by the British.

An estimated 40,000 people were imprisoned at Natzwiller, with 10,000 –12,000 executed or dying from disease or malnutrition.

At his trial at Belsen, Kramer didn't deny that prisoners had been gassed under his command, but he denied responsibility for selecting victims.

That claimed distinction did not impress the court. He was found guilty of all charges and was hanged in Hamelin Prison, about 25 miles southwest of Hannover, on December 13, 1945.

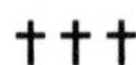

Epilogue 4

If ever a building could be described as resilient, St. Anne's Church in Warsaw qualifies.

It is named after Anne, princess of Mazovia – a lowland region of central Poland that includes Warsaw – who commissioned building the church. Construction was completed in 1454. The church's exterior could be described as architecturally eclectic. It is principally Baroque garnished with touches of Gothic and Classical. The interior is Baroque – exclusively and opulently.

Disaster first struck the church when fire swept through it in 1515. By 1521, it had been completely rebuilt. During a 1650-1655 war between Sweden and Poland, St. Anne's escaped widespread destruction – only to be victimized again by fire two years after that war ended. Arson was suspected.

The church next was in jeopardy during World War II. Threatening it were the Nazi occupation, the Warsaw uprising, and Hitler's subsequent order to raze Warsaw. Only 15 percent of Warsaw's buildings survived that apocalypse, and St. Anne's was one. Most of its roof collapsed but its walls and colorful interior suffered little.

Today? The sturdy, resilient church sits among trees, and its courtyard, with a pleasant, warm-weather outdoor café, provides a view of the Vistula – the river that Russian troops declined to cross until after German forces had crushed the Poles' uprising.

EPILOGUE 5

After World War II, Cleveland Indians shortstop and player-manager Lou Boudreau continued to enjoy a fine major league baseball career. In 1948, he achieved his long-sought goal: his Indians won the American League pennant. They also went on to win that year's World Series.

After Boudreau retired, he received baseball's highest honor when he was elected to the Major League Baseball Hall of Fame in Cooperstown, New York in 1970. In attendance was a Catholic priest who flew in from Arizona.

Boudreau died August 10, 2001 at age 84.

Acknowledgements

As I went about structuring this book, several friends provided crucial research assistance, and they did so with remarkable enthusiasm, speed and thoroughness.

I owe a special debt of gratitude to my long-time friend, Peter Bloomfield. He was born in 1933 in London and raised there. He shared first-hand knowledge of what it was like to be a young boy during the Battle of Britain. Yes, as depicted in the book, Peter did, in fact, watch aerial dogfights. He also possesses – and shared with me -- intimate knowledge of London's World War II hospitals, knowledge gained as a result of his needing an emergency tonsillectomy during The Blitz. He also was one of the many London children evacuated to rural areas – a happening which enabled him to watch the buildup of men and equipment for the D-Day invasion. In addition, he recommended other background sources, including books and movies. Peter graduated from Sandhurst, Britain's military academy and has retained a lifelong interest in World War II history. Together, we have visited the D-Day Museum in Portsmouth and Tangmere Air Base. He lives in Petworth, a village about an hour's train ride south of London.

I owe another special debt of gratitude to long-time friend Elaine Russell-Reolfi of North Canton, Ohio. As we were discussing my plans for Warrior Priest, she told me about her visit to the Natzwiller concentration camp, and she offered to loan me her English-language version of a book on the camp that was written by former inmates. The book includes not only first-hand accounts of camp experiences but also photos and diagrams.

I owe still another debt of gratitude to good friend Laura Ramaschi who lives in Ribeauville, France with her husband Kristoff and son Frederic. She obtained and sent to me a detailed and annotated – in English – map of Ribeauville. Laura and her family live in a delightful house that was built in 1513 and that she and her husband have lovingly restored. During my most recent visit, I told them I wanted to be invited back in 2013 to help celebrate the house's 500th birthday.

There are several others who must be thanked:

- Roscoe Armstrong of Dallas, Texas who advised me on the names of 1940ish side-by-side two-seater airplanes and provided me with addresses for web sites that show photos of the planes. Roscoe owns and flies his own WWII vintage plane.
- Sally Stevenson Hays of Shelby, Ohio who provided me with the first name of Dr. Wilson Kingsboro. Sally's late father and late uncle were pharmacists who for decades ran a legendary drug store and soda fountain in Shelby and Sally, in her words, "got to know everybody."
- Marzena Witek of Sosnowiec, Poland who provided me with a fact about St. Anne's Church that was proving elusive: the year in which its construction was completed.

As the book neared completion, I was considering the question of a title. There were several possibilities, and I decided to explore them with a diverse group of friends who enjoy reading and whom I know to be thoughtful. I presented them with five possible titles, and they replied with thoughtful opinions. I am very grateful for their thinking. They are: Peter Bloomfield, Petworth, England; Alexandra Dinita, Bucharest, Romania; John Edwards, Somerset, Ohio; Terry Gamble, Canton, Ohio; Mel Helitzer, Athens, Ohio; Bill Hincher, Tampa, Florida; Jodi Hutchison, Madison, New Jersey; Andrea Johnson, Columbus, Ohio; Lynne Johnson, North Canton, Ohio; Jean Riley Lash, Shelby, Ohio; Jodi Seaton Lowery, San Mateo, California; Dee Dee Milligan Oman, Aurora, Ohio; Dick Parrish, Shelby, Ohio; Laura Ramaschi, Ribeauville, France; Elaine Russell-Reolfi, North Canton, Ohio; Pat Reynolds, Twinsburg, Ohio; Theresa Roman, Canton, Ohio; Anne Lafferty Stock, Vermilion, Ohio.

To Lynne, my loving wife of 36 years, I owe a huge debt of gratitude for everything she did to prepare the manuscript for publication.

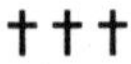

Sources

- American Heritage New History of World War II – Stephen Ambrose & C.L. Sulzberger.
- Atonement – Ian McEwan
- Battle of Britain – Len Deighton
- Battle of Britain – the movie
- A Bridge Too Far – Cornelius Ryan
- A Bridge Too Far – the movie
- Concentration Camp – Natzwiller-Struthof – written by the National Committee For The Erecting And Preservation Of A Memorial For Deportation At The Struthof
- D-Day: 24 Hours That Saved The World – Editors of TIME magazine
- The Doolittle Raid – Carroll Glines
- General Patton: A Soldier's Life – Stanley Hirshson
- Historical Maps of World War II – Europe – Michael Swift & Michael Sharpe
- Is Paris Burning? – Larry Collins & Dominique LaPierre
- The Longest Day – the movie
- Normandy 1944 – Stephen Badsey
- On-line biography of General Stanislaw Sosabowski – written by his son
- Past Forgetting – My Love Affair with Dwight D. Eisenhower – Kay Summersby Morgan
- Uprising – the movie
- World Book Encyclopedia – World War II

ROSTER OF REAL-LIFE PEOPLE

- Peter Bloomfield (as a boy)
- Lou Boudreau
- Alva Bradley
- Sir Alan Brooke
- Lieutenant General Frederick 'Boy' Browning
- General Dietrich von Choltitz
- Colonel Charles Codman
- Major Julian Cook
- General James Doolittle
- General of the Army Dwight Eisenhower
- Lieutenant John Fitzgerald
- Admiral Hans Georg von Friedeburg
- Lieutenant Colonel John Frost
- Lieutenant Colonel Stanislaw Jachnik
- Colonel General Alfred Jodl
- Ken Keltner
- Dr. Wilson Kingsboro
- Commandant Josef Kramer
- Captain Charles Mason
- Brigadier General Anthony McAuliffe
- Lieutenant James McCarthy
- Father Michael McFadden
- Captain Marc Mitscher
- Field Marshall Bernard Montgomery
- Bea Patton
- General George Patton
- General Stanislaw Sosabowski
- T/5 Robert Thompson
- Major General Roy Urquhart
- Seaman Robert Wall

†††

INSPIRATION

The inspiration for this story was Reverend George Reinweiler. He was born in 1914 in the village of Milan in northern Ohio. Upon ordination from the Josephinum seminary in Worthington, Ohio in 1941, he was sent to Arizona where he spent his entire career, serving several communities, including Douglas, Clifton, Tolleson, Tempe, Ajo and Globe, as well as Indian missions. He died in Arizona in1979 and was buried on Good Friday in Milan. As a youth, he enjoyed sports, playing both baseball and hockey. As a priest, he enjoyed camping, fishing and hunting, including mountain lions, and he also loved golf and bowling, a sport in which he excelled -- he was a member of several national amateur championship teams. For several years, he flew his own plane, a gift from an affluent benefactor. But he never became an Army chaplain, nor did he ever travel outside the United States, nor did he befriend the real-life people depicted in this book. He did secure a role as an extra in the movie The Great White Hope in return for permitting the film's producers to change the doors of his Holy Angels church in Globe which was to be included in the background for a fight scene. Father Reinweiler was a very cool guy. He also was my uncle.

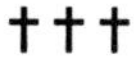

Reverend George Reinweiler

1915-1979

About the Author

From the 1960s onward, first as a soldier, Mike Johnson combined strong interests in military history with extensive travel. He journeyed often to the Korean DMZ, visited Nazi death camps and walked the streets of towns and villages once occupied by the Wehrmacht. Johnson is an alumnus of Ohio University, Marshall Law at Cleveland State University and Stanford University's Graduate School of Business and has worked for three global companies. He is working on a second historical novel.

Printed in the United States
112976LV00005B/201/A

9 781420 889475